# BITTERSWEET

FREDDIE LEE JOHNSON III

ONE WORLD
BALLANTINE BOOKS • NEW YORK

This novel is a work of fiction. Neither the characters portrayed nor the events depicted are real, and any similarities between them and actual persons or incidents are entirely coincidental. Also, though the locales mentioned in the narrative exist, many geographical and topographical details have been altered for the sake of story and dramatic effect. Accordingly, they should be regarded as entirely fictitious.

A One World Book
Published by The Ballantine Publishing Group



www.ballantinebooks.com/one/

Library of Congress Control Number: 2002094705

ISBN 0-345-44597-X

Cover design by Dreu Pennington-McNeil
Cover painting by Gary Kelley

Manufactured in the United States of America

First Hardcover Edition: January 2002
First Trade Paperback Edition: January 2003

1 3 5 7 9 10 8 6 4 2

DEDICATED TO
ILAR-DORIS HATCHER-FREEMAN,
MY MOTHER, MY INSPIRATION, MY HEART

He answered and said unto them: "When it is evening, ye say, it will be fair weather, for the sky is red. And in the morning, it will be foul weather today, for the sky is red and lowering. O ye hypocrites, ye can discern the face of the sky, but can ye not discern the signs of the times?"

—MATTHEW 16:2–3

# THE ACHIEVER

# CLIFFORD

IT'S A BRIGHT, BEAUTIFUL MORNING AND WE'VE JUST HIT CRUISING ALTITUDE, FLYING home from Walt Disney World to Pittsburgh, when Demetria turns from the window and stares through me.

"I'm not happy," she says.

I smile and pat her hand. "Next vacation will be better."

"I'm not talking about that! It's this marriage. Clifford, I'm not in love with you anymore. I'm not sure I even like you."

I sit riveted to my seat. Invisible hands squeeze my head from the outside while a seventy-car pileup rattles it from the inside. "Baby, what did you say?"

She jerks her hand away. "You heard me! I want out of this marriage. And I don't wanna talk about it!"

She turns back to the window, suddenly determined to become the world's most knowledgeable cloud expert. I caress her shoulder, wondering why it's been so long since I've noticed its softness, its beauty. Demetria slaps my hand away as if it were some leprous claw.

"Demmy?"

She doesn't answer, so I lean closer and whisper. "Demetria?"

"Leave me alone!" she snarls, snapping her head around and narrowing her eyes. She glares at me, then turns away.

I count the steel-gray hairs of the man in front of me. He and the woman sitting next to him are leaning against each other, snuggling and whispering.

"Sir, would you like something to drink?" The flight attendant's voice is a small echo that gradually gets louder. "Excuse me, sir. Would you like something to drink?"

I try to answer, but my throat's too tight.

The flight attendant leans close and pats my shoulder. "I understand," she says. "But there's no need to be afraid. Flying is still statistically safer than driving."

She empties a miniature bottle of scotch into a cup and hands it to me before I can tell her I don't drink. "On the house," she says. "Will you be okay?"

I nod and look at myself in the polished metal of her food service cart. The reflection scares me.

ON THE GROUND, WE FIGHT OUR WAY THROUGH THE CRUSH OF HUMANITY TO THE BAGgage claim, then to the airport shuttle.

Our little boys, five-year-old Bradley and seven-year-old Barry (I call them Braddie and Bear), are in the seats directly across from us in the shuttle bus, playing with their Disney-toy loot.

Braddie lowers his voice into a poor imitation of James Earl Jones's bass as he pretends to be the elder lion, Mufasa, from *The Lion King*. And Bear imitates the son, Simba, who after much consideration and agonizing has decided to eat his longtime warthog friend Pumbaa after all.

"Dada, are we gonna pick up Scratch?" asks Braddie, the excitement in his voice proving that he's *really* missed our lovable mongrel.

"I'm petting him first!" declares Bear.

I force a smile. My face feels like it's cracking from the effort. "Don't worry, guys. We'll stop by Grandy's on the way home and get him."

They whoop their approval and return to their Disney fantasizing. The driver's voice scratches out over the intercom, "Please call out the row and section number where you're parked."

"Twenty-six-C!" I shout.

The driver gives a thumbs-up and winds his way through the parking lot, eventually letting us off at our brand-new Toyota Camry. Demetria and the boys get in while I load the luggage into the trunk. When I shut it, new-car showroom freshness whooshes into my nostrils, flooding my mind with memories of the day we bought the car.

There's Demetria, pulling me across the showroom floor, talking fast as she explains how the four-door will be better for us since the boys are getting bigger. Here's the salesman, talking such a smooth line, it feels good to believe him. There's Demetria, pulling into the driveway, the sleek vehicle looking like it was designed around her panther body.

"Clifford!" Demetria calls. "What're you doing back there?"

"Nothing," I say, forcing the words out past the lump in my throat. I get in and we start off.

I turn onto the expressway for the forty-minute drive first to Momma's house, then to our upscale town house rental in Penn Hills Commons.

In no time at all the boys fall asleep, exhausted from too much fun and too much travel. I'd better try and get some answers now. Once we're home, they'll be causing so much commotion that having any kind of serious discussion with my wife will be next to impossible.

Demetria's seat is reclined and her eyes are closed but I know she's awake. "Demmy?"

She exhales in an exasperated huff. "I knew you were gonna do this."

"Do what?"

"Hound me."

"Baby, don't you think we need to talk?"

"No!"

"Sshh! The kids."

"No, I do not think we need to talk," says Demetria, her voice a harsh, rasping whisper. "I told you how I feel. What else is there to know?"

I look at her and say, "Are you serious?"

Demetria's eyes flap open like shutters. She returns her seat to the upright position and looks at me with hard, loveless eyes. "I'm dead serious. What made you think I wasn't?"

"I don't know what to think," I say, swerving back into my lane. "That's why we need to talk, baby. I need to know what's going on."

"Clifford! I don't see what the problem is. I told you I'm not happy. I told you I don't love you anymore. I don't even like you. How much simpler can I make it?"

"But, baby . . ."

Demetria sounds like she's growling when she says, "Stop calling me baby!"

My forearm muscles bulge as I tighten my grip on the steering wheel. "Demetria, why're you doing this?"

"Doing what?"

"What's made you suddenly want to destroy this family?"

"Suddenly?" Scornful laughter bubbles up from her throat. "There's nothing sudden about it."

She looks at me with twinkling eyes, like she's having fun and she knows I'm not. Then her expression softens, like it's dawning on her that *I don't understand what she's talking about.* "You honestly don't know, do you?"

"No!" I whisper hoarsely. "I don't have the slightest idea."

She stares straight ahead. "It's about truth, Clifford. It started just before we left on vacation, with a conversation that Nolan, Tammy, and I had at work. . . ."

Them again. I should've guessed that Nolan and Tammy were somewhere at the bottom of this crap. Ever since Demetria started working at 21st Century Polymers I've had my suspicions about them and their viral influence. Especially that crud Nolan.

I've told her time and again about letting *their* opinions interfere in *our* marriage but she insists that it's no different from the so-called interference from my brothers, Nathan and Victor.

"We were talking about what people would do if they were *really* told the truth," says Demetria. "So we decided to try it, just for fun. But the conversation turned serious when Nolan shared with us what he was gonna tell Elaine. . . ."

She rambles on about Nolan, who routinely seeks her out as confidante, counselor, and comforter. Whenever his love life is in crisis, Demetria always nurses him back to health.

". . . so when Nolan finished talking, I told him he deserved someone that he could not only love, but be *in* love *with*. Someone he had things in common with, could have fun with, and who would be there for him when he needed them. I told him he was crazy to stay in a relationship where his needs weren't being met."

Demetria pauses and lets the words sink in. I keep my eyes on the road.

"Is that all?" I ask.

"No," she snips. "On vacation, I realized that I'd been talking about myself."

Demetria looks at me and I glance at myself in the rearview mirror. Bowling balls of sweat are rolling down my face.

"Clifford," she goes on. "I don't wanna live like this anymore. I want true love, excitement, and fun. But not with you. *I want a divorce.*"

The words fall from her lips like late autumn leaves that have been waiting, waiting, waiting for winter finally to come.

"Clifford. Clifford!"

"Yeah, ba . . . I mean, what?"

"Why are you driving in two lanes?"

I get back in my lane and check the dash digital readout. A green light comes on, indicating a temperature adjustment. Downward. I glance at the source of the chill.

"Demetria?"

"What is it, Clifford?" Her tone tells me that she wishes I *and* this subject would just dry up and blow away.

"Couldn't you have decided this *before* we bought the car?"

Demetria's face darkens with a disgust so profound, I feel like I've been slapped. "If all you're worried about is the car, I'll take over the payments."

"I'm not worried *only* about the car," I snap. "But do you expect me to believe that your wanting to dump me for true love, excitement, and fun *one lousy month after we bought this thing* is some kind of accident?"

"I don't care what you believe. I told you where I stand and that's that!" She closes her eyes and turns away from me.

"Demmy, can we *please* talk about this?"

"No!"

I spot Braddie and Bear in the rearview mirror, both awake and looking scared. "Go to sleep!" I order.

Their eyes snap shut but I hardly expect them to sleep. This is ridiculous. If I were my brother Victor, I'd pull onto the shoulder, drag Demetria out of this car, and *make* her talk to me. But I'm not Victor and I can hear him ridiculing me again.

*Cliff, you sorry chump. Why're you lettin' her punk you?*

I tune into a soul oldies station. Maurice White of Earth, Wind & Fire is singing "That's the Way of the World." I glance in the rearview mirror. My face looks stupid and weak.

After nearly a half hour of riding in this arctic silence, I almost miss the exit that puts me on the road to Momma's house. I get off the expressway, go through the intersections, and turn onto Momma's street. As we get closer, I see that her garage door's open, so I know she's home.

I hope Demetria comes inside. If she doesn't, Momma will not only be insulted but will start asking a lot of questions that I don't feel like answering.

For the most part, Momma and Demetria have a decent relationship. But they've had their moments, most of them related to matters of child rearing, like the time Momma threatened to spank Braddie and Bear.

Demetria was furious, railing about them being traumatized and calling Momma's methods regressive and counterproductive.

"She should've given them a time-out or had them watch one of the Love My Buddy videos," she complained. "That's why we bought them. To teach the boys alternatives to aggression."

"Demetria, I agree with you," I said. "But since Momma gave them a warning instead of a spanking, don't you think she's as sensitive to the issue as you are?"

"No, Clifford. I *never* would've threatened them. And I don't understand your nonchalance. Aren't you concerned about your children growing up desensitized to violence?"

"Of course I'm concerned. But trust me when I tell you that Momma's *nothing* like she used to be. The only kind of warning Nate, Victor, and I ever got was a thunder roll."

I finally got Demetria to agree that a threatened spanking wasn't likely to transform Braddie and Bear into Mob hit men, but only after I assured her that I'd talk with Momma about practicing the kinder, gentler version of parenting advocated by the "experts."

I pull up in front of Momma's house, park, and am relieved when Demetria gets out with the boys. By the time I'm out of the car, Braddie and Bear are at the front door, their faces glowing with expectation now that they're mere seconds away from our dog, Scratch.

I try to lighten my step as I approach the house, doing my best to calm the tornadoes shredding my heart. The last thing I need is Momma using her hyperintuitive-shared-family-spirits baloney to get in my business. But even if she senses something, I'm not obliged to explain. No matter how much my family might want to interfere, I'm going to work this out in *my* way, in *my* time.

The only person I don't have to worry about is Victor. He'll equate Demetria's departure with finding a cure for cancer. I'm lucky he's in Cleveland. Digging my way out of this mess will be hard enough without having to hammer through his hostility.

Scratch barks as soon as Demetria rings the doorbell.

"Coming!" Momma answers. She opens the door and looks right past me and Demetria to the boys. "How's my precious pair?" she says.

Braddie and Bear holler back, "Grandy!"

Momma's hair is pulled back into that French roll Daddy always said made her look exotic and beautiful. He was right. And her diligent commitment to whatever workout routine she's been following down at that health spa has resurrected some of the curves and indentations that make me glad she's a churchgoing woman.

Scratch, his tail going like a turboprop, starts spinning in tight circles behind Momma. She glances at him, smirks, and says, "I'm *so* glad you all are back to take this crazy dog."

She talks tough, but Momma's the only person who loves Scratch more than the boys do.

Braddie and Bear rush in and bombard Scratch with petting. Momma plants her hands on her hips and assumes the tired-of-talkin' stance that never failed to send me, Nate, and Victor fleeing for safety.

"How dare you dirt-monsters run in here without first giving me a kiss?" says Momma, the love in her eyes belying the indignation in her voice.

The boys forget Scratch and rush to Momma, who's already bending down and offering her cheeks for their loud, smacking kisses. She hugs them both, making them squirm and giggle.

"I've got something for you two," she announces.

"Tell us! Tell us!"

"Look downstairs."

The boys zoom off to find their treasure, with Scratch following close behind. Momma shakes her head and chuckles as she watches them scramble through the door.

"They're so full of energy," she says.

"You should've seen them at Disney World," Demetria confirms.

Momma's eyes meet Demetria's and, to my further relief, they summon smiles for each other and exchange a perfunctory hug. Then each retreats quickly into the safety of her space.

"So did you all have fun?" Momma asks.

"Absolutely!" I blurt. "We're already planning our second trip. Right, baby?"

"No, Clifford. We're not!"

Momma's eyes dart from me to Demetria, and back to me. Demetria glances at her watch and I study my feet.

I look hard at Momma and force out a laugh. "Demetria's right, Momma. After spending a week chasing Braddie and Bear all over the Magic Kingdom, it's way too soon to think about the next trip."

Demetria purses her lips and rolls her eyes, brightening her expression in time to meet Momma's eyes.

"Mother, is it okay if I use your phone?" she asks. "I need to call some friends and tell them I won't be meeting them for dinner. All that 'fun' has left me more drained than I'd expected."

I catch myself before asking who Demetria was planning on meeting for dinner. She never mentioned anything about it during vacation. But then, with the kind of revelations she's just dumped onto me, why would she?

"Sure," says Momma. "You'll have to use the one in the kitchen. I'm surfing Carnegie Mellon's research library on my laptop right now so the living room phone is tied up."

I glance around and see Momma's laptop sitting on the dining room table. It's surrounded on all sides by books, index cards, pens, tablets, diskettes, and journals, all of it proof that she's been slugging away at her doctoral dissertation. If she maintains her pace, she's certain to make her oral defense in time for graduation in December.

"Thanks, Mother," says Demetria. "I won't be long."

She saunters off and Momma turns to me, opening her arms wide. We embrace, the familiarity of her arms reminding me of a time when one of her hugs was all it took to make things better.

"I'm glad you're back," says Momma. "I missed you."

"I missed you too."

I start to pull away but she holds me tight and whispers, "What's wrong?"

I kiss her cheek. "Nothing, Momma. Everything's fine."

Momma steps back and looks hard at me. Her expression remains soft and smiling, except for the split second when her nostrils flare, proof that she's smelled my lie.

I quickly gesture toward the table and her laptop. "Looks like you're making progress on the research."

"You'd better believe it. I'm almost finished with chapter four, and Dr. Karovic is certain that this'll be published as a book."

I hug her again. "I'm very, very proud of you."

She strokes the back of my head. "As I am of you, Clifford. How much longer before you finish your MBA?"

"One more class, then the thesis project."

Momma pushes me away and grips my arms firmly. "You can do it, sweetheart. Just remember to stay focused and never, ever quit!"

I glance into the kitchen at Demetria. "I will, Momma. I promise."

"Mommy! Dada! Look!" shouts Braddie, clambering up the steps.

He charges into the living room, carrying a bag from Kaptain Krazy's toy store. Bear and Scratch race in behind him.

"Grandy got us kites!" Bear exclaims. "Just like the ones on TV!"

"This one's called the Windrider," adds Braddie.

"And this is the Cloudskipper."

"Let me see them!" I say, boosting the excitement in my voice to match theirs.

They hurry over and I whistle and say, "Wow! These are great-looking kites."

"This one'll fly higher," Bear challenges.

"Will not!" Braddie counters.

"Will too!"

"Will not!"

They continue debating as they take off to go show Demetria. I stand and watch till they're gone.

"Momma," I say, "I really wish you wouldn't spend so much on them. They're spoiled enough as it is."

She dismisses my comment with a wrist flick. "Clifford, they're just kites. No harm done."

It's pointless to pursue my complaint and I remind myself to once again tell Braddie and Bear how fortunate they are to know *this* version of Momma rather than the one their uncles and I had as kids. Not that Momma was a whip-cracking torturer, but she also didn't tolerate any foolishness. There was simply no time for it.

Once Daddy got killed in Vietnam, there was no option but for her to go back to work. She returned to the classroom as both a teacher and a student, eventually getting two master's degrees. Her considerable teaching talent landed her in the principal's chair at a school where the students cared little, and the parents even less. Within two years she'd cleaned up the mess, and educators from across the state were visiting and wanting to know Momma's "secret."

That first year after Daddy's death was hard on everyone, especially Momma. By day, she was a pillar of confidence and competence, running her life and her school with tough love. At night, we listened to her cry herself to sleep. Nathan sought comfort through women and sex before finally turning to God. I took refuge in books and academics, excelling in all things concerning the mind. And Victor found strength in anger, working out his resentment over Daddy's absence by straying farther and farther into the streets.

After a while, we shifted into our new rhythm of living, growing up faster and learning as best we could the universe of things boys need to know as they become men. We became for each other the anchor Daddy had been for us all. Then one day we were finding it hard to remember a time when the Matthews family hadn't consisted of just Momma and her three hardheaded sons.

Braddie and Bear blast back into the living room with Scratch once again bringing up the rear.

"Okay, Dada," says Bear, thrusting his kite toward me. "Here! It's yours!"

Braddie mimics Bear's gesture. "Yeah, Dada. Here!"

I smile at the boys. "Why don't you guys hang on to your kites, okay? That'll make it easier for me to get Scratch and all his stuff into the car."

"This is *your* kite!" Braddie declares.

"And this one!" Bear adds.

"Huh? What're you guys talking about? Grandy bought those for you."

"So we could give 'em to you!" Bear insists.

I look at Momma, who shrugs. "Don't look at me. They called me after they got home from the last day of Vacation Bible School . . ."

"The day before we left for Florida."

"Yes. That day. Anyway, they called and asked if I'd buy them kites."

"But, but why?"

"Clifford, stop being silly," Momma admonishes. "These are my grandbabies. It's my pleasure to make them happy."

I start to point out that Braddie and Bear just spent an expensive "happy" week at one of the world's most famous theme parks, but focus instead on the day before we left.

I remember working late. Demetria picked the boys up from Vacation Bible School at Nathan's church. We finished packing for Disney World. Braddie and Bear wanted to go to the toy store. I refused, turning their pouts into smiles by warning that they were blowing their chance to romp with Mickey, Donald, and Goofy. Then they disappeared into their toy room to play video games, and that was that. Or so I thought.

"Thanks for letting me use the phone," says Demetria, stepping out from the kitchen. "It turns out that this was a bad night for Nolan and Tammy also."

I glower at the mention of those names, notice Momma studying me, and quickly look back at Braddie and Bear. Demetria excuses herself into the bathroom.

"Here, Dada!" says Braddie. "You have to fly it."

"Soon!" adds Bear.

I give an exasperated sigh and shake my head. "Okay, you guys. Give me the kites."

They hand them over, then charge back downstairs where Momma keeps a video game unit, set up and ready to go for whenever they come over. Scratch barks at the kitchen door that opens into Momma's garage.

"Let him out so he can do his business," says Momma.

"Why have you been letting him go in your garage?"

"Clifford, you know how much I hate having piles of dog poop in my yard, killing my grass. And Scratch is a good dog. He uses the paper just like I told him."

I'll have to see this for myself. The only time Scratch uses the paper at home is when he hits it by accident. If he hadn't finally learned to let us know when to let him out, he'd have been on death row down at the pound.

"Clifford, while you're out there, you might as well get his bowls, toys, and leash," Momma says.

"Yes, ma'am."

Demetria calls to the boys as I gather up Scratch's stuff. "Braddie! Bear! C'mon so we can go!"

I clean up behind Scratch, chuckling as I ask myself who's the master and who's the dog.

Demetria's voice cuts through my lighthearted introspection. "Braddie! Bear! Did you hear me? I said to come on!"

I rush inside. The increasing frustration in Demetria's voice makes it imperative that I be close by to ensure that Momma doesn't reach any embarrassing conclusions about something being wrong.

"Braddie! Bear! You guys c'mon so we can go," I say.

"Okay, Dada!" they shout. And for clarification Bear adds, "There's only one more big boss to beat, then Luke Skywalker saves the planet."

Those boys know I'm a *Star Wars* fanatic and they're exploiting my weakness. Demetria's glare communicates clearly that she's not enjoying the delay.

"No!" I holler. "You guys come up here now!"

"Pleeeease," Braddie whines. "We're almost done."

Momma, sitting at the table and staring intently at her laptop screen, turns slightly toward the basement and speaks in a tone just above conversational.

"Braddie. Bear. You dirt-monsters get up here *now*."

The pandemonium of laser blasts, rocketing ships, and intergalactic explosions vanishes, and Braddie and Bear come clomping upstairs.

Demetria's face is fully flushed with frustration. The moment the boys explode through the door she says, "Get in the car! And take Scratch with you!"

"Don't forget his stuff," I add, nodding at the food bowls and doggie toys.

Momma's eyes seem focused on her laptop screen, but I know better. She's taking in every gesture, word, glance, and grunt as evidence of the cloud hovering over me.

The boys give Momma quick hugs and kisses, then bounce out the door with Scratch following. Demetria snatches up Scratch's leash and heads for the door.

" 'Bye, Mother," she says, her smile a modified grimace. "And thanks for keeping Scratch."

"You're welcome," Momma answers, standing up. "You take care."

I grab the kites and kiss Momma's cheek. "See you later, one and only. I'll call you in a day or so."

I turn to leave, stopping when Momma grabs my arm. I glance outside at Demetria, busy getting everyone into the car, then face Momma. "What's the matter?" I ask.

"Why did you lie to me?"

"I'm sorry, Momma."

"Apology accepted. Is there anything I can do?"

"No ma'am. It's just a little quarrel. No need for you to get involved."

"It's too late for that."

"What do you mean?"

"Prayer, Clifford! I'm constantly praying for you, Nathan, Victor, and your families." Moments like this leave me wondering how Momma can navigate the intellectual minefield of a doctoral program and still be so spiritual. In a few seconds she'll be describing her latest vision, the deli clerk's interpretation, and how it was confirmed by the ring around her bathtub. Lucky for me, Demetria facilitates my escape with a beep of the car's horn.

I kiss Momma again and we head outside together. "Momma, I appreciate your prayers but I can handle it. I'll call you later."

" 'Bye, Grandy!" shout the boys.

Demetria waves, then sits back and closes her eyes. I get to the car, find space for the kites, then wave to Momma.

"I love you. We'll talk later."

She nods confidently and says, "I know."

I'VE BEEN TRYING TO HAVE A CONVERSATION WITH DEMETRIA EVER SINCE WE GOT HOME. But after she told me that her planning to meet Nolan and Tammy for dinner was none of my business, it's been one obstacle after another.

First, she took a nap. Then she was busy going through the mail. An hour later, she picked up a family pack from King Kluck Chicken. Then she and the boys ate. Then she washed her hair. And while she was at it, she decided to take a nice, long bath. Then it was getting late and she was too tired to talk. I asked her again, "Please, can we deal with this crisis?"

"The crisis is yours, not mine."

"Demetria, how can you just throw away this marriage?"

"Since when has it been a marriage?"

"I'll do anything you want."

"Then shut up and leave me alone."

Then she got on the computer to check for e-mail. And my too-tired-to-talk wife spent the next two hours surfing the Net. When I asked Demetria again to "please help me understand," she answered, "You'll get it when I'm gone."

I tried to follow her into our bedroom, but she slammed the door in my face. I banged on it and hollered, *"Why?"*

She threw something at it and hollered back, *"Why not?"*

BEFORE PUTTING THE BOYS TO BED I EXORCISE ANOTHER "MONSTER" FROM THEIR closet, pulling out all their toys to make sure I get even the teeny-tiny creatures. Braddie points to the kites leaning against the wall just outside the closet door.

"Dada, when are you gonna fly the kites?"

"Soon, Braddie. We'll fly one in a little while."

"Just one?"

"Yeah. We'll take one, practice and get good, then we'll fly the other one."

He smiles a toothy smile. "Okay. But *when*?"

I smile, poke him in his stomach, and say, "Really soon. How's that?"

Braddie glances at the kites. "Okay, Dada. But it's gotta be soon."

Braddie's suddenly a lot more serious than his normal five-year-old self. But he's probably just tired. After all the excitement of Disney World, the flight and drive home, and picking up Scratch, his energy should be almost gone.

I tuck him in, kiss him and the already snoring Bear good night, then go to get in bed. Demetria's down in the living room, laughing and talking on the phone with Tammy, it sounds like. Knowing that she's conversing with that saboteur is irritating, but at least it's not Nolan. That would cause a confrontation, and given the delicacy of my situation, that's the *last* thing I need.

Demetria addresses Tammy directly by name a few times, satisfying my curiosity, and I go get in bed to wait for her. And wait. And wait.

I know Demetria won't feel like talking, but *we have to*! Before today's flight, I'd hoped we would spend our first night back drowning in each other's love juices, especially since we didn't make love on vacation. But

Demetria's made it clear that she means to keep her juices to herself and make me stew in mine.

Before long, I doze off. Then I'm startled awake by a siren blasting somewhere in the neighborhood. I check the digital readout on the alarm clock. Almost two hours have passed and Demetria's still not in bed.

I get up and tiptoe into Braddie and Bear's room. Demetria's asleep in Braddie's bed, holding him so that his head is snuggled deep between her breasts where *my* face should've been two hours ago. I shake her gently and whisper.

"Demmy. Demmy."

She grunts and stirs. "Wha, what's the matter?"

Her soft tone surprises me. It's like she's forgotten that she hates my guts. Then she remembers. "Why're you bothering me?"

"Come to bed, sweetheart."

"I'm fine sleeping here."

She shifts into a more comfortable, and permanent, position.

"Come on, baby," I say. "Braddie's got to learn to sleep by himself."

"Be quiet before you wake him."

Braddie yawns, switches his sucking thumbs, then returns to deep slumber. When he stops moving, Demetria rolls him onto his stomach, then nestles her head into the pillow.

"Demmy . . ."

"Good night, Clifford."

I kiss her cheek. "I love you."

I back away, taking a mental snapshot of the scene. As soon as I step into the hallway, Demetria wipes my kiss from her cheek.

THE CLOCK READS 4:13 A.M. I GET UP, GO INTO THE ADJOINING BATHROOM, CUT ON THE light, and stare at myself in the large mirror. Have I changed that much? Could it be something physical that's adding to Demetria's frustrations?

At five feet eleven inches, I'm not tall but I'm also not short, and it's the same height I was when we got married. I've got a slight married-guy's paunch, but can handle that through exercise. I've kept all my hair, although there's flecks of gray here and there. My chest and arms could use some toning, but nothing's sagging or flabby. And aside from a few laugh lines around my eyes, my face is still mostly youthful.

I get back in bed and study the ceiling shadows, asking myself again: "Is Demetria serious? Is she really going to flush me and this marriage for 'true love, excitement, and fun'?"

I'm not a wife beater, child abuser, or pet torturer. She's never had to beg me to go to work. I make a decent dollar. I don't smoke, drink, or do drugs. If it's the twelve pounds I've gained, I'll lose them. If it's a status issue, I'll have my MBA soon and maybe a promotion. If it's sexual, I'll practice better ejaculation control or get a penile enhancement.

And what's all this stuff about being in love? I'm still in love with Demetria. But our love has grown, matured, and endured. It's taken life's best shots and kept plugging along. Isn't that what love's all about? Isn't that love succeeding? And what about being there for her? I haven't been anywhere *but* there. In the delivery room. By her sickbed. In the trenches during her times of frustration. On her side during her family's squabbles. Where is the "there" she's talking about?

Braddie and Bear! Sweet mother of mercy. I've never even considered their growing up without me. But here it is. We're on the verge of becoming statistics so Demetria can go rainbow windsurfing. A tear rolls from the corner of my eye.

This can't be real! I've got to focus and see the big picture. What's *really* happening is that Demetria's fighting some "thing" she can't articulate and I've got to discover the source and restore order. All it'll take is some investigation, some skilled corrective action, and *voilà*! Things'll be back to normal.

# THE GLADIATOR

# VICTOR

ANY MAN WHO LOVES HARD IS A FOOL. A STONE-COLD, SHO'NUFF FOOL. IF THAT SOUNDS cold-blooded, tough! I mean, it ain't like I'm sayin' people shouldn't fall in love and whatnot, but *NO* man should let a woman get her hooks in him. Hey, baby, I know whut I'm talkin' about. I've seen it too many times. When a dude falls in love, wham! Dead meat. The babe starts moanin' and groanin' about any and everythang. He's borin', ain't tall enough, don't make enough money, ain't got the right kinda car, ain't got the right kinda job, don't pay enough attention, don't spend enough time, or somethin'. And it's always somethin'. Then one day, she just ups and decides she ain't bein' loved enough so, boom! It's over. 'Bye! See ya!

That's when they start havin' fun, hearin' the dude babblin', "But, baby. Can't we work it out?" And not havin' nothin' but some punk excuse, they hide behind "If you don't know, I ain't tellin' ya." Throwin' in some cheap shot like "Your needin' to ax just proves you weren't payin' no attention." Just thinkin' about it pisses me off. Anyway, there the sucka is, layin' in the middle of the street, wonderin' did anybody catch the number of that bus. And do people care? Not no but *HELL NO*! They act like, hey, you a man. Never mind them tire marks on your face. Be strong and deal with the pain. Not me, baby.

I ain't givin' up nothin'. Specially my emotions. I've been through too many changes. You share your dreams, fears, and secrets and then they wake up one mornin', pissed cuz you ain't Denzel and can't sing like Luther, and wonderin', where's Toto and why ain't this Kansas? And it ain't no use tryin' to satisfy 'em. When they get restless and wanna go North to freedom, I pack their bags and send 'em on their way. Just look at my baby bro, Clifford. I could see if he was like me. I chase booty and don't care if the babes know it. At least I ain't like some'a these clowns, blowin' smoke up their butts with junk like "Yeah, baby. I love you for your mind." And then they start givin' up that booty like rabbits on crack. But Cliff, he's out there bein' Mr. Fambly and Demetria's got him chumped into thinkin' the lower half of her body done went on strike. He's my blood and I love him, but he's one naive sucka for lettin' her run that game on him. But hey, that's him. I'll tell you one thang. If she'da tried that foolishness with me, I'da sent her scraggly butt to Canada.

So I don't waste *no* time figurin' 'em out. Where they been, what they want, where they goin', and how they gonna get there ain't got a thang to do with me. My big brother, Nate, is all the time hasslin' me about risky livin' but at least I'm honest. When I lay my dong in the cut there ain't *no* mistakin' my intentions. And besides, they use me too. No matter how tight I watch my back, I still end up light in the pocket. But not always, cuz I don't b'lieve in spendin' no whole lots a money. That way, when they come down with the you-ain't-treatin'-me-rights, I point 'em to the door and tell 'em don't look back. So like I said, I ain't in'trested in love. It costs too much and I ain't payin'.

JUSTINE'LL THROW A FIT IF SHE WAKES UP AND SEES ME SMOKIN' IN HER BED AGAIN. SO whut! If I wanna kill myself smokin', that's *my* business. Thousands of people are gettin' whacked every year by muggers, drug dealers, and psychos and the po-leases come after smokers and jaywalkers.

So I don't care how many laws they pass. I'll use my seat belt when I feel like it. If I wanna drink and drive, that's whut I'ma do. I'm watchin' every violent movie and TV show I can find. And I'll smoke when I want, where I want, includin' Justine's bed.

She rolls over, wiggles her nose, then boings into a sittin' position and grits on me.

"Ice! I *know* you ain't layin' in *my* bed smokin'!"

I take a drag and blow. "Well then, you know wrong."

"Fool! How many times I gotta tell you not to be smokin' in my bed?"

"As many times as it takes. And who you callin' a fool?"

"You! Fool!"

Justine shifts and the covers fall off 'a them nice jugs. Too bad her head's on this body. Cuz she can definitely roll that booty, but she ain't got the brains of a basement brick.

"Now why you wanna go callin' me names?"

"I wouldn't be callin' you no names if you didn't ask for it. I don't know how many times I've told you not to be smokin' in my bed."

She gets up and snatches her robe off the chair. I swear, her booty belongs in a hall of fame. I feel like grabbin' that big, round thang.

"Don't be mad, baby," I say. "But with the way you screw, I gotta smoke just to calm my nerves."

She crosses her arms and narrows her eyes, gettin' more pissed and lookin' beautiful.

"Ice, don't *even* start. You ain't never had no bad nerves."

I stand up and grab my dong, the Dipper, and point him at her. "C'mon and gimme some more lovin', baby. The Dipper's complainin' about bein' hungry."

"You lucky I don't kick that toothpick into space."

"Justine, don't try chumpin' me. With the way you was moanin' last night, this 'toothpick' musta been hittin' a nerve."

She laughs like she knows somethin' I don't. "I was fakin'."

"No you wasn't."

She shrugs and says, "Believe what you want."

She leaves the room and comes back with half a toothpick. "So this is what you were scratchin' me with."

A heat wave zooms up the back of my neck. "Slut!"

Justine grabs a book off the dresser and throws it at me. It misses but it's close enough for me to feel the *whoosh* before it slams into the wall.

"Get out, Ice. Now!"

I stay cool and start puttin' on my clothes, watchin' Justine from the corner of my eye. Ain't no use bein' stupid.

While I'm watchin' her, I'm checkin' myself out in the mirror. Ev'rythang's still tight. My stomach's got them washboard muscles, my chest is cut, and my skin's all stretched nice over this six-foot-two-inch frame. My crotch bulge is its own best advertisin' and, accordin' to the babes, my tiny diamond earring gives me that look of a jazz player.

Justine keeps watchin' as I get my stuff, then follows me into the kitchen. "What're you doin'?" she axes.

I start settin' up the coffeemaker. "Want some coffee?"

"I told you to leave. Don't make me have'ta call the po-lease."

I walk over to her and look into them big, sleepy eyes. "Baby, I don't want you doin' nothin' you don't wanna do."

I palm one'a them nice, juicy casabas. Justine half slaps my hand away and I palm the other one. I slip my arm around her waist and pull her into me.

"Ice, what part of *NO* don't you understand? Or are you just crazy?"

I try kissin' her but she leans back. I squeeze one'a them hamhock booty cheeks and pull her treasure box into the Dipper, who's awake and ready.

"C'mon, baby. Just one kiss 'bye," I say, doin' my best Barry White.

Justine's eyelids droop and I imagine the Dipper diggin' in her treasure box.

"I hate you," she says. Then she kisses me, suckin' my tongue so hard it pulls at the root.

NOTHIN' BEATS STARTIN' THE DAY WITH A NICE SHOT OF BOOTY. SPECIALLY SINCE I gotta face them clown passengers on my bus. One'a these days, I'ma quit this job, move from Cleveland to Atlanta, and hook up with the transit dudes down there. Now *that* would be livin'. Spendin' all day watchin' them fine southern babes shimmy down the aisle. The only thang I'd have'ta do is set up a booty network. I guess Cliff ain't the only one'a the Matthews boys worried about his next lay.

That weak-minded fool gets on my nerves. I don't know why he thinks Demetria's the only woman he can get with. The last time I was home in Pittsburgh, I tried hookin' him up with Vanessa but he acted like he was too good for the women I know. And it wasn't like Vanessa was some street ho. She just prefers married men. That way, she gets the pleasure without the problems.

I get down to the RTA lot, clock in, and head out to my assigned bus. I'm just about finished with my walk-around safety inspection when Corey, our punk lot supervisor, comes waddlin' up, movin' like somebody's broke a broomstick off in his butt.

Six months ago, Corey was just another workin'-stiff driver like me. But now that he's finally brown-nosed his way into management, he's been actin' all uppity, demandin' to be called "Mr. Jackson." He ain't had no love for me ever since I told him I wasn't bowin' and scrapin' for *nobody*. And he really got pissed the day I grabbed the Dipper and told him, "C'mon and Mr. Jack *this*!"

Corey was gonna write me up, till I reminded him that I had the goods on him belly-bumpin' with his secretary, Claudia. When I mentioned that I might one day slip up and say somethin' to his so-called fiancée, Francine, he got the look-of-the-stupids and backed off. Since then, Corey's been keepin' his distance. As long as he stays cool, Francine won't never have'ta know that the only "paperwork" he uses after hours is a napkin to wipe Claudia off his chin.

Corey waddles closer and calls me. "Ice! Can we talk for a minute?"

"Why? We ain't got nothin' to discuss," I say, continuin' my inspection.

"The district manager's been on my case to reprimand you for that accident."

"Corey, why're you sweatin' me? I told you it wasn't my fault."

"But didn't you rear-end the guy?"

I stop and stare hard into Corey's eyes. "Look! I told you the dude slammed on his brakes. And even the po-leases said he was drunk."

Corey swells up like someone's pumpin' him full'a gas. "You need to watch your tone of voice."

"Or what?" I say, facin' him directly.

Corey's Adam's apple jiggles, then he spins around and stomps off, mumblin' somethin' about mothers. I oughta jerk a knot in his butt for that, but forget him. I finish my safety inspection, check out with the dispatcher, and hit my route.

---

EVEN THOUGH THESE DRUNK DRIVERS AND CRACKHEAD PASSENGERS SOMETIMES PISS me off, gettin' hooked up with the Cleveland RTA was definitely the right thang to do. It's a sittin' job for a change. The work ain't too hard. The pay ain't too bad. And best of all, I get to see Edie. Watchin' her get on the bus every day with her little baby girl, Karenna, lookin' just like my Jewel back in Pittsburgh, always brightens thangs up.

I make my first few pickups, turn onto Superior, and see Edie, standin' like always at the bus stop in front of her buildin', and holdin' that little cutie-pie. Which reminds me, I gotta make sure I'm in Pittsburgh for Jewel's birthday.

I swing over to the curb and hit the brakes.

"Can't you drive no better than that?" yells some wino from the back.

That sucka's lucky I ain't runnin' back there to drive my fist into his big mouth. Edie gets on and I pull out the lollipop I brought for Karenna. When she sees it, she squeals with some serious joy.

"Bus driver's got candy!"

Before handin' it over I check with Edie. "Do you mind if she has it?"

Edie smiles. "No. But from now on, get her Gummy Bears so we can both have something we like."

"That's why I'm here."

Edie blushes and looks away, like she's searchin' for a way to escape the spotlight. Before she runs off, I reach down beside my seat and pull out her present. Her eyes fill up with happy, matchin' the sunshine beamin' from her smile.

"A rose!" she says.

"Why can't you do stuff like that for me?" axes some crow, jabbin' her elbow into the grumpy-lookin' dude beside her.

"Should we just get out and walk?" bellyaches the punk who complained when I hit the brakes.

Edie steals a mean glance at that fool and I grit on him as she takes the empty seat behind me. Once she's sittin', I pull into traffic and try again to figure out how I'ma get her to go out with me.

"Thanks for the rose," she says. "That was very sweet of you."

"Sweet thangs for a sweet woman."

"How do you know that I am?"

I shrug and say, "I trust my instincts." I glance into the overhead mirror and see Karenna. "Besides. Ain't no way you coulda gave birth to a gem like Karenna if you was mean."

Edie blushes. "I have my moments."

"Don't we all?"

We ride for a couple'a blocks in silence, and I turn my head just far enough to where I can talk low over my shoulder while keepin' my eyes on the road.

"So, Edie, when're we goin' out?"

Edie don't answer right away. I glance up into the overhead and see her lookin' stiff-jawed and serious. And I'm wonderin' what I coulda said that's slapped me back to square one. Her eyes meet mine and we're locked for a hot second before I have'ta focus back on the road.

"Ice, you seem okay," Edie says. "But I don't think that's a good idea."

I have'ta bite my tongue to keep from cussin' my disappointment until Edie says, "At least, not right now."

"That's cool," I say, turnin' my head again to make sure she hears me. "But can I ax you somethin'?"

"Sure."

"Are you afraid or somethin'? Cuz if you are, I wanna set your mind at ease."

Edie leans forward and says, "Fear has nothing to do with it. But I'm not a woman who plays at relationships . . ."

*RELATIONSHIPS?* All I'm axin' is to go out on a date!

Edie finishes with, ". . . so let's just say that before I spend any time with you, I'll trust my instincts."

AFTER I DROPPED EDIE OFF, THE DAY SLID STRAIGHT INTO THE TOILET. FIRST THERE WAS that drunk, baggy-pants lowlife who puked in the aisle, and them hoodlum kids who threw rocks at my bus, breakin' one'a the windows. Then while I was eatin' lunch with my RTA partners, Clyde and Brantley, I caught some junkie pissin' on my tires. The finishin' touch was havin' to listen to them passengers all afternoon, whinin' and cryin' about smellin' vomit.

I get back to the lot, fill out some incident reports, then head to the locker room to shower and change into my civvies. Cleveland traffic's still light but that won't last, so I gotta hurry. After today, the last thang I wanna deal with is road hassles.

And speakin' of today, I could use some unwindin'. So I'ma go home, catch some *Zs*, then swing on down to Benny's. If ain't no booty action happenin', I'll call it a day. If there is, well, it'll be a good night.

I start out across town, see a Toys "R" Us, and jet into the parkin' lot. Now's as good a time as any to buy Jewel one'a them Misty Maidens dolls she's been talkin' about. The other night on the phone, she was bouncin' off the walls about the latest one, Magic Maiden.

"Nero, will you get me Magic Maiden?" she axed.

"Baby, I'll get you anythang you want."

I love the way she says "Nero" even though I ain't too crazy about her reasons for sayin' it. She just started callin' me that durin' one'a my visits. I got a chance to ax why when my nosy ex, Lynnette, finally left the room.

"Jewel, why's you callin' Daddy 'Nero'?"

"Because Mommy does."

"Whutch'you mean, baby? Tell me z'actly whut she says."

"She says you're a good-for-nuffin' Nero."

I got on Lynnette's case about bad-mouthin' me in front'a my baby, but it didn't do no good. And I had to stay cool cuz all she had to do was sneeze and them Children's Services thugs woulda chopped my visitation for good.

Nate and Cliff think I'm paranoid when I tell 'em those suckas are programmed to assume I ain't never right and Lynnette can't do no wrong. But like Momma always used to say, Cliff and Nate "don't b'lieve a black cow gives white milk." If they ever have to deal with them bouncers, they'll know the real deal.

Anyway, in a few weeks when I go home it'll be cool givin' my baby four presents for her turnin' four years old. One present for each year of joy she's gave me, no matter how hard Lynnette's tried to screw 'em up.

Seein' Jewel always reminds me that I got somethin' to live for. But I swear, I'd pay big money to be allowed visitations without havin'ta put up with Lynnette's big mouth.

I WAKE UP FROM MY NAP AND CUT ON CNN. SOME TALKIN' HEADS ARE JAWJACKIN' about them Congress clowns votin' theyselfs a pay raise. That's how it goes. Them fools line their pockets with *my* tax money, claim they can't raise the minimum wage, and think I'm too stupid to notice.

I start gettin' dressed to head on down to Benny's, splashin' on some'a that Winter Mirage cologne Justine bought me. That stuff is good. And accordin' to the commercials, once the ladies get a whiff I oughta have platoons of 'em linin' up to drop their panties. Since Justine don't get off at the auto plant till late, I just might get lucky before she arrives.

I grab a couple'a condoms, stuff 'em in my wallet, and head out. Just as I'm passin' the phone, it rings. My caller ID says it's Momma, but I don't feel like foolin' with her right now so I let it roll over to the answerin' machine.

I check myself in the mirror, start toward the door, and my pager goes off. The message says: ANSWER ME—MOMMA. Then the phone rings again. And this time I know I'd better pick up.

"Hi, Momma."

"Hello, Victor. I'm glad I caught you before you started your evening of catting around."

I gave up a long time ago tryin' to figure out how she knows stuff. That's what made growin' up around her so tough. She couldn't be lied to. I'd bet money she's why Nate became a preacher. He prob'ly figured that the only way he could get Momma out'a his head was to get in good with the Big Sky Boss.

"How're you doing?" axes Momma.

"I'm fine. What about you?"

"Busy. I'm just about finished with my dissertation, which means I'll be on time for December graduation."

"Congratulations, Momma. Just lemme know when and where, and I'll have my face in the place."

"I certainly shall."

I check my wall clock. It's almost time for Ladies Hour to start and I ain't about to miss none'a that action.

"So Momma, whut's on your mind?" I ax.

"Are you in such a rush, you can't even spare a minute to talk with me?"

"Naw, Momma. I was just . . ."

"Well then at least wait for me to get to my point."

"Yes, ma'am."

"That's better. Now. When was the last time you talked with Jewel?"

"The day before yesterday. Whuts'up? Is she okay?"

"She's doing fine. I just wanted you to know that I called to ask Lynnette if Jewel could come over here for a sleepover with Braddie and Bear."

"That oughta be fun."

"It will be. Those dirt-monsters are such good boys."

"Yeah. How those cool little dudes ever popped out'a Demetria is somethin' them *Unsolved Mysteries* dudes oughta check out."

"Victor, stop being cruel."

"That ain't cruel. It's the truth. Anyhow, whut'd Lynnette say?"

"She said she'll think about it, but I'm sure it'll be all right. She'll get a whole evening's break, and Jewel will get to spend some quality time with her cousins."

That's just like Momma, givin' the benefit of the doubt. She talks like Lynnette might act'chally say "Yeah!" when it ain't gonna be nothin' but "No!" Cuz Lynnette'll figure that bustin' Momma's bubble will get at me.

But I don't wanna piss on Momma's parade, so I just say, "Lemme know whut she says."

"I will, Victor. It would help if you could keep the peace. I'm sure Lynnette will be much more agreeable if she's not angry."

"Momma, b'lieve me. Lynnette ain't hardly one'a the people I wanna talk to. If she catches an attitude and squashes your plans, it won't be cuz'a me."

"Well, all right," says Momma, soundin' like she ain't too sure about b'lievin' me. "It's just that these kids don't see enough of each other. And I want them to grow up knowing that we're a loving family."

"With a grandma like you, that won't be no problem."

Momma chuckles. "Okay, Mr. Charmer. Anyhow, I'm sure they'll all have fun. Now that Braddie and Bear are back from vacation, they should have plenty of stories to share."

"Where'd they go?"

"Disney World."

"It must be nice."

"What must be?"

"To have money for that kinda vacation."

"What're you talking about? Clifford saved up for that trip. And he got the best economy package available."

"Economy!" I say, laughin'. "Momma, you know good'n well that stuck-up-stiff-neck-tight-butt Cliff didn't stay in no low-rent district. Not even at Disney World."

Momma don't say nothin', and I can almost see her shakin' her head, wonderin' if I'ma ever straighten up and be good.

"Victor, I know you love Clifford. Why must you always attack him?"

Here we go again. Big bad wolf Ice is abusin' Momma's little Clifford. What I wanna know is, how come she ain't never axed Cliff about his attackin' me? Always carryin' on about whut he's got and how together his life is, like I woke up one mornin' and decided I wanted to be alone, broke, and diggin' a hole to nowhere. But later for all this drama. I gotta get down to Benny's cuz Ladies Hour has started.

"Momma, I gotta run."

"Wait! Jewel has been asking about you. You need to come see her soon."

"I'll be there in a few weeks. Her birthday's comin' up. I ain't forgot."

"You need to see her more often. Lynnette said it's been nearly a month."

"Momma, I can read a calendar!" I say, gettin' loud. "And you *know* I'm back there to see Jewel every chance I get."

"Will you just hear me out before you go flying off the handle? I know you and Lynnette have had your differences. But you all need to put those aside for Jewel. It's not good for that baby to know her parents are so hostile toward each other."

I'd tell Momma that there ain't enough words or time to describe my hostile-ness for Lynnette, but I keep quiet. Time is passin' and the ladies are gatherin'.

"Victor, are you listening to me?"

"Yeah, Momma. But whutch'you want me to do? Act like nothin' happened? Pretend that all them changes Lynnette put me through was just some joke?"

"What you're supposed to do is be a better man than she is a woman. You need to see past her and think about Jewel."

That's whut don't nobody seem to understand. Jewel is *all* I can think about. Specially her havin'ta grow up without her daddy like I grew up without mine. I lose sleep every night, knowin' she's gettin' her life lessons from that street-ho Lynnette. And blood pours from my eyes everytime I hear Cliff's echoin' voice, accusin' me of chumpin' my responsibilities just cuz I moved to Cleveland.

I could tell Momma all'a that but she wouldn't hear me. So I just say, "Momma, you don't understand."

"Yes I do! More than you know. And I realize that Lynnette can be difficult. But she's still Jewel's mother, who . . ."

"Who'll do anythang she can to make me miserable, includin' usin' Jewel as a weapon."

"Victor, please don't interrupt me."

"I wouldn't if you wasn't talkin' stupid. But whutch'you want from me? You think I like bein' apart from my baby?"

There's a throat-chokin' silence comin' from the phone and I can see Momma jammin' her hands onto her hips, her nostrils flarin' and her foot tappin'.

"Momma, I'm sorry. I didn't mean to get smart."

She don't say nothin' and I know she's pissed.

"Square business, Momma. I ain't meant nothin' by it."

"Don't you ever talk to me like that again. *Understand?*"

"Yes, ma'am."

"And tonight while you're out fornicating, you just think about winding up with another Lynnette. There'll be no one to blame but *yourself*."

"Yes, ma'am."

She pauses and sighs. "Victor."

"Yes, Momma."

"I just don't want to see you hurt again. Believe me, sweetheart. You don't want to spend your life cleaning up the mess from one-night stands. You're too precious for that."

And this is why there ain't nobody in this world like Momma. Cuz she knows how to make a sucka down in the dumps feel like a king. So I tell her she's right, that I'ma try and do better, that I'll be in Pittsburgh soon, and I miss her a lot.

Then we hang up and I hurry on down to Benny's to see about gettin' some booty.

---

I DON'T EVEN GET PAST THE RAGGEDY JUKEBOX AT BENNY'S FRONT DOOR WHEN SOMEbody's hollerin' my name.

"Hey, Ice! Whuts'up, baby?"

Ricky. Whut's that punk doin' here?

"Come on and have a sit-down," he says, wavin' me over to his booth.

I slap five, funky-handshake, and cool-hug with some'a the brothas on my way across the room. Ricky's sittin' with this *fine* hefty-chested babe and I'm suddenly glad he's got a big mouth and likes to brag. I squeeze in and slap him five.

"Whutch'you been up to?" he axes.

"Hey, man. You know the deal. Just fightin' the battle."

I take a long look at Ricky's woman. Anybody else might get pissed, but Ricky don't care. He figures she's makin' him look good.

"Say, Ricky. Intro me so I can tell her what a dog you are and save her some grief."

Ricky laughs and waves me off. "You ain't got no room to talk, Mr. Slab'em'n Jab'em."

He looks at the babe, then cuts his eyes at me. "Simone, this trash-talkin' wolf is Ice. Ice, this"—he pauses like a drumroll's comin'—"fine lady is Simone."

She gives a weak smile, tryin' to be cool. But I can tell she likes whut she sees.

Vernon yells from behind the bar. "Ice! Whutch'you drinkin'? You know Benny don't play lettin' suckas stay who ain't buyin'."

"Vernon! Quit axin' stupid questions and bring my usual!"

Ricky's laughin' cuz me and Vernon go through this every time I come in here. I peep at Simone and shiver. She's starin' at me like a dog scopin' a T-bone. Vernon brings my beer and I pay him.

"Where you been hidin'?" axes Vernon.

"Hey, man. I been on the case."

"You are a case," says Vernon, walkin' off.

"Don't forget to bring my change!" I holler. "You know you on parole."

Vernon flips me the bird and Ricky laughs. Simone's starin' at me so hard she prob'ly needs to change into some dry panties. I'ma *definitely* get me some'a this booty.

Ricky jumps up and grabs his stomach. "Hey, Simone. Ice. Ya'll're gonna have'ta 'scuse me. I feel a big one comin'."

"Man, why're you so foul?" I say, frownin'. "Go on, before you start stankin' up the joint. And you better hope that funk don't peel the paint off'a Benny's bathroom walls."

Ricky takes off, holdin' his stomach. And I stare into the valley of Simone's giants.

"You got a problem?" she axes. Her voice is filled with all kinda bad attitudes.

"Yeah, baby. I'm tryin' to figure out how I'ma get all that in my mouth."

"You is pitiful."

"And you is fine, baby. F-i-n-e. Fine!"

She shifts. Those balloons jiggle. And I drool!

"Look, don't *even* start," says Simone. "I ain't in the mood to be hearin' no lame lines from a lame clown."

I drink some'a my beer and chuckle.

Simone gets a cigarette and lights up. "What're you laughin' at?"

"Nothin' much. I'm just wonderin' how Ricky found hisself such a skeezin' freak."

Simone grabs my drink and throws it in my face. I grab her drink and throw it between them mountains. She gasps like someone's punched her in the stomach.

I smile and say, "That's whut I wanna hear when I slide into you."

That *really* pisses her off and she flies across the table and starts whackin' me up'side my head. Vernon's laughin' with some'a the brothas at the bar. I grab one'a Simone's arms and find out what it's like to hold an out'a-control fire hose. Then she tries slammin' a knee into my balls. This is gonna be some *good* booty!

"Hey, Ice! You want me to call 911?" hollers Vernon, laughin'.

"Get him off'a me!" screams Simone.

"Shut up!" I holler.

"Make me!"

Simone yanks one arm free, gives my head a star-spinnin' whack, then pulls me close and drills her tongue down my throat. I ram my tongue into her mouth like a piston and palm one'a them giant boobs. She shoves me back, pulls out a cosmetic mirror, and starts fixin' up her hair and makeup.

"Dog, baby," I say, tryin' to hear myself over that ringin' in my ears. "Why was you tryin' to win the boxin' gold medal on my head?"

"Cuz you asked for it."

I scope out every inch of cleavage in that jigglin' brown Jell-O and feel the Dipper wakin' up.

"What about Ricky?" she axes.

"I ain't in'trested in him."

Simone lights up another cigarette and blows smoke in my face.

I fan it away and say, "So why don't you gimme that phone number?"

"Why should I?"

I kick off one'a my shoes and rub my foot along Simone's calf and up her thigh. She's tryin' to be cool, but I can see through the swirlin' smoke that she's lovin' my big toe.

"Ice!"

Vernon nods toward the back, lettin' me know that Ricky's on the way up. The ash from Simone's cigarette gets longer and her eyes glaze over as my big toe massages the other lips I'd like to kiss.

"Hey, Vernon!" hollers Ricky, bein' loud and stupid as usual. "Get me another scotch and water and Simone some'a that nerve tightener Benny made up. And, oh! Get my man Ice another beer."

Simone stamps out the cigarette and dabs her forehead with a napkin. Ricky gets to the table just as Simone's puttin' her pen away and I'm puttin' her number in my pocket.

# THE PROPHET

# NATHAN

VICTOR IS CONSTANTLY BUGGING ME ABOUT FIXING HIM UP WITH "ONE'A THEM BIG-BUTT church girls." When I tell him he oughta come to church and fix his soul up, he backs off. That's Victor for you. He'll drive from Cleveland to Pittsburgh to fornicate, but he won't drive the extra few minutes to church to worship. Knucklehead. He's bent, and Clifford's a bourgeois, intellectual snob. But they're my brothers and I love them.

Becoming a Christian brought some wonderful changes to my life. Especially in my relationship with Brenda. Before we got married, she'd compromised her values and slept with me as the price for my so-called love. Then light entered my life and I saw the world through her eyes and realized how wrong I'd been. I'm glad she stuck beside me, but I've got to be truthful. With what I now know of God's love, His words, and His wrath, I'm not certain I'd have done the same for her. No one is worth that kind of trouble. Which brings me back to Victor.

He's always bragging about his women, but compared to me when I was "out there" he's a rank amateur. After Jesus, I had to learn to resist temptation's knock. I still struggle, and I ask God every day to strengthen me against my flesh. But that's nothing compared to the battle for people's souls. It's like stirring the Atlantic with a teaspoon, and I wonder sometimes if God did the right thing by calling me to pastor Divine Temple. Everyone has some special need. Lovely Sister Dawkins wants to divorce Percy for messing around. Brother Loudon's searching desperately for a job. Sixteen-year-old Keishawn Newman is pregnant. Sweet old Mother McCoombs, my spiritual mother, is terrified that her gangster grandson, Raymond, is gonna end up a chalk outline. And then there's my wild brother Victor. He keeps me in prayer.

Thank God for Brenda. Few women could've dealt with all she's endured. Accepting the necessity of me splitting time between family and flock. Getting called at all hours to comfort someone caught in the grip of tragedy. The constant cries of the community. Someone of lesser understanding would've forced me to choose between her and God and gotten her feelings hurt. Not Brenda. She's let me tend to the Lord's business. And I appreciate that because I refuse to be found lacking when Jesus asks me to report on the shepherding of his sheep.

---

JUST AS WE DO EVERY YEAR, ON THE SAME DAY AT THE SAME TIME, AT NOON, WHEN THE sun is highest and the day brightest, making it impossible to hide the truth of my crime, Brenda and I walk toward the grave site. I don't know why she comes. If the situation were reversed, I'm not sure I'd be here for her. But she is for me. And because she is, I know her love for me goes deep.

She stops just before we get there, letting me finish the last few steps alone, shambling into the arms of the guilt, shame, and pain that have been awaiting my arrival. I place the flowers in front of Syreeta's headstone then kneel to pray the prayer I've uttered for nearly twenty years.

"Father, God. Please forgive me."

It wasn't that I didn't care about Syreeta. But Brenda was the one I was most serious about, the one whom I intended to marry—after I finished having my fun. That's what all the veterans urged me to do before I lost my freedom.

"You'd better get it out'a your system, boy," they'd laugh. "Once you're wearing that ring, you won't get time off for good behavior."

I took their advice to heart. It was just too soon to give up freaky Lolo who, to borrow her words, liked "those really naughty things." And I'd miss Amber, her money and her Cadillac, and the thrill it gave me when we traveled to planet ecstasy, where her heart-attack-prone husband no longer dared venture.

I can scarcely believe I used to be that person. Life was good, or so I thought. And it wasn't like Brenda and I had made any real commitment to each other. Even so, I had to hide my sneaking around from her. Brenda had substance and was serious about life and love. She would've left me and I couldn't have had that. And Syreeta, well, I knew she loved me. But that was her problem. Being a "real" man, I expected her to manage her emotions, no matter how many times I bled them.

To all my "real" men friends, I joked that Syreeta was just another "rode woman," a flesh highway upon whom I drove myself to pleasure. She knew about the others. I made sure of that. Unlike my approach to Brenda, with Syreeta I kept nothing hidden. I thought she understood that we were just "friends." I expected her to understand that having sex with my "friends" was just a part of friendship. But she kept talking about *relationship*.

I told Syreeta to stop dreaming. I tried to let her down easy. But she kept pressing me, shoving me into a corner until the day she forced me to strike back.

"Yes, Syreeta!" I hollered. "I'm in love with someone. And it's not you!"

It was her own fault. At least, that's what I told myself. And she cried the way she always did, with a quiet elegance and dignity that troubled my numbed nerves of shame. She never took her eyes off me, staring through tears that, I realize now, were the distilled sorrows of angels.

"But Nathan, don't you have any feelings for me?" she asked in a whisper.

"Of course I do, Syreeta. You're nice and everything, but this can't go anywhere."

"Why, Nathan? What have I done?"

What could I tell her? That she was fun and a good lay, but I could never spend my life with someone so easy. Brenda had given herself too, but it had taken almost a year. She'd made me work.

"Doesn't it matter that I love you?" Syreeta asked, the hurt in her voice leaving me breathless.

Of course it mattered. I needed her to love me, so she'd lie down whenever I wanted. She was so unlike Brenda, who, after the first time we did "it," refused, telling me she wouldn't abuse the Lord's love again. That's how I knew I needed Brenda.

Momma had taught me, Clifford, and Victor the qualities to look for in a future wife. Being God-fearing ranked at the top, even though at the time, it mattered little to me. I needed a bigger reason to love Christ. His merely saying "Follow me" wasn't good enough. I needed something spectacular, and it came.

I was in my apartment with Lolo when Syreeta called that night. Marvin Gaye was setting the mood, insisting that we hurry and "Get it on." The wine had flowed freely and Lolo was ready for "naughty things" when the phone rang.

"Hello?"

"Nathan, it's me, Syreeta."

"Can't talk now. I'm busy."

"Nathan, I'm pregnant."

Marvin Gaye's voice was drowned out by the thumping in my ears as my blood pressure surged.

"Says who?" I asked.

"Says the doctor."

"So! Why're you calling me?"

"You're the father."

"How do you know?"

"You're the only one I've been with."

It was a lie. Syreeta had given herself too quickly. With standards like that, I couldn't have been the only one.

"You're a liar."

"Why would I lie, Nathan?"

"Good question, Syreeta. Why don't you tell me?" Lolo's lust was losing its heat and I was losing my patience. "Syreeta, the baby's not mine. Go trap somebody else."

"Nathan, we need to talk about this."

"No!"

And I hung up, right as she was saying, "For God's sake, Nathan! Please don't . . ."

There was ice on the roads that night. And Syreeta was distraught. That's what her mother later said at the funeral.

Syreeta was on her way to confront me, reason with me, and urge me to do right. But she drove too fast, and the ice was unforgiving. Her car rolled several times, killing her and the baby. Blood tests later showed the child was mine.

Momma held me as I cried into her lap. "I killed her, Momma. Just as surely as if I'd used my own hands."

She didn't say a word, letting my conscience condemn me like no earthly judge could. I wanted Momma to whisper something, *anything,* absolving me of blame. But she wouldn't do that. She'd raised us to know better, to be accountable, and to do unto others as we'd have had them do unto us.

I prayed for God to ease my pain, even at the price of taking my life in exchange for Syreeta's. And then in the small morning hours when angels gather the last breath of some and grant a reprieve to others, I looked up and found my Christ waiting. Eternity opened its arms and the old Nathan passed away and all things became new.

The next day, I told Brenda of my lies, bracing myself for her tears and departure. But she stayed, granting me a mercy and love that I'd never shown to Syreeta. That was twenty years ago. I know of Christ's love, but I still haven't forgiven myself for Syreeta.

I hear Brenda, crying, close behind me. She's been here every time. And always, I've asked her, "Brenda, why do you come?"

And always, she's answered, "Because Syreeta was my friend."

Brenda and I ride in silence on the way home, each of us struggling again to work through a tragedy that years of reflection haven't made any clearer. Of my guilt for Syreeta's death, there's no doubt. Someday I'll accept the Lord's forgiveness. His love and mercy know no end. But what humbles me most is Brenda. She considered every lie I told about everything that happened and forgave them all. Victor called her stupid. Clifford called her illogical. Momma called her precious. From that day forward I called her *wife.*

She looks over at me and says, "Nathan, are you happy with me?"

I take her hand. "Sweetheart, absolutely! Except for the Lord coming into my life, you're the best thing that's ever happened to me. Why do you ask?"

She shrugs. "No reason. I just wanted to know."

Brenda knows how much I love her. But sometimes when we come from

Syreeta's grave, I can tell she's wondering if vestiges of the old Nathan are still alive and kicking.

"There's no other reason?"

"No. I guess I just wanted to hear you say it."

We ride for a few minutes in silence until I say, "Are you happy with me?"

Brenda smiles and taps her chin with her forefinger. "Hmmm. Let me think about that."

"What's there to think about? That should be an automatic yes."

She laughs. "Maybe. But it doesn't hurt to do a quick review."

"And what's your conclusion?"

"That overall, you'll do."

"That's not encouraging," I say, with an exaggerated pout.

Brenda leans over and kisses my cheek. "Poor baby. You should be happy. After all, I said 'You'll do.' Isn't that better than saying 'You're done'?"

I chuckle. "You've got a point." I give her a lingering glance. "Seriously, sweetheart. I love you with all my heart."

She squeezes my hand. "I know, Nathan. But sometimes it just needs to be said, so we both can know." She shakes her head. "With so many members of the congregation getting divorced, it makes you wonder who'll be next."

"Do you mean us?"

Brenda hesitates, then says, "Yes."

"Bren, the only way that can happen is if you decide to leave me. Because I promise you, I'm not going anywhere."

She lets go of my hand and massages the back of my neck. "Baby, I'm not going anywhere either."

"So there you have it. I'm not going anywhere. You're not going anywhere. I love you. You love me. It sounds like we're a marital success."

"After eighteen years, we'd better be." She is silent for a few moments, and then she says, "How long have Beverly and Percy been married?"

I think for a second, then answer with "Almost eighteen years."

"That's scary."

"You're right, sweetheart. But you've got to look at the whole picture. With everything that Beverly's been through, it's a miracle she's lasted this long. Everyone's in prayer that the Lord will knock some sense into Percy. But you know how Christ approaches these matters . . ."

"I know. If He doesn't force people to accept salvation, the most important decision in their lives, He won't force them to accept the blessings of a fulfilled marriage."

I nod in agreement. "I just hope Percy wakes up before it's too late."

"It's already too late. How long do you think a woman as attractive as Beverly will remain by herself?"

"About a half hour. And I'm probably off by twenty-five minutes."

Brenda looks at me directly and says, "Do you think she's attractive?"

I keep my eyes dead ahead. "Yes, I do. But all the women in our congregation are stunning. Beverly's just another rose on the bush."

From the corner of my eye I see Brenda's eyebrow arch. "That may be true. But you've got to admit, Nathan, she's a very attractive rose."

I keep my response short, simple, and to the point. "Agreed."

Brenda stays focused on me while she continues massaging my neck.

"Mmmm. That feels good," I say, rubbing her inner thigh.

She slaps my hand away. "Stop being fresh."

"Would you prefer me stale?"

She rolls her eyes. "That was soooo corny."

"Well, would you?"

She closes her legs on my hand. "No. I prefer you fresh. And in the oven."

I look over at her, see the glint in her eyes, and say, "What time are Corrine and Nate Junior due back from their trip?"

Brenda pulls the bus-trip schedule from her purse. "Let's see. This year's nature outing for the church's Young & Gifted program won't be back for another couple of hours."

I squeeze her inner thigh, moving my hand closer to her crotch. "Are you in the mood for some baking?"

Brenda moves my hand deeper into her crotch and whispers, "The oven's already warm."

AFTER MAKING SWEET, SLOW LOVE, BRENDA AND I TAKE A SHOWER, FRESHENING OURselves up in time to get dinner ready before the kids arrive home. She gets out first and rushes downstairs to start cooking while I indulge myself a few extra moments, letting the warm water massage me. Then I get out and start drying off.

I wipe away some condensation from the bathroom mirror and check my hairline. I'm definitely getting thin on top, but Brenda says it looks distinguished. As for the rest of me, I'm fortunate that my metabolism's remained high enough for old friends to still call me "Nay-thin," although I'm nowhere near as thin as I used to be. My salt-and-pepper mustache, even neatly trimmed, is still nice and thick. And even though I wasn't blessed with Victor's six-two height, I nevertheless value the five feet ten inches God gave me.

"Nathan! Come on, handsome!" Brenda calls. "The kids will be here any minute."

"Okay, baby!"

I finish getting myself together, then go help Brenda with dinner. We're through with only minutes to spare before the kids get home. I greet Corrine and Nate Junior at the door and tell them they're just in time to eat. We go into the dining room, the kids interrupting each other as they recount the high, low, and funny points of the nature outing.

"The best part were the reptiles," says Nate Junior. "Dad, you oughta see how those boa constrictors eat their food. It's *really* cool!"

"It's disgusting," counters Corrine. "Swallowing those poor baby rabbits whole. Those snakes are cruel."

He rolls his eyes. "Do you know how dumb that sounds? Snakes aren't cruel. They're just snakes."

"Whatever," Corrine says. "They're slimy, stupid, and cruel."

Nate Junior opens his mouth to offer a rebuttal but his mother interrupts. "Okay everyone. Enough about the snakes. Dinner's ready. Let's eat."

We sit down and, as always, hold hands before we pray. I look into each of their faces and am humbled again by the wondrous way God has blessed me. Then we bow our heads and I pray.

"Father God, thank you for this food we are about to receive. Bless the hands that prepared it and purify the food that we may partake of it. In Jesus' precious name, amen."

Everyone says amen and we start eating.

"Dad, pass the rolls, please," Nate Junior says.

I hand him the basket and marvel as he casually grabs four. If he's eating like this at twelve, I can only guess what he'll be consuming at sixteen.

"There's something important you need to mark on your calendar," says Brenda, looking at me.

"What's that?"

She looks at Nate Junior and says, "Tell your father the good news."

He blushes. "Aw, Mom. It's no big deal."

"He's right, Dad," Corrine agrees. "It's no big deal."

Nate Junior makes a face at Corrine and she returns the favor. Brenda ignores them both and beams a smile at me.

"Honey, our son, Nathaniel Christopher Matthews Junior, is this year's winner of his school science club's Young Einstein trophy."

I give him a light punch to the shoulder. "That's great, tiger! Which one of your projects won the competition?"

He grins and says, "The one demonstrating how to capture and store solar energy more efficiently."

I look at Brenda, who's glowing, and ask, "From which side of the family do you think he gets his brains?"

"Mine, of course!" she answers, faking indignation.

"What about Uncle Clifford?" asks Nate Junior. "He's kinda brainy."

Brenda smiles and pats Nate Junior's arm. "Finish your dinner, son."

Corrine looks like she's about to explode with an announcement of her own. "Mom. Dad. Is it okay if I go out this weekend with some friends?"

"What friends?" Brenda asks.

Corrine purses her lips and says, "Jenna, Byron, and . . . Tyrone."

Brenda looks at me and I say, "Corrine, how many times do we have to go through this, pumpkin? I don't think Tyrone Ballard is someone you should be spending time with."

"But, Dad. It's not like I'll be alone with him. Jenna and Byron will be there too. And we're only going to the movies."

"Corrine, listen, baby. I know it seems like just a harmless date. But that's how most trouble begins, as a harmless something-or-other. I just don't feel right about Tyrone, not yet anyway. So I'd like you to follow my wishes and stay away from him, okay?"

Corrine pouts. "Okay."

That little exchange dampens the atmosphere for a moment, but we're soon talking and sharing as before.

"Did you call the church today?" Brenda asks.

"Yeah, sweetheart. Those construction guys are making progress, but I'm going to have to take a closer look at how the bathroom rework is going. The last thing the Lord's house needs is the smell from clogged toilets."

"Dad!" Corrine cries. "I'm trying to eat!"

"Oops. I'm sorry, pumpkin." I wink at Nate Junior and his eyes fill with mischief. "So, Nate. Tell me once more how a boa constrictor eats its food."

Corrine's fork clangs onto her plate. "Dad!"

"Okay, okay." I chuckle. "I'm just joking."

"Well, I wish you'd joke *after* dinner," admonishes Brenda.

I poke out my lower lip and give a mock sniffle. Nate Junior follows my lead.

"You two are so silly," says Brenda.

Corrine rolls her eyes. "Mom, they're just men."

"And what's that supposed to mean?" I ask.

Corrine bites into her roll and between chews says, "Testosterone."

My sip of juice goes down the wrong pipe and I start coughing. Brenda laughs.

"Tes-what?"

"Not tes-what, Dad. It's called testosterone." Corrine says it like an impatient instructor talking to a student who should know this material.

"And what *about* testosterone?"

"It's why guys do what they do."

"And just what exactly does that mean?"

Nate Junior waves his hand excitedly. "I know! I know! C'mon, Dad. Ask me!"

Brenda shoves the basket of rolls in front of him. "Have another roll, Nathan."

He looks into her eyes, sees this is a bad time to protest, and adds a fifth roll to his plate.

I look at Brenda and she shrugs. "Don't blame me," she says, smirking. "These are *your* children."

I look back at Corrine and study her face. She's fifteen now, looking more like a woman than my little girl, and that constantly ringing phone is proof that others have noticed. I don't mind most of the callers. But Tyrone Ballard's a different matter. In addition to being eighteen and a smoker, and not having a steady job or plans for college, he's already fathered a child. And worst of all, Tyrone's not a Christian. It's not that he's a bad kid. From what I'm told, he somehow manages to take care of his child, and he is enrolled in an evening vocational program. So I applaud him for trying. But he's not the best for my baby—and that's what she deserves.

I look at Corrine and say, "Hmph! Testosterone!"

Corrine gives me a sly smile. We're gonna have to have a long talk.

AFTER DINNER, THE KIDS WANDER OFF INTO THEIR INDIVIDUAL WORLDS AS I WASH THE dishes and Brenda dries and puts them away. When she reaches up to shelve some glasses, her butt sticks out. I double-check to make sure the kids aren't around, then position myself between Brenda's cheeks, move in, and wrap my arms around her. She leans back into me and says in a teasing voice, "Why Reverend Matthews. Are you trying to lead me into temptation?"

"Never! But I was hoping you'd give me my daily bread."

"You just finished dinner," says Brenda, using her butt to bump me away. "But it feels like you're still hungry." She turns around and plants her palms against my chest, applying just enough pressure to keep me from leaning all the way in to kiss her.

"I know I just ate," I say. "But as you know, man does not live by bread alone."

Brenda wraps her arms around my neck and softly grinds her pelvis against my blooming erection.

"According to the Bible," I say, "he's supposed to live by every word that proceedeth forth from the mouth of God."

She grinds a bit harder. "Mmmm. What part of God's word caused this?"

"The part where He commands us to love one another."

Brenda giggles softly. "Are you sure you didn't misread that as a command to *lust after* one another?"

I straighten up and put on my official theologian's face. "Never!"

Brenda gives me another grind. "So, what're we gonna do about this?"

"Why Sister Matthews, what on earth could you be referring to?"

Brenda kisses my eyelids. "Poor baby. You really don't know?"

I shake my head. Then all playing ceases and we kiss, wrapping our tongues into a moving passion knot.

Brenda pulls me toward the bedroom and yells to the kids. "Corrine! Nathan!"

"Yes, ma'am."

"Answer the phone if it rings. Your father and I have some things to discuss."

"Yes, ma'am."

Brenda looks serious, like all her mental energies have focused onto a single thought.

"You think they suspect?" I ask.

"Do you care?" Brenda answers.

We close the bedroom door and start "talking."

IT'S ALWAYS NICE WHEN BRENDA AND I MAKE LOVE TWICE IN THE SAME DAY. THE BEST part is falling asleep in her arms afterwards. This is so serene, lying here with her, shielded from a world that's sometimes so harsh I can hardly bear to face it. God truly blessed me in letting me have Brenda. I'm so much more fortunate than poor Beverly Dawkins, struggling to hang in there with Percy. She's as strong as she is beautiful, and I pray daily for her marriage to succeed. Percy's not making it easy for her, but at least she knows I'm here for her.

*Pray.*

The word knifes through my thoughts. If it's God, I'll obey immediately. But there's only silence, so I inhale the scent of Brenda's lilac-perfumed body and sailboat into sleep.

*Pray!*

This time, it's definite. I wiggle away from Brenda and grab my robe. The Lord's rarely spoken with such urgency and I'm wondering what could so upset the Creator of all life, the Master of the universe, the One with no beginning or end. Brenda whispers that she loves me and rolls onto her side. I kiss her cheek, cover her up, and tiptoe into my den. The answering machine's light is blinking and I . . .

*PRAY!*

I fall to my knees. "For whom, Lord? About what?"

Why am I bothering God with this? I know of enough situations to keep me in prayer for years. So I ask the Lord to protect Mother McCoombs's grandson. To help Brother Loudon find a job. To bring peace to lovely Beverly Dawkins. To remove the violence from our streets and . . .

*Pray for Clifford.*

Clifford? If God had instructed me to pray for wild man Victor, well, that'd be different. But Clifford? He's got a great job, a beautiful wife, and two adorable boys. He is about to get his MBA and is raking in success with an ease that's always left me baffled. And—Father, forgive me—envious. What need of his could command the Lord's urgent attention?

*He needs Me!*

I pray.

I'VE ASKED THE LORD TO STRENGTHEN EVERY ASPECT OF CLIFFORD'S MARRIAGE. SPIRITUAL. Physical. Sexual. Financial. I've asked Him to give Clifford and Demetria a love for each other unlike any they've known before. I've implored Him to equip them not only to fulfill Braddie and Bear's physical needs, but to guide those boys safely into Heaven's arms. And just as I'm asking Him to keep outside influences from defiling their marriage bed, the phone rings.

I grab the phone and glance at my desk clock, wondering who's calling this close to midnight.

"Hello?"

"Hello, Nathan."

It's Momma. Her calling this late could mean trouble, but I stay calm. "Hi, Momma. This is a nice surprise. What are you doing up so late?"

"Working on my dissertation," she answers, sounding very tired. "Once this project is over, I'm taking a month to catch up on all the sleep I've lost."

"Hang in there, Momma. We're all looking forward to celebrating at your graduation."

"Thanks, sweetheart. And rest assured, I *will* be walking across that stage. But look, I know it's late, so let me not keep you too long."

"Okay. What's on your mind?"

Momma pauses, then says, "Clifford."

I purse my lips and slowly shake my head. "Yeah. I've been thinking about him too. Did he, Demetria, and the kids get back from Disney World?"

"Yes. They came by earlier to pick up that crazy dog." There's a lighter tone in Momma's voice when she mentions Scratch.

"Was everything all right?"

"Yes and no. I can't say exactly what's going on, but something's bothering Clifford. Either way, please stay in prayer for him."

"Momma, we're on the same wavelength. I was praying for Clifford when you called."

"Good. Just keep it up. And don't forget Victor."

"Not a chance."

After a slight pause, Momma asks, "Did Brenda go with you to Syreeta's grave?"

"Yes, she did."

"She's darling. I hope you remind yourself daily of how blessed you are to have her."

"I do, Momma. I cherish Brenda more than anything. Along with you."

She chuckles softly. "That's okay, Nathan. She's your wife. Love her as you do yourself. Just save a little bit of room for me."

"Momma, there'll *always* be room for you. And not just a little bit."

I can feel her smiling through the phone. "That's good to hear." Momma yawns. Hearing her, I do the same. "Okay," she says. "It's time for me to get in bed."

"My feelings exactly. And don't worry, Momma. I'll keep Clifford and Victor at the top of my prayer list."

"Don't forget your own situation."

"My situation? What're you talking about?"

"Nathan, you're a senior pastor. That's a huge responsibility the Lord's entrusted you with and it should be handled with care."

"You're right, Momma. But don't worry, because I'd never . . ."

"Satan's a hungry lion, seeking whom he may devour. Don't let your holiness fool you into thinking that that doesn't include you."

"I won't, Momma. I promise."

"Good night, baby."

Momma and I hang up. And I'm baffled. Because for as much as I'd like to think I understand her, I have no idea what prompted her to say what she just said.

# TROUBLED WATERS

# CLIFFORD

I KICK OFF THE COVERS, STRETCH, AND LISTEN TO THE SATURDAY MORNING PULSE OF THE Matthews household. Demetria's got the radio tuned to some station spouting a steady cloud of intelli-crap instead of listening to the more substantive excellence of National Public Radio. And Braddie and Bear are downstairs, laughing, vrrroooming, and kabooming with their latest video game favorite, "Troll Warrior." So far, so normal.

I can't believe we've only been back a week. Whatever the length of time, I could use another vacation.

"Braddie! Bear! Turn off that video game and go eat!" yells Demetria.

That's normal. But after what she said about divorce, how can anything be normal? She hasn't mentioned it since we got back, but the fact that she mentioned it at all means that things can't possibly be "normal." But then, I could've blown everything out of proportion. Yeah. That's probably what happened. Demetria was just letting off steam and I took it to the extreme.

"Braddie! Bear! Don't make me come down there!" shouts Demetria.

She's coming down the hallway, so I pretend to be asleep and watch her through slitted eyes. She hurries into the room, takes off her robe, and searches her closet for an outfit. A blouse slips from its hanger and Demetria bends over to pick it up.

After nine years, I've still never seen a woman's butt as attractive as Demetria's. Even in plain white panties, she's an exquisite sight. She pulls off her bra and goes to her dresser for another. I can't take any more of this.

I get up and hug her from behind, cupping one of her breasts. I know she feels my erection, but she doesn't move. That's normal. She keeps searching through her dresser drawer, ignoring my sofly grinding hips. That's normal. I kiss her neck and cup both her breasts, making my hip movements more emphatic until she thrusts her butt backwards, shoving me away.

"Stop that!"

"Stop what?" I say, pretending innocence.

I reach for her and she sidesteps me, putting on her new bra as she goes back to the closet. The hypnotic undulations of her butt make my nature throb. I'm going into the fourth week of this dry spell.

"Demmy, do you wanna make love?"

"Can't you see I'm getting dressed?"

"Sure I can. But I'd be more than happy to undress, then redress you if that'd help." I ease closer until Demetria's eyes lock onto mine. I freeze. So does my blood.

"I *do not* want to make love," she says, her voice low and menacing.

I sit on the edge of the bed and watch her finish dressing. "What're you getting ready to do?"

"I'm going to the market. Braddie and Bear need some cereal, and Scratch is almost out of dog food."

Which reminds me, I've gotta pick up Scratch from the vet. After being left for a week at Momma's, then last night at the vet's, the poor mutt's probably starting to wonder if we're trying to get rid of him.

I watch in silent admiration as Demetria adds a light touch of makeup to her face and inspects herself.

"Demmy, you are truly beautiful."

"I'm gonna go now," she says.

"Okay. I'll take the boys and get Scratch."

"Don't forget the pickup slip."

"I won't."

She inspects herself once more and turns to leave. "I'll be back in a while."

"Maybe later?" I say.

"Maybe *what* later?"

"Maybe we can, you know, make love. Later?"

Demetria sighs in exasperation. "We'll see."

She leaves and I glance at my once proud nature, now deflated. Yup! Things are *definitely* back to normal. And I can't help grimacing as I hear again something Victor once said that fits this moment.

*Cliff, one'a ya'll is stupid. And it AIN'T Demetria.*

Right now I'm feeling very stupid. I used to wave bones in front of Scratch, laughing at how he followed my hand. It was like manipulating a puppet and I loved watching his eyes glaze over for just a sniff or lick.

I don't do that anymore.

I START WASHING UP AND CRACK THE BATHROOM DOOR SO THE BOYS CAN HEAR ME. "Braddie! Bear!"

"Yes, sir."

"You guys get your socks and shoes on. We're gonna leave in a minute."

"Yes, sir."

The phone rings.

"I'll get it!" yells Bear.

"Okay," I answer. "Braddie! Turn that TV down!"

When he does, I realize just how loud it was. I hope their listening habits change by the time they're teenagers and listening to that P-funk or whatever they're calling music these days.

"Dada, phone," Bear says.

"Who is it?"

"Uncle Nathan."

Nathan! What a pleasant surprise!

"Okay, Bear. Tell him to hold on."

I finish wiping my face and pick up the bedroom phone. "Hello?"

"Hey, Mr. Clifford."

"Big Nate! How's my favorite theologian?"

"Great! And you?"

"Still trying to recover from vacation."

"Recover? You should be rested and itching to get back to work."

"In your dreams. You know how it is. It takes a week to catch up on the rest you *didn't* get on vacation."

"True enough." Nate laughs. "Anyway, welcome back. I've got some great news for you."

"Let me hear it. I could use some good news."

"The kids in the Young & Gifted program have voted you Mentor of the Year."

"They have! That's wonderful."

"I'll say. You've done a great job, Clifford. I've never seen anyone connect with them the way you have."

"Thanks, Nate. I'm glad to hear it." And I really am. If only I could connect the same way with Demetria.

"So, is everything all right?" Nate asks. "I mean, with you, Demetria, and the kids?"

"The boys are doing great. I'm hanging in there. And Demetria, well, she's being Demetria."

Nate hesitates before continuing. "Is there anything I can do to help?"

"Forget it, Nate. Nothing's happening out of the ordinary. How's Brenda?"

Nate pauses as if he's processing my previous statement. Mercifully, he doesn't ask for clarification. "Brenda's doing fine. Thank God she's here. Without her I'd have been overwhelmed by this pastor's position."

"It's a lot of work, isn't it?"

"*That,* little brother, is an understatement. But you know, in many ways it's exciting."

"How so?"

"Clifford, it's amazing to see God's blessing in so many areas. A little truly becomes a lot when it's placed in the Master's hands. . . ."

I'm hearing loud and clear what Nate's saying. He's talking about the kind of thing I need to have take place within myself, would like to see in Demetria, and would love to apply to this marriage. But how?

". . . and that's why I'm certain everything's gonna be all right," Nate says, finishing.

"Nate, of course it's gonna be all right. God's got a good man in charge."

"Flattery will get you nowhere."

"I'll keep that in mind, if you ever do something I can flatter you about," I say with a chuckle.

"Touché. You're getting pretty good with your comebacks."

"I was taught by two of the best. Speaking of which, have you heard from Victor?"

"Yeah. He called the other night from Justine's."

"What! He's still with her? That makes what, five months? Are we witnessing the birth of stability?"

"Clifford, instead of joking, you should be in prayer for him."

"I know, Nate. And I'm sorry. But I still can't help wondering how we all came from the same gene pool."

"Will you stop! Man, listen. No matter what, he's our blood."

"So you've said. I guess we'll have to live with that reality."

Nate sighs and says, "Anyway, he called from Justine's. He said he'll be home soon for Jewel's birthday."

"Where's he gonna stay?"

"Probably with Momma. I'd like for him to stay with us, but I'll have to check with Brenda first."

"Well, it'll have to be with one of you or a motel because there's no . . ."

"I know, I know," says Nate, his voice full of judgment and accusation. "There's no way you'll let him stay at your house."

Nate's self-righteous, finger-pointing tone slams my anger button. "That's right! Just like you wouldn't if you knew he'd hassle Brenda."

"Huh? Why're you catching an attitude? I only meant to say that . . ."

"I know you think me harsh for telling Victor the last time he stayed here that he'd never be invited back. But that doesn't mean I disowned him. I put him out for disrespecting my wife, which, according to you, is *exactly* what I should've done in placing my wife before my family."

Nate's quiet. Too quiet. And I'm getting thoroughly irritated at the likelihood that he'll act like the suffering party when *he* made me lash out at *him*.

"Clifford, I'm not accusing you of disowning Victor," he says, "especially since I know you love him the way Momma taught us—more than yourself.

All I meant to say was that I know he put you in a tough spot, and I felt terrible that you were left with no other choice."

That's what Nate's saying now. A moment ago, his tone was saying something far different, most of it having to do with blame.

"Believe me when I tell you that I was speaking out of love," Nate says. "If it didn't sound that way, I apologize."

As much as I want to stay angry, I can't. I hate it when Nate paves over my thunder with Christian goodness.

"Forget it, Nate. I just need you to understand my side of things. Even though Victor rarely visited, when he left, Demetria would be crabby for days, and the boys would act like they were competing for juvenile delinquent of the month."

"What do you mean?"

"Take those vulgar Marine Corps songs of his. He actually taught one to Braddie and Bear, and they loved it. Especially Braddie. Do you know how embarrassing it is to be out with a five-year-old who's singing, *'I know a girl who lives on a hill. She won't do it, but her sister will'*?"

"I can't say I've had the experience."

"Well, you didn't miss anything, except for public humiliation."

"No doubt," Nate observes. "Victor definitely marches to his own beat."

"Yeah. Probably to the sound track of the latest *Deep Throat* porn video." I hold my breath, hoping Nate doesn't ask how I know about such "art."

"Well, Clifford, time's moving on," he says. "I've got to work on this Sunday's sermon, visit some sick and shut-in, then get down to the church and check on the progress of renovations."

"How's that going?"

"Like clockwork. These contractors really know their stuff. By the time they're through, Divine Temple's gonna have a brand-new look."

"For what they're charging, it's supposed to."

Nate laughs. "I won't disagree with you there. Anyway, I'd better get moving."

"Okay, Nate. I'll talk to you later."

Several awkward seconds pass until Nate says, "By the way, Clifford, you were right to place Demetria before your family. It's consistent with the Lord's Word in Genesis 2:24, when He says, 'Therefore shall a man leave his father and his mother, and shall cleave unto his wife: and they shall be one flesh.' "

"Thanks, Nate. I appreciate your saying that."

And I really do. It's so different from other occasions, when he's used the Bible to point out everything I'm doing wrong. I've usually listened politely and quietly during those soapbox lectures, but I've always wondered how sanctified Nate would be if Brenda played sexual Russian roulette with him. How holy would he be if, like on some game show, every time he wanted to make love he had to guess the secret password?

"Well, Clifford. Take it easy. Keep your chin up and all that sort of stuff."

"You too, Nate."

Then we hang up.

# VICTOR

I DON'T LET NOTHIN' KEEP ME FROM MY MORNIN' TAI CHI WORKOUT. IT'S ONE'A THE FEW good thangs to come out'a me sweatin' my balls off with the Marine Corps. But it wasn't till Celia dumped me that I got in'trested in martial arts.

After bein' together since high school, we was gonna get married and make that thang permanent. Then in boot camp I got this Dear John letter, with Celia explainin' how some fool named Delroi had been callin' her, pourin' his heart out, and confusin' her feelin's for me. I felt somethin' risin' in me that I knew was bad but didn't wanna stop. So I wrote and told her to don't never write me, call me, or say my name again.

Since then, and except for Lynnette, I've been involved but never serious. It's better that way. Cuz babes may not leave today or tomorrow, but sooner or later they do. And when they do, I intend for 'em to be leavin' somebody *else*.

Right as I'm movin' into another tai chi form, I hear Justine yawnin'. I shouldn'ta let her stay last night. Lately, every time she comes over, she's wantin' to play house, cookin', cleanin', and sendin' me to the store for her napkins. And then there was that time she offered to wash my clothes.

I told her, "Not no but *hell no*!"

I didn't mean to jump off like that, but when a babe gets to where a dude don't mind her seein' the skid marks in his funky drawers, that's *too* close. Pretty soon, he's at some altar, mumblin' "I do!" and wonderin' how he got there.

"Ice, why don't you fix some coffee?" calls Justine from the bathroom.

"Cuz I don't want none."

"What if I do?"

"Then you know where everythang is."

Justine steps into the livin' room, lookin' sexy in one'a my old dress shirts.

"Why're you bein' so mean?" she axes.

"Justine, don't start. I ain't in the mood."

"You ain't never in the mood unless you tryin' to scheme your way between my legs."

I hurry through the last tai chi movement. Ain't no use tryin' to do it right with my concentration gone.

"Justine, whaddyou say when I'm at your place? 'Get it yourself, Ice. I ain't your momma.' 'Do it yourself, Ice. You ain't no guest.' 'Ice, my name ain't spelled m-a-i-d.'

"Now, if you think I'm bein' mean for actin' like you, then we're both mean."

"You a lie. I do way more for you than you do for me. Includin' puttin' up with your stanky attitude."

"You keep talkin' and you gonna see a for-real stanky attitude."

"I ain't scared of you. And I'm tired of this. You can't just treat me like I'm—"

Justine's singin' the you-ain't-treatin'-me-right fight song makes my head pound with what Lynnette said just before Jewel was born. "Shut up!" I holler. "I know I can't just treat you like any old body! I know you can do bad all by yourself! And I know you can take care'a yourself *and* your baby!"

"Baby?" says Justine, soundin' puzzled. "I ain't got no baby." Then her eyes narrow and her voice comes out like a cat hissin'. "I don't believe this! You been up here screwin' me, had me runnin' around like your play-wife, and all this time you've been thinkin' about that *ho* back in Pittsburgh!"

I shake my head, tryin' to get it from the *then* back into the *now*. Justine stomps into the bedroom, then seconds later comes out, dressed and cryin'. She normally dresses sharp but right now she looks like a bag lady. Her tears fall like garden hoses are pumpin' water through her eyes.

"You probably don't care," she says between sniffles, "but . . . I love you."

I shouldn't let this happen. But this is how it goes. Sooner or later, they always leave. Justine's just the latest one sayin' good-bye.

"Ain't you got nothin' to say?" she axes.

"You know the way out."

Justine grabs her purse and runs out the apartment. I watch from the window as she gets in her car and squeals tires, pullin' away. Her taillights flash a couple'a times in the distance. And then Cleveland swallows her up.

I PULL INTO THE HUNK-A-BURGER PARKIN' LOT AND WAIT. IT'S TOO BAD STUFF GOT UGLY with Justine, but it ain't no thang. Any sucka with half a brain knows to have some backup, and I got mine. *Simone!* And just as soon as she gets here this plan'll be in motion.

I should'a stopped by a sportin' goods store and got myself a helmet. Cuz when she unsnaps that bra I'ma need some protection from gettin' slapped, smacked, and face-dribbled by them bouncin' bowlin' balls.

I wish she'd come on. This ain't exactly the safest place for a meetin' but Simone said we had to meet here or not at all. She's prob'ly sendin' me through these changes cuz'a some dude she's slammin'. Hey, it's cool. Before anythang happens, she's gonna tell me whuts'up. A sucka can't never tell when he'll be lookin' down the business end of a pistol. And as much as I like booty, I ain't dyin' for it! But I gotta admit, when I heard Simone's silky voice, remembered them king-sized knockers, and thought about her screwin' me with the same energy she'd used to whack my head, I got instant agreeable.

The dash clock shows only ten minutes have passed, but it feels like years. Simone needs to hurry up. After describin' in down-to-the-stitch detail whut she's gonna be wearin' and where it's gonna be grabbin', she's got the nerve to make me wait. I know she's gamin' me but it don't matter. It's workin'!

I wonder how many other suckas'll get trickbagged before the day's out. Nate's the only person I know who prob'ly won't. But I bet Brenda sometimes has him wishin' he could sneak off and get some strange. And Cliff! Demetria's had him by the balls from day one.

The first time he brought her home, she was yappin' about "*pah*-tee-ing" with her sorority sisters in Georgetown in D.C., borin' us to tears about the Porsche she was gonna buy "one day," and her plans to visit Wendell, her friend-of-the-fambly-ex-boyfriend, stationed in Italy with the Air Force.

Nate and Momma just sat there, noddin' and smilin' like drunk crash dummies. Cliff was disgustin', grinnin' and blinkin', face shinin' like a lightbulb. And it wasn't no surprise that Demetria was in charge cuz Cliff was always smarter about books than women. So when Demetria started jabberin' about visitin' that Wendell punk I got to rememberin' how Celia chumped me into defendin' democracy while she screwed for world peace and decided this wasn't *even* gonna happen. Not to *my* baby bro.

I said, "If you'n Cliff is so tight, why're you still moonin' over this clown in Italy?"

She looked at me like some furry, thousand-legged creature had crawled down into her panties.

Momma said, "Victor! Hush your mouth!"

Nate said, "Victor, c'mon, man. Not now."

"Naw, man," I answered. "Cliff's up here mumblin' about them gettin' married and whatnot. If she's gonna be in the fambly we need to know what kinda game she's runnin'."

"Victor, I'm not telling you again," said Momma, soundin' like she did them times she made me go out back and get my own switch.

Then Cliff added his two cents. "Victor! Back off!"

He wasn't playin', cuz his voice was rumblin' and he looked like if he'd had a baseball bat, my head woulda been in some serious trouble. But he *didn't* have no bat, so I looked at him and said, "Or what?"

"Or I'm gonna kick your sorry black—"

"Clifford!" Momma shouted. "Not in my house you don't!"

We was all starin' bug-eyed at Cliff, cuz he didn't hardly never cuss. And everybody in there knew he couldn't beat up hisself, never mind me. But when he jumped up like he meant to try, I knew he musta really loved Demetria to risk one'a my whoopin's. So I headed for the door.

Right as I gripped the knob Demetria hollered, "Wait!"

"Whutch'you want?" I axed, turnin' around.

She stood up and locked eyes with me. "Personally, I don't think my relationship with Clifford is any of your business. But he's told me how close you all are so I'll say it again. Wendell's just a friend! I'm in love with Clifford. I hope you can believe that. If not, you'll just have to deal with it!"

I coulda slapped that knobby-kneed bimbo into the next Wednesday, but remembered Momma hollerin' that she'd beat me into butter if I ever laid hands on a woman. I looked around the room and felt like pukin'. Cliff was wipin' his eyes. Nate was grittin' on me like I *really* was the devil. And Momma was shakin' her head like I'd got caught pissin' in the principal's coffee.

I looked at Demetria and said, "I ain't gotta believe nothin' cuz I ain't the one marryin' your scraggly butt. And *hell no*! I don't believe you. If Cliff was gonna visit some friend-of-the-fambly-ex-girlfriend you'd be pissin' all over yourself, cryin' about it bein' unfair and wantin' to break up. I think he's stupid for swallowin' that crock, but he has, so too bad for him!"

That almost broke Cliff and Demetria up for good, but Cliff did some championship beggin' in them next few weeks. I got so tired of hearin' him, *I* almost called Demetria to apologize! But Cliff hung in there, showin' some guts I didn't know he had. When they hooked back up, he was happier than a lotto winner, dancin' around, callin' Momma "Mother dear," and tellin' everybody how great love is. I was tired of gettin' accused of bein' jealous of Cliff's findin' true love and decided to lay low.

And then I spent that weekend with Jocelyn.

IN HIGH SCHOOL, ME AND JOCELYN USED TO SPEND HOURS SHOOTIN' HOOPS. SHE GOT A full ride to the University of Maryland and one weekend invited me down to College Park for a Greek step. Jocie said the "step" was some kinda convention where eggheads from all over came to watch fraternity pledgees perform like drill teams, only with lots more cool, funk, and soul.

I almost puked when I found out Demetria was goin', talkin' 'bout she had to be there cuz her sorority was supportin' one'a the frats. She even chumped Cliff into goin', givin' him the jitters with all her good-male-friends-who'll-be-there talk. Cliff punked out so bad he flushed his plans to attend some student political trainin' conference in Baltimore. I wasn't happy 'bout bein' in the same place with Demetria but got over it cuz I wasn't *even* gonna let her stop me from tappin' some'a that college booty.

After the step, Jocie and some'a her girlfriends snuck me and some other dudes into a dorm full'a so many fine sisters I was gettin' whiplash watchin' 'em. The lights got low, the music got loud, and we had us a par-tay! Some'a the brothas and sisters paired off, disappearin' into closets, corners, and bathrooms for some pokin'n strokin'. Jocie stepped off to another dorm party with some other sorority babes and I made my move on the melon-chested honey who'd been eyein' me. We tipped on down to her room and I stood outside while she checked to make sure her roommate was gone. That's when I heard yellin' from across the hall. Miss Melons was takin' her time, so I eased across for some prime-time eavesdroppin'.

"Getting married!" hollered a dude. "What about us?"

"What're you talking about?" yelled a babe. "It's been over between us! Why can't you understand?"

"What I understand is that you're rolling me for some jerk you hardly even know!"

"I love him!"

"No! You love me!"

"Wendell! I do love you. But not that way."

I tried tellin' myself that I was gettin' it all wrong. But two-plus-two was slappin' me with an in-my-face FOUR! So there wasn't nothin' to do but . . . believe.

"How can you do this?" yelled Wendell. "I laid everything on the line for you!"

"I know, Wendell. But I'm *in* love with Clifford."

There was a slap, a cry, then scufflin'. The door flew open and there stood Demetria, wrapped in a skimpy towel, and loverboy wearin' nothin' but his drawers. She saw me and screamed. I saw her, and Wendell, and went overload.

"Who're you?" hollered Wendell.

"The brother of the dude whose fiancée you just slapped!"

Then I was all over Wendell, slingin' him from one side of that room to the other.

"You sorry faggot!" I hollered. "Didn't yo' momma teach you about not beatin' up on the ladies?"

Right as I was jammin' his head down the toilet, he broke free and tore out the room, zoomin' past Demetria who was huddled in a corner and wringin' her hands.

Demetria cried up a storm, beggin' me not to tell Cliff. "Please, Victor. This didn't mean anything. It was just, just . . ."

"Just *what*, Demetria? A sayonara screw?"

She put her face in her hands and started blubberin' and groanin', mumblin' and moanin', apologizin' and gettin' saved, but she wasn't sayin' squat.

"You sorry slut!" I hollered. "I knew you wasn't nothin'! Now Cliff's gonna know too!"

"Victor, try and understand," she moaned. "I didn't know Wendell was coming."

"What he do? Shoot his load in secret?"

"My mother told him I was staying here with friends."

"Did she tell you to screw him?"

"I told Wendell it was over."

"Then gave him some booty cuz you was sincere."

"I didn't mean for it to happen."

"But you was thinkin' of Cliff the whole time." I scoped the room, lookin' for any'a Cliff's stuff. "And where is Cliff anyway?"

"At that political training conference."

"Liar! Cliff said he wasn't goin'!"

"He decided at the last minute."

"Demetria, you must think I'm King Stupid to believe that lame story. How'd you ditch him?"

She flopped into a chair and started wringin' her hands and cryin' so hard I thought her eyes was gonna blow out her head.

"It's true, Victor. We were gonna go to the step. But Clifford changed his mind. Then Wendell showed up—"

"And one thang led to another and you just *had* to grease his pole."

"It was a mistake. Victor, please. I'm sorry. It'll destroy Clifford."

*That* hit a nerve. Cuz Cliff loved Demetria like it wasn't nobody's business. And there wasn't no denyin' that she'd told panty-wipe Wendell about bein' in love with Cliff *before* I crashed her party.

I was confused and pissed cuz I knew Momma, Nate, and Cliff was gonna twist thangs around to where *I'd* made Demetria give Wendell some booty. Then Demetria took one'a my hands into both'a hers and looked at me with eyes pleadin' so hard they glittered.

"Victor, please," she said. "I promise, *it'll never happen again.*"

And stupid me, I bought that sorry line, becomin' Demetria's silent partner in settin' Cliff up for a slow grillin'. When I tried tellin' Nate, he started prayin' for God to free me from spirits of jealousy, carryin' on about how if I didn't clean up my act I was gonna get thunderbolted onto the express train to hell. And Momma, she just started cryin' and axin' me whut I had against Cliff's bein' happy. I told her I ain't had nothin' against it and was about to tell her that his happiness was whut I was tryin' to protect when she cut me off and told me to never bring it up again.

So Cliff and Demetria got married. And now it's been nine years and plenty'a pains later. And even though ain't nobody said too much, everybody knows that the *last* thang Cliff is these days is happy.

# NATHAN

I NEED TO FOCUS ON PREPARING FOR THIS SUNDAY'S SERMON. BUT THOUGHTS OF CLIFford and Demetria keep interfering with my Bible study. It's no secret they've been having problems, but this is bad, really bad. Clifford's barely shaken the vacation dust from his feet and he sounds like he just spent six months as a galley slave. Not that a mere vacation could've produced a radical change in their relationship. But the different surroundings, the excitement of getting away, and a break from the pressures of modern living should've sent them home with improved perspectives. Knowing Clifford, though, he probably spent the vacation agonizing about the mountain of paperwork piling up on his desk.

I'm going to have to talk to him. But how many times will it take? He's so driven to succeed, subordinating the things in life that really matter to the pursuit of his next credential or merit increase. That drive's been great for the kids in the Young & Gifted program, but not so great for Demetria, Braddie, and Bear.

Clifford's Saturday morning Y&G leadership classes are just one layer of a work schedule that sometimes has him traveling for days, conducting round-the-clock training for a three-shift operation, and pursuing an MBA. Once the usual headaches over sex, money, and kids are added to the equation, it's no wonder disaster's stalking his marriage.

I've got to find someone to replace Clifford in the program. That'll at least free up his Saturdays. I hope I won't have to tell him to spend them with his family. But then, maybe I will. For all his drive and intelligence, Clifford can be a rock when it comes to the obvious.

I add a few final thoughts to my rough-draft sermon, set it aside, and press the PLAY button on my answering machine. It's picked up several times while I've been studying but I'd turned it down to minimize the interruptions. I grab a pen and jot down notes as the messages replay.

Message 1: *"Reverend Matthews, this is Syd, from Monitor Construction. We found a way to reroute that plumbing in the church men's bathroom at no extra cost. Just thought you'd like to know. See ya."*

Message 2: *"Pastor, dis here is Mother McCoombs. They's gonna put me in the hospital for some tests. Please ax the church fambly to pray for me. And keep prayin' for my granbaby, Ray. Bye-bye, now."*

Message 3: *"Pastor, this is Bev Dawkins. I just wanted to thank you again for meeting with me last Tuesday. I appreciate your taking the time and look forward to our next counseling session. You've been a great help and I really value our friendship. Love you. 'Bye."*

I smile at the last message. The "Love you" ending is a bit too friendly but warming nonetheless. My skin tingles and I look up and see Brenda standing in the doorway with a cup of coffee. I croak out a hollow chuckle and reset the answering machine.

"Brenda! You startled me. How long have you been standing there?"

Brenda's smiling, but there's a touch of frost. "Who was that?"

"There were three messages, Bren. Which one are you referring to?"

"The one from the woman who loves you."

I chuckle again. This time it sounds even more hollow. "Oh, that! That was Beverly Dawkins. She was just thanking me for meeting with her last Tuesday."

"Is she still getting divorced?"

"I'm afraid so. She's taking it really hard."

Brenda hands me the cup of coffee. "Is there anything I can do?"

"Naw, baby. I've got it under control."

"Even the part about her loving you?"

I feel a sheen of sweat on my forehead. "C'mon, Brenda. That's just friendly counselor-client small talk. There's nothing to worry about."

Brenda takes hold of my chin and stares deep into my eyes. "Nathan, are you sure she's not getting too close?" Her face is placid but her eyes are smoldering.

I stand and hold Brenda by her shoulders. "C'mon, sweetheart. Beverly's emotions are just a little exposed right now. She just needs some gentle support. Don't worry, Bren. I only have eyes for you."

I hug Brenda, kiss her, and smile. She doesn't smile back.

# CLIFFORD

SCRATCH CHARGES ME, JUMPS ON MY LEG, AND STARTS PEEING. I LEAP OUT OF THE WAY as Braddie and Bear laugh. I scowl at Scratch, but it's impossible to get angry with him when he's this happy. I kneel down and pet him as he nuzzles my face.

"Scratch! So help me, I'm actually glad to see you."

Braddie and Bear hug and pet Scratch, grab his leash, and get in the car while I pay the vet attendant. On the way home, I stop at Pederson's Drug Mart. Before the boys and I go in, I point a threatening finger at Scratch.

"Scratch, you'd better not chew up my floor mats this time." He barks back something sounding like "Up yours!" then lies down.

In the store, Braddie and Bear go to the video games section, right across from the florist and Hallmark cards section where I'm headed. I can keep an eye on them from there.

It's time to go into Phase II of Operation Keep Demetria. Especially since Phase I, giving her a card a day, seems to have been as successful as attempting to boil the ocean.

I select some more cards, making sure this time they're not too mushy. I might've come on too strong with that last batch, so a measured approach'll be better. One rose and a card a day will let her know she's on my mind but, more importantly, *keep me on hers.*

When the boys and I get home, Demetria's in a foul mood, folding the grocery bags like she's spanking them. Grocery shopping sometimes does this to her, but I'm at a loss for what to do.

The last time I shopped, it was to show her that I didn't consider the task solely hers. She complained for the next week about my not using coupons, and lectured me on how I'd been snookered into buying name brand, the insanity of buying two- versus four-ply toilet paper, etcetera. So I said "never again." Banishment from the grocery store wasn't exactly a career setback, and in the long run it worked out better. Now she gets what she wants and I'm not judged a moron for buying the wrong bag of green beans.

But still, I've got to do something. Everything going wrong during Demetria's day usually diminishes lovemaking possibilities for the night, especially if she's had a crappy day at work. And while I can't control conditions on her job, I can do something about conditions at home. So I tell Braddie and Bear that Mommy's not feeling well and that if they make noise,

I'll get them. Their eyes fill with fear and confusion since they were already playing quietly. Guilt spreads over me and I want to explain. But what can I tell them?

*Boys, Dada's REALLY horny and wants to screw Mommy until her nose bleeds. But I can't do that if you guys upset her, so please be quiet or I'll sew your lips to your belly buttons.*

It doesn't matter. They're just gonna have to deal with their predicament. If they don't, tonight I'll be dealing with mine.

FOR SOME REASON, DEMETRIA "FORGOT" TO MENTION THAT 21ST CENTURY POLYMERS was throwing a cocktail party and dinner tonight to celebrate its most profitable quarter. She also "forgot" to mention that she'd planned on riding to the event with Tammy and wanted to leave early so they could dress together. And she almost "forgot" to ask me if I wanted to go. But I declined, especially seeing as how she'd asked only for the sake of marital correctness. Not to mention that I could see she was dreading the possibility that I'd accept.

Besides, I prefer spending the evening with Braddie and Bear to watching Nolan's eyes map the contours of Demetria's butt.

Sometimes I wish I had Victor's wild boldness. He'd have stuffed Nolan's head someplace where all he could do was watch his bowels move. And as for Tammy, he'd make her bite herself so she could inject herself with the same poison she's been dumping into Demetria's head and onto my marriage.

I race Braddie and Bear into their room, faking frustration when they "win."

"Dada, you're old!" Bear says, laughing.

"And fat!" Braddie adds.

I chase them around the room. "Old and fat! I'll show you who's old and fat!" I wrestle them to the floor and check my watch. We're right on schedule for bedtime. "Okay, you guys," I say. "Let's do it!"

The boys hop to their feet and stand at attention. Victor, during one of his visits, had fascinated them with stories of how Marine recruits get into bed. So now they insist we do it "Uncle Victor's way."

I turn off the light and stand in the doorway, letting the hallway light silhouette me and my hands-on-hips Marine drill instructor's posture.

"All right you insects . . ."

"No, Dada," Bear interrupts. "You're supposed to say *maggots*."

Thank goodness Demetria's not home, or we'd certainly bypass this part of the hittin'-the-rack ritual. I clear my throat, lower my voice, and start over.

"All right, maggots! On your knees!"

The boys drop to the floor.

"Listen up, people," I growl. "You will now pray!"

"Whose turn?" Bear asks.

"Did I give you permission to speak, schoolbum?"

"No, sir!"

"Well then, keep your bubblegum-chewing mouth shut!"

"Yes, sir!"

I point at Braddie. "You, toy-lover! Pray!"

"Which prayer, Dada?"

"That's Sergeant Dada to you, mudpie-maker!"

Braddie giggles. "Which prayer, Sergeant Dada?"

"The Children's Prayer, milk-drinker!"

Demetria and I have followed Nathan's advice and alternated between the Lord's Prayer and the Children's Prayer so as to teach the boys both. Braddie brings his palms together with a loud smack.

"Ready!"

Bear and I bring our palms together with loud smacks. "Ready!"

After a long second I command them, "Pray!"

"Now I lay me down to sleep. I pray the Lord my soul to keep. If I should die before I wake, I pray the Lord my soul to take. God bless Mommy, Sergeant Dada, and Scratch. And help us to be good, and get the new 'Troll Warrior II' video game, and, um, amen."

The boys hop to their feet and resume their sloppy positions of attention.

"All right, Jell-O-slurpers! Get in those racks!"

They scramble into bed and beneath their covers, then lie in the position of attention. I perform a quick visual inspection, grunt my satisfaction, then stand back in the doorway.

"Ready! Sleep!"

Braddie and Bear snap their eyes shut in the best tradition of the United States Marine Corps.

I can't help smiling. Victor's Marine recruit game is ridiculous, but it's impressive to watch the boys' rapid, disciplined responses. It's also revealing. If they can play this well at being disciplined, then they can do it for real.

I stand back in the doorway and take another mental snapshot. I may need these images to remind myself that, once upon a time, I tried to be a good father.

"Dada?"

Bear, true to his pattern, is already fast asleep, so this has to be Braddie. I look at his face in the soft glow of the night-light and all of my drill instructor's menace melts away. He's not a fearless Marine anymore but a little boy, *my son,* needing some extra help keeping the night creatures away.

I smile. "What do you need, Braddie?"

He motions for me to come close and I sit on the edge of the bed.

"What's the matter, son?"

"Nothin'."

"Well then, why'd you call me?"

Braddie stares hard into my eyes. "Dada, when are we gonna fly a kite?" he asks.

I smile and muss Braddie's hair. "Don't worry, Braddie. We'll fly one someday."

I pat his leg and start to leave, but he grabs my arm. "No, Dada! You have to fly one soon!"

As sometimes happens, Braddie doesn't know playtime is over and I have to get stern. "Braddie, I said we would. Don't worry. There'll be time."

"No, Dada. You have to fly it soon! Then he'll fix us."

He'll fix us? Who'll fix us? And why is "he" sending weird messages through my baby boy? Talk about rotten luck. Demetria's been urging me to get lost, and now I've got a total stranger suggesting that I go fly a kite.

I take firm hold of Braddie's shoulders. "Braddie, who said this to you?"

Braddie's expression shapes into a portrait of compassion so profound that I nearly wilt under the weight of its love. "It's I Am's promise, Dada. Uncle Nathan said I Am would fix us."

I almost ask who "I Am" is and then remember. "I Am" is the name God gave when Moses asked who he should say had sent him to bring the Hebrews out of Egypt.

A brick-sized lump fills my throat and I struggle to choke it down. "Braddie, when you say, 'fix us,' do you mean me and Mommy?"

Braddie nods excitedly. "Yeah, Dada. If you and Mommy get fixed, then we'll be all better."

I pull him into me and hug him tight. Braddie wraps his arms around me and pats my back.

"Fly the kite, Dada," he says softly. "Fly it soon. Then I Am will fix us."

ON MY WAY DOWNSTAIRS, I DECIDE TO CALL NATHAN SO I CAN FINALLY FIND OUT WHAT the heck is going on with the boys and these kites. Nate's got to know *something*, since Braddie mentioned him in connection with this confusion. Beyond that, he's a trained counselor, so there's no reason I should pay some child psychologist for an opinion when my own brother can give me one for free.

While Nate's phone is ringing, I consider the best way to ask my question so that it doesn't come out as an invitation for him to preach.

"Matthews residence," Brenda answers.

"Hello, beautiful sister-in-law of mine."

"Clifford! What a wonderful surprise."

"Not as wonderful as hearing you answer the phone."

"You've just earned yourself another hug. How are you?"

A grim, mischievous part of me wants to tell Brenda that—aside from the mounting feeling that my life's falling apart, that I envy her marriage, and that I'd like to stake out a lunar homestead—everything's great.

But I settle for saying "I'm fine. How about you?"

"Rushed. I was about to go pull my shift at the annual Y&G sleepover."

"It's at Holy Covenant this year, isn't it?"

"Yes. And a good thing too, especially with all the renovations going on down at Divine Temple."

"Well, don't be late on account of me. I was just calling to holler at Brother Nate."

"Clifford, there's always time for you. . . ." Brenda says.

And I'm wondering what it must be like to be Nate, married to someone as big-hearted as Brenda, to have her working *with* and not *against* him, and to be secure in the knowledge that his life partner will be just that: *his life partner.*

". . . and Nathan's down at the church," she finishes.

"Okay, Bren. I'll talk with you later. Have a good time."

"We always do. 'Bye."

We hang up and I call Nate.

"Divine Temple. Pastor Matthews speaking."

"Hey, Nate. It's me."

"Clifford! Twice in one day! God's truly blessing generously."

Nate's being so happy to hear from me after I bit off his head this morning leaves me not only feeling like a slug, but recalling things he's said about forgiveness. Especially with regard to marriage: "Clifford, no matter how badly Brenda and I disagree, we take our problems to the Cross where we find the power to love and forgive each other *through Christ.*"

That's okay for Nate, but Demetria and I need something that's rational, logical, and immediately applicable. Leaving matters in the hands of a deity who sometimes seems to enjoy running the world like a bad circus act is hardly a preferred solution.

"Got a minute?" I ask.

"Sure. I was just putting some finishing touches on this Sunday's sermon. What's on your mind?"

There's no great way to begin, so I plunge ahead. "It's about Braddie and Bear."

"What happened? They're okay, aren't they?"

"Yeah. They're fine. But Braddie, he's . . ."

Nate sighs. "Thank God. You sounded so serious. I thought something was wrong."

"Sorry, Nate. But they're fine, really. I'm just wondering if you can tell me anything about their sudden fascination with kites."

"Huh?"

I relate how the boys, and Braddie in particular, have been carrying on about kites and I Am since we returned from Disney World.

". . . and a little while ago while I was putting them to bed, Braddie told me that *you* said something about I Am promising to 'fix us.' "

A long silence answers me, and I'm wondering if Nate's still there.

"Nate?"

"Yes."

"Do you know what Braddie's talking about?"

He hesitates, then says, "It was the last day of Vacation Bible School."

"Okay. So what happened?"

"We wanted to do something the kids would really enjoy. Someone suggested flying kites. It sounded like a good idea, and they had a blast."

This all sounds warm and wonderful but doesn't answer the question. "And how does I Am fit into all this?"

"To tell you the truth, Clifford, He fits in perfectly," Nate answers, his tone firm and unapologetic. "On the way to the park, Braddie and Bear rode with me and some other kids. I told them that, when we're in trouble, God wants us to look up to Him just as we'd look up to a kite."

I feel a sermon coming on but need to hear the rest, so I stay quiet while Nate continues.

"I told them that He who calls himself 'I Am' had promised to guide, comfort, and heal us if we'd simply obey and look up to Him in prayer."

A still, heavy silence hangs between us. And it should. Because Nate knows *exactly* why Braddie and Bear have taken his message and twisted it to their needs. And I know he knows, but I refuse to confirm his suspicions.

Then Nate goes on, not only showing himself to be a gentleman but addressing my spoken and unspoken concerns in a way that almost has me believing Momma's shared-family-spirit malarkey. "Clifford, growing up can be pretty stressful, even for little guys like Braddie and Bear. They're probably just trying to cope with all the changes confronting them right now. Why not go ahead and fly their kites? It'll be fun, and it will assure them that they've obeyed I Am and give them some hope that help is on the way."

For a long moment I consider Nate's suggestion. "I don't know, Nate. Won't that just be feeding their fantasy?"

Nate exhales heavily. "Clifford, what I *think* is that it'll calm their fears. What I *know* is that if you look to I Am during this time of trouble, He'll guide, comfort, and heal you."

It's time to go. So before I mess up and tell Nate more than I want to reveal, and he reveals knowing more than he wants to let on, we say 'bye and hang up.

---

AFTER MULLING OVER NATE'S WORDS, I SCOUR THE HOUSE FOR BACK ISSUES OF Demetria's *Career Moms* magazine. So far, I've found only two copies and a book Nate loaned me, *The Architecture of Marriage*.

I've started reading it several times but never finished. This time, I will. It's hard admitting that I need to read books and magazines on how to be married, but I've got to do something. With the way this relationship is melting down, I can't afford haphazard solutions. So maybe the "experts" can tell me what I haven't had the brains to figure out on my own.

Sticking out from between the pages of the book is an old bulletin from Nate's church, announcing a marriage retreat. They're already planning the next one and Demetria and I *definitely* need to go. But after the one we attended two years ago, I'm not so sure that's a good idea.

It was fast-paced and lots of fun, and I felt great afterwards but was aware that something dangerous still simmered inside Demetria. And after the wonderful weekend we'd had, that really puzzled me.

We'd spent three days in a resort hotel, sat through hours of fun, to-the-point instruction on the dynamics of Christian marriage, and eaten two candlelight dinners; and for once we weren't hassled by kid-caused coitus interruptus. And after all that, Demetria's mood *still* stunk.

I asked her over and over, "Baby, what's wrong? Baby, what's wrong? Baby, what's wrong?"

And over and over she answered, "Nothing. Nothing. Nothing."

So I let it go. I guess I should've asked again.

When I hear the garage door opening, I stuff the magazines and the book into my desk and hurry to greet Demetria. She steps inside and I do a double take.

"Baby, you look stunning!"

Demetria's dressed in a new, sharp-looking outfit and her hair is fixed in a cute but daring style that frames her face like she's a living fashion portrait. She's carrying a Boland's Exquisites shopping bag, which further explains the new outfit and why she left early to go to Tammy's. Boland's is the most expensive store in the mall, but Demetria seems happy so I'm not saying a word.

"How was the party?"

"Fine."

I can't resist the urge to hug her. Her body stiffens, but I suppress my fear, kiss her cheek, and say, "You look gorgeous."

Demetria resists with a gentle but unmistakable please-get-off-me shove.

I step back and let my eyes travel slowly up and down, then down and up Demetria's willowy form. "Oooh, Demmy. You're *wearing* that outfit. I'ma have to keep my eye on you."

She waves me off and smiles. I mean, really *smiles.* The skirt is shorter than her normal knee-length and I'm guessing the effect it's already had on the male co-workers who've seen it on her round, compact butt.

"My, my, my," I say. "Whose attention are you trying to get?"

Demetria smiles again. "Just the person who can give me what I want."

I laugh. "Oh! You mean me."

Demetria checks the wall clock, looks at me, and rolls her eyes. "Clifford, it's late and I'm getting tired. If you still wanna make love, come on."

I gesture toward the steps with a sweep of my arm. "After you, baby."

I know she said not to call her "baby," but I'm not letting her intimidate the affection out of me.

BEING INVITED TO MAKE LOVE WITH "IT'S LATE AND I'M GETTING TIRED" ISN'T THE MOST promising of beginnings but, like Scratch, I'm in no position to complain about the bone I'm thrown.

By the time I'm out of my clothes and freshened up, Demetria's beneath the covers with her eyes shut! I've got to hurry before she falls asleep like the last time. I try to remain calm. Frantic displays of desire disgust Demetria, and knowing that reduces my dignity to a compost pile. She opens one eye, glances at me, and shakes her head.

"Are you ready?" she asks, her tone about as warm as the computer voice aboard the starship *Enterprise.*

"More than ready!" Stupidity drips from my voice and I know I'm wearing the idiotic smile of the mentally abandoned. I scurry into bed, lifting the covers so I can see her beautiful, curvaceous outline in the soft glow of the night-light.

I kiss her cheek, her neck, and move to her ear. She jerks her head away, reminding me that she doesn't like tongue-in-ear, so I move my hand to her equatorial region and play in her rain forest. The forest is dry and the land beneath it remains determinedly still. But that's okay. Her forest will soon ooze with the dew of love and quake with desire.

*What makes you think that, fool?* asks Victor's chuckling voice in my head.

My hands are at work and my "thing," as Demetria calls it (saying the word like it carries the taste of a truck-stop toilet), is brick hard. I kiss her soft but unyielding lips, getting more excited at the thought of being inside her.

"Stick it in!" she orders.

And like Scratch, I obey and "stick it in," hating myself with each probing thrust.

I'm not stupid. Demetria despises me filling her inner spaces, and no more understands letting me return than I can comprehend my desire to plunge into this abyss that swallows my pride. But I pretend to be welcome in this place of hostile passion, and Demetria remains as detached as a painting watching from the wall.

Supernova energy bursts from my body and I call out the name of God. Tears roll from Demetria's eyes and I realize that instead of a moment of ecstasy, this has been the scene of a crime.

"I love you," I say.

Demetria wipes her eyes and says, "I know," adding ominously, "I have to go."

Then she kisses me, not passionately but with feeling, and hurries into the bathroom.

Twenty minutes later, I'm sitting outside the bathroom door, listening as Demetria cries inside.

"Demetria, what's the matter, sweetheart?"

"Oh, my God," she groans. "I tried. But there's nothing left."

"Nothing left? What do you mean?"

"Forget it, Clifford. Just leave me alone."

"No, Demetria. You're my wife. If you're in pain, so am I. Please talk to me."

There's more sniffling, then a choked sob. "Only if you promise to do as I say."

I consider her proposition, gulp, then say, "Anything."

"Get out of my life."

I lean toward the door, my mouth barely an inch away. "Demetria, please forgive me."

"For what?"

"Because I've just lied to you."

# VICTOR

IF SIMONE DIDN'T HAVE SUCH JUICY-LOOKIN' JUGS, I'DA DUMPED THIS HASSLE A LONG time ago. And the second I see a brand-new Corvette turn into the Hunk-a-Burger parkin' lot, I *know* my big evenin' of nipple nibblin' is busted.

Simone said she'd be drivin' a sporty car but she didn't say nothin' 'bout it bein' no 'vette! Specially a new one. But wait! The 'vette whips into a parkin' space near my econo-cart and I see a dude behind the wheel. Good! Ain't nothin' worser than havin' a ride bummier than a babe's. One look and she knows dinner'll be served at a drive-thru.

When Simone finally pulls up I see that her car ain't much better'n mine, so it ain't no thang. She gets out and hustles over, them knockers jigglin'n jooglin' all over the place. She gets in and we kiss. My eyes lock onto them watermelons like cruise missile radars lockin' on target. They're beggin' me to help 'em out'a that over-the-shoulder-boulder-holder and my mouth fills with drool.

"I can't do nothin' tonight," says Simone.

My jaw hits my lap. "Whut! You know how long I've been . . ."

Simone opens her door to get out.

"Wait!" I holler. "Whutch'you doin'? Where you goin'?"

Simone closes her door and locks me down with narrowed eyes. "You'd better watch how you talk to me."

I put myself in check and smooth out my voice. "Okay, Simone. I'm cool. But dog, baby. I was really wantin' to get with you."

She turns so all her front is showin', then unbuttons her shirt halfway. I'm like one'a them cartoon characters whose body parts fall off, a piece at a time. Simone shakes her shoulders and them bazookas jiggle'n bounce till I can't stand it! I jam my face into the cleavage and moan. Simone strokes the back of my head and talks soft'n sweet.

"You gotta be a good boy if you wanna play with Mommy's toys. Okay?"

I nod into that pillowed valley.

Simone lifts my head, takes my hands, and guides 'em over her mountains for a fast feel. Then she buttons up her shirt, kisses me, and is gone.

---

SINCE SIMONE HAS GIVEN ME THE SHAFTIN' I'D PLANNED ON GIVIN' HER , AIN'T NOTHIN' else to do but roll on down to Benny's. And even though there's plenty'a my partners in here and a couple'a babes with some marvelous mountaintops, it ain't enough to shake my bad mood. Cuz I had my lips all primed, tuned, and ready to slurp and slobber my way up'n down Simone's slopes.

Vernon sets a beer down in front'a me and leans on the counter. "Why're you sittin' there grittin' at them peanuts?"

I grab the bottle and take a long pull. "Got stood up, man."

"By who?"

"That Simone babe."

Vernon frowns as he tries to remember. Then his face lights up with a smile. "Oh! You mean the babe with the twin towers."

"Don't rub it in, man."

Vernon laughs. "Ice, you's one greedy sucka. Instead'a bein' pissed about not gettin' some strange booty you oughta be drivin' your sorry self over to Justine's." He starts wipin' the counter, then refills the peanut dish. "And you need to be rememberin' what I've told you about dippin' your johnson into so many honey pots."

"Look, Vee. If I'd wanted a safe sex lecture I'da call my older brother, Nate."

Vernon slaps me up'side my head. "Don't spar with me, punk! I'm talkin' to you as a friend, not just the dude who twists the cap off your beer. You're gonna catch somethin' and not know it till the day your joint falls off in the shower."

I shake my head and finish my beer. "Vee, do you hassle all your customers like this?"

"Only the ones I care about."

Our eyes lock for a moment, then we smile and slap five.

"Okay, Vee. I'm cool. And you're right. I'ma hang with Justine. Lemme use the phone."

Vernon's face, all smiles and friendship a second ago, freezes over. "Ice, you know Benny don't play lettin' customers use the bar phone."

"Man, just gimme the phone!"

Vernon grabs the phone from beneath the counter and sets it down in front'a me. Now I'm wishin' I'da handled that misunderstandin' with Justine differently. Cuz now to patch thangs up I'ma have'ta go through some stupid apology routine just so she'll know that I know I messed up. But if that's what it takes to get some trim, so whut.

I move down from people as far as the cord'll let me and wait through six rings, gettin' worried that Justine might not be home. Then she picks up, laughin'.

"Hello?"

"Hey, baby. Whuts'up?"

Justine's laughin' chops off into nothin'ness. "What do you want, Ice?"

It don't take no genius to figure out that she ain't glad to hear from me. But it ain't no thang. I'll just admit I was wrong, fill her ears with some sweet talk, and she'll be rollin' out the red carpet.

"How you been?" I ax.

"Ice, I can't talk now."

"You on your way out?"

"That's none'a your business."

Heat's buildin' at the base of my neck. "Whutch'you mean it ain't none'a my business?"

"Just what I said!"

I start to fire back when I hear a voice in the background. And it don't sound like somebody from a girl's choir.

"Justine! You got somebody there with you?"

"That ain't none'a your business either."

"Who is it?" I holler. "I'll come over there and kick . . ."

"Listen up, punk!" says a deep, *really deep,* voice. "You ain't gone do nothin'."

Whoever this is sounds hard enough to back up his words, but I ain't lettin' this sucka chump me. I'll go over there and teach him some pain even the Marine Corps don't know about.

"Who is this?" I holler. "Put Justine back on!"

Vernon's evil-eyein' me from the end of the bar. "Ice! Don't be yellin' in Benny's phone."

I grit on Vernon and grip the phone tighter. "Listen ya Darth Vader–soundin' beagle-breath cum-stain! Where's Justine?"

"I'm right here," says Justine, soundin' like she's sittin' on a laugh she can't wait to enjoy.

"Justine! What're you doin'? Why're you doin' this to us?"

"Listen, picklehead!" says Darth. "You been fired. So don't be callin' here no more!"

I'm grippin' the phone so tight my knuckles hurt. "Justine! Who'zat? Why're you doin' this? Justine!"

Justine and her dude laugh, just before I hear the double-click of two phones hangin' up. I slam the phone down and Vernon snatches it away.

"That's the last time you use it!" he hollers.

From down the other end of the bar, that bubble-lipped comedian wannabe, Ezell, yells, "Ice, you sho' got a way wif da womens."

I put a cheesin' smile on my face and smooth-stride on down to him. "Whutch'you say, Ezell?"

Ezell glances around to make sure all his boys is lookin'. Once he sees they're starin' at him like he's some hero, he speaks reeeaaal slow, like he savorin' each word fallin' out'a his big mouth.

"I said, you-sho'-got-a-way-wif-da-womens."

Ezell's boys laugh and he joins 'em, lookin' away and slappin' five with a couple of 'em. When he looks back, his face punches my fist. Then he slides off his bar stool like a greased noodle.

"Ice!"

It's Vernon. He's holdin' a bat and lookin' like he's ready to rumble. "Ice, you a friend, man. But Benny ain't havin' no brawlin' in his joint."

Vernon sounds like he's sorry about havin'ta do this, but I know he ain't playin'. And if I wasn't so mad, I'd tell him I'm sorry about makin' him do it.

I ease over to the door and say, "You got it, Vee."

"Man, go home," says Vee. "Get some sleep. It'll be all right."

I leave, get in my car, and hit the highway, drivin' as fast as I can push my puzz-mobile. I can't believe this. After everythang we've been through, Justine's just gonna slam-dunk me. I drive faster, knowin' this could get me busted and my bus license pulled. But so whut! I gotta get away. Maybe I'll get lucky and end up someplace that'll help me forget. Then I remember.

*I ain't never been lucky.*

# NATHAN

BEFORE CLIFFORD CALLED ASKING ABOUT THE BOYS AND THOSE KITES, I WAS PRETTY sure that things had gotten worse between him and Demetria. Now I'm certain. I'd be willing to do whatever it took to make his situation better, but the only thing I can do right now is pray. So I do, asking the Lord to keep Clifford safe in the hollow of His hand, and to do the same for Demetria, Braddie, and Bear. I ask Him, above all, to let them remain a loving family. It's bad enough dealing with marital disintegrations in the church family. It's torture to see it happening to someone whose blood I share.

I finish praying, glance at the clock on the far wall of my church office, see that it's almost eight, and stretch. Beverly Dawkins should be here soon.

I normally wouldn't hold a counseling session this late, but with the church renovation adding more chaos to my already hectic schedule—tending to the needs of my parishioners, serving as community liaison for Pittsburgh PD's Drug Free Streets task force, and getting the Y&G kids situated for tonight's sleepover at Holy Covenant—this was the only time available.

Thank God Brenda's helping chaperone the sleepover. She thrives on all the round-the-clock game playing, singing, crafts, and skits. So do Corrine and Nate Junior. As for me, once I'm through talking with Beverly, I'm going to drag my tired self home, take a shower, and get in bed.

I edit a few more lines of Sunday's sermon, shut down the computer, and straighten up my desk. When Beverly gets here, I don't want anything distracting me from our conversation. During our last session, she indicated that she was growing more frustrated with Percy and his foolishness. If conditions have deteriorated further I'll need to pay full attention so I can give her my best advice.

I notice the new church directory and once again pause to admire the cover. The printers did an excellent job of making the church look like a house located in Heaven.

I flip through the pages, stopping at a picture of Mother McCoombs. She's smiling, but her eyes look so tired, like her eighty-three years of struggle chose that Kodak moment to take their toll. But they're also filled with strength. After living through the Depression, a world war, Jim Crow and the Klan, and the deaths of two Kennedys and a King, she's never taken her eyes off Jesus, never once wavered in her belief that He'll make things right. It's a real blessing to see her live the faith I'm trying to grow.

I flip forward, then back a few pages, taking a last look at the printer's master craftsmanship. Then I see Beverly's picture. She's absolutely gorgeous. Almost every Sunday someone—and that includes women as well as men—comments upon her beauty. Even Brenda's mentioned that Beverly looks not only much younger than her own forty-two years but considerably younger than Brenda's thirty-nine.

And as to why Percy's cheating on Beverly, it's anybody's guess. She's elegant, sophisticated, and charming, while Percy bears the unmistakable stamp of someone who's spent hours on street corners, holding his crotch and guzzling beer. People meeting them for the first time usually leave wondering how Beverly ended up with "that!" Sweet Beverly needs the care and attention of far more tender hands like—*perish the thought!*

I'M SITTING IN MY FAVORITE COUNSELING CHAIR, ACROSS FROM BEVERLY, WHO'S ON THE couch, looking very fragile and upset. For the last forty minutes, I've listened in silent amazement as she recounted Percy's latest antics. And I'm convinced more than ever that he's either blind or a complete fool to ignore someone as lovely, warm, and wonderful as Beverly to go chasing after other women.

"I'm tired of fighting this battle," says Beverly, her voice trembling. "Percy's driven me to the point where I just don't care anymore."

The more she talks, the more she struggles against her tears. And the more she struggles, the more I want to hold and comfort her.

"And nothing you've tried has worked?" I ask.

"Nothing!" Beverly's eyes flash. "I've gone out of my way to create a more seductive home atmosphere with candles, incense, and soft music. I've worn skimpy lingerie, even begged him to touch me, but . . ." She chokes back a sob, then continues. "But he still rejects me, calling me a frigid prude and other horrible, humiliating things."

My anger at Percy for being so mean to this gentle, sweet woman is building, but I suppress it and merely say, "You don't deserve that."

"In my head, I know you're right," Beverly agrees. "But it still hurts here," she says, softly tapping the center of her chest.

I keep my gaze up and away from where she's touching her breasts so that my mind stays focused. But then she crosses her legs and her skirt draws back, revealing more of her wonderfully smooth, shapely thighs.

She shakes her head, the movement tossing her hair into a shimmering cloud. "Am I that ugly? Am I that undesirable?"

"Absolutely not!" I answer quickly. "Beverly, you're a stunning, attractive woman with much to offer. Percy's inability or unwillingness to appreciate your inner and outer beauty is *his* failure and *his* problem."

She balls her hands into fists and closes her eyes tight, squeezing out tears. "I've been such a fool. What did I ever see in Percy? What made me think he knew anything about being a man?"

"C'mon now, Beverly. You're being too hard on . . ."

"And now, after all these years, after investing so much time in a relationship that should never have been, I, I . . ."

Beverly's voice trails off as she succumbs to her tears. I rush from my chair over to the couch, put my arm around her shoulders, and hug her. She turns toward me and buries her face in my shoulder, her sobs coming strong and hard.

"Shhh, shhh," I say, stroking her hair. "C'mon, don't cry. I know it's painful, but everything's going to work out. You're still young and beautiful enough to find someone who'll love you, just the way you want and just the way you need."

"But I'm afraid," she says, looking up at me and sniffling. "After this, I don't know if I'll ever be able to give my heart again."

I wipe the tears from her cheeks. "Stop talking like that. Of course you'll be able to give your heart again. And this time, you'll get back all the love you give."

She smiles bravely, the profound sadness in her eyes making her look more beautiful than ever. "Do you promise?"

I nod and look deep into her glistening eyes. "If only you could see yourself as I see you."

"And how is that, Nathan?"

It's the first time she's ever spoken my name and it sounds wonderful, like her voice is kissing my ears.

I wipe her moist cheeks and say, "I see you as a rare and precious jewel who deserves nothing but the best."

"And you're a wonderful, sensitive man who deserves nothing but love." She strokes my cheek and says, "A man who deserves all of my love."

We look hard into each other's eyes, our faces coming closer and closer until our lips meet in a tender kiss. It's good, so very good, and burning passions ignite.

Beverly breaks the kiss and holds my face in her palms. "It's been so long," she says, her voice husky and urgent. "I've been aching for so long."

We kiss again and Beverly lies back, pulling me toward her as we slide down a slope of lust toward a point of no return.

I slip my hand beneath her sweater and she stiffens for a moment, relaxes, then places her hand over mine and guides it to her breasts. I unsnap her bra and squeeze her breasts, kissing her harder and grinding my pelvis against hers, pushing my erection against the warmth of her pleasure canal. I slide my hand beneath the underwire support of her bra and start caressing and kneading the soft, supple flesh, my throbbing erection stiffening harder with the sweet pain of desire. She shifts her position and reaches down and rubs my crotch, stroking the length of my hardness, gripping and squeezing as a prelude to what she'll do once I'm inside her.

I kiss Beverly's ears and neck, slowly moving down to her breasts, squeezing and sucking them, licking her nipples to hardness, then giving them soft, gentle bites.

"I need you," she says, gasping. "I need you so much."

I slide my hand between her legs and she opens them wide, giving me room to feel and caress her moist sacred spot. When I touch her, she trembles and moans.

"Make love to me," she urges. "Do it to me. Now!"

"I will!" I say, growling out the declaration.

I unbuckle my belt and start unzipping my pants, Beverly's gyrating hips delaying my progress, the delay increasing my desire. I help her out of her panties as I struggle to free myself. And just as I'm about to succeed, I freeze.

From the corner of my eye, I see Brenda staring at me from her picture on my desk, her gaze penetrating and knowing. I also hear the gentle voice that speaks to me so often, still filled with love but now rumbling with anger.

It says: *Nathan, be ye not deceived, for God is not mocked. Whatsoever a man soweth, that shall he also reap.*

A chill blows over me and I look back at Brenda's picture, staring into her eyes and imagining the tears that will pour from them if she ever discovers what's happening here. I have to stop it *now*.

I pull away from Beverly, her hips still undulating sensuously in anticipation.

"What are you waiting for?" she asks. "I'm ready!"

I scramble to the opposite end of the couch, hastily fixing my clothes and fighting to breathe through my fear as I realize the terrible mistake I've made, and was about to make.

"What's the matter?" Beverly sits up, looking puzzled. "Why did you stop?"

"Beverly, I, I can't. I'm sorry, but this isn't right."

"But, but I thought you wanted me. I thought . . ."

"This shouldn't have happened. And it's my fault for taking advantage of your vulnerability. Please forgive me."

Beverly looks away in shame. "So then . . . you're rejecting me too?"

"No, Beverly! Don't take it that way. I'm not rejecting you, but what we were doing was wrong, something that could hurt both of us."

Beverly hurriedly puts on her panties, grabs her purse, and rushes to the door, keeping her eyes averted.

"Wait!" I say, catching her by the arm. "Please, Beverly. We've got to talk about this, so that there's no misunderstanding."

She jerks her arm free and runs out of the office.

I PULL INTO THE GARAGE, CUT OFF THE MOTOR, AND SIT, TREMBLING AS I CONSIDER WHAT my near-fornication might have cost—and still might cost me—in terms of my marriage, my family, and my spirit.

Brenda's gaze flashes before me again, this time so very sad. She's asking, *Nathan, why?*

My eyes mist over and I place my head on the steering wheel. "Father God, please forgive me," I whisper. "In the name of Jesus, *please forgive me.*"

The gentle voice that normally answers remains silent. I sit up and wipe my eyes dry, knowing that in shutting me out God is exercising His declared refusal to look upon sin. And right now, I reek of it.

What was I thinking, me a married man and servant of God, about to fornicate with another man's wife—and in the Lord's temple? How could I have forgotten the words I'd hurled from the pulpit every Sunday morning concerning such dangers? Why didn't I consider the cataclysm that this could bring upon my wife and family?

I want to confess everything to Brenda right now and let her do what she will. But that's false bravado, since she's with the Y&G kids at the sleepover. And knowing that drives my guilt deeper.

Brenda's the bedrock of my ministry. She's the one who gave me the courage to not only patch up our church but expand the effort into full-scale renovation. She's the one who urged the police to accept my offer to work on their Drug Free Streets task force, asserting that there wasn't a stronger, more capable advocate for the community than me. She's the reason I didn't eliminate the every-other-year Y&G sleepover rotation between Divine Temple and Holy Covenant. She insisted that the kids really enjoyed it and that it would help strengthen church relations. Without Brenda I wouldn't be succeeding. She's my world, my life, and my dream.

So how could I have been so stupid? Should I tell her? As hard as it will be to keep this mistake hidden inside me, should I risk losing all I have just to ease my guilt? Even if I don't tell her, will she sense that something's wrong? Will the Lord reveal to her that the husband she's loved completely and without reservation has betrayed her?

I can't do it! As bad as I feel about what I've done, I'd feel even worse about causing Brenda that kind of pain. Besides, the only person I *really* have to confess to is Christ, and I've already done that. And even though the Lord said that if we confess our sins He'd be faithful and just, forgiving and purifying us from all unrighteousness, I don't feel forgiven and I certainly don't feel pure. Which means I need to exercise faith.

I'm simply going to have to remind myself that the Lord's words and promises are true, even for me. I'll have to strengthen my belief in the knowledge that Jesus' death on the Cross washed away *all* the sins of humanity, including mine. I'll have to deepen my trust in the certainty that God will welcome me into His kingdom as long as I've been cleansed by the blood of Christ.

I bow my head and pray, thanking God for putting me in remembrance of His promises. I thank Him for saving weak sinners like me from an eternity of torment and doom. And I promise Him, in the name of Jesus, to be on my guard from now on, at all times, in all places, in all ways, so that I won't put his love, forbearance, longsuffering, and grace to the test. Amen.

I slowly get out of the car, hit the garage-door button, and check the mail. A pair of headlights pulls into the driveway and, once my eyes adjust, I see it's Demetria. I go over and open her door. She's dressed in her baggy around-the-house sweat suit, and her eyes are puffy.

"Hey, precious," I say, hugging her. "How're ya doing?"

Demetria smiles bravely. "Fine." She looks at me quizzically and says, "Are you okay?"

I force a smile onto my face. "Sure! I'm just a little tired. What're you doing out so late?"

Demetria looks away, nervously shifting her weight from foot to foot. "I was out driving around and decided, I mean, there's a lot on . . . I need to talk with Brenda."

"I'm sorry, Demetria. Brenda's chaperoning the Y&G kids for their annual sleepover."

She doesn't answer, staring trancelike straight through me. I duck down slightly and look directly into her eyes.

"Demetria? Did you hear me? Brenda's chaperoning the Y&G kids."

Demetria blinks and looks at me like I've suddenly popped into view. "Huh? What did you say?"

I touch her forehead. "Are you feeling well?"

She rolls her eyes and smiles. "Of course I am, silly." She pushes up on her tippy-toes and kisses my cheek. "I'll see you later. Tell Brenda I stopped by."

"Okay."

She starts back to her car, slowing when I call, "Demetria, what's wrong?"

She wilts, slumping against the car. I rush to catch her.

"I don't want to hurt him," she sobs. "I don't want to hurt him."

"What? Hurt who?"

"Clifford!"

"But . . ."

"He loves me. I *know* he does. But it's too late. Too late!"

"Demetria, what's going on? Whatever it is, it's never . . ."

"I need you to understand, Nathan. If anybody'll understand, you will."

"Now, c'mon Deme . . ."

"You've got to explain it to Clifford, please!"

"Explain what?"

"I can't pretend anymore. There's too much pain."

"Wait, Demetria! C'mon inside. Let's pray together. Let's put this in God's hands."

"I have prayed. But how long, Nathan? How *long*? God's not listening to me!"

"No, Demetria! He is! But the Lord moves in His own time."

"No! *I can't!*" she sobs. She tears herself away and gets into the car. "Don't hate me, Nathan. Please don't hate me."

"Demetria, you're my sister in Christ and family. I could never hate you."

She starts the car, rolls down the window, and says, "Be there for Clifford, Nathan. Promise me you'll be there for him."

"I promise, Demetria. But please, can't we at least . . ."

She backs away into the street, leaving me standing there mortified and grimly aware that Clifford's present troubles could be my future.

# DARKNESS DESCENDS

# CLIFFORD

A MONTH AGO, DEMETRIA MERELY COULDN'T STAND ME. NOW SHE FEELS CONTEMPT. And more and more, I'm asking myself, "Why am I fighting so hard?" That question, and a bunch of others just like it, led me to start seeing Dr. Crennick.

Marriage counseling is one part of the company's health and welfare benefits I never thought I'd be using. But it's free and available, so I might as well take advantage. I'm already scheduled for an appointment and I talked to Demetria about coming, but she flatly refused, telling me that counseling was for couples that had a chance of surviving.

"I told you, Clifford," she'd said, exasperated. "We *don't* have a chance."

I finish brushing my teeth, rush downstairs, and holler to the boys. "Braddie! Bear! C'mon, you guys. Time to go."

Demetria yells from the dining room. "No, Clifford! I'll drop them off at day care."

"That's all right. It's been a while since I've taken them."

"Will you just let me do it?"

"Demetria, what's the big deal? Why are you acting like you're the only one who's qualified to do this?"

"Because I'm usually the one who does."

She's got me there. The one, maybe two days during the week that I either drop the boys off or pick them up isn't enough to dispute her point.

"Well then, why don't you take one and I'll take one?"

I kick myself as soon as the words escape my mouth. Demetria looks at me like I've suggested renewing our vows.

"Clifford, don't be silly! Just take care of *yourself,* like you normally do."

A heat wave shoots to the top of my head. If what Demetria says is true, then my taking the boys just this once won't threaten her self-deluded status as the goddess of mothering martyrs. And why am I letting her make me negotiate this anyway?

"Demetria, I really want to do this. Why're you being so hostile?"

"You're only making things worse."

"Making what worse? How is this worsening your life?"

Demetria levels her gaze and speaks with chilling calm. "I'm not talking about me."

Several crackling seconds of hostility pass as we stand opposite each other. I snatch my briefcase off the dining room table and head for the door.

This is crazy! I'm doomed to listen daily to Demetria's complaining about dropping the boys off, picking them up, coming home, cooking, cleaning, and playing mommy. But whenever I try to help, she fights me. And when she's not fighting me, she's lobbing snide reminders that these are my kids too, and that taking care of them is as much my responsibility as it is hers, and that when I do it's not "helping" her but doing my job as a father. Hearing that crap's bad enough, but what's worse is being scolded like some ignoramus who's devoid of parental instinct because I never carried a baby.

The thoughts clattering around my head coalesce and fall from my mouth in a muttered expletive.

"Don't mumble," says Demetria. "If you've got something to say, say it!"

I stop at the door and look back. "Believe me, Demetria. You don't wanna hear it."

She cocks her head to the side and smirks. "Yeah. You're probably right."

Victor wouldn't take this. He'd whiz across the room and give Demetria some quick street facts. But Victor's not here and I'm not him. So being me instead of him, I open my legs wide and let her slice my testicles that're still bleeding from our last clash.

She gets her car keys and says, "And, Clifford, don't forget that you're supposed to pick up the boys so I can go shopping and get my hair done."

And Victor's laughing echo says, *Like I said, Cliff. One'a ya'll is stupid. And it ain't Demetria.*

IT'S ALMOST NOON, WHICH MEANS THAT IN A FEW HOURS I'LL HAVE TO GO HOME. AND that's gonna take all my strength. Calling that house "home" is making less and less sense. Especially with all the fights about who'll move out.

During the last one Demetria said, "That's why I'm leaving you, Clifford. I'm sick and tired of your selfishness. You know it'd be better for Braddie and Bear to stay here and not have to move, start at a new school, and make new friends."

"Selfishness! Demetria, as the galactic queen of self-centeredness, you're in no position to point fingers. And for the last time, NO! I'm not leaving Braddie and Bear with the memory of their father walking out. And since when did *you* get so concerned about their adjustment, before or after deciding to turn them into children from a broken home?"

"I'm gonna have my lawyer make you move."

"Go ahead!" I roared. "And be sure to have him prepare you for a custody fight!"

Demetria gasped, as if an invisible hand had snatched her throat. "You wouldn't dare!"

"Try me!"

"Braddie and Bear are coming with me."

"Maybe. Maybe not. Since you're destroying their home for 'true love, excitement, and fun,' I'm guessing that the court will decide on *not*!"

"What's the matter with you?" Demetria hollered. "Don't you care about subjecting the boys to that kind of trauma?"

"Demetria!" I bellowed. "Lest you forget, *you're* the one who wants the divorce."

Demetria cursed and stomped out. Thank God I didn't invest in a home with her. I'd go berserk if I was ever made to pay for a house I couldn't live in.

THE ONLY THING WORSE THAN WORKING *THROUGH* LUNCH IS HAVING THE TELEPHONE ring *during* lunch. I should let it roll over to my voice mail, but what the heck. I'm here. Lunch is blown. And that obsessive achiever's desire Nate's always warning me to moderate compels me to answer.

"Erie Aerospace. Clifford Matthews speaking."

"Clifford, it's me."

"Hold on, Demmy."

With the kind of "discussions" we've been having I can't assume that this one won't end up being a shouting match, so I transfer the call from my cubicle to an empty office with real walls. I hurry inside, shut the door, and grab the phone.

"Okay, Demetria. Go ahead."

"I've made arrangements for us to attend a class. It'll be starting soon and it's really important that . . ."

"Huh? Wait, Demetria. Wait!"

"Clifford, I don't have time to get into a long discussion. Tammy's waiting outside for me so we can go to lunch."

"Forget Tammy! There'll be plenty of time for her to coil around, suffocate, and swallow her lunch."

"Clifford, I wish you'd stop insulting my friends. Tammy hasn't done anything to you and I don't see why . . ."

"Maybe it's those three sixes branded into her forehead."

Demetria exhales an exasperated huff and says, "What's your question?"

"What kind of class did you sign *us* up for and why do *we* have to go?"

"It's to help kids cope with divorce. We're scheduled for separate sessions."

And so I was wrong. Just when I thought I'd run out of bones for Demetria to break, she found another.

"How very thoughtful of you," I say. "To schedule me for classes I've no interest in taking. And after all your complaining about me spending so much time in classrooms and libraries."

"Clifford, why're you being so unreasonable? Getting some help on how to cope with this will be good for us."

I crumple the soda can I'm holding. "Good for us! Demetria, what'd be good for us is to not have to go through this crap. Or hasn't Tammy advised you to consider *that* option?"

"No one's advising me on anything. And I don't know why you're acting like it's someone else's fault this marriage is ending. We're the only two people getting divorced."

"*We* may be getting divorced but *you're* the only one who wants it."

"Clifford, please. This isn't easy for me. And it certainly won't be for Braddie and Bear. Can't you understand that it's better for us to help them deal with this than to make them grope for stable ground?"

"And can't you understand that the most stable ground for them is their *family*? All of us! Together!"

Demetria sniffles and says, "Don't you think I know that? But it can't be that way."

"Why, Demetria? Why can't it be? Just tell me what you want and I'll make it happen."

And then in a voice filled with fury, she says, "Clifford! How plain do I have to make it? I don't love you! I can barely stand the sight of you! And I refuse to stay in a bad marriage for the sake of the kids!"

Time stands still. My hand goes limp, almost dropping the phone. I've taken a lot of low shots from Demetria. But this one leaves my ears ringing and my logic center short-circuiting as I struggle to comprehend how the wife of my memory mutated into the mean-spirited harpie at the other end of the line.

The silence lengthens, and I imagine Demetria wide-eyed with surprise, hardly believing what she just said any more than I can. But if she's surprised, she recovers quickly.

"Is that direct enough for you, Clifford? By the way, I might be home late."

"What about tonight's parent-teacher conference for Braddie?"

"It's your turn, Clifford. Now you'll see how it feels to go alone."

# VICTOR

COREY, THE RTA LOT SUPERVISOR, IS LUCKY THAT THIS CLANKIN' RATTLETRAP HE'S GOT me drivin' today hasn't made me late for my lunchtime honey-watchin' hour in Moody Hollow Park with my fellow drivers Clyde and Brantley. I told that fool the bus was actin' up. Then he put on his big-boss "Mr. Jackson" face and said, "Take it anyway!"

That really pissed me off. But as soon as I saw Edie, standin' on her corner and holdin' Karenna, everythang smoothed out. One'a these days, I'ma get Karenna and Jewel together and see just how much they favor each other.

As for Corey, he better not press his luck.

I'd hate to get a brotha in trouble, but he's gonna mess around and have me blabbin' everythang I know. By the time he's through gettin' whooped by Claudia's King Kong husband, and chewed up by them sexual harassment po-leases, the only thang he'll be bossin' are the memories of slurpin' Claudia's slot. And from what Clyde and Brantley tell me, he's had his head jammed up in there so tight, his face is startin' to get a crease down the middle.

By the time I get to Moody Hollow, Clyde and Brantley are already eatin' lunch. It ain't no thang cuz I'm still early enough to catch our babe show. I hope that redbone with the three miles of legs comes out. She's so fine, I could almost see myself doin' some old-timey stuff like layin' my jacket down across a puddle so she don't get her feet wet.

I take my seat on the park bench, start grubbin', and wait for the honeys.

"Did ya'll read the 'We the People Speak' section in this mornin's paper?" Clyde axes.

Me and Brantley shake our heads no.

"Was there somethin' important?" I ax.

"Yup! The dude writin' the piece says that since we done got away from the church, we're like driftwood. No direction, no purpose. Just bein' floated along by anything."

"So what," says Brantley. "Floatin's better'n sinkin'."

Clyde looks at Brantley like he just farted out his ears. "That ain't the point, youngster. If you ain't got no spine to resist bein' pushed, then you can't resist bein' dragged under. With no anchor to common sense, you'll just end up rotted driftwood."

Brantley's about to fire back when Clyde's eyes get big and he points to the high-rises. "Here they come!" he shouts.

The honeys come out, first in ones and twos, then in groups of four or five.

"Where'zat redbone you was all pumped up about?" axes Clyde.

I shrug. "Don't know, man. She didn't mail me her schedule for this week."

Clyde flips me the bird and we keep lookin'.

"There she is!" shouts Brantley.

We all get lightheaded watchin' the redbone strut to the Galleria. Just as she gets to the door, she stops and looks over her shoulder—straight at us!

"You see that!" Brantley hollers. "She scoped me, man. I'm in love!"

"She wasn't lookin' at your nappy-headed, scraggly butt," Clyde says. "She was lookin' at *me*. A star like that needs somebody older, somebody more mature, who knows how to treat a woman *right*!"

"The only thang you got right so far is 'old,' " I say.

Clyde tries smackin' me up'side my head but I duck. And Brantley's still swearin' up'n down that he was the one the redbone wanted, so I decide to set him straight.

"I don't know why you hopin' so hard. You can't afford no woman like that."

"What you tryin' to say, man? I'm workin' every day."

"And that child support and the IRS is eatin' you alive, just like it's doin' me."

Hearin' "IRS" makes Clyde choke. He grits on me and says, "Why'd you have to go and bring them up?"

"Don't tell me you're still hopin' they all get alien-abducted," I say, laughin'.

"Let me tell you somethin'," says Clyde, lookin' more pissed about it than usual. "I'd join the Nazis and march on Gay Pride Day if it'd help get rid of 'em. But they's already actin' like Nazis, and done took the little bit'a pride I had." Then he takes a lion-sized bite out'a some oozy pastry he's been eyein', and grins. "But I still ain't got it as bad as you two suckas. Dealin' with the IRS is *way* better than dealin' with them child support gangstas."

I can't say nothin' cuz Clyde's dead-on-the-money right.

Clyde grins wider and says, "I told you youngsters about pokin' your peckers where they ain't got no business."

Brantley looks at me like his eyes is gonna start sparkin' and sizzlin'. "I don't know where you get off talkin' trash! Pretty soon, *you're* gonna be the only one payin' child support."

I laugh. "Whut! Is you special now? Or maybe Tawnee just up and decided that you was such a nice guy, she went and told the court to let go of your nuts."

Brantley ain't just grittin' no more. He's lookin' like he just might leap into my throat. When he finally speaks, his voice comes out soundin' like a Rottweiler's if it could talk. "I don't care what she's told the court! She ain't gettin' another cent till she quits playin' head games with my son. Chumpin' him into thinkin' I'm the boogeyman or somethin'."

Me and Clyde get quiet, and I'm feelin' stupid cuz I shoulda known better. Of all the thangs that coulda pulled Brantley's chain, this is the worsest.

"Always claimin' he's over at her sister's on the days I'm s'posed to get him. Naw, man. She ain't gettin' nothin' till I'm seein' Tyrell on a reg'lar schedule."

Clyde don't look like he's wantin' to get into this, but Brantley's his friend, so he clears his throat and jumps in anyway.

"Brant, listen, youngster. You gotta pay it or they'll . . ."

"I don't care what they do!" Brantley shouts. "The courts talk all that yang about the 'welfare of the child.' How's my child's welfare bein' looked after if he ain't allowed to see his daddy? Him knowin' he's got a daddy is as important as him havin' a roof over his head! Him knowin' he's got a daddy makes a difference in how he sees hisself!"

Clyde tries again but Brantley shuts him down. Then I get into it, cuz even though Brantley's my partner, he ain't stopped to think that when clowns like him don't pay, it makes life hard on us who do. It's bad enough them snake politicians and thug social workers treat divorced fathers like their pictures is hangin' beneath post office WANTED signs. We don't need Brantley givin' 'em more reasons to bust our balls.

"Brantley, listen to me," I say. "I know whutch'you sayin', man. But you gotta pay."

Brantley ignores me and keeps on gripin'. "The courts figure that, hey, if you have'ta stand while you piss, then you is *guilty*!"

"Brantley, why you wanna go crazy like this?" I ax. "You know that if you don't pay, they'll haul you to the slam."

"That's 'zactly what I'm talkin' about! How's a sucka s'posed to do what the court's tellin' him if he's countin' wall bricks in lockdown? They throw you in the slam and say, 'Pay!' Then they rag on you for not earnin' no money while bein' in the slam *they* threw you in. That's why it's called justice. It means 'Just Us'!"

I try to get in a word but Brantley cuts me off. "We're just pickin' a new kinda cotton," he says, snarlin'.

"Whutch'you talkin' about?" I ax.

"Think about it, Ice! With no more slavery and segregation, somethin' had to be invented to cripple the brothas. And look at how slick it is. Besides Old Marse still keepin' our kids from us, he's got us on the ropes for ten, fifteen years. By the time a sucka's through, he's past his prime and out'a time. Just another has-been field hand."

"What about all them fools cripplin' *theyselfs*, havin' two and three kids by two and three different women?" axes Clyde. "It ain't right for them to be let off the hook."

"And it ain't right for me to be gettin' jammed cuz'a *them*," Brantley counters.

"Brantley! Will you shut up for a minute?" I shout. "You ain't gotta convince me. I told you whut happened the day me and Lynnette went to domestic court."

Brantley grits on me like whut I gotta say better be good.

"The judge listened to Lynnette like she was quotin' Jesus. But when my time came, he did all the talkin', hittin' me with that same 'welfare of the child' bullet. I never did get a chance to tell him that me bein' concerned about my child's welfare was why I was standin' in front'a him in the first place."

Right then, my mind starts hasslin' me. *Again.* So there I am, goin' through the front door of me and Lynnette's apartment. Jewel's not in her room and my heart's jackhammerin'. I step into my bedroom and my life changes.

Lynnette's in bed, layin' butt-naked next to a dude whose hair looks like he poured engine oil on it. A line of drool is hangin' from his lip and his dong's pointed to the edge where two little hands grab the sheet and pull until Jewel's standin' up. She sees me, smiles, then looks at the dude's dong like it's a new kinda toy.

I'm hittin' the dude. He's standin' like a wet dishrag and Lynnette's dialin' for the po-leases and hollerin' at me to stop hurtin' the punk. I try grabbin' the phone but she jumps out the way, gettin' some help from the dude, who tries to hit me. I punch, kick, and hammer-blow the sucka till he's screamin' like a wounded pig. Then I throw, thrash, and thump him till he's yelpin' like a mutt.

Po-leases bust in right as I drop the dude to his knees, put two fingers into his nostrils, and lift his head back to get a clean throat shot. A wallopin' pain slams into the back of my head. I stagger and see three cops, one holdin' a nightstick, the others reachin' for their pistols. I step toward 'em and Officer Nightstick clonks me once, twice, and the world turns black. . . .

"Ice! ICE!"

Somebody's shakin' me and I look up and see Brantley. "C'mon, man. Snap out of it."

"Lookit how he's sweatin'," Clyde says.

"Ice. You okay, man?" Brantley axes.

"Yeah. I'm cool."

We're quiet for a long time till Brantley says, "I'ma get me one'a them sactomees."

"A what?" Clyde axes.

"You know. One'a them operations where you can't have no more kids."

I jam my thighs together and Clyde rolls his eyes.

"You big dummy," he says. "You talkin' about a vasectomy."

Brantley don't even rise to Clyde's name-callin'. He just says, "Yeah. One'a them."

"Man, if you don't want no more kids, why not just wear a rubber?" I ax.

Brantley answers in a tremblin' voice. "Cuz I wanna be sure."

"Sure! Whutch'you got to be *that* sure of?"

"That I don't never again love a child that the government and the courts can take away and all I can do is look."

Brantley grabs his stuff and leaves. Me and Clyde follow, not even stoppin' when we see the redbone struttin' back to her buildin'.

# NATHAN

MOTHER MCCOOMBS LOOKS UP AT ME FROM HER HOSPITAL BED AND SMILES.

"Now, Pastor, you stop worryin'. The Lawd's got ev'thang under control."

I give her a halfhearted smile. This is the second time Mother's been admitted to the hospital for testing. It's worrisome, but with her complaining about chest pains there wasn't much choice.

I step aside as a nurse comes in to check Mother's blood pressure. After the nurse finishes, I put another pillow behind Mother's head, lean over, and kiss her cheek.

"You'd better hurry and get well," I say. "Your work at the church is starting to pile up."

She squeezes my hand and smiles back, her eyes filling with mischief. "Didn't I tell you? When I get out'a here I'm goin' on vacation."

"Vacation! What vacation?"

"I'ma take one'a them cross-country train trips."

I'm barely able to suppress the grin that's trying to take over my face. "You'd better not be going with another man."

Mother McCoombs pinches my cheek and shakes it gently back and forth. "Now don't you be gettin' jealous. I told you that you wasn't the only one I was seein'."

I slap my forehead and feign heartbreak. "How can you do this to me? After I've given you"—I glance at my watch—"the best forty minutes of my life!"

We laugh and I hug Mother. "I love you," I say.

"I love you too, Pastor."

I'm about to suggest that we pray for her speedy recovery when she takes my hand and starts praying herself. "Lawd, please comfort my Pastor. And continue givin' him wisdom as he grows stronger in You and his faith. Lawd, show him there ain't *nothin'* you cain't handle and that, just like you said in olden times, all thangs'll work together for your glory. In Jesus' name, amen."

I say amen, kiss Mother again, and prepare to leave.

"Don't worry, Mother," I say. "These are just routine tests to make sure those chest pains aren't anything serious."

"I ain't worried," she says serenely. "If the Lawd should call me home right now, I'm ready to join Him." Then she winks and says, "But if He wants to wait till next week, that'll be okay too."

We laugh again and I start for the door.

"Pastor," she calls.

"Yes, Mother."

"Please keep prayin' for my granbaby Raymond. My daughter says they had a big fight and she ain't seen him for days. He's run off like that before and she's at her wits' end. She mighta even throwed him out this time. That poor chile. With four other mouths to feed, that boy oughta be helpin' her."

I agree but keep my opinion to myself. Mother's got enough to deal with right now without engaging in prolonged discussions about her gangster grandson. "Mother, I'll keep praying and so will the church family. And I'll be sure and have Brenda's Intercessory Prayer Team keep him at the top of their list."

She smiles and relaxes, settling her head deep into the pillows. "Thanks so much."

"You're welcome. I'll see you later."

She nods and her eyes close as she starts to doze off.

IT'S A QUICK DRIVE BACK TO DIVINE TEMPLE, BUT STILL LONG ENOUGH FOR ME TO RECALL the details of my close call with Beverly. Thank God she and I reached a workable, albeit imperfect, understanding.

After our "incident" she dropped out of sight for a while, but eventually she returned my phone calls and, after much coaxing, agreed to meet with me to get things straight. It was an intense encounter.

I felt the same attraction to her, strong and surging. But I'd promised God to mend my ways and I stayed anchored behind my desk while she sat a nice, safe distance away on the couch.

I opened the meeting by saying, "Beverly, please forgive me for what happened. I betrayed your trust and I feel absolutely miserable about it."

She was looking down, studying her lap, and I remembered the shamed expression she'd worn that unfortunate day. Long seconds passed and she said nothing.

Then she slowly lifted her head, stared directly into my eyes, and in an unnervingly calm voice said, "Nathan, I will not forgive you."

My mouth went dry and my heart began hammering. "Beverly, please, I . . ."

"I won't forgive you because nothing needs to be forgiven," she said, smiling softly. "I love you, Nathan."

I sank back into my chair, relieved and alarmed.

"I won't say that I wasn't embarrassed and angry with you," she continued.

"But you don't know how much I adore you. Knowing that you wanted me made me feel good. It made me realize that the problem wasn't me but Percy preferring those sluts he chases after."

"Beverly, it's good you've reached that conclusion, but . . ."

"Please let me finish."

I nodded, and she continued. "Because of what happened, I know I'm still desirable. I know that with the right man, I'll find the love I deserve."

It was sounding more and more like Beverly was preparing to name *me* as the "right man" and I had to stop her before she made the identification.

"Beverly, wait! Please listen to me closely. I'm glad your outlook is more positive, but we can't have that kind of relationship. It's not right and wouldn't be helpful to either of us."

She chuckled. "Relax, Nathan. I know you're married." I was about to give her an emphatic nod of agreement when she said, "But I also know that you still want me."

That was the last straw. I searched for the words to tell Beverly that I could no longer be her counselor. I worried that she might get angry and make threats, but the situation was too risky and I decided that it was better to risk her wrath than to chance another mistake. Especially since she was right about part of me still wanting her.

"Don't look so alarmed," Beverly admonished. "I'm not going to do anything that will risk what we have. All I ask is that you not shut me out. As long as I can see you, that'll be good enough."

I studied her face, taking in each beautiful feature. "Beverly, I'll keep working with you, but only if we establish some definite ground rules."

"Name them."

"First, that we keep this strictly professional counselor-client relationship."

"Agreed."

"Second, that we keep the focus on helping you manage your way through this situation with Percy."

"Agreed."

"And third, that you forgive me for what happened and accept my pledge that it won't ever happen again."

Beverly frowned but after a moment said, "Done."

A considerable amount of weight lifted from my shoulders when Beverly smiled. We talked a little while longer, then she said she had to leave. She stood up and I went to shake her hand, but she hugged me. I tensed for a moment, relaxing when she released me and headed for the door.

"Beverly, wait," I said in a low voice.

She stopped and faced me, circling her arms around me as mine engulfed her.

"Thanks for understanding," I said.

We held each other briefly. Then she was gone. And I was overjoyed to have dodged a bullet.

Ever since then, things have been pretty much okay. Beverly and I have formed a great friendship of respect and affection, and it's been purely professional and aboveboard. As for Brenda, she's irritated that Beverly's started calling me by my first name. I explained that Beverly had simply gotten comfortable with me and that it would be a mistake to correct her on such a small matter, possibly compounding her emotional troubles. Brenda still doesn't like it, but I've decided that it's far better to have her irritated about Beverly's liberal use of my name than to have her learn about my liberal exploration of Beverly's body.

WHEN I GET TO DIVINE TEMPLE, HELEN, MY CHURCH SECRETARY, MEETS ME IN MY OFFICE with her notepad and begins running down the list of tasks she's scheduled for me.

"Pastor, Sister Matthews called to remind you to mark your calendar for Nate Junior's science club award ceremony."

I reach for my calendar and Helen says, "I've already made the notation."

I sit back and watch Helen have fun demonstrating her efficiency.

"Syd from Monitor Construction called to schedule a meeting about the next phase of church renovation."

I glance at my calendar and Helen says, "Already done."

"Sister Dawkins called and said something about deciding to 'move ahead to the next step.' "

I purse my lips and nod. The "next step" Beverly's talking about is filing for divorce. Helen averts her knowing-the-next-step eyes from mine and continues.

"Mr. Timothy Rasmussen of Mid-Atlantic Robotics & Cybertech says he'd love to meet with you and the Y&G board members. And finally"—Helen moves closer and lowers her voice—"Sister Carlene Newman and her husband, Chet, are waiting to see you."

"Okay. Give me a couple of minutes to get situated, then send them in."

Helen snaps her notepad shut, wheels around with almost military precision, and strides out. I use the moment alone to prepare myself. Sister Newman's warned me about Chet and his temper, convincing me once again that hotheads like him are one of the reasons why God gave humans the weapon of prayer. Before this meeting's over, I may have to use a lot of it.

There's a knock on the door and I invite them in to take a seat. Chet's eyes are smoldering and Carlene is a ball of tension, wringing her hands and biting her lower lip. There's no easy way to tell Chet what he has to hear, so I start at the beginning.

"Brother Newman, I asked you here today at your daughter Keishawn's request."

Chet frowns and leans forward in his chair. "Keishawn's request?"

I nod.

"What're you talkin' about, Rev? I thought I was here fo' my wife. What's goin' on?"

He cuts his eyes sharply over to Carlene. She looks like she'll bolt from the office at any moment.

"Carlene, what's this all about? You seein' a man on the side and usin' Keishawn and this fool to tell me?"

My jaws tighten and I pray for patience. "Brother Newman, there's no need . . ."

"I ain't no Christian, so stop callin' me 'brother.' "

"All right. Can I call you Chet?"

"You can stop wastin' my time and get on with it."

"Very well. As I was saying, Keishawn asked me to meet with you to discuss a very serious matter."

"What's she done!" Chet hollers. He glares at Carlene. "Carlene, if you been holdin' out on me, I'ma . . ."

"Chet, please!" I say. "Please. That's what we're here for. To get this all out in the open."

"Get it in the open! Are you out'a yo' mind? Ain't nobody askin' you to stick yo' nose into my fambly's business. This don't make no sense. I'ma go down to that high school, snatch Keishawn out'a class, and find out fo' myself what this is about."

"Chet, honey, please wait," says Carlene.

Chet springs up from his chair. "What's goin' on, Carlene? I ain't askin' again."

I jump up and race from behind the desk. "Chet! Chet! C'mon now. There's no need to behave like this."

He gets in front of Carlene and jabs his finger in her face. "Don't you sit there lookin' stupid! Tell me what's happenin'! What's that no-count girl gone and done now?" He grabs Carlene's collar with one hand and swings his other arm back in a wide arc. "Answer me, woman!"

"Chet! NO!" I holler.

Carlene dives from her chair and out of Chet's grip. I get a grip on Chet's wrist, put it into one of the martial arts locks Victor once showed me, and start applying pressure. When Chet's gaze meets mine, his eyes tell me that his plodding brain has figured out that he's made a big mistake.

Chet sinks to his knees and says through clenched teeth, "Whats'a matter with you? This ain't no way fo' a preacher to be actin'."

I squeeze harder. "You're right, Chet. I should be acting like a preacher, so I'm gonna share some of the Lord's wisdom with you."

Chet groans. "C'mon, man. You gonna break it."

"Chet, the book of Ephesians, chapter five, verse twenty-five, says, 'Husbands, love your wives, even as Christ loved the Church, and gave himself for it.' Now, since you're not a Christian, that probably doesn't mean much to you so I'll explain." I add some pressure. "Are you listening to me?"

"Yeah, man! C'mon, you hurtin' me."

I ease off and continue. "You see, Chet, to Jesus, the church is precious beyond description. He cares for it, nurtures it, lifts it up, protects it, provides for it, and shields it from all of life's dangers. He loves it completely and without reservation."

I add some pressure.

"I'm listenin'!" Chet screams.

"Okay. So the lesson is that if husbands love their wives like Christ loves the church, then you should care for Carlene, nurture her, lift her up, protect her, provide for her, and shield her from all life's dangers. She should be precious to you beyond description and you should love her completely and without reservation. Understood?"

"Yeah. *Yeah!*"

I lean down and whisper in his ear. "Okay, Chet! You've heard from the Lord. Now listen to me. If you ever again touch Carlene for any reason other than to bring her comfort, it'll take the prayers of every Christian in Pittsburgh to keep me from waxing your sorry butt and dragging you downtown to the slam. Got it?"

*That's enough!* a voice whispers.

I release Chet and step back. He's massaging his wrist as he stands up and locks his murder-filled eyes on me.

"You done went too far, preacher man. You think you can just humbiliate me in front'a my wife and gets away with it?"

Other self-defense lessons Victor taught me rush from memory, but I remain still. Chet balls his hands into fists and steps toward me, but then he hears the soul-stirring voice of Sister Danielle Henshaw, rehearsing for her solo in this coming Sunday's service.

Sister Henshaw's clear, strong voice has never failed to leave worshipers crying tears of happiness, lifting their arms toward heaven, or clutching their chests in rapture. The glory of Christ blossoms from her throat as she sings "Amazing Grace." Chet glances at the Cross on my wall, the Bible on my desk, and slowly unballs his fists. Sister Henshaw lifts her voice into higher ranges and the power pulsing from her words rains holy strength and boldness down upon Carlene.

Chet glowers and says, "Look, preacher. Religion don't make me no difference one way or t'other. But since Carlene and Keishawn is all wrapped up in yo' mumbo-jumbo, I'ma let you keep your teeth. This time!"

I step toward Chet and extend my hand to shake. "I appreciate that, Chet."

He glances at my hand like I'm handing him a rotting fish, then turns to leave.

"C'mon, Carlene!"

Carlene stays put, her granite expression communicating clearly that she won't be leaving until *she's* ready.

"Did you hear me?" says Chet, getting loud.

Carlene walks quietly but resolutely up to Chet and stares hard into his eyes.

"Whats'a matter with you, woman? Don't make me have'ta . . ."

"Chet, sit down and close your mouth!" says Carlene, her voice calm but filled with iron resolve.

I move closer and off to the side, making sure Chet not only sees me in his peripheral vision but knows how close I am. He throws up his hands in frustration and plops into his chair. Carlene takes her time sitting down, faces Chet, and speaks slowly and directly.

"Chet, Keishawn is pregnant."

She stares him down, waiting for him to explode, but Chet just blinks.

"She was afraid to tell you, so we, I, decided to break the news like this. Chet, Keishawn wanted to tell you but was scared. How do you think it made her feel, knowing that when she needed her father most, he wasn't there for her? What do you think it did to her, knowing that the person who claims to love her so much was the *last* person in the world she wanted to tell?"

"My baby. Pregnant?"

"She's not a baby anymore."

"But how?"

Carlene scowls. "You oughta know the answer to that. But since you don't, I'll explain. Afterwards, we're gonna talk about preparing for our grandchild."

I sit down and listen.

IT'S HYPOCRITICAL, BUT I STILL HAVE TO PERFORM THIS NEXT DUTY AND DEAL WITH MARcus. So I again remind myself that I've confessed, God's forgiven me, the slate's been wiped clean, and I'm well within my rights and responsibilities to take action.

I'd wanted to do this either right before or immediately after meeting with Keishawn's parents and get this situation out of the way once and for all. But Marcus couldn't get off work any earlier, and now that I think about it, I'm glad. It's given me time to strengthen my spirit for what has to be done. It'll take everything I've got.

Marcus has ridden with me across country when I've spoken at other churches. He filled in as Sunday school superintendent after Valerie Burton left. He arranged a tour of his job at Tri-River Chemicals to help Corrine with her science project. He and his longtime sweetheart, Denise Atwell, helped us launch our Young & Gifted program. And Brenda says that Marcus is one of the church's best administrators. But what hurts most is that Marcus is my friend.

There's a soft knock on my office door. I glance out the window and say, "Lord, please give me the right words."

There's another knock, followed by, "Pastor, it's me. Marcus."

"Come on in. It's open."

I wave Marcus in and ask him to have a seat. Anxiety must be written all over my face, enough for Marcus to get concerned.

"Pastor, are you feeling well? Is something the matter?"

He's looking at me with a mixed expression of worry, caution, and suspense. It's cruel to keep him in the dark, so I move to the chair opposite him and expose him to the light.

"Marcus, I've met with Keishawn Newman and her parents."

He looks at me as if that information has no meaning to him.

"They know she's pregnant."

"Pastor, I don't understand. What's that got to do with . . ."

"Marcus! Don't!"

He glares at me and I pray for the courage to stand firm against the defiance and deceit staring through his eyes. Then something in him gives way, and he bleats out, "Pastor, you've gotta understand. It, it just . . . happened."

I'm painfully capable of identifying with Marcus's last statement. But that doesn't remove the necessity of what must be done.

I have to talk fast. The blood's surging through my veins. My vision is blurry and my throat's so tight I have to push out the words. "Marcus, I've got to take action. You're relieved of your duties as chairman of the usher board."

"I didn't mean to do it," he sobs.

"You're restricted from working with the kids in the Young & Gifted program."

"Oh, God! It was an accident."

"You'll need to turn in your keys and anything regarding church business, building access, and operating programs."

"This wasn't supposed to happen."

"I've arranged for you to meet with Keishawn and her parents. I'm strongly advising you to make arrangements to provide support for Keishawn and your baby."

"I never meant for it to go this far."

"I've also arranged for you to meet with some Christian counselors who specialize in this type of crisis. And of course I'll be available whenever you want to talk."

"What'll I tell Denise? I was gonna ask her to marry me."

"Marcus, this'll have to be reported to the police. I'll go with you, if you want. But either way, it'll have to be disclosed. You've had sexual relations with a minor and that has legal implications."

Marcus is sobbing. He covers his face with his hands to muffle the wail that spirals out from his throat.

I wipe my cheeks and manage somehow to continue. "Marcus, are you listening? Please, man. I know this is hard but you've got to hear what I'm saying."

"What about Denise? I was—"

"Marcus, you'll need to get a lawyer."

"Denise, baby. Forgive me."

I stand and pull Marcus to his feet and hug him. Once he starts settling down, I whisper the last of my message into his ear. "Marcus, this needs to be taken care of. Soon! What's done is done, but the Lord will see you through. What you've got to do now is take responsibility and do the right thing for Keishawn and your baby."

Marcus sniffles. "I'll do whatever you say."

He hands me the keys to the usher board office, plops into the chair, and stares into space as fresh tears wash down his cheeks. "Pastor?"

"Yes, Marcus."

"What'll I tell Denise?"

I try and find words that'll help ease his pain. But only one comes to mind: "Truth."

# CLIFFORD

THAT EXTORTIONIST SUNSHINE KIDS DAY CARE CENTER CHARGES FORTY-FIVE DOLLARS per kid for each half hour past 5:30 the parent picks up the kid. Those prices, added to their monthly wallet gouging, make me wonder sometimes if I oughta dump grad school and get into the day care business. I sign the boys out at 5:30 on the dot. One more minute and POW! Ninety bucks!

At home I fix a quick dinner while the boys watch *Toon Heroes*. Then it's off to the parent-teacher conference for Braddie.

I meet the teacher, Ms. Banks, in the nature lab so we can talk in relative privacy while the boys occupy themselves with a rabbit in its cage, a rhyming cockatoo, and lizards in a terrarium.

Ms. Banks tells me that Braddie's schoolwork, while still very good, has recently lost some of its stellar glow.

"It's not that I'm worried," she says. "But Bradley is one of my most talented students. I'd hate to see anything distract him from doing his best."

She pauses as if waiting for me to fill in the blanks. She waits in vain, eventually cutting her eyes over at Braddie and lowering her voice further.

"What I'm most concerned about is the downward trend in his behavior."

"Excuse me?" I say, truly puzzled. "What do you mean? Braddie's never been a discipline problem."

"And I'm not saying that he is now, Mr. Matthews. But there's no denying that something's changing within him. Just yesterday, at recess, he started calling names and pushed another little boy down on the blacktop."

I sit back in my chair, stunned. "Braddie did this? My Braddie?"

She nods gravely. "I was as shocked as you are. Up till then, I'd have easily picked Bradley as one of the sweetest students in this school. And it made me wonder again about what's going on in his life that could so alter his behavior."

She pauses, searching my face again, and again waiting in vain.

"Isn't it possible that it was just a minor playground scuffle?" I ask, hoping that the defensive lightning bolts shooting through my stomach aren't arcing into my voice.

"It's possible," Ms. Banks answers. "But it still doesn't explain Bradley's reaction. One minute, the kids were playing kickball; the next, Bradley was shoving someone to the ground when his team lost."

I force a chuckle. "Well, Ms. Banks, Braddie can be pretty competitive. You should hear him when he's playing that 'Troll Warrior' video game with his brother."

Her face remains serious. "I appreciate Bradley's competitive spirit, Mr. Matthews. But because of his outburst, we had to enroll him in a special anger-management program."

*"What?"*

"It's standard procedure," Ms. Banks continues quickly. "A year ago the district instituted a zero-tolerance policy on violence. It mandates that any child displaying violent tendencies be sent to anger-management sessions."

"You've got to be kidding!" I rasp, glancing over at Braddie, who is talking softly to the cockatoo.

"I appreciate your distress, Mr. Matthews. But with all the school shootings over the last few years, educators across the country have been under tremendous pressure to identify children who might be at risk."

"At risk." How I hate that label. It's the modern equivalent of being called a leper. It's also the category I've repeatedly told Demetria our sons will be banished to as the price *they* pay for her towering selfishness.

Ms. Banks glances at Braddie and shakes her head. "He's such a good boy. And I really wish there'd been some other way, but my hands are tied."

I look over at Braddie, who is laughing with the cockatoo, and I can't help but feel that the rope tying Ms. Banks's hands is the same one that's slipping a noose around my family's neck.

I STAY JUST UNDER THE SPEED LIMIT GETTING OVER TO MOMMA'S, HOPING WITH ALL MY might that she'll be able to suggest something that'll help me keep Braddie from getting stigmatized as one of America's future incorrigibles.

She answers her door quickly, surprised at seeing us and happy about being surprised.

"You boys want some cake?" Momma asks.

"Yes!" they shout in unison.

"Go on in the kitchen, sit down, and I'll be right there."

I glance at Momma's laptop, the screen split, one side filled with text and the other side showing a pie chart.

"What're you working on?" I ask.

"I'm working up a comparative distribution on the number of African American children being overdiagnosed as ADHD."

"Isn't that attention displacement . . . ?"

Momma smiles, but she answers in the firm tone of a master educator. "No, no. It stands for attention deficit hyperactivity disorder. There's a staggering number of black children who're being sidetracked into special ed programs, branded as intellectually deficient and their self-esteem ruined."

I want to grab Momma and hug her for already being at the center of my concerns about Braddie. "That's what I need to talk to you about," I whisper.

Momma frowns in confusion until I nod toward the kitchen and silently mouth Braddie's name. Her eyes widen and her jaw stiffens.

"Hold on, Clifford. Let me take care of these dirt-monsters first."

The tone of her voice leaves me feeling sorry for whoever answers the phone tomorrow when she calls Braddie's school to investigate his "at-risk" classification.

I scan her work while she's laughing and talking with the boys. It looks good, really good.

"When you're through, there's a new game I bought for you downstairs," she says.

"Which one is it, Grandy?" asks Bear.

Momma lets the suspense build, then says, "Troll Warrior II."

The boys scream their joy, forget about their cake, and hustle downstairs. Momma's chuckling softly as she saunters back into the living room.

We've barely sat down when the noise of troll warriors battling smelly dragons and slobbering giants echoes up from the basement.

"So how and why was Braddie determined to be at risk?" Momma asks.

I tell her what Ms. Banks said about Braddie's minor little scuffle, insisting that the anger-management class is nothing more than an overreaction to boys-being-boys.

Momma listens intently, her eyes focusing on me so hard it feels like my skin's being heated. "Well, Ms. Banks is right about the zero-tolerance policy," Momma says. "She didn't have much choice there."

"C'mon, Momma. We're talking about Braddie here, not a kid from some drug-infested inner-city wasteland."

Momma scowls. "Clifford! Stop being a snob!"

"But . . ."

"There's as much drug abuse in the suburbs as there is in the city. Probably more! Just because it's not publicized doesn't mean it isn't a problem. So take your nose out of the clouds and tell me the truth about what's going on with Braddie."

"Huh? But Momma, I *am* telling you the truth."

Her eyes narrow. "Clifford, I've known Arlene Banks for ten years. She's one of the most competent, compassionate teachers in this school system. She probably cried about having to send Braddie to those classes. So I *know* she didn't just do this willy-nilly. Now stop beating around the bush and tell me what's going on."

I stare down at my lap until Momma pushes my chin up with her index finger and we're looking eye to eye. Long seconds pass while I summon the courage to speak words I've been trying not to think.

"Momma, Demetria's leaving me, and I don't know what to do."

Momma wipes my cheeks with tender palm strokes, her own face remaining passive, even peaceful.

"And the kids, Momma. What about the kids? Look at what we're already doing to Braddie."

Momma keeps wiping my cheeks, ignoring her own tears while drying mine.

"Are you two still talking?" she asks.

"I guess you could call it that."

"Good. Keep on talking. And I mean *talk*. You don't want to crowd her. She's probably scared and confused and trying to figure out what to do."

"But . . ."

"Clifford, you need to love Demetria through this. And pray that God will guide you both to the right conclusion."

"Yes, ma'am."

"Do you still love her?"

"Yes, I do. It's been hard, but I still love Demetria with all my heart."

"And have you been praying?"

"Well, not ex . . ."

"Love and prayer, Clifford! Understand! Lots of love and continuous prayer."

"But Momma, I've been doing all I can and nothing . . ."

"Clifford, this is a woman's heart you're dealing with, not some engine where if you do *this* it'll do *that*. If you rely only upon yourself and what you know it'll be like trying to catch the wind. You'll lose her. Understand?"

"Yes, ma'am."

Momma takes my face into her hands. "Clifford, tell me the truth. Is there someone else?"

Nolan's face flashes across my mind, then is blotted out by an image of me pounding him into the ground. But no matter how much I distrust him, I know Demetria. And even though she's acting like her mean, evil stepsister twin, I can't imagine her doing such a thing.

"No, Momma. I don't think Demetria's having an affair."

"I was referring to you."

"Me!"

Momma stares hard into my eyes, like she's drilling to the center of my mind and watching my thoughts swirl into an answer.

I think of the department secretary, Cheri. We've often eaten lunch together, talking about books and the latest movies. But in addition to Cheri's being married, Demetria knows her and I've always been open about my conversations with her.

I return Momma's stare. "No. There's no one else. Only Demetria."

Momma nods slowly and smiles. "Then fight for her, Clifford. Fight for her and your family. But remember what I said: much love and much prayer."

"Yes, ma'am."

"In the meantime, I'll see who I can talk to about getting Braddie out of those sessions. But I'll be honest, he'll probably still have to go. Things have gotten to that point."

I look down, shake my head, and mutter beneath my breath. "Maybe I should fly one of those doggone kites."

"What did you say?" asks Momma.

She looks puzzled as I start explaining, her expression smoothing out when I get to the part about "I Am" and how the boys believe flying the kites will move Him to "fix us."

Momma arches an eyebrow and says, "Well, then, maybe you should."

# VICTOR

I'M GLAD THIS WORKDAY'S OVER. IT WAS BAD ENOUGH HAVIN'TA FOOL AROUND WITH that hunk-a-junk bus. What made it worser was Brantley's kickin' me down memory lane.

I cut off the locker room shower and hear somebody singin' that old Chi-Lites hit, "Coldest Days of My Life." From the way it's bein' mangled, it sounds like Boots. I hope he doesn't bring his silly self over here cuz I ain't in no mood to talk. But here he comes, dippin' and slidin' like he's practicin' his second-job pimp walk.

"Ice! Whuz*zup*, player?"

"Nothin', man. Long day. Glad it's over."

"Must'a been. Why's you lookin' so down in the mouth?"

"I'm cool, Boots. Just got thangs on my mind."

I sit down in front'a my locker and start gettin' amazed, for the umptazillionth time, at how marryin' Lynnette jacked up my life in so many different ways.

"You hungry?" Boots axes.

"Naw, Boots. Why?"

"I'm just wonderin' why you got that bag of lollipops in your locker."

"They're for Karenna."

"Karenna?" says Boots, scrunchin' up his face. "Who'zat?"

I stand and finish gettin' dressed. With Boots's mouth as big as it is, I ain't hardly tellin' him none'a my business. Once he sees I ain't answerin' his question, he shrugs.

"Okay, man. It's cool." Then he says, "So did you, Clyde, and Brantley do lunch out in Moody Hollow today?"

"Yeah."

Boots punches his palm with his fist. "Aw, man! I wish my route took me out that way. I'd have me more numbers than the Cleveland directory."

"And one day you'd be sorry you ever axed for 'em."

Boots's eyes get stupid big to match the stupid look on his face. "Hold up, man. Is this *Ice* I'm talkin' to? Whuts'up bro? Love life done went sour?"

"Boots, I ain't in the mood. Okay?"

Boots raises his hands in pretend surrender. "Okay, Ice. You got it. I was just bein' friendly."

"No problem. We cool."

Boots gets quiet, but he's still here, so I know more of his bull is on the way.

"So who's Karenna, man? I mean, is this some new move you usin'? You found a babe who goes for lollipops?"

"Yeah, Boots. She goes for 'em big time."

"Is she fine?"

"Looks just like a baby."

Boots stomps his foot and lights up the locker room with a big toothy smile. "Ice! My *main* man! You's one smooth brotha!"

"Yeah, man. Real smooth."

"Are you gonna bring her around? You gonna let us see your latest addition?"

"If I do, I'll be carryin' her."

The smile falls off'a Boots's face and his bumpy brow tells me he ain't understandin'.

"Carryin' her? She been in an accident or somethin'?"

"Naw, man. She can walk. Just not too good yet."

Boots is lookin' seriously confused, and I'm suddenly glad he's here, cuz seein' his silly face is makin' me feel lots better.

"Ice, you is one raw dude. If they's blind, crippled, or crazy, it don't make you no difference, do it?"

"Naw, man. Not one bit."

Boots shakes his head and I'm about to bust out laughin' when he walks off sayin', "Ice, you is cold-blooded."

I FINISH GETTIN' DRESSED AND HEAD OUT TO MY CAR, STOPPIN' TO CHECK MY MAILBOX on the way. The only thang in there is a note from Corey, cancelin' my vacation for the week I'm goin' to Pittsburgh to see my baby girl.

After today's lousy lunch, havin' to break up two fights, and gettin' cussed out by some stanky-breath-blue-haired-hoola-hoop-earring-wearin'-booger-bear, this is the *last* thang I wanna be dealin' with. But since Corey's playin' games, I ain't got no choice. Cuz I swear, if him or anybody else wants to make me miss out on seein' Jewel, they're gonna need some good, up-to-date medical insurance.

I step out quick-time for Corey's office and see somethin' through his window that's better than all the whoopin's I could ever put on him. He's sittin' there with his fiancée Francine!

She and him are eatin' dinner, laughin' and tappin' each other like a couple'a love-struck-bout-to-get-married fools. Corey looks up, sees me comin', and looks like he just found out he owed twenty-five years of back taxes. I walk in smilin'.

"Hey, Corey. Whuts'up?"

"Uh, Ice, my brother. What can I do for ya?"

I look at Francine and pretend not to remember her. "Ain't you Corey's fiancée?"

"Yeah, man," answers Corey, cuttin' in. "We're gettin' married. Francine, this is Ice. Ice, Francine."

I shake Francine's hand. "Oh, yeah. Now I remember. How could I forget somebody as drop-dead good-lookin' as you?"

Francine blushes. Corey grabs my elbow and pulls me toward the door.

"Ice, we're discussin' wedding plans, so . . ."

I snatch my arm back and talk loud. "I don't wanna mess up no plannin', so I'll be quick. I'm takin' them extra vacation days. With pay!"

Corey puts his hands on his hips and gives me his meanest "Mr. Jackson" look. His face is contortin' so bad his chin is up where his eyebrows oughta be.

"Are you crazy?" he axes. "You can't make those kinda demands."

Francine looks from me to Corey and back to me as I sit down beside her. "Hey, Francine. You oughta make Corey take you to the Claudia Café. That's where he likes to eat."

Corey wheezes, grabs a chair to steady hisself, and falls over it. Francine and me help him up while he's sputterin' and gaspin'.

"Corey, you all right, man?" I ax.

He grabs my collar with a death grip. "You, muthu . . . muthu . . ."

Francine rubs Corey's shoulders. "Corey, baby. What's wrong?"

Corey's face scrunches up as he coughs his answer. "I'ma, I'ma kick yo' . . ."

I start laughin'. "Corey, stop showin' off for Francine. You can't even kick a habit right now, much less anythang on me."

Francine glances at Corey suspiciously, then smiles like she's caught on to his attention-gettin' scam. She winks at me, then looks at Corey with sincere, lost-in-love eyes.

"Don't worry, baby," she says, kissin' his forehead. "Francine'll make it all better."

I stare, straight and hard, into Corey's eyes. "So then, you's agreein' to gimme them extra vacation days, right, Corey?"

Corey's expression makes me glad he ain't no ax-murderer. Francine kisses his forehead again.

"Go on and say yes, baby."

Corey grits but doesn't say nothin' until I tap Francine's shoulder. "Corey says you gotta lick the plate clean at the Claudia Café."

He starts hackin' and sputterin' again, finally chokin' out, "All right, man. You got it."

I pat Corey's head. "Thanks, brotha."

Then I help Francine up and give her a good-bye kiss, on the lips. I wink at her and head out the door, bustin' my sides laughin' when Francine axes, "So, what's with you and this Claudia Café?"

I AIN'T BEEN ON THE ROAD TOO LONG BEFORE I'M THINKIN' ABOUT BRANTLEY AND THAT depressin' lunchtime conversation. I swear, from now on if he's gonna mess up my lunchtime honey-watchin' hour he can eat by hisself, cuz I don't need no help gettin' bummed out.

One'a these days he's gonna get it through his block-head that it ain't about bein' fair, hearin' his side, and makin' people do right. Like Nate's always sayin', a dude's gotta check the fruit on the tree. And since the politicians is the ones makin' the rules on divorce and child support, if I check the fruit on the tree, I'm in for a rotten-to-the-core disappointment.

They's always pretendin' to school us up on thangs like integrity, fairness, and freedom. That's about as stupid as hearin' a car salesman talk about honesty. And all that smoke-blowin' about bein' concerned for suckas like me and Brantley is about as believable as an insurance company tellin' a dude with AIDS, "Don't worry. You covered."

I'd like to see how sanctified them suckas would be if one day *their* "forever" loves dropped the bomb on 'em, sayin' it's over, talkin' about needin' to find theyselfs, how they just ain't got that same old "feelin'," and that the guys'd better be cool if they wanna see their kids again. And then, just to make sure thangs is completely stupid, right as their "forever" loves is kickin' 'em out the door, they hear, "And don't forget to send the check!" I betcha they'd understand then.

Replayin' all that frustration pisses me off to where I almost run a red light. But I see it in time and stop. My attitude gets lots better when this cute honey steps off the sidewalk and struts across like she *knows* she's fine. And she is!

Specially that tight, grabable booty! It ain't like some of 'em where their owners think that just havin' some meat piled up back there means they got it goin' on. But this babe definitely does, cuz her rumpshaker's like Jell-O in a bad wind, wigglin' and stayin' in place all at the same time.

I keep my eyes locked on all'a that Dipper-delightin' cheek-action till it's out'a sight, then notice I'm just a few blocks from Edie's apartment building. I shouldn't oughta do this, but so whut! After the kinda day I had it won't harm nothin' to pump myself up with a quick drive-by of the buildin' containin' one'a the finest, most ladylike women I know. Besides, with the way Edie's stallin' me, seein' her buildin's about as close as I'll ever get to *her*.

The light turns green and I zip on through, take some shortcuts to Edie's, then slow down when I get near. Just as I'm cruisin' past, the front door flies open and Edie busts out, high-steppin' and lookin' mad. Some dude dressed like a fashion ad and yellin' somethin' hurries out behind her, grabs her arm, and spins her around. Edie tries jerkin' away, then slaps the piss out of him.

I swing over, park, and jump out my car. By the time my foot's hit the ground everythang the Marine Corps taught me about ATTACK! has zoomed into focus.

"Lyle, leave me alone!" hollers Edie.

"No!" shouts his *GQ*-ness, grabbin' her again. "We've gotta talk about this. We're gonna sit down and discuss this like civilized adults. How do you think this looks? Carrying on like common street trash."

Street trash? He prob'ly means everyone who ain't dressed like him in his yuppie-buppie threads, usin' day-long words and tryin' to outrun the repo man. A minute ago, I'da been satisfied with tellin' Lyle to let Edie go. Now, I'ma have'ta thump him. He sees me stridin' up on him and points his finger.

"Don't interfere here, Kareem. This is none of your affair."

Kareem? I'ma stuff his head where the sun don't shine. Edie's boo-hooin' and my head's poundin'.

"Let her go!" I say.

"Look, Kareem. I don't want any trouble. This is a purely personal matter."

"If you don't let her go, I'ma give you a purely personal whoopin'!"

Lyle's eyes are full of homicide. But he ain't as stupid as he looks, cuz he lets Edie go.

"You've got some pretty big balls to be interfering in my affairs, Kareem."

"Call me 'Kareem' again and my pretty big foot's gonna interfere up yo' duke chute!"

Lyle pulls out a hundred-dollar bill and waves it at me. "Tell ya what, Kareem, Malik, Mustafa, whoever you are. Why don't you take this hundred, go buy yourself some drugs, and get high."

I step toward Lyle and Edie jumps between us, facin' me and jammin' her palms into my chest.

"Please, don't!"

Lyle's still wavin' the hundred, smirkin' like he just *knows* I'ma snatch it and take his advice. He reaches for Edie but she hops over to me. I move in front, makin' sure she's completely behind me, and look straight into Lyle's face.

"Looks like you been fired, punk!"

Lyle grits on me, then Edie. "You're out'a your mind, choosing this loser over me."

I step toward him and he flies into a candy-apple-red BMW, fishtailin' as he speeds away. And I start tremblin'. Not from fear but wonderin' why I let that sucka talk to me like that.

Edie grabs my arm with a Terminator grip and says, "I don't wanna be alone."

No intro. Nothin' fancy. No game playin'. Edie just lays it down straight in a way I ain't used to.

I look at her and say, "I won't let you be."

# NATHAN

BEFORE HE LEFT, MARCUS SAT QUIETLY WHILE I CALLED AND SET UP THE MEETING WITH him, Keishawn, and her parents. Given Chet's abundant reserves of hostility, I'll have to pray long and hard before that encounter. What a mess.

For weeks now, a few members have been looking for a new scandal to seize upon and turn into a public humiliation. Keeping people focused on our church renovation and other important projects in such an environment has been difficult. But some, like Beverly Dawkins, have shown a strength and depth of character that's left me impressed and grateful. Beverly's beauty truly goes beyond being skin deep.

Just as I'm considering what to do next about the turmoil surrounding Keishawn, the telephone rings. I start to let it roll over to Helen's line, remember she's not here, and answer. It's Helen. And she's crying.

"Helen! What's wrong?"

"Pastor, it's the hospital. They said . . ."

I grab my keys and blast out the door. The hospital's not that far from the church and my speeding makes the distance even shorter.

I burst out of the elevator and race past the nurse's station and down the corridor leading toward Mother McCoombs's room. An irritated voice chases me around the corner.

"Hey! No running in the hospital!"

Several blue- and pink-coated people whiz past me and dart inside Mother McCoombs's room. I charge in behind them. Once inside, my legs turn to rubber and I stagger sideways, knocking over a table full of flowers. A squad of hospital workers buzzes around Mother McCoombs, yelling to each other in their special healers' jargon.

"She's going into arrest!" hollers a rail-thin woman in a white coat. It's Dr. Salazar, Mother McCoombs's physician. "Where's that unit?"

"On the way!" someone in a blue coat answers.

I weave my way through the busy staff until I'm at Mother McCoombs's head. I stroke her hair and start praying.

"Hey!" yells one of the workers. "Whaddya think you're doing?"

"Leave him alone!" Dr. Salazar orders. "He's her pastor."

Someone in a pink coat rushes in, pushing a defibrillation unit. "It's here!"

"Hurry up!" Dr. Salazar shouts. "We're losing her."

"Reverend Matthews!" I look up and see Nurse Gordon. She's a good, strong Christian woman and has tended to every detail of Mother McCoombs's comfort since the day she arrived. She looks hard into my eyes. "Pastor, thank God you're here!"

"It's ready!" someone shouts.

"Let's do it!" Dr. Salazar answers. She looks around at everyone and orders, "Clear! You too, Reverend Matthews."

I step back as Dr. Salazar jams two oblong metallic objects against Mother McCoombs's exposed chest. Mother McCoombs jitters and shakes and her eyelids flutter.

"Clear!"

The monitor beeps, then ba-beeps. Mother McCoombs's eyelids slit open and she looks at me and gives a weak, lopsided smile.

"Pastor?"

"Yes, Mother."

Her eyes widen with sparkling wonder. "There's so much love."

Then the monitor flatlines. All I can do is weep.

*PASTOR, PROMISE ME YOU'LL LOOK AFTER MY GRANBABY.*

*I will, Mother.*

And so, since there is no answer at Mother McCoombs's apartment, I hit the streets and start searching. Hour after hour, street after street, alley after alley, asking any and everybody if they know where I can find Raymond McCoombs. Evening turns to darkness. The capitalist lords of the day flee toward the safety of their high-rises and their suburbs, surrendering the streets to the hollow-eyed wraiths of the night. Somewhere in this pandemonium of horns, sirens, blasting music, arguing lovers, crying children, panhandlers, and silent sufferers, Raymond's waiting to be found.

At the Straight Shooters pool hall, no one knows anything. So they say. But I'm not one of them. I don't belong. I can't be trusted. Then a burly, shade-wearing giant speaks up.

"Go home, preacher. Anybody in they right mind don't wanna find dat fool."

The pool hall fills with laughter. I leave. More walking. More streets. Block after block. My feet ache. My stomach growls. A man selling clothes from his rusting car's trunk pulls a switchblade.

"Look, man! I don't know da dude. Now either buy somethin' or get out'a my face!"

More streets. A raspy voice calls from a dark alley.

"Is you a real preacher?"

"Yes."

A choked sob, the voice filled with sorrow. "I was a good man. Once."

"And you still are. Trust in the Lord. He's the God of second chances."

"It's too late, Pastor. Crack took my soul."

"But Jesus died so that . . ."

"Get away from me!"

More walking. My feet throb. I get a coffee and a Danish from a greasy spoon. Just outside the door, a woman calls.

"Hey, baby. Want a date?"

"No! Are you ready for your date before the Judgment Throne?"

She laughs. "I don't believe in God."

"And yet you believe in his enemy, Satan."

"I don't believe in him either."

"Then why serve him?"

"Get lost."

"Get found."

"Hey, sucka!" says a lanky man dressed like a fashion fugitive from the seventies. "If you ain't buyin', git ta steppin'!"

I hurry away. Despair nips at my heels until I remember friends on the police force who might be willing to help. Mother McCoombs's description of her streetwise grandson suggests that he spends his time evading the police. And he'll probably resent my using them to find him, *if* they can. But I gave Mother McCoombs my word. Somewhere in this pandemonium, Raymond McCoombs is waiting to be found. Please God, don't let me fail.

I END UP AT MY FRONT DOOR. BRENDA GASPS WHEN SHE SEES ME. HER EYES ARE RED and puffy.

She throws her arms around my neck, her tears mixing with my own.

"Oh, Nathan," she says, kissing me softly. "I'm sorry. I'm so, so sorry."

I try to control my voice. "She's gone, Bren."

"I know, baby. I know."

"I was there when she . . ."

"I know, Nathan. The nurse from the hospital, Sister Gordon, called and told me."

I squeeze Brenda tight. "What am I gonna do?"

She takes my face into her palms, kisses the tears from my cheeks, and says, "Pray. Then let me love and comfort you."

# CLIFFORD

IT'S PAST TWO IN THE MORNING WHEN DEMETRIA GETS HOME. I WANT TO FOLLOW Momma's advice about not crowding her, but right now I'm just too PISSED. Demetria opens the door and jumps when she sees me standing there.

"Clifford! Don't scare me like that!"

"Where have you been, Demetria?"

She shoves past me and starts up the stairs to our bedroom. I grab her arm and spin her around.

Momma's voice says, *What did I tell you about manhandling women?* and I let go.

"Demetria! I want to know where you've been."

"None of your business."

"Wrong, Demetria! As long as we're living under the same roof, it's *all* my business."

Demetria crosses her arms and cocks her head to the side like an opponent considering the pros and cons of beating me to a pulp now or later.

"Okay, I'll tell you, not that it's any of your business. I went to meet Nolan and Tammy at The Hub. I felt like dancing and having some fun. You *do* remember what fun is, don't you?"

"Demetria, I remember. But I don't appreciate your coming home at all hours, disrespecting me. And I especially don't like your being out with that slug Nolan."

"Clifford, he's not a slug. And I'm not disrespecting you."

"Yes you are! And I'm telling you right now, I won't stand for it!"

Demetria stares at me with that "assassin's look" Victor says women get when they're through with you. Then she pulls a notepad from her purse, stomps into the living room, and plops down onto the couch.

"I was gonna do this later," she says, her voice tight with anger, "when it would be easier for you. But now's as good a time as any."

"Demetria, what're you talking about?"

"The same thing I've been talking about for weeks now. *Leaving you!*"

My legs turn to water and I lurch into a chair.

Tears fill Demetria's eyes as she glances at the notepad.

"I've been to see a lawyer," she says. "He recommends that we go for a dissolution. It's easier, faster, and cheaper. And since money'll probably be tight until after this is over, it'll be best."

I hold myself, close my eyes, rock back and forth, and whisper, "Don't let this happen. Please don't let this happen!"

"A dissolution avoids the nastiness of a full divorce action, which I definitely don't want. That is, unless you want to contest anything."

I don't answer and Demetria flips another page, her words coming in starts and stops as she fights through her tears.

"Clifford, I . . . I don't wanna hurt you. And this'll be . . . just as difficult for me because I, I've never . . . been out on my own. I went from home to school to marriage."

I stop rocking and look hard into her eyes. "Demetria, are you serious? Are you destroying our family because you missed some stops on the carnival-of-life tour?"

She flips a page and presses on. "I'd . . . like for *you* to . . . move out as soon as possible. And I'd . . . also like for us to try and remain . . . friends."

"Friends! Are you *serious*?" A pain bubble claws its way up and out of my throat as a foghorn of a moan.

Demetria pulls a tissue from her purse, blows her nose, clears her throat, and speaks with more composure. "Please don't . . . don't say anything to the boys, until it's close to your move. It might affect their schoolwork."

I dig my fingers into my sides. Visions of Braddie and Bear's faces changing as they grow into manhood whisk through my mind. Cackling voices whisper that I won't see those changes.

Demetria wipes away the tear snailing down her cheek and presses on. "I've seen ex-married 'couples' that get along fine and ones that hate each other. I would like for us to be the former."

I look up at Demetria, and it suddenly strikes me how absurd she looks, being "bothered" when she's gotta be having one rollicking good time. This is it! Her big moment to get back at me for every jibe, snipe, quip, cut, insult, wrong, right, up or down thing she thinks I ever did to her. And she's loving it! So her sitting there looking like some morally challenged headsman, distraught at my decapitation, is more than I can bear. I start laughing, loud and hard.

"Right, Demetria," I say. "Why would I wanna hate you?"

I laugh toward the ceiling. "Let me get this straight. Your big plan to win my friendship is to dump me, make my sons grow up without their father, and have the law make me finance your trip to Oz."

I face Demetria, chuckling as I wipe laugh tears from my eyes. Her eyes dart nervously from side to side as she fumbles with her Secret Agent Man notepad.

"Don't worry," I say. "I'm sure we'll be bosom buddies."

Demetria presses on. "You can see the boys anytime you want, and they can come see you anytime they want. We'll alternate weekends. If during the week they want to . . ."

I scoot to the edge of the chair and drill Demetria with my eyes. "Who are you to tell me when I'll see my sons?"

"Clifford, please. I'm only trying to explain . . ."

"I don't care about your explanations, Demetria. What I *do* care about is Braddie and Bear. And like I've told you before, you've got one helluva fight coming if you think I'm gonna just roll over and give them up."

She lowers her eyes and sobs, her body shuddering. She balls her hands, twisting the notepad. She calls upon God, asks Him for strength, then looks up at me, her eyes red, wet, and incredibly sad.

"Clifford, I'm sorry you're upset," she says, speaking slowly and softly. "And I know you don't believe me when I say I *do not* want to hurt you. But I'm dying inside. Please try and understand. I need to do this, before I turn into someone neither of us recognizes and we both hate."

I want to tell Demetria that on that last point, she's already crossed the line. But even now, even though she's roasting my heart over an open pit, I can't bring my emotional self to hate her the way my intellectual self is commanding me to do.

"I know this is hard to hear because it's hard for me to say," continues Demetria, her voice suddenly smoother and stronger. "But now that it's said, at least the worst part's over."

I stare at her through tear-blurred eyes. "No, Demetria. The worst part is that I still love you."

Then I grab my keys and dash into the night.

# VICTOR

WHEN ME AND EDIE WALK INTO BENNY'S, VERNON STARTS GRINNIN' AND WHISPERIN' TO Bochamp and Deke, sittin' at the bar. Then he yells over to our booth. "Ice, you know Benny don't play lettin' nobody stay who ain't buyin'."

Edie's holdin' back a laugh as I get up and hustle to the bar.

"Vee, whuts'a matter with you? Can't you see I'm with somebody?"

Vernon gets a big "SO!" look on his face, glances at Edie, and lets out a long, slow whistle.

"Good gosh-a-mighty! Man, she is *fine*. Why's she hangin' with your rusty butt?"

"Just shut up and gimme a brew."

"What kind?"

"Any kind! Why you bein' such a pain?"

Vernon gets my beer, then reaches into the mini-fridge and pulls out a brew that, just from the look of the bottle, has gotta be way better than the rotgut he's been sellin' me.

"Let her try this," says Vernon. "Benny had it special-delivered from Germany."

"Vee, you's a sorry chump. Whenever I've axed if Benny gets the imported stuff you always told me no."

Vernon nods at Edie. "If you looked like her, I'da told you different."

I slap my money down on the counter and turn to leave when Vernon grabs my arm.

"Whuts'up with you, man?" I ax.

"Ice, you need to go easy with her," says Vernon.

"Vee, whutch'you talkin' about?"

Vernon's grip tightens and he looks at me real serious. "Whut I'm talkin' about, fool, is that you need to go easy with her. There's somethin' different about this woman. Somethin' special. Even from over here I can tell she ain't like them other skanks you usually bring up in here."

I wink at Vee and say, "Thanks for the warnin'. I'll call if I need help handlin' thangs."

Vernon's jaw tightens and I'm wonderin' if he's gonna grab a bottle and smash it over the top'a my head.

"Ice! I'm serious, man. If you's too stupid to not appreciate somethin' good, specially after all that headache Lynnette put you through, then you deserve every emotional whoopin' you get."

I check out Vernon's eyes and see that he's downtown, for real, serious. But I ain't got *no* idea of whut's got into him. Cuz Vee has cussed me out, watered down my drinks, cheated me out'a my change, sicked bouncers on me, and hooked me up with booger-bears so ugly they made that Medusa chick look good. But he ain't never looked out for me, not like *this*!

So instead'a tellin' Vee to mind his business I just say, "Okay, man. You got it."

I hurry back over to Edie, hand her her beer, take a pull off'a mine, and say, "So tell me, Edie. Whuts'up with Mr. *GQ* slingin' you around like that?"

She stares into her beer like the answer's there. "It was a misunderstanding."

"A misunderstandin'!"

I oughta shake her myself, givin' that lame answer after I was about to risk gettin' clonked by the po-leases for fightin' in the street.

Edie sighs and looks up. "Okay. It was more than a misunderstanding. Lyle wants to get back together."

I take a second to recover from that brick to the chin and say, "Oh."

"And thanks for butting in," says Edie.

I nod and take a swig'a my brew. "Edie, you mind if I ax you somethin'?"

"Go ahead."

"How come you ain't never said yeah to goin' out with me? I mean, why'd it take all this to finally stop gettin' the cold shoulder?"

Edie raises an eyebrow and gives me what Nate calls one'a them devilish smirks. "First of all, if it hadn't been for all *this*, I still might've been making my mind up. And second, why should a cold shoulder bother someone nicknamed Ice?"

Now *I'm* starin' into my beer.

VERNON BRINGS A COUPLE'A SLICES OF PIZZA OVER TO THE TABLE AND SETS 'EM DOWN in front of Edie.

"I didn't know ya'll served food here," I say.

Vernon shrugs. "New policy."

"New? How new?"

Vernon grins at Edie, grits on me, and says, " 'Bout five minutes."

I grit on Vernon as he takes my money and glides away. Edie grabs a piece of pizza, offers me the other one, and we keep talkin'.

"Lyle's a cybergeologist with NAER, North American Energy Resources," Edie says.

"A whut?"

"A cybergeologist. He searches for oil and gas deposits with computer radar imaging technology."

I ain't got no idea whut she just said, but whatever it was, I know I'm outclassed. No wonder that sucka was wavin' hundreds at me to go get high. I ain't *even* gonna chump myself into thinkin' I got a chance with Edie.

Edie sighs and kinda sniffles. "When I told Lyle I was pregnant, he exploded and left. And now, almost two years later, he calls saying how wrong he was and pleading to see Karenna. I didn't want to, but Mother convinced me to let him see her. Now he wants to pick up where we left off."

"Whut! You ain't gonna do it, is you?"

I ax the question with a lot more in'trest than oughta be had by a dude thinkin' he ain't got a chance. Edie laughs and my ears soak up her voice.

"Not in a million years," she says. "Lyle's a boy impersonating a man. I'm already raising a child. I don't intend to marry one."

The way Edie says that makes me feel like somebody's laid me out under a microscope. And *hers* is the eye checkin' me out. She smiles, remindin' me of a construction job I once worked for some extra cash. I tore down a wall, one brick at a time, just like her smile's doin' me right now.

"So, Ice. Tell me about yourself," says Edie.

My brain warns me that the more info a babe's got, the faster a dude'll be divin' for cover. But my lips start flappin' anyway. And we don't stop talkin' till that pain-in-the-neck Vernon says, "Ice, time to go. Benny ain't runnin' no bed'n breakfast."

I WALK EDIE TO THE FRONT DOOR OF HER APARTMENT AND SHAKE HER HAND 'BYE. AND *that's* how I know she's different from them funky skanks I'm use'ta dealin' with. With one'a them, we'da been slobbin' each other down, crashed through the door, tore off our clothes, knocked over furniture, and got down to some serious slammin'. But Edie's got some class I ain't never experienced. And even though I gotta make sure she don't get too close, I wouldn't mind hangin' out with her.

"Edie, can I see you again?"

She don't answer right away. I can feel a big N-O comin' and my shoes are fillin' with sweat.

Then Edie says, "Why?"

I ain't used to this. Most times my face, body, and below-the-belt bulge are enough to catch a babe's in'trest and get me whut I want. Lots of 'em even ax *me*. But I ain't *never* had to explain *why*. The Dipper's hollerin' for me to step off cuz Edie ain't about givin' up no booty but puttin' a ring in our nose, tyin' us to a post, and cuttin' off our balls. But the Dipper ain't never had no heart to risk gettin' broke or a mind to keep gettin' flattened by babe scams. So I tell him to be cool cuz Edie's somethin' new, different, and special and I need to find out more.

So I say, "Cuz, Edie, I like you."

"Ice, the teller at my bank likes me too. But I'm not going out with him. Why should I treat you any different?"

This woman must be out'a her mind, talkin' to me like that. But then I hear Momma say, *Now you know how it feels,* and I back off'a my attitude.

"Look, Edie. You'n I both know that if I said I loved you, I'd be lyin'. It would blow my chances. And I could carry on about how fine you are, but that's just street talk and wouldn't do me no good neither. So it's like this. I've told you I'm divorced, got a kid, and live pretty much from paycheck to paycheck. I moved to Cleveland to get a new start. I see my baby girl when I can, all I can, which ain't *never* enough. Sometimes my money's up, sometimes it's down. I've done the datin' game but I'm tired of playin', just like you."

"How do you know that?"

"Cuz'a these changes you're puttin' me through."

Edie ain't smilin' but neither am I.

"There ain't no reason you should trust me, and there ain't no reason I should trust you. We've both been through some thangs, but I know we could do right by each other. The only way we'll know is to try."

I pull out my keys and get ready to zoom to my econo-cart. "So there it is," I say. "No games. No double-talk. I like you and I'd like to see you again. Will you let me?"

The steel in Edie's eyes melts and she smiles. "Sure."

And just as I'm thinkin' I might get me a kiss after all, Edie says, "'Bye," and ducks out'a sight.

I go home to my sardine can apartment, get inside, and see the answerin' machine light blinkin'. I change clothes, fix some coffee, grab the latest issue of *Ebony* magazine, and sit down and hit the PLAY button. Corey's voice booms out first.

> *"I'ma get you, you lowlife gutter rat. Francine's been buggin' the daylights out'a me about the Claudia Café, wonderin' why she can't find it in the Yellow Pages. Have a good laugh, funny man."*

I laugh until I hear the next voice, floatin' out the machine like smoke.

> *"If you want the thirty-eight-double-Ds on this hundred-and-ten-pound body, you'd better call."*

Thirty-eight-double-Ds! I knew Simone had some warheads but them nukes are huge! I grab the phone and dial so fast sparks fly off the keypad.

Simone answers with a yawn. "Hello?"

"Hello. Yeah, Simone. This is Ice."

"Who?"

"Ice."

"Who?"

"Ice!"

"I know who you are. You lucky I ain't hung up. I called hours ago."

"Simone, don't be like that, baby. I was . . ."

"Don't go tellin' some lie you gonna have to babble your way out of."

"I ain't lyin'!"

"Yes you is. The only men who ain't lyin' is dead."

I ask myself if thirty-eight-double-Ds is worth all this and the Dipper shouts, "YES!"

"Simone, why're you givin' me such a hard time?"

"Cuz you ain't gave me one."

"I wanna give you all the hard I got, baby. Honest!"

She laughs like I just told her I'm a man she can depend on. "Forget it," she says. "You ain't serious about gettin' together."

"C'mon, Simone. You know how bad I wanna get with you. Why would I mess up my chances by runnin' a scam?"

Hearin' that pleadin' in my voice makes me glad no one, specially Cliff, can hear me.

After some nerve-janglin' seconds, Simone keeps talkin'. "Look! I'm arrangin' for us to spend a few days together. So be ready. Cuz when I call, I don't want no half-steppin'. I just want you to come."

"I plan to, baby. Over'n over again."

Simone laughs. "You so full of it."

"And, baby, the day I'm gnawin' your mountains into molehills, you will be too."

We laugh and hang up. I sip some coffee, take a look at the fine sisters *Ebony*'s selected as this year's most eligible bachelorettes, and get a mule-kick to the head. I drop the magazine, shut my eyes tight, and grit my teeth. After a couple'a minutes, the mule-kicks are just poundin', then plain old throbbin'.

I reach for the phone and dial Cliff's number.

# NATHAN

I BOLT UPRIGHT IN BED AND STARE INTO THE DARK. MY PAJAMA TOP IS SOAKED. MY throat's dry. And the telephone's ringing.

"Hello?"

"Hello, Nathan."

"Hi, Momma."

"Something's wrong with Clifford."

"Yes, Momma. I know."

"Keep praying."

"I will, Momma."

I hang up and give Brenda a gentle shake. The phone rings again. Please God, don't let this be Victor.

"Hello?"

"Hi, Uncle Nathan."

"Braddie?"

"Yes, sir."

"Me too, Uncle Nathan."

"Bear?"

"Yes, sir."

"What are you guys doing up so late?"

"Mommy's sleep," Bear answers.

"And Dada's gone," Braddie says.

Then they both say, "Dada's in trouble."

"Yes, boys, I know."

"Are you gonna talk to Jesus?" Bear asks.

"Yes. And I want you guys to pray too."

"We have been," says Braddie.

"That's good, you guys. And never forget, Jesus has the power to . . ."

"Tell Dada he should fly the kite," Braddie interrupts.

"Huh? What did you say, Braddie?"

"I Am will fix us if Dada flies the kite."

"It's true, isn't it, Uncle Nathan?" asks Bear. "If Dada looks up at the kite, I Am will make us better, won't He?"

I hear the desperate pain in my nephews' voices.

What Braddie and Bear are saying is essentially correct. The Lord will fix all things for the good if Clifford humbles himself, looks up, and calls upon the name of God. But the "fix" may not be what any of us expect, and it may not come in the way or time we'd desire. And how do I tell that to these boys who, more than anything, just want their family to be healed?

"Braddie. Bear. The best way you guys can help your dad right now is to go to bed and get some rest. Okay?"

"Yes, sir."

"Don't worry, you guys. I Am knows where your dad is and will keep him safe. Now go on to bed."

"Yes, sir."

We say good night, and I ask the Lord to comfort and keep them. Then I look at Brenda on her knees beside our bed. Seeing her there, acting on her faith to pray for a family member of mine, drowns me in guilt. I'm also gripped by fear, knowing that the turmoil smothering Clifford right now could just as well be encircling me.

The phone rings again. It sounds as though its normal jangling has been injected with a bad-tempered demand for immediate attention.

"Hello?"

"Nate! It's me."

"Victor! How're ya doing?"

"Never mind that! What's hap'nin' with Cliff?" Victor's abruptness isn't personal. It's just who he is.

"I don't know. What have you heard?"

"I called his house. He ain't there. Somethin' ain't right, so start talkin'."

"Victor, I really don't know the details."

"Come off it, Nate! If I felt somethin', I know you did. So quit playin' stupid!"

I stare into space, slack-jawed, and think, "Oh my God!" Now I know what was pulsing through the phone. *Rage!* Years of caged ferocity that's escaped and is now feeding upon its former master.

"Demetria's rollin' him, ain't she?" growls Victor.

I hesitate, then answer, "Yes."

For a long second, there's only silence. Then Victor's voice explodes from the phone like crashing winds. "I WARNED ya'll, didn't I?"

"Lord help us."

"I told ya'll that one day she'd do him! And now you're callin' God, like some arsonist who's set fire to hisself!"

"Victor! Listen! You can't interfere here. Only God can . . ."

"Shove it, Nate! God had His chance! If He ain't gonna do somethin', *I will*!"

The phone's call-waiting beeps.

"Victor, please try and understand . . ."

The call-waiting beeps again.

"Hold on, Victor! *Please!* I'll be right back."

I press the button. "Hello?"

"Nate?"

"Clifford. Thank God you're . . ."

I'm blasted by a babble-filled wail.

"Clifford! *Clifford!* Hold on. Let me get Victor off the other line."

I click back over to the other line. "Victor? *VICTOR?*"

The dial tone answers. And I'm afraid. Very, very afraid.

BRENDA HANDS ME AND CLIFFORD OUR CUPS OF COFFEE, FIXES ONE FOR HERSELF, THEN joins us at the kitchen table.

Clifford sips his coffee and sniffles. "Nate. Brenda. I'm really sorry about dropping by so late. Thanks for taking the time."

I take hold of his hand and give it a firm squeeze. "It's all right, Clifford. You know we're here for you."

"Nate, I don't know what to do," he says. "Demetria wants me to move out. But I can't just up and leave Braddie and Bear. I can't have them grow up like we did."

This has got to be devastating him. He, Victor, and I spent a mostly fatherless childhood wondering what it would've been like if Daddy had survived Vietnam. We love Momma dearly and agree she did a wonderful job. But we always resented having to learn our manhood lessons from surrogates.

A shiver races along my spine as a hissing voice in my head says, *Maybe your children will be fatherless too—cheater!*

"Why is this happening?" asks Clifford, his face a tortured mask as a tear spills onto his cheek.

I reach across the table and pat his arm. Brenda grabs a napkin, wipes her eyes, and rubs Clifford's back in slow circular motions.

"When was the last time you had a good night's sleep?" I ask.

"I can't remember. I've been too busy countermaneuvering Demetria."

"What's she doing?"

"The more appropriate question is, what *isn't* she doing? She's been seeing more and more of that grub, Nolan . . ."

"Nolan! Isn't he one of her co-workers?"

Clifford purses his lips and nods. "She spends hours on the phone with Tammy, talking about singles clubs, dating, finding a good man . . ."

"She's talking like that? In front of you?"

Clifford smiles ruefully. "Oh yes. She's like a hyperactive kid on Christmas Eve."

I hesitate before asking but push on and say, "Clifford, do you really think Demetria's having fun? I mean, this is a huge step she's taking and I can't imagine her . . ."

For an instant, a chilling, eternal instant, the face I'm looking into snatches my breath. It's not Clifford's. Its fury is palpable. Its mouth opens and speaks with Clifford's voice, but the words are soaked with Victor's venom. Until this bone-chilling moment, I never realized how much alike they look. Brenda and I glance at each other and she moves closer to me.

"Just shut up, Nate, before you start sounding as stupid as Demetria, telling me how this isn't meant to hurt me and how I shouldn't take it personally."

"I wasn't going to . . ."

"What about me?" shouts Clifford, pounding the table. "What about Braddie and Bear? What am I supposed to tell them? Who's gonna teach them what they need to know about becoming men? Should I just hope that someday, somebody'll float through Demetria's revolving door and love them? Guide them? Instruct them? Discipline and watch over them? How would you feel knowing that *your* kids were gonna be exposed to a boatload of panty-sniffing lowlifes? Huh?"

*That's how Brenda will get even with you!* snickers the voice.

Clifford springs up from his chair and starts pacing, his arms flailing. "Demetria thinks she's the only one who has those boys at the center of her heart. She thinks she's the only one who couldn't live without them. But she finds nothing wrong with doing to me the very thing that would destroy her if she were in my shoes. She finds nothing wrong with destroying me! So what about me, Nate? *What about me?*"

# REALITY 101

# CLIFFORD

NOW THAT DEMETRIA'S FORMALLY CONSULTED WITH A LAWYER, I'VE GOT TO TALK TO MY boss, Trevor. Not that he can do anything, but he should know what's going on, in case I need some time off. I'm sure he'll understand. He's working on his third marriage and rumor has it that he might soon be eligible for a fourth.

I step into Trevor's doorway and knock. He's brain-locked with his computer and doesn't take his eyes off the monitor.

"Whatcha need?"

"Got a minute?"

"I'm kinda busy."

"It won't take long."

"It better be good."

"It's not."

Trevor looks at me quizzically. "Is this some kinda joke?"

"Not unless you think natural disasters are funny."

Trevor scowls. "C'mon, Clifford. I'm really busy. Get to the point."

"Divorce."

Trevor's face sags like someone's grabbed his cheeks and pulled down. "Shut the door and have a seat."

An hour and a half later, I step from Trevor's office knowing more about his previous marital explosions than I'd ever have figured to ask.

Well, now it's official. As long as only I knew, it wasn't real. But by telling Trevor, I've put the wheels of bureaucracy into motion, and Clifford-the-married-guy will now have his paperwork modified to reflect his new identity as Clifford-the-marital-failure.

I can just imagine how it'll probably go. Trevor will double-check to make sure I've directed our much maligned slaves in Human Resources to make the necessary paperwork changes. They'll inform Payroll, who will inform the Information Services geeks. After that, everyone will know. But what could I expect?

This is the real world, where dirty little secrets like mine can't be kept. It'll be embarrassing, but at least people will understand when they see me arguing with the pencil sharpener. And I'll understand when groups of laughing, talking people suddenly remember they have important things to do when I show up.

I get back to my cubicle, grab the phone, and start to call Dr. Crennick's office to schedule another counseling session. My finger hovers over the phone as I ponder the wisdom of continuing to see him.

At first, it was good having Dr. Crennick to talk to. But after my last appointment, I left wondering if he wasn't working for Demetria. Instead of being *my* advocate and seeing *my* side of things, he started floating off into theoretical fantasyland, droning on about Demetria struggling to find her personal space, rejuvenating her inner child, and nurturing her right to be a whole person, blah, blah.

That's all well and good, but I need for him to tell me that I'm right, Demetria's wrong, then help me develop a strategy to end this madness. Maybe he was just trying to get me to be more objective, something I'm finding emotionally difficult but I know is good intellectually. If that was the case, then Dr. Crennick's still worth my time. I punch the numbers on the phone and make the appointment.

# VICTOR

I PASS THE PITTSBURGH CITY-LIMITS SIGN RIGHT AS JAMES BROWN'S OLDIE-BUT-GOODIE "The Payback" starts pumpin' from the radio. The Godfather of Soul is throwin' down, the title and words sayin' all that needs to be said about my reasons for comin' home. I almost didn't make it, foolin' around with that punk Corey and his supervisor ego. He was gettin' all caught up bein' MR. JACKSON again, tryin' to bust my balls cuz I was takin' vacation earlier than planned, even after I told him I had a fambly emergency. Then I said "Claudia Café" and he got instant agreeable.

Now that I'm here, I'ma fix it so Demetria don't get no more opportunities to jack up my fambly. I feel bad that Cliff's gotta go through his misery, but now that he's seein' the true colors of that sluttin' bottom-feeder, he'll be better off.

In a weird whacked-out kinda way, Demetria's made my job easier. With her decidin' to walk, all I gotta do is make sure she keeps steppin'. And I *definitely* gotta make sure that Cliff's spine don't turn to jelly if Demetria decides that bein' a out-the-closet ho ain't so good after all. Cuz even if she stays, she's still gonna be the same schemin', rotten, nasty walkin'-VD-bomb that she's always been. Like the babes're always tellin' me, a dog is a dog is a dog, and Demetria's one'a the biggest bow-wows of 'em all.

At least I'll get a chance to see my precious baby Jewel, along with Momma, Nate, and his crew. I'll check out Braddie and Bear if I can, but with Cliff's action bein' so raggedy, I ain't puttin' no money on it.

I glance over at the Magic Maiden doll and some other toys I bought for my baby. I can't wait to see her face when she gets 'em. When I told her I'd bought the doll, she was off-the-chart happy.

"Nero, when can I have it?" she axed.

"Soon, baby. I'll be there real soon and it'll be all yours."

"Are you bringing Magic Maiden's castle and flying horsey?"

"Jewel, Daddy ain't got the money to—"

"Pleeeease, Nero. Magic Maiden has to have her castle and flying horsey."

It wasn't like I didn't wanna get her the stuff, but after that payday muggin' from the IRS and them child support pirates, I was left with more month than money, and was wonderin' if I could even keep the lights on. I'd also taken a pay advance so I wouldn't have'ta deal with Cliff's evil-eyein' me for beggin' and borrowin' from Momma. But what can I say? Jewel pushed the right button, so I hit up Clyde and Brantley for some dollars, bought the castle and flyin' horsey, and reminded myself that nothin's too good or expensive for my baby.

I even thought about axin' Lynnette to let me take Jewel down to that Chuck E. Cheese playland joint that was just built near Momma's neighborhood. Then I got pissed about havin' to ax to take *my own daughter* someplace fun and decided that it wasn't worth the argument. Specially the part where Lynnette would enjoy remindin' me that I still ain't allowed to see Jewel unsupervised, and that the only way I could take her was if Lynnette came with us.

I didn't even try foolin' myself into thinkin' I could stomach that stress, so I flushed the idea. And it made me wonder again if them Children's Services pencilnecks ever ax theyselfs if it don't seem stupid that I ain't allowed private time with my baby, while them lowlife germs slimin' through Lynnette's revolvin' door get to spend all the time they want.

The disc jockey puts on an old Isaac Hayes hit, "One Big Unhappy Family," and I get down with Ike as I turn onto Steepleton Road and see a sign for 21st Century Polymers.

When me and Cliff last talked and he was whinin' about Demetria's coworkers, Nolan and Tammy, he mentioned that her company was changin' locations.

Cliff was cryin' about how Nolan's always sniffin' up Demetria's thigh and how Tammy keeps Demetria's attitude even more stanky. It's his own fault. I'da got some'a the brothas and took 'em both to an empty warehouse and "explained" to Nolan the dangers of "not keepin' yo' mind off my baby's booty" and "convinced" Tammy to "keep yo' advice to yo'self!"

I should keep goin', but I'd be a chump to be this close and not ruin Demetria's day, specially after all'a the trouble she's pissin' onto my fambly. I turn into the parkin' lot, go inside, and stop in the lobby to check the directory for Demetria's name. I don't see it and I diddy-bop up to the receptionist's desk.

"May I help you, sir?" axes a babe, lookin' like she needs a free spa membership.

"Yeah. Don't Demetria work here?"

"Do you mean Miz Matthews?"

"Miz?" I roll my eyes. "Okay. We'll play it your way. Don't *Mizzz* Matthews work here?"

The receptionist grits on me. "Is she expecting you?"

"Do turkeys celebrate Thanksgivin'?"

"Huh?" says the receptionist, frownin'. Then she figures it out and grits even harder. "I'm sorry sir. I'm not allowed to . . ."

"Wait a second, baby. I ain't in'trested in none'a your snivelin' red-tape-don't-bug-me-cuz-I'm-too-tired-to-think excuses. Just tell me if Demetria's here!"

Some voices echoin' down the hallway gimme my answer. From all the talkin' and laughin' it sounds like they're havin' one serious par-tay. They turn the corner and there's Demetria! She and some two-dollar-ho-lookin' babe and a dude steppin' like he's her pimp are walkin' together, laughin' and carryin' on like life ain't nothin' but a ball. It oughta be. Cuz just like Lynnette's doin' with me, Demetria's buildin' herself a day'n night funland, right on top'a Cliff's back.

The baby killer whale receptionist says, "Sir, unless you have an appoint . . ."

"Shut up, Free Willy!" I say, dismissin' her with a wave.

That really frosts her butt and she starts stabbin' the numbers on her phone.

I beeline for the laughin' group and say, "Demetria! We gotta talk!"

Demetria stops so fast her pumps are prob'ly leavin' skid marks on that shiny hallway floor.

"Demetria! What's wrong?" axes the dude.

I gotta give the brass panty leech credit. I had her off balance, but she recovers quickly and says, "It's okay, Nolan. It's just Clifford's Neanderthal brother Victor."

"That's Ice to you, *slut*! Only fambly members call me Victor. And from whut I'm hearin', that don't apply to you no more."

Demetria's eyes narrow and she nudges the two-dollar ho. "Tammy, go get security," she says.

As Tammy hustles back down the hallway I point at Demetria, my finger, hand, and arm lookin' like one big mad arrow.

"Lissen up," I say. "This ain't just about you doggin' Cliff. You're messin' with *my blood*! So just do whutch'you gotta do then get the hell out'a my fambly!"

Nolan steps forward, but he's a smart sissy and makes sure it ain't too close. "Look, Victor, Ice, whoever you are. Keep making threats and you're gonna be in big trouble."

"And if you keep jumpin' bad, you's gonna be in Emergency."

"Hey!" shouts a rent-a-cop, hustlin' up behind Demetria and Nolan. "What's going on here?"

"He barged in here and started threatening Ms. Matthews," Nolan says.

"That's right!" Free Willy adds.

"I want him arrested!" commands Demetria.

"For whut?" I ax. "I ain't done nothin' but told you get out'a my fambly. Just like I would to any other skank!"

That *really* pisses Demetria off, cuz her face twists into a kinda ugly that even them Hollywood special-effects dudes ain't dreamed up.

She starts shoutin' at the rent-a-cop, "Don't just stand there! Arrest him! I want that bastard buried beneath the jail!"

"But Ms. Matthews, he hasn't . . ."

*"I said ARREST him!"*

I glance around, see an exit that offers escape into a part of the parkin' lot close to my puzz-mobile, and start easin' over to the door.

"Freeze!" shouts another rent-a-cop, runnin' up and mumblin' into his radio.

Tammy's trottin' up behind 'em, all that hustlin' makin' her jugs flop'n bounce in a way that makes me wish I had some time to check her out.

The first rent-a-cop pulls out his nightstick. "All right, you! Up against that wall. Hands up. Legs spread wide."

"Not a chance, punk!" I say, glancin' at the exit. "Besides, you ain't my type."

The rent-a-cops charge and I fly out the exit, scramble into my car, and jet away, leavin' those fools coughin' on exhaust, dust, and stankin' smoke from burnt rubber.

OKAY. MAYBE THAT THANG BACK AT DEMETRIA'S OFFICE WAS MORE THAN I INTENDED happenin', but I ain't broke no laws. Ain't nobody got hurt and wasn't nothin' stolen. So these two cop cars shouldn't be zoomin' up behind me like the Untouchables, their abba-labba lights whirlin' and flashin', puttin' *all* my business in the street. This better be good, cuz I ain't ran no STOP signs. I ain't cut nobody off. I ain't been cruisin' over the speed limit. I ain't drunk. I don't fool with no drugs. And last I looked it wasn't Hassle-a-Brotha month. So the *only* thang these po-leases can ticket me for is DWB—Drivin' While Black!

I pull over and a voice blasts from a PA speaker. "Get out of the car and lie facedown on the ground."

Get on the ground? This sounds more serious than plain old DWB. I swear, every time one'a my they-all-look-alike cousins goes'n does somethin' stupid the po-leases think *I'm* the suspect.

"Get out of the car! Now!"

I get out with my hands up and face the Thumpers, *reeeeaaaal* slow.

"Be cool, man. I ain't packin' no heat. Why're ya'll sweatin' me?"

"Facedown on the ground!"

I go to take off my sunglasses then *stop*! Ain't no sense givin' these fools an excuse. I can hear the news report now: *Po-leases say the suspect was pullin' a gun from his nostril.*

Gettin' hassled by these Thumpers reminds me of stuff I don't need to be rememberin'. Not now! But my mind's got a mind of its own, so there's Lynnette, standin' behind a Thumper, wearin' her *"Gotcha!"* grin. And Jewel's hollerin' and reachin' for me, but Lynnette won't let her come. The evil grinnin' booger-bear down at Children's Services, tellin' me it ain't none'a my business how Jewel's child support money is spent. And that smart-aleck social worker, tellin' me over and over, like each word was slow-meltin' chocolate, that, no, I couldn't see Jewel unsupervised. Then months of threatenin' child support letters, when I'd *never* missed a payment.

"Get on the ground! Now!"

Even though my mind's tryin' to find its way out'a what happened *then*, my eyes ain't so stupid as to mistake what's happenin' *now*! So I drop to the ground, understandin' lots better whut Nate means when he says I oughta be keepin' myself "prayed up."

# NATHAN

"SISTER DAWKINS, WOULD YOU OUTLINE THE PLAN FOR MR. RASMUSSEN?"

Mr. Timothy Rasmussen, founder and CEO of Mid-Atlantic Robotics & Cybertech, has taken his seat directly across from me, proof once again that God answers prayer. Now I need Him to answer another and help with this proposal. If Rasmussen agrees, the teens in the Young & Gifted program will have a tremendous opportunity to pursue an apprenticeship with one of the fastest-growing robotics manufacturers in the East. I nod toward the end of the table.

Beverly makes quick eye contact with the other Y&G board members and beams her brightest, winningest smile at Rasmussen. "Mr. Rasmussen, it's truly an honor to have you here and we're delighted that you've taken time from your busy schedule to meet with us." She glances at me for a lingering second. "And I'd like to thank Pastor Matthews for nominating me to chair this project."

Rasmussen nods curtly and glances at his watch. Beverly doesn't miss the cue and plunges into the presentation.

When she finishes, Rasmussen's face is a masterpiece of inscrutability. He cracks his knuckles one at a time, something I'm told he does when he's deep in thought. After knuckle number seven he looks at me and smiles.

"Rev'rend Matthews," he says, speaking slowly in his soft Virginia accent, "I do b'lieve this is just what the doctor ordered."

"Straight from the eternal medicine cabinet, Mr. Rassmussen."

Rasmussen chuckles. "So it is. So it is. Well, if you'll allow me, I'd like to help out."

"Great!" I exclaim. "I can't tell you how much this'll mean to the kids."

Rasmussen's face takes on a soft, reflective glow. "Oh, I think I've got an idea. Ya see, I wasn't always up to my eyeballs in money. Anytime I hear of a sound project that'll help out some young folks, I'm glad to support it."

Beverly's beaming. She gives me a thumbs-up.

Rasmussen drinks her in with his eyes. "My compliments, Miz Dawkins. Your knowledge of the high-tech business is truly impressive."

Beverly blushes and demurs. "Why, thank you, Mr. Rasmussen. But I owe it all to Pastor Matthews. He's my inspiration."

She smiles at me and my chest swells. Brother Otis Trayne, sitting beside me, hands me a note, keeping his hands just below the table. It's from Brenda, sitting opposite Beverly.

*Nathan, stop gushing over Beverly. You're making us both look like fools!*

I TURN ONTO OHIO AVENUE AND PULL UP TO THE LIGHT. BRENDA AND I ARE HALFWAY TO Deacon Cabell's house, where we're going to check on him, see how he's recovering from his chemotherapy, and have a word of prayer. But with all the strife tornadoing in this minivan, we'd do better to let Deacon Cabell pray for himself.

"Brenda, why're you making such a big deal out of nothing?" I say. "All Beverly did was express appreciation for being given a chance to play a key role in getting Rasmussen's support."

I'm gripping the steering wheel so tight, my knuckles hurt. I've got to end this argument before Brenda senses that Beverly and I have exchanged more than glances.

"Nathan, it wasn't just 'nothing.' You should've seen yourself. With the way you and Beverly were making eyes, someone might've thought you were newlyweds."

"This is ridiculous. I don't even know why I'm dignifying your paranoia with a response."

"Paranoia!"

"That's right. Paranoia. I've done everything I can think of to set your mind at ease about Beverly. *You* were the first one I consulted about nominating her as chairperson. *You* were the one who gave her the strongest endorsement. *You* were the one who said it would benefit the ministry to have her more involved. So what happens? I nominate Beverly. The board approves. She does a great job. She proves that everything *you* said about how much of an asset she'd be is correct. And all I get from you is grief and accusation. Now tell me, how much sense does that make?"

"Nathan, you're missing the point. It's one thing to . . ."

"No, Brenda! You're missing the point! There's nothing going on here but you allowing your jealousy to run wild. And to be honest, I'm getting sick and tired of being blamed for the ghosts haunting your hyperactive imagination."

Brenda's eyes narrow. "Oh! So now I'm hallucinating! Is that it?"

Mercifully, the car phone rings. It's Helen.

"Pastor, quick!" she cries. "You've gotta hurry!"

"Huh? Slow down, Helen. What're you talking about?"

"Your brother Victor!"
"What about him?"
"He's been arrested."
I say a quick prayer for Deacon Cabell and rocket through the red light.

# CLIFFORD

I'M TALKING WITH CHERI, THE DEPARTMENTAL SECRETARY, ABOUT ME AND THE BOYS finally going kite flying tomorrow, and ask if she's got any tips.

"Not really," she answers. "As far as I know, you just run and pull the kite behind you until it starts flying."

"That's pretty much what I figured."

"You'll want to make sure the boys are far enough apart so they don't get their lines tangled. You know how selfish kids can be about their possessions."

I almost start to tell Cheri that the boys gave *me* the kites so the issue of "their" possessions isn't even a concern. But I don't want to get into all that "I Am" hokum and the boys' believing that kite flying will somehow "fix us." So rather than answer directly, I drone on about how it'll give me a chance to show Braddie and Bear some real "dad stuff."

Back at my cubicle, I'm jolted by an overwhelming feeling of dread as I sit down. I've joked often enough about Momma's belief in our shared-family-spirit, but this feeling is real. And it concerns Victor.

I start to call Momma. But she'll already know if something's wrong. If it isn't, I'll be sending out a false alarm, causing her unnecessary worry. Instead I call Nate's office. Helen, his church secretary, says he should be in his car. I dial his car phone and moments later I'm zooming toward the highway.

I RUSH INTO THE POLICE STATION, LOOK AROUND FOR NATHAN, AND SEE HIM SITTING IN one of a row of chairs along the far wall, looking nervously in the direction of an office with the nameplate DETECTIVE G. TALLAMETTI outside. He sees me and waves me over.

"What happened?" I ask.

"We're still sorting it out," Nate answers.

"We?"

"Brenda's here with me."

I spot Brenda over at a pay phone, looking sober and determined. What a woman. Not only is she down here for this crisis, she's apparently as worried as Nathan and I am about our errant brother.

"Would you mind keeping an eye out for Victor?" Nate says. "I'm gonna go get some coffee."

"No problem," I answer, sitting down.

Nate takes off and I assume the vigil. Detective G. Tallametti's door opens long enough for me to glimpse Victor's back. Facing him is a silver-haired bulldog of a man chomping on a cigar as he speaks. Quick hand motions accompany his words. From Victor's slouching posture and the tilt of his head I can tell he's giving Detective G. Tallametti the look of a rabid wolf.

Even here, in the midst of a force that has him outnumbered, outgunned, and generally overwhelmed, he's standing his ground. It's a small piece of ground, but it's his. And it's a glaring contrast to all my kowtowing and giving up miles of territory every time Demetria's yawned, sneezed, or burped.

Brenda's still at that pay phone, calling and hanging up. Whatever's going on, it's not making her happy.

Nate walks up and hands me a cup of vending machine coffee. It tastes like liquid cardboard.

"We should hear something soon. Gino, er, Detective Tallametti and I are on the DFS community task force."

"DFS? What's that?"

"Drug Free Streets."

"You've never mentioned anything about being on a task force."

Nate shrugs. "I guess it's just never come up."

I shake my head and take a sip of coffee. "I don't know how you do it."

"Lots of prayer, a loyal secretary, and a well-organized planner," says Nate, chuckling.

"No, Nate. How do you keep Brenda's support?"

Nate doesn't answer, so I drop it. Besides, Detective Tallametti's on his way over. Victor follows him, his expression and body movements just shy of outright defiance. When they reach us, Detective Tallametti stands off to the side while we hug and greet Victor.

"What did you do?" I ask.

"I ain't done nothin'," Victor answers. Then, speaking just loud enough to be obnoxious, he says, "Unless bein' born the wrong color is a crime."

Seeing Detective Tallametti's scowling face, Victor smirks, the taunting grin expanding until he glances toward the entrance. Then his eyes get big, his shoulders droop, and he says, "Oh no."

Nate and I look toward the door and are vacuumed into Victor's dread. It's Momma. And she's not happy, not at all.

"Lord, protect us," says Nate.

I finish with, "Amen."

Detective Tallametti follows our gaze, sees Momma, then looks back at me and Nathan.

Nate reads the question on his face and says, "She's our mother."

"Also known as the Enforcer," I mumble.

Victor looks down at his feet and shakes his head, finally worried.

"Can I help you, ma'am?" asks a uniformed officer as Momma beelines toward us.

She breezes past him, shifting her pocketbook from one arm to the other like she's preparing to throttle someone.

She glares at Victor, who's looking down at his feet. Then she turns her attention to Nathan and me.

I say, "Momma, I didn't wanna worry you. That's why I didn't . . ."

She sticks her finger in my face and I shut up. She looks at Nathan and says, "And you knew that I'd sense something was wrong. Thank God Helen was there to fill me in. It's fortunate that I got a cab so soon after discovering that my car wouldn't start."

Nate opens his mouth but she cuts him off with, "Never mind!" Looking at me she says, "Our spirits are connected whether you believe it or not!"

The smile on Detective Tallametti's face testifies to how much he's enjoying this scene. He grabs Momma's hand and pumps it enthusiastically. "Ma'am, I'm so very happy to meet you," he says, cutting his eyes at the now contrite Victor.

"Is he going to jail?" Momma asks.

"No, ma'am. As a matter of fact, I was just about to release him into Reverend Matthews's custody. But I see no reason why he can't be released to *you*."

Victor grimaces.

Detective Tallametti gestures toward a side room with an OUTPROCESSING sign hanging on the door. "You can wait with him in that room over there, ma'am."

He looks at Victor, who is obviously in discomfort, then back at Momma. "I can have the outprocessing officer wait till after you two have talked, if you'd prefer."

"I would!" snaps Momma.

She marches off to the room and Victor trudges after her, his feet dragging and his eyes downcast.

"Okay, Reverend Matthews," says Detective Tallametti. "Lemme fill ya in on the details concernin' your brother."

He's starting to explain when a stressed-out-looking uniformed officer hurries by and shoves a piece of paper into his hand. He glances at it, then says to Nate, "Looks like one of our snitches has some info on that McBloom kid you were askin' about."

"Don't you mean McCoombs? Raymond McCoombs?"

Detective Tallametti holds the paper close to his eyes, squints, and shrugs. "So it is. Well, anyway. We've got a lead on him."

"Great! Any idea how long it'll take to find him?"

"No tellin'. But don't worry. The moment he's picked up, I'll call."

"Thanks, Gino. I appreciate anything you can do for him—and for my brother."

"As for your brother," Detective Tallametti says, "I had to promise the Chief to name my first grandson after him, but he's agreed to reduce everything to a third-rate disturbin' the peace."

"How does that translate, Gino?" Nate asks.

"He's gettin' a warnin'."

Nate pumps Detective Tallametti's hand. "Thanks, Gino! Thanks a million. I owe you big time!"

"Nothin' doin'. Although I'd appreciate you puttin' in a word with the Big Guy upstairs for the Steelers this season." He glances over at the out-processing room. "That brother'a yours is one hard case. We coulda used him in Vietnam."

"He's an ex-Marine."

Detective Tallametti's eyebrows hike up a notch. "Well, that explains him."

"So, then, is everything all right?" I ask.

Detective Tallametti glances at me and gives me a quick once-over.

Nate says, "Gino, this is my brother Clifford."

He gives me a cursory nod, then refocuses on Nate, his eyes serious and his voice official. "Reverend Matthews, your brother's gettin' off easy, butcha better make him understand. Under no circumstances is he to go near Ms. Matthews again."

"What!" I blurt.

Nate grabs my shoulder and forces me down into one of the chairs behind us.

"Which Ms. Matthews, Gino?" Nate asks. "There are several."

Detective Tallametti frowns. "Dolores? No, that's not it. Deidre? Naw. That's not it either." Then he snaps his fingers. "Demetria! Yeah, that's her name."

"That's my wife!" I spring to my feet. And for a moment I'm certain that this isn't *my* life I'm living but one belonging to the main character in a sadistic cartoon.

Detective Tallametti looks at me. "Oh she is, is she? Well, maybe you oughta try makin' peace between her and your Marine brother."

"Will you *please* just tell me what happened?" I say.

"Easy, Clifford," cautions Nate. He reaches for my elbow and holds tight. "Gino, any details you can give us would really be appreciated," he says.

"Your brother apparently went to Ms. Matthews's place of employment and threatened her."

"Threatened!" I blurt. "There's gotta be some mistake. I mean, it's true that Victor and Demetria don't exactly get along, but he's not crazy enough to . . ."

"According to Ms. Matthews and some others, he's reached a new level of insanity."

The door to the outprocessing room opens and Momma comes out, followed by a considerably subdued Victor. I rush over, shove him back inside, and close the door behind us.

"Why, Victor?" I rasp. "What possessed you to go threaten Demetria?"

"Clifford, what's the matter with you?" asks Momma, opening the door. "Haven't we had enough trouble for . . ."

"Momma, *please*!"

She gets quiet, probably surprised not only at my words and their urgency, but that I had the nerve to direct them toward her. I'll apologize later. I yank the door shut.

"Whutch'you talkin' about, Cliff?" Victor asks. "I didn't threaten Deme*trash*."

I walk up on him until we're almost nose to nose. "Liar! Several people heard you."

Victor's jaw hardens. "First of all, you'd best get out'a my face. Second of all, the only people who heard anythang was that Nolan clown and the Tammy skeezer who's been sabotagin' your action."

"Stop playing, Victor! Detective Tallametti said they heard you issue a threat."

"Cliff, lissen at yourself!" Victor growls. "After all you been through, why's you blindly b'lievin' suckas who's tryin' to whoop you into dog sweat?"

My raging frustration makes my hands tremble, requiring all my strength to keep from grabbing Victor and shaking him into putty. How can I make him understand? If Demetria's behind this, then she's definitely moved to some cold, distant place from which there may be no return.

"Victor, don't you see how this looks? I just can't believe that Demetria would . . ."

"Just like you never b'lieved that she'd one day roll your naive butt!" he snarls. "But it's happenin', *ain't it*?"

The question brings everything into brutal clarity. And its implication is equally clear. The rules of what I once considered normal have changed. And I'm no longer in a position to predict what Demetria will or won't do.

Demetria's had little trouble treating me like something that needs to be scraped from the bottom of her shoe. And I'm her husband! The man she's loved, lived with, and had kids by. If she could turn on me, she'd have no trouble turning on her nemesis, Victor. As for Nolan and Tammy, their being mixed up in this sewer-swirl is no surprise.

But I still refuse to believe that Demetria had a part in this. Not so much out of concern for Victor, but for *me*. The only way to find out is to ask.

I storm out of the room and run into Nate and Brenda.

"Nathan, we need to get home," Brenda is saying. "No one's answering the phone."

"Take it easy, Bren. The kids just probably have their music turned up too high."

"Maybe so. But I still want to check on them."

Brenda looks at me. "Clifford, what's the matter? You look like . . ."

"I'm fine!" I answer, sidestepping her and Nate.

"Where are you going?" Nate asks.

"To find out what happened."

I stop and look back at Nate, Brenda, and Victor, who's leaning against the doorway of the outprocessing room. Momma walks up beside him. For an instant, I have the strangest sensation that each of them is sharing some portion of the agonies tearing me apart. Then I rush off to the pain-pit I loosely call home.

I WHIP INTO THE DRIVEWAY, DASH TO THE HOUSE, AND *CAN'T GET IN*! I DON'T BELIEVE this. Demetria's added another friggin' lock to the door, and it looks like a deadbolt. What kind of drugs is she on? This is still *my* house, where *my* money's helping pay the rent, where *my* kids live, and she's got the audacity to lock me out!

"Let me in!" I holler, banging on the door.

A second later, a second too long, the door's still closed. I leap over to the dining room window, punch out the screen, and climb in. Scratch growls and barks, until he sees my face. He tucks his tail between his legs and slinks downstairs. Braddie and Bear stare in openmouthed amazement.

"Where's your mother?"

Demetria's laughter floats down the steps before they answer.

I look at the boys and point to the basement. "Go!"

They snatch up their toys and vanish. Demetria's giggling yanks me by the ears and spits in my face. My throbbing head pounds harder, like it's getting whacked by the frenzied palm slams of a delirious bongo drummer. The world slows to a speed my brain knows isn't possible but must accept. Another giggle and the world speeds up. The world spins faster and I'm at the top of the steps. It stands on its head and I'm at the bedroom door. It flies off its axis and I crash Demetria's phone party. Her head snaps around, her face showing the remnant of a fast-fading smile as she looks me up and down.

"How'd you get in?" she asks.

"Never mind that. I wanna talk to you."

"Later."

"Now, Demetria!"

She turns away. "Go ahead, Nolan," she says into the phone.

I blur across the room and snatch the phone. "Did you have Victor arrested?"

Demetria snatches the phone back. "No! He had himself arrested."

"Demetria! Don't play games. This is serious."

Nolan shouts from the phone. "Demetria! Are you all right? Talk to me!"

I snatch the phone again and speak in a way that leaves no doubt I'm related to Victor "Ice" Matthews.

"Whaddya wanna tell her? How sorry you are that she's murdering her marriage, but you'll be there to screw her through the rough spots? How it's so terrible you've had to wait to get in her panties? Or maybe you wanna tell her that if she's ever down in the mouth, you'll be glad to fill it with your joy?"

"Hey!" hollers Nolan. "Who do you think you're talking to?"

"A *worm* who can suck the sweat from my balls!"

I slam the phone down and glare into Demetria's slitted eyes. "Did you, or did you not, have Victor arrested?"

"What if I did! After putting up with all his crap, it was the least I could do."

"Have you lost your mind?" I shout. "Victor's gone out of his way to avoid you since I banned him from the house. He didn't deserve this, and you know it!"

"Don't tell *me* what I should or shouldn't know! You and no one else is gonna tell me what to think, how to be happy, or . . ."

*"Shut up!"* I bellow. "You've talked enough! All you've done since Disney World is talk! About what you want! About your dissatisfaction! Your unhappiness! Always about Demetria! Demetria! Demetria!"

Demetria stomps toward the door. "I'm not gonna sit here and take this."

I yank the phone from the wall and hurl it into the dresser mirror. The glass shatters and Demetria dives for cover. When the pieces have clattered to the floor, she stands and looks at the mangled mess.

The dresser was one of the first pieces of furniture we bought, back when our marriage was young, made in Heaven, and would last forever. Back when we looked into the mirror, kissed, and promised never to become the people now staring back at us from a still-hanging shard.

"I hate you," Demetria says.

"The feeling's mutual."

"I'm divorcing you. As soon as possible."

"Demetria, *I could care less!*"

I face her directly, stare hard into her eyes, and speak slowly and clearly, so there's no misunderstanding. "Life is too short to spend with a miserable creature like you, so I'm moving out. If you're gonna divorce me, *just do it*! Until then, stay the hell out'a my way till after it's done!"

Tears gather in Demetria's eyes but don't fall, as if they're being held in place by the raw suction power of her anger. I step toward her and she holds her ground. Good! Because I need her to hear each and every word I'm gonna say.

"Demetria, I'm saying this once, and *only* once. Don't hurt my family! Do whatever you're gonna do to me but, I'm warning you, *leave the blood alone*!"

Demetria thrusts out her chin. "Or what?"

I step closer. "Or . . . you'll find out!"

I look her up and down with my own withering contempt and storm out.

# VICTOR

I AIN'T STUPID ENOUGH TO THINK THAT THAT FUSSIN' OUT MOMMA GAVE ME DOWN AT the po-leases station is the last of her mouth, so once I drop her off at home I'm makin' moves to get out'a here. I've got one foot in my car when I see her standin' at the front door.

"Where do you think you're going?" she axes.

"Uh . . . I was gonna go . . ."

"I want to talk to you."

"But, Momma, I . . ."

She walks into the house before I can finish. I lock the car door, hurry inside, and see her sittin' at the table, foolin' around with her laptop computer.

"Victor, why'd you come home?" axes Momma, still starin' at her computer screen.

"Huh?"

"Why'd you come home?"

"Whuch'you talkin' about, Momma?"

She looks up from the computer, sits back, and crosses her arms tight over her chest.

"Victor, it's not a hard question. Why did you come home?"

"To celebrate Jewel's birthday early."

Her eyes narrow. "Victor, don't you lie to me."

"I ain't lyin', Momma. You axed a question, I answered it. Why're you sweatin' me?"

Now why'd I go and say that? Cuz she jumps up, blitzes across the room, and starts jabbin' her finger in my chest like it's some cookin' fork checkin' the meat. "Don't you raise your voice to me! Understand!"

"Yeah, Momma. I gotcha."

"You're not going to take your frustrations out on me. Not after I carried you for nine months, wiped your stinky butt, and loved you through all your uglies. You *and* your brothers are going to show me respect! Is that clear?"

I just nod. Cuz as pissed off as I am, it's best I don't say *nothin'*.

Momma plants her hands on her hips and shakes her head. "You're so hardheaded."

Then a soft smile creeps onto her face and she opens her arms, invitin' me in. I accept the invitation and hold her tight, wishin' that her huggin' me and pattin' my back would last forever.

"I'm sorry, Momma," I say.

"That's okay, Victor. You've just got to remember that I know when you're lying."

She pushes me away and holds my face in her palms. "Now, you tell me why you came home. And don't you use Jewel as an excuse. As close as Cleveland is to Pittsburgh, you could've left the morning of her birthday and been here in plenty of time. Now, why are you here?"

I look straight into Momma's eyes and say, "I came to take care'a Cliff and Demetria."

Momma plops onto the couch and looks at me like I just told her she's won a nude photo contest. "Victor, what's going through your mind? You can't just walk into your brother's house and dictate conditions."

"Momma, if I'da had *my* way this wouldn't even be a discussion."

"You're not going to do this. Understand?"

I don't say nothin'. I grit on the wall behind Momma. She grabs my hands and yanks me down beside her.

"Did you hear me? I forbid you to do this. If you want to help Clifford you can talk to him, support him, be there for him, and encourage him. But you cannot do this!"

I get up and start pacin'. "What're we s'posed to do, Momma? Just stand around playin' dumb while Demetria slices Cliff up, gettin' him ready for a domestic court quick-fry?"

"No, sweetheart. What we're supposed to do is love Clifford through this process. And love him hard! So that every time he thinks he's alone, he'll run into the love coming from one of us."

"C'mon, Momma! Cliff's our blood! We can't just sit back and shadowbox this thang. Howzit s'posed to help if his own fambly's tellin' him that that drillin' sound he's hearin' ain't really him gettin' screwed."

Momma closes her eyes and sighs. "Victor, I'm so sorry. After all these years, I thought you'd finally let it go."

"Let whut go? I ain't doin' nothin' but protectin' my brother. Just like *you* taught us." I sit down beside Momma and talk soft, hopin' this sugar approach'll work. "Listen, Momma. All I wanna do is see whuts'up with Cliff and Demetria. Once that's done, I'm back in Cleveland, one-two-three. No pain, no fuss."

Momma's lookin' at me so hard it feels like her eyes is borin' holes into my head. "This has nothing to do with Clifford, does it?"

"Whutch'you talkin' about? This ain't about nothin' *but* Cliff."

She pats a spot beside her. I scoot closer and Momma takes both my hands into hers. Then she speaks slow and steady. "Victor, I know your heart's breaking over what's happening with Clifford. So is mine. But there's more to it than you realize."

"C'mon, Momma. You're soundin' like them flimflammin', mumble-mouthed counselors I was seein' after Lynnette flushed me."

Momma squeezes my hands. "That's exactly what I'm talking about! Lynnette hurt you. And it's still hurting, isn't it?"

I try pullin' my hands away but Momma squeezes tight and holds on. "You can't tell me she didn't. Because I saw you, and felt you, and carried your pain. Just like I'm carrying Clifford's."

I stay quiet, starin' at our knot of hands.

"Victor," she goes on, "the hurt from Lynnette, added to what happened with your father, has turned you into a tower of anger."

"I don't wanna talk about this!" I yank my hands out'a Momma's.

She grabs 'em again and scoots closer. "Good! Just sit there and listen. You and your brothers may have the fire of the Matthewses but you've got the heart of my family. And that's unfortunate."

I try standin' but Momma pulls me down.

"Momma! I don't wanna hear this! Whut's the point? Whut're you tryin' to do?"

"Be quiet and listen!"

She strokes my cheek with the back of her hand. "Maybe it couldn't be helped, you all learning to love the way I do. Total. Hard. And complete. I prayed desperately that none of you would love blind. But you did, all of you. Just like I loved your father."

A tear falls on my hands. I turn away and fight with everything I've got to keep from boo-hooin' like some punk.

"Momma, it wasn't right whut he did. Writin' from Vietnam to give you the ax by mail. Then gettin' waxed in an ambush, scammin' me out'a my chance to beat out his brains and make him tell us *why*."

Momma strokes my hair and speaks soft'n tender. "Victor, you don't know how many times I wished you hadn't been home that day I received his letter. I never should've let you see me react like that. You were so young. And so brave, obeying my wishes that you not say anything to Nathan and Clifford."

I push Momma away, but not hard. "And whut for, Momma? Whut was the point in not tellin' 'em the truth?"

Momma sighs. "You all loved your father so much. It was bad enough seeing what *you* went through. I couldn't bear the thought of seeing Nathan and Clifford hurting the same way. So I tried to protect them. I only wish I could've done the same for you."

"But why, Momma? *Why?* Didn't he say he ain't wanted you? Or us? Cliff and Nate had a right to know whut kinda snake he was, talkin' all that yang about lovin' us and how we meant so much to him. He made us all look like clowns, *includin' you*!"

The words rocket out'a my mouth before I can stop 'em. Momma stays cool, lettin' me get away with spoutin' off like that for this first, and no doubt last, time.

Then she says, "Now, Victor! You listen to me. You all didn't need to know why. Lee Matthews may have been *your* father but he was *my* husband and I loved him. Part of me still does. I'm not saying that it didn't hurt or that I didn't hate him. For a long time, I did. And I wanted to go on hating him. But it just wasn't in me. And every time I looked at you boys, I'd remember what Lee and I once had, how we'd loved each other so much, and I decided to hang on to that memory. No matter what happened at the end, we had more years of happiness than hardship. And I refused to let myself become bitter when God had blessed me to know that kind of love."

I jump up from the couch and try walkin' away, but Momma's holdin' my wrist with a grip that oughta be had by someone with lots more muscles.

"Victor, please! I know you want to protect the family. But that's the risk of loving. You took that risk when you loved Lynette. It's the risk Clifford and Demetria took in loving each other. That same risk exists even for Nathan and Brenda. That's what makes love so beautiful. And that's why it can hurt so much."

I snatch my hand from Momma and head for the door, stoppin' when she calls.

"Victor!"

"Yes, ma'am."

"I don't want you interfering in Clifford's business."

I don't answer, lettin' my silence do my talkin'.

"Victor, did you hear me?"

"Yes, ma'am."

"And?"

"And, I'll do whatever you say. After there ain't no more risk."

MOMMA AIN'T SPEAKIN' TO ME NOW, CUZ I AIN'T PROMISED TO NOT MEDDLE IN CLIFF'S business. Too bad! This time I'm doin' thangs *my* way. And speakin' of thangs goin' my way, Cliff's pullin' up, right as I'm pullin' out. I get out of my car and wait for him to walk up. I can tell from his face that he found out whut he didn't wanna know.

"How'd it go?" I ax.

"About as good as your experience."

If Cliff wasn't so knees-to-nuts whooped, I'd smack him up'side his head for that. But he's seriously gloomin', so I'ma cut him some slack.

Momma passes us, stompin' to her car and grumblin' that she's goin' to meet with the dude guidin' her big writin' project. Cliff pulls her off to the side and they talk kinda low, but I can still hear some'a what they's sayin', and ease a little closer so I can hear more.

"Clifford, *of course* I'm upset," says Momma. "One of my sons was arrested."

"But Momma, Victor shouldn't have gone down to Demetria's job."

"Why are you defending her? You said yourself that she didn't try to stop it."

"I'm *not* defending her, Momma. I'm only saying that Victor didn't help matters."

Momma tightens her lips, like she's holdin' back a storm of cussin'. "Listen, Clifford," she says. "I'm going to support you in every way possible, and respect your right to handle things *your* way. But don't expect me to be happy about malicious acts directed toward my children."

"Yes, ma'am."

"Do you have someplace to stay for the night?" axes Momma, already figurin' out that Cliff ain't but a couple'a steps away from livin' in a box.

"Well, I . . ."

"Stay here for the night," says Momma. Then lookin' at me and bustin' my so-called slick eavesdroppin', she says, "And Victor, you remember what I said."

Momma says 'bye, then leaves. Me'n Cliff watch her drive off, then go inside, sit down at the kitchen table, and start piecin' thangs together.

# NATHAN

BRENDA HURRIES INTO THE HOUSE AND CALLS, "CORRINE! NATHAN!"

No answer. We check their rooms, the bathrooms, downstairs, and out in the yard. Everything's in order and looks normal, *too* normal.

"Maybe they left a note on the fridge," I say.

We both look. Nothing. We call several neighbors, asking if Corrine and Nate Junior are over at their houses, or if they noticed them leaving or anything odd. Nothing. We call several of their friends. Nothing.

"You think they're down at the park?" I ask.

Brenda grabs her keys. We speed down to the park and drive slowly through each section, stopping every now and then to check the wooded areas on foot. Nothing. We stop by the skating rink, the basketball courts, and a fifties-style soda shop and flag down some of their other friends. Nothing!

"Maybe they're home by now," I say.

Brenda nods and blinks back the tears gathering in her eyes. We get home, park in the garage, and hurry off to check through the house again. We tromp through the house and meet back in the living room. Brenda's expression matches my rapidly expanding fears. Then a minivan pulls into the driveway.

It's Sister Nandi Briscoe of our church grounds committee. In the van with her are a bunch of kids, laughing and talking excitedly. Nate Junior gets out, waves a casual good-bye to his friends, then strolls toward the house, smiling and whistling. He slows down once he sees me standing in the doorway.

Sister Briscoe waves and smiles. I kind of smile and wave back, making a mental note to speak to her about her part in this confusion. Nate Junior slinks inside and launches immediately into his own defense.

"Sister Briscoe stopped by to see if I could go to a skating party and Corrine said . . ."

"Corrine!" I snap. "Who are you supposed to listen to, Nathan?"

"You, but . . ."

"And what're you supposed to do when we're gone?"

Nate Junior's mouth twists down at the corners. "Stay inside and not have any company."

"And did you do that?"

"No, sir. But when Sister Briscoe asked if . . ."

"We've been worried sick!" says Brenda. "Why didn't you at least call on the car phone or page us?"

"I, I was gonna do it," stammers Nate Junior. "But you guys are always saying that since Corrine's the oldest she . . ."

"Boy!" I nearly holler. "Sit your little skinny butt down and be quiet!"

Nate Junior's mouth snaps shut and he zips into the nearest chair. Brenda steps over to the living room window, looks out, and says, "Nathan!"

I hurry over and look out to where she's pointing. A car's pulling into the driveway. It's Tyrone Ballard. And sitting beside him, hip to hip, as if they were lovers who couldn't stand to be even inches apart from each other, is my little girl, who along with growing into a woman has decided to become a rebel. They sit talking for a few moments, so engrossed in each other that they don't even check for signs that Brenda and I might be home. Tyrone leans over and kisses Corrine on the cheek—the first of many steps on the road to his getting her pregnant. And abandoning her, *just like I did with Syreeta*!

I charge out the front door and, pulling my voice from some deep place I've never dug before, holler, *"CORRINE!"*

Corrine's and Tyrone's eyes snap over to me and they know they're witnessing holy thunder. Tyrone shoves Corrine out of the car and is already backing out of the driveway before she can shut the passenger door. He zooms down the street, his clattering, smoking jalopy sounding as desperate to get away as he must be. Corrine doesn't face me for a long time, her fear freezing her in place. Then she slowly turns, her face already pleading.

"Dad," she says, her voice trembling, "we only went to get a burger. I didn't think you'd mind, since . . ."

I point to the front door. "Get inside!"

I follow Corrine inside and am preempted by her determination to get in the first word.

"Dad, you've gotta give me a chance to explain."

"Corrine, I don't have to do anything. But *you*, young lady, are gonna have more than enough to do, starting with household chores."

"Don't you even want to hear my side?"

"No!" I bellow. "There's only one side that's important here: *mine and your mother's*!"

"Dad, please! If you just let me ex . . ."

"Corrine! How many times do I have to tell you? *I don't wanna hear it!* I told you that under *no* circumstances were you to go out with Tyrone Ballard." I glance at Nate Junior, then back at Corrine. "And both of you know better than to have company or leave the house when your mother and I are gone."

Tears well up in Corrine's eyes and she starts sobbing. She sounds truly pitiful. And I want to hug my baby, tell her I forgive her, and have her promise to never do it again. But now's not the time. Corrine's getting too big for her britches and she needs to understand that I mean what I say.

"Corrine, I don't care how many tears you cry. You're grounded."

"What about Nate Junior," she whines. "He left the house too."

"Don't worry about Nate Junior. He'll get his punishment."

"But why are you grounding me and not him? I'm the oldest."

"That's right!" I shout. "You're the oldest. Which means *you* should've kept Nate Junior at home and had the good sense to respect my wishes and stay away from Tyrone."

Corrine hollers, "You never let me do anything! You don't like Tyrone because he has a baby. But I'm not gonna get pregnant! Why can't you trust me?"

"Corrine! That's not the point. I mean, that *is* the point. And how can I trust you when you can't even follow simple instructions like staying home when we're gone?"

"It's not fair!" she shouts. Then she stomps off toward her room.

"Corrine! Don't you walk off when I'm talking to you."

"I hate this house!" she hollers, still stomping away. "Why do you always have to treat me like a baby?"

I grab Corrine's arm and spin her around. "I told you not to walk away from me."

She yanks free from my grip and slaps the wall. "I'm sick and tired of this prison. Just as soon as I'm eighteen I'm getting out of here."

"Prison!" I holler. "Is that what you think of your home, Corrine?" Brenda eases up beside me, takes firm hold of my elbow, and pulls me back from Corrine. "If that's how you feel, I can arrange that," I say. "Along with being grounded, you've lost your TV, Internet, and telephone privileges."

Corrine merely glares when I declare she is losing her TV and Internet privileges. But when I say "telephone," she's horror-stricken. She looks at Brenda. "Mom! Please do something!"

The flagrant appeal to Brenda makes my blood boil. "You can also forget dating, allowance, weekend stays with friends, and anything else not connected with school or housework."

"Now, wait a second," Brenda says. "Don't you think that's going overboard?"

"Brenda! This *isn't* a debate and now is *not* the time!"

Corrine fights through her sobs and asks, "When do I get my privileges back?"

"When you start living by God's standards and obeying the rules of this house."

Corrine works her jaw back and forth, suppressing her fury for as long as she can. And then, she just can't.

"Are *you* living by God's standards when you're always making goo-goo eyes with Sister Dawkins?"

Brenda gasps. My mouth falls open. Then I lunge past Brenda and slap Corrine with all the boiling anger of a hypocrite whose cover has been blown.

Corrine staggers back into the wall and slides to the floor.

"Nathan!" Brenda shouts.

I stand paralyzed, staring at my hand. "Corrine, baby. I'm sorry. I didn't mean to . . ."

"Don't talk to me! Ever!"

Brenda shoves past me and hurries to Corrine, kneeling down to hug her and stroking the back of her head. Corrine sobs into Brenda's chest.

Brenda looks up at me and her eyes fill with fire. "Get out!"

My heart falls into my stomach. "Brenda! What're you saying? Shouldn't we at least talk about this before . . ."

"Nathan! This *isn't* a debate and now is *not* the time!"

I grab my keys and leave.

# CLIFFORD

VICTOR EXPLAINS THAT THE POLICE TOLD HIM TO STAY AWAY FROM DEMETRIA OR RISK doing time.

"But that's against the Constitution," I say. "The law says . . ."

"Cliff, I don't wanna hear it. The law says thiefs are s'posed to go to the joint. Except if they're on Wall Street or in the government. The law protects and serves the ones who can afford it."

"Victor, I don't believe that. I know it's been rough for you but I can't accept . . ."

"In a minute you gonna be sorry them Thumpers didn't keep me."

"But . . ."

"But nothin'! The only law you know, you learned from *Dragnet* reruns. The law I know is whut I saw in them pistol barrels today."

We sit staring at each other for a few moments, then Victor starts laughing, gets up, and grabs himself a diet soda from Momma's fridge.

"What's so funny?" I ask.

He pours the soda into a glass, takes a few swigs, and sits down. "You."

"Me?"

"Yeah, Cliff. You!"

"Why?"

He finishes off the soda, lets out a long, rolling burp, and tosses the can into the recycling bin. "Man, ain't you never realized that I've been tryin' to protect you ever since Demetria's paw first crossed Momma's doorstep?"

I just sit and stare at Victor, probably with that expression he calls the look-of-the-stupids.

"Never mind, Cliff. The bottom line is that Demetria's dumpin' you . . ."

"Look, Victor. Just because we're separating for a little while doesn't mean Demetria's dumping me."

"Y'all're separating? It sounds like gettin' dumped to me."

In all honesty, it sounds like it to me too. But I'm not about to admit that to Victor.

"Like I was sayin'," he continues, "I need to get you ready for whut's comin' after you get rolled."

"Forget it, Victor. Buying into your philosophy amounts to giving up.

And no matter how bad it seems, I owe it to those boys to try and work things out."

"Whut about workin' it out for you? Ain't you worth it?"

I don't answer and Victor smiles in triumph. "Well, maybe *you* can work it out. But Demetria ain't even tryin' to hear none'a that."

"How do you know?"

Victor leans forward and speaks with gripping intensity. "Cliff, why can't you see? Demetria's in it for Demetria! Has been from day one. You weren't married to her for nine years. She just let you hang around. And now she wants some new friends, and you gots-ta-go!"

How I wish, with all my heart, that Victor's words weren't true. But after the thrashing my heart's sustained over the last few weeks, it's all it can do to keep beating, never mind pumping life into fantasies.

"Tell me somethin'," says Victor. "Whut'd she say to get it out in the open? I mean, whut'd she say that moved it from her just thinkin' it, to doin' it?"

"It's not important."

"It's not, huh? Well, just keep tellin' yourself how important it *ain't* when they're hackin' that child support from your check. Keep tellin' yourself how important it *ain't* the first time you pick up those boys and see some other sucka's car parked in the driveway and . . ."

"She said she wanted 'true love, excitement, and fun.' But not with me! Okay? Are you satisfied? Will you shut up now?"

I sit back in my chair and listen to my heart beating like a gong. And the normally unflappable Victor, who's seen some of everything and done even more, is sitting across from me with his eyes wide and mouth hanging slightly open.

"Man, that is cold-blooded," he says.

"Tell me about it," I answer.

# VICTOR

CLIFF GETS BUSY FIXIN' SOME COFFEE AND I SAY, "HAVE YOU TALKED TO BRADDIE AND Bear?"

"About what?"

"About you and Demetria breakin' up."

"No."

"Why not?"

Cliff turns around, leans on the counter, and crosses his arms. "Because we're not breaking up. We're having some problems, Victor. Nothing more. Nothing less."

I jam my eyes shut, bite my lower lip, and start countin'. "Man, whuts'up with you? Are you writin' a book called *Dumb Cuz I Wanna Be*? Ain't you stopped to wonder if them boys ain't noticed ya'll treatin' each other like dirt?"

"Of course they've noticed! But that's no reason to go scare them with warnings of their parents splitting up. Not when I have no intention of letting that happen."

"So I guess your movin' out is just some kinda game you and Deme . . ."

"Victor, I told you. We're having some problems. Okay? It's no big deal. We'll work it out. Married couples go through this. Sometimes."

Cliff sounds real convincin', up to where his voice trails off and he says "Sometimes." I check out his eyes. He ain't lookin' at me but at hisself in Momma's glass cabinet behind me. I smile and shake my head.

Cliff frowns. "What's so funny?"

"Man, as bent as I've always thought you was, I ain't never been able to figure out how you could be so win-the-prize smart and pork-butt dumb at the same time."

Cliff turns around to finish makin' the coffee and says, "Forget you, Victor."

"I don't mind bein' forgot cuz I'm used to it. But why're you forgettin' your boys?"

Cliff spins around with a spoon in his hand and starts jabbin' the air. "First of all, I'm not bent. Second of all, it's irresponsible to scare Braddie and Bear about something that's not gonna happen."

I jump up and stomp over to Cliff, jammin' my chest up against the spoon. "I'ma tell you whut ain't responsible. It ain't responsible for you to put Braddie, Bear, and the rest of us through these hassles cuz you're too stubborn to read your pink slip. It ain't responsible lettin' Demetria fill them boys' heads full'a her twisted trash." I slap the spoon out'a Cliff's hand. "It ain't responsible lettin' her hurt them boys any more than she's plannin'."

Cliff shoves me away and says, "Get out'a my face!"

"I'ma get in more than your face if you don't protect my nephews from that broom-rider."

"Victor, I'm ending this discussion."

"Whuts'a matter? Truth hurtin'?"

"Not at all. But the truth of the matter is that you, as usual, don't know what you're talking about. Demetria has her faults but she loves those boys." He looks into Momma's glass cabinet again and adds, "Far more than she ever loved me." Then he throws me an ugly grit. "So I refuse to accept your sludge about Demetria doing something to hurt Braddie and Bear. She loves them, provides for them, and has nothing but their best interests at heart."

I look at the ceilin' and shake my head. "Cliff, would you let *me* raise Braddie and Bear?"

"What kind of question is that?"

"One needin' a simple yes or no."

"Well, yeah, I guess, if something happened to me and . . ."

"No! Let's say nothin' happened to you and Demetria, and that Momma and Nate could take care of 'em, but all of you decided it was too much. Would you let *me* raise 'em?"

The sweat beads bubblin' up on Cliff's forehead get bigger.

"I'll make it easy for ya," I say. "*No!* You wouldn't let me raise 'em. Even though you know I love them boys, and would provide for 'em, and have nothin' but their best in'trests at heart, you still wouldn't let me raise 'em. And ya know why?"

Cliff's lookin' at his feet, not sayin' a word.

"Cuz'a how I live. Even though I ain't pushin' drugs, robbin' banks, pimpin' ho's, or dialin' 1-900-SUC-MINE, you still wouldn't let me. All cuz you think the way I look at life, get thangs done, treat people, and my minute-here-minute-gone relationships would be a bad influence on 'em. Teach 'em ideas about life'n love you ain't agreein' with."

Cliff sniffles but he ain't gettin' off that easy.

"I'm right, ain't I?"

Cliff brings a hand up to his eyes and starts mumblin'.

*"Ain't I?"*

Cliff's head barely moves but it's a nod. I hate breakin' him down like this, but after whut he said about that fight between him and Demetria I *know* that evil heifer has put her gettin' a new life plan into overdrive.

"Cliff, whutch'you think them boys is learnin' about life'n love right now, watchin' you and Demetria? Whut they gonna learn watchin' their momma's minute-here-minute-gone relationships? Whutch'you think they gonna learn when they figure out that while they was playin' video games she was splittin' it wide and bronco-bustin' the baloney-pony?"

I take hold of his chin and lift his head so that we're looking eye to eye. "And don't kid yourself, man. Anybody lookin' for 'true love, excitement, and fun' ain't talkin' about findin' it at a sewin' circle."

Cliff wipes his nose and nods.

I pat his shoulder. "It ain't all about food, clothes, and roofs, Cliff. It's also about how Braddie and Bear's minds is bein' shaped. Demetria could be the biggest drugged-out, violent, nasty-habit, triflin' skeezer on the planet and the court ain't gonna think twice about grantin' her custody. So she, her loverboys, and all her can't-find-a-good-black-man-cuz-they're-all-in-jail-on-drugs-or-faggots bashin' friends is gonna be their main mind shapers till they leave home. Think about it, man. Whutch'you think them boys' minds is gonna be like after listenin' to years of *that*?"

I snatch a paper towel from the roll hangin' over the sink and hand it to Cliff.

He blows his nose and says, "Thanks."

"Cliff, you ain't gonna have much say-so. And much'a what you do say'll get flushed. So if you wanna thank me, talk to them boys. Talk to 'em quick! Cuz ya know whut?"

"What?"

"You can bet your bottom dollar, Demetria already has."

# NATHAN

I SHOULD DRIVE DOWN TO THE CHURCH, BUT I'M TOO UNCLEAN TO BE IN THE LORD'S house. That contradicts everything I've told people about how God will take them as they are, dirty or clean, rich or poor, educated or ignorant. But my Master expects more and better from me and I just can't face Him, not now, not yet. What a mess! And I know what Brenda must be thinking.

If Corrine's child eyes have noticed something suspicious, then the eyes of more sophisticated, conspiracy-hunting adults most certainly have. And God only knows what the gossip must be. People being people, church members probably haven't been able to resist "accidentally" letting Brenda know that something's rotten in Denmark. And they've probably done it in the cruelest of ways, a whispered comment here, a snicker there, as they wonder how long it'll be before Brenda finally sees what they see.

I still can't believe I slapped my baby. And what am I gonna tell Momma? She and Brenda are so close, they could very well have been biological mother and daughter. When Momma saw how Brenda forgave me after that mess with Syreeta all those years ago, she fell in love with her. And now this.

I should stop delaying the inevitable and go explain what happened. But before I do, I'd better call and see what kind of mood Momma's in.

I punch the speed-dial button for her number on the car phone and wait a couple of rings. Victor answers. After a second, I find my voice.

"Victor?"

"Whats'up, Nate?"

"Weren't you're supposed to be seeking refuge?"

"I was, till Momma decided to fuss me out again."

"How'd it go?"

Victor chuckles. "She thinks she won."

I smile. At least he's in good spirits. Usually, when Victor's will clashes against Momma's, it registers a seismic 10.0.

"Is Momma around?"

"Naw. She's off meetin' with her chief egghead."

"You mean her advisor."

"If you say so. Whut's she writin' about anyway? I keep forgettin'."

"She's analyzing the impact of culturally biased testing and psychological evaluation upon African American students over the last twenty-five years."

After a long pause, Victor says, "No wonder."

"No wonder what?"

"No wonder a sucka's gotta sometimes have an interpreter to talk with her."

We laugh and I say, "Have you heard from Clifford?"

"Yeah. He's right here." Victor barks at Clifford, ordering him to pick up Momma's living room phone.

"Hey, Nate. How're ya doing?" Clifford asks.

"I've had better days."

"Ditto."

"Man, I'm hungry," Victor says.

Clifford chuckles. "Victor's ability to disengage emotionally is incredible. After spending the last few minutes clubbing me over the head with his *reality* hammer he's suddenly preoccupied with his stomach."

We listen while Victor rummages through Momma's refrigerator, complaining about her food selection. "Momma ain't got nothin' in here but veggies, fruit, and yogurt."

I say, "She's trying to eat healthier."

"So am I. That's why I need some meat!"

"Well, unless you're into fish or soyburgers, you're out of luck," Clifford says.

"C'mon, man. Let's go get some *real* food."

"Where?" he asks.

"I know a little joint. It's in the hood. With black people. Remember them, Cliff?"

Clifford must be giving him that look Victor calls a grit, because Victor chuckles and says, "Don't look at me like that, man. You know you sometimes forget."

"Let's just go!" Clifford snaps, hanging up none too gently.

"How about you, Nate? You comin'?"

I almost decline, but I know I'd better eat now, while I still have an appetite. And especially since I probably won't be a welcome presence at tonight's dinner table.

"Okay. But you still haven't told me where you're going."

"You know where the Grits'n Gravy is?"

"Yeah. It's been a while but I remember them having some dynamite food."

"They still do."

"Okay, then. See ya in a bit."

"You got it," says Victor. Then we hang up.

I turn around in a vacant lot and head toward the Grits'n Gravy. That name brings back memories.

Brenda and I first went there as newlyweds. We were so young, so new in the ministry, and so broke! What a blessing it was to find a place that not only served cheap, scrumptious meals but piled the plates high. But that was a lifetime ago, before time, lust, and temptation kicked, slapped, and battered my faith to the edge of doubt.

I stop at a light and focus on composing myself before meeting my brothers. I still can't believe how angry I was with Corrine. My baby's exposing me as a clay-footed pigeon hurt in ways I'd never have imagined. But what hurts all the more is that *I'm* responsible for her losing more of her childhood innocence. I'll make it up to her. I promise.

# SHARING JEREMIAH'S CUP

# CLIFFORD

THE INSTANT VICTOR AND I STEP INTO THE GRITS'N GRAVY DINER WE'RE SMOTHERED IN the smells of frying chicken, barbecued ribs, steaming crabs, baking pies, bubbling gravy, hamhock-seasoned collard greens, and onion-sautéed potatoes. Smoke not sucked away by the overhead fans billows up from the grill, bounces off the ceiling, and hangs obstinately over the heads of the patrons.

"Well ain't this nothin'!" booms a dark, gelatinous giant, grinning at Victor.

"Big Black!" shouts Victor, his face bursting into a smile. "My *main* man!"

Big hustles from behind the counter as fast as his girth will allow and rushes toward Victor. They slam into each other, laughing, talking loud, and pounding each other's back as they hug. Then they go through a blinding series of wrist-grabbing, finger-twining, hip-bumping, elbow-knocking gestures that, I guess, means "Hello."

"Big, you still bribin' the health inspector to keep this dive open?" asks Victor, grinning.

Big jabs Victor with his meaty elbow. "An' it's gettin' downright expensive."

Victor gestures to me and says, "Big, this is my baby bro, Clifford."

I extend my hand to shake. Big grabs me and squeezes the air out of me with a powerful bear hug.

"Any baby bro of Ice's is a baby bro of mine," growls Big, slinging me side to side.

Then he frees me from his steel-trap arms and motions me and Victor toward a booth he calls "Ice's spot." It's separated from the others by Big's kitchen, so it has a little more privacy. An absolutely bald, thuggish-looking, shade-wearing man at the end of Big's counter spots Victor, balls up his fist, and taps his chest. Victor returns the salute.

"That dude looks familiar," Victor says to us. "But I can't place him."

Several people enter, and see Victor.

"Hey, Ice! Howzit hangin' baby?" one calls out to him.

"Draggin' the dirt'n diggin' a ditch. Whuts' up Two-Step?"

Two-Step shrugs and says, "Hey, man. You know the deal."

"See there!" exclaims a guy, grabbing his friend's shoulder and pointing at Victor. "There's proof that surgery can't cure ugly."

"Donovan! I *know* you ain't talkin' no smack!" shouts Victor, laughing. He flips up his middle finger and says, "Ugly this!"

A gum-popping woman dressed in bright yellow and green, her reddish-tinted hair swirled into a mountainous, platinum point, hollers to Victor. "Ice, why're you flippin' up that old bony finger? You don't *even* know how to use it."

Victor fires right back with, "Candy, all I know is that it's been two years since I got with you and that rotten fish smell still won't wash off."

Big Black and most everyone else in the diner roars with laughter as Victor and his tormentors trade insults. When the commotion finally starts to settle, Victor sits down.

# VICTOR

I SCOOT INTO THE BOOTH WITH CLIFF AND NOTICE HIM GIVIN' ME A STRANGE LOOK. "Why's you starin' at me like that?" I ax.

"Like what?"

"Like you're fixin' to kiss me."

Cliff shrugs. "I don't know. I guess I'm just proud of you."

"Proud? For whut?"

Cliff bites his lower lip, like he's got the answer but don't know how to say it. "Victor, I'm proud of the way you've bounced back after Lynnette. You've carved out a life for yourself and built a circle of friends who, from the looks of it, really care about you." He looks down and adds, "People who've cared about you far better than I have."

I reach across the table and grab his wrist. "Cliff, don't talk like that."

"Victor, all I'm trying to say is that . . ."

"Look, man. I know whutch'you sayin'. And yeah, it's been nice havin' a deep bench of friends, but I ain't never doubted that my blood was backin' me up."

Cliff stares straight and hard into my eyes. "Victor, I'm sorry. I didn't realize that . . . I mean, I had no idea of everything you . . . I'm, I'm just sorry."

"Aye, Cliff. It's cool. You couldn'ta known. Nobody could. Most folks look at divorce like racism, poverty, and crime, the kinda stuff that happens only in the other dude's neighborhood. They don't get in'trested till they wake up one mornin' and see one of 'em sittin' on their chest, grinnin'."

I start to give Cliff some more encouragin', but chop it when I see this fine, slim-hipped, bowlegged waitress comin' our way.

"What can I get ya'll?" she axes.

Cliff checks out the menu while I check out how baby doll's Grits'n Gravy T-shirt is grabbin' her knockers. She throws me a grit and I wink.

"I'll have the special," says Cliff, actin' like he ain't noticed them headlights.

"And you?" says the waitress, glarin' at me and soundin' all crabby.

"Gimme the special too," I say. "And tell Big I want the *breasts*."

She rolls her eyes, writes down our orders, and stomps off to Big. Cliff starts raggin' on me about bein' crude when he's cut off by Big.

"What!" hollers Big, lookin' at me. "Ice! I *know* you ain't *even* tryin' to order some grub, with your sorry, moochin' self. Specially since you ain't paid from the last five times."

"Hey, Big!" I shout. "They ever find the dudes stealin' all that restaurant equipment?"

Big's eyes get BIG and he fumbles with a giant cookin' fork, almost droppin' it onto the grill.

"Two Barnyard Buzzard Specials, comin' up!" says Big.

Cliff chuckles. "You sure have a way with people."

"Everybody's got buttons, man. I just make sure I know whut ones to push."

Someone walks up to our table and says, "Got room for one more?"

Me and Cliff look up and see Nate.

# NATHAN

CLIFFORD GIVES ME A WEAK SMILE AND SAYS, "HELLO."

And true to form, Victor skips the formalities and gets to the point. "Whuts'up with that long face, man? Is God havin' a party and you ain't invited?"

"No, Victor. Nothing like that. I'm just finding out what it's like to go from being a prince to a pauper in the eyes of my baby girl."

Victor grins. "It's a short trip, ain't it?"

"Not funny."

Victor stands and pinches his nostrils. "Skeeee-uuuuse me, while I leave you'n your stanky attitude to go take a piss." He steps off, grumbling to himself.

I slide into the booth and Clifford offers a weary, lopsided smile. "You look like I feel," he says.

"And how's that?"

"Like the dead atheist who finds out there's a God after all."

Before Clifford can ask what's bothering me, I quickly question him about what happened after he left the police station. Victor sits back down as he's finishing.

". . . then she said she was definitely divorcing me. And I told her I was moving out and that if she was going to go through with this to stay out of my way until it was done."

I hesitate before responding, taking care to not sound judgmental and give Victor ammunition to accuse me again of looking down my "stuck-up heavenly nose" at them. "Clifford, nothing will be resolved if you reflect hostility back at Demetria."

Clifford nods, his expression remorseful. "You're right, Nate. I even thought about that during the fight. But I was *so* angry!"

"And it's about time!" says Victor.

"No, Victor," I admonish. "Proverbs 15:1 says, 'A gentle answer turns away wrath; but harsh words stir up anger.' "

"Don't blame it on anger, man. This is all cuz'a Cliff's sayin' 'I do.' "

"That's beside the point," I counter. "Clifford and Demetria are married and that's that! What they need now is to restore the love in their precious union."

Victor looks at me like I've announced that my women's choir sings topless. "Precious union? Man, you must be buggin'. Has Cliff told you about Demetria's plans for findin' 'true love, excitement, and fun'?"

"Yeah. And so?"

"And so, do that sound to you like Demetria's wantin' to patch thangs up?"

"It sounds like a marriage needing lots of prayer."

Victor rolls his eyes and looks at Clifford. "Man, you're toast."

"You'd better be careful," I say. "God doesn't like doubt and He most certainly won't tolerate being mocked."

"I ain't doubtin' *or* mockin' God. I believe He can do whatever He wants, anytime He wants. But Cliff's vampire started suckin' nine years ago. Where's God been all that time, out in Vegas shootin' craps?"

Victor's irreverence has sunk to such new lows, I can only stare at him in disbelief.

"Stop calling my wife a vampire," says Clifford.

"Whutch'you call her?" challenges Victor. "The light of your life? The joy of your world? If you do, then you live on one screwed-up planet."

"Victor, I'm gonna pray for you," I say.

"I thought you already was."

"I'm gonna pray more!"

"Good! Cuz I need all the help I can get to win that lotto."

# CLIFFORD

THE WAITRESS FRESHENS OUR CUPS OF COFFEE, TAKES NATHAN'S ORDER, AND LEAVES. Victor takes a sip and grunts approvingly. Nathan sips his and relaxes into the seat.

"Wanna talk about it?" he asks.

I shrug. Part of me does. A lot of me doesn't. Most of me knows I should. So I say, "I'm worried about Braddie and Bear."

"How so?"

"If Demetria goes through with this . . ."

"Whutch'you talkin' 'bout 'if'?" Victor interrupts. "It's as good as done."

Nathan gives Victor an admonishing glare. "Can't you at least pretend to be a little more sensitive?"

Victor glares back. "And howzat gonna help? Nate, you better get a grip cuz this thang's for real. Demetria's kicked Cliff into her Helluva Shame amusement park and is laughin' herself silly watchin' him ride the Crush'n Flush."

"Listen, Victor," says Nate, his voice a tight rasp. "Everyone's getting hurt by this. Even Deme . . ."

Victor's palm snaps up in Nate's face like a traffic cop declaring "HALT!" "Nate, you can stuff that pile back up the bull. Demetria ain't doin' nothin' but actin' like the selfish slut she's been from the day she learned to say 'Gimme!' And since robbin' suckas is against the law, she's doin' the next best thang, *bleedin' one.*"

Nate looks at me, his eyes pleading that I'll back him up. "Clifford, surely you don't agree with him?"

My shoulders droop. "Nate, all I know is that it hurts. And I'd give anything to make it stop."

Victor sits back and smiles with grim approval. "Don't look so bummed out, Cliff. Believe me, man. Once you see how that use'ta-be-caged slut is cuttin' a fool when she's free and on the loose, you'll know you didn't get out a second too soon."

"Victor, how can you be so caustic?" Nate asks. "Aren't you even concerned that Clifford might still care about Demetria?"

Victor's smile widens. "You better b'lieve I'm concerned. Cuz it don't make no sense for him to be carin' when all Demetria wants is to fart him into her past."

"He's got a point," I say.

"C'mon, Clifford!" urges Nate. "Even now, after all that's happened, the Lord can still put things right between you and Demetria."

Victor laughs. "Nate, for once you'n me is agreein'. Cuz the way I see it, the Lord's already put thangs right between Cliff'n Clap. She's takin' herself out'a Cliff's life *and* our fambly. Now we can finally clean up the mess and forget her."

"I've got to figure out how to get custody of Braddie and Bear," I say, staring into my coffee.

Victor chuckles. "Cliff, why not just jump off the Empire State Buildin', flap your arms, and see if you'll fly?"

Nate's about to take Victor to task, *again,* when we hear someone behind us.

"Psst! Psssst! Pastor Matthews!"

We turn toward the sound of running water, clattering dishes and silverware, and see a guy wearing an apron, rubber gloves, and a hair net waving to get Nate's attention.

"Who'zat?" asks Victor.

Nate signals to the guy that he'll be right over, then turns back to me and Victor.

"That's Brother Loudon, one of my parishioners. He got laid off recently. I've been trying to get him into a program for some retraining and career development, but he's scared to death of computers."

"That's gonna make his transition tough," I say.

"You got that right," Victor agrees. "Even bus-drivin' suckas like me has gotta know about computers."

Nate nods. "Yeah. Computers are an occupational reality these days." He slides out of the booth and says, "I'll be right back. I just wanna check and see how Brother Loudon's getting along."

"We'll be here," says Victor. "I ain't goin' nowhere, and Cliff ain't got nowhere to go."

Nate looks at Victor, shakes his head, and says, "You're impossible."

# VICTOR

NATE AIN'T BEEN GONE A HOT MINUTE WHEN THE BALD, SHADE-WEARIN' DUDE AT THE counter gets up, throws some money down for his meal, and diddy-bops our way. He takes a toothpick, flicks somethin' from between his teeth, and gets close enough for me to finally recognize him.

I call out his name right as he's callin' mine.

"Cruiser!"

"Ice!"

I get up and we give each other the soul brother's handshake and a hug.

"I thought they was tryin' to get criminals off the streets," I say, laughin' and slappin' Cruiser's back.

"They gotta catch 'em first."

"Cruiser, it's good seein' you, thug. How long has it been?"

"Couple'a years at least. Last I saw you, you was packed up and beatin' feet for Cleveland."

I sit back down and tell Cruiser to grab hisself some butt-leather. He slides in next to Cliff so we can talk face to face. Cliff's lookin' all cockeyed, not even tryin' to hide that he's starin' at Cruiser's shinin' bald head.

"Why's you lookin' at my head like dat?" axes Cruiser.

"Don't pay him no mind," I say. "He just ain't never seen no eight ball that could talk."

We laugh, slap five, and I jerk my thumb at Cliff. "Cruise, this is my baby bro, Cliff. Cliff, this is Cruiser."

"Pleased to meet you," says Cliff, extendin' his hand.

Cruiser latches onto it and goes through the first few eye-blurrin' motions of the newest version of the soul brother's handshake, whizzin' around Cliff's stiff, unmovin' fingers. When he sees that Cliff don't know whuts'up, he shakes his head and slaps his hand away.

I check out the sweet watch on Cruiser's wrist and say, "Ain't that a Rolex?"

Cruiser nods, smilin' like the cat who ate the canary *and* the goldfish. "Nice, ain't it? It's a gift from Rufus Calloway."

Gift my foot! With the kind of fanatic Rufus is (or was) about his jewelry, I *know* he didn't just give it up. Specially not no Rolex watch!

"How bruised up was he when he 'gave' it you?" I ax.

Cruiser grins. "C'mon, Ice. You know dat after all'a them changes Rufus took me through, he had more'n just a reg'lar whoopin' comin'. Besides, you know I'm into collections. Rufus owed. I collected. End of story."

Cruiser glances at Cliff, sittin' there with his mouth hangin' open and eyes bugged out. "Say, Ice. Is it safe talkin' in front'a Mr. Suburbs?"

"Yeah, man. He's cool. Ain't that right, Cliff?"

Cliff nods so fast, it don't even look like his head moves.

Cruiser checks him out for a few seconds, says, "Cool," then looks back at me. "So Ice, whutch'you doin' back here? Are you just visitin', or hidin' out after scammin' one'a them Cleveland babes?"

"Neither, clown. I'm here to see my daughter and help out my baby bro. His skeezin' wife's takin' him through that divorce grind."

"Victor, I'd really prefer not having my business put in the streets," says Cliff.

I wave him off. "Man, pretty soon your business is gonna be what they call public record. All a sucka'll have to do if they wanna see your dirt is go downtown and ax."

"Dat's a low blow," says Cruiser.

"It's a for-real blow. Specially since she's rippin'-off his sons and gonna make him pay her for doin' it."

Cruiser snaps his toothpick in half and his eyes get real dark and mean. Cuz I know he's thinkin' about how his old lady disappeared with his boy when she discovered the real deal about his "business."

Cruiser looks at Cliff and speaks like his blood just went to slow boil. "Look, man. Doin' women ain't my thang, but me'n Ice go way back. If you want your boys, I can convince dat ho to see thangs your way."

Cliff blinks, licks his lips, and chugs some'a his water, his hand tremblin' so bad some of it sloshes out the glass.

"Cruise, why's you tryin' to get my baby bro jacked up with the poleases?" I ax, chucklin' and hopin' it'll lighten thangs up and put Cruiser's focus back on me.

Cuz it's one thang for Cruiser to blow this kinda smoke my way. But Cliff! He ain't got no heart for thuggin'. And I ain't got no heart to let him even pretend that he wants to deal with that kinda trouble.

I start to tell Cruise that it's a no-go when Cliff says, "Nah, no thanks. I, I'll work it through the system."

Cruiser looks at me like someone just wired his nuts to an electric generator. "Is he serious, man? He's gonna depend on dat blindfolded babe carryin' the sword and scales down at the courthouse?"

I shrug. "I guess so, man."

Cruise looks at Cliff real serious for a long, long time. Then he busts out laughin'. He slides out the booth, slaps me five, and says, "Ice, good seein' you, bro."

He tears off a piece of napkin, writes his pager number on it, and jams it in Cliff's shirt pocket.

"Call when you want some *real* justus," he says. And then he steps off.

# NATHAN

BROTHER LOUDON TEARS OFF HIS GLOVES AND APRON AND WE HUG.

"My God, Pastor," he says. "It's good seein' you."

"It's good seeing you too, Walt."

Brother Loudon's face clouds with shame. "I ain't meant for you to catch me bustin' suds for a livin'."

"C'mon now, Walt. The Lord values all labor. Just so long as it's honest and done to His glory."

He nods in agreement with the concept, but I know he wishes it were working itself out in someone else's life.

"Have you given any more thought to my suggestion about the community college?" I ask.

"Yeah, Pastor. I've been thinking about it a lot. That's why I called you over." He lowers his eyes. "I was wonderin' if you wouldn't mind goin' down there with me next week and help me sign up for some'a them classes."

I smile and give Brother Loudon's shoulder an approving squeeze. "You'd better believe I will. Just let me know what day and time."

Thank God for this moment of success. I'm humbled and grateful to know that, even with all the disgrace I've brought upon myself over this mess with Beverly, the Lord's still using me to accomplish His work.

"Thanks, Pastor," says Walt. "I appreciate it."

"It's my pleasure. And you'll see, everything'll work out just fine."

Brother Loudon scowls and snorts. "I wanna believe you, Pastor. But I wouldn't be in this fix if they hadn't done me wrong." He presses his lips together, doing his best to maintain control. "It ain't right how they done me, Pastor. I was a supervisor. Twenty-four years' service. Never missed a day. Came up from the bottom doin' some'a every kinda job. Now look at me."

"Listen to me," I say, speaking firmly. "The Lord has heard your prayers and knows of your faith. Especially by your being here."

"Huh?"

"Walt, the evil one came and took your job. But you didn't give up. You went out and found this job and are still looking for one better, believing the Lord will provide. When we take action upon the Lord's promises, He honors our faith with blessings abundant, pressed down, and running over."

Brother Loudon smiles and my heart lifts as I suddenly realize what God just did. In using me to encourage Brother Loudon, he's also encouraged *me*!

"That's bad news sittin' at your table," says Brother Loudon, staring past me and out into the dining area.

The warm Christian love filling his eyes just a moment ago has been replaced with the steel, concrete, and cold of Pittsburgh's streets.

I look to see what he's glaring at, and he's right. It *is* bad news, and its name is Cruiser Allen. He's standing up and slapping five with Victor while Clifford sits there wide-eyed and mouth agape.

"Excuse me, Walt," I say. "I've gotta get back over there. Those are my brothers and I can't have bad news getting that close to them."

# CLIFFORD

AS I WATCH CRUISER LEAVE I'M STILL TRYING TO RECOVER FROM THE SHOCK OF WHAT I'VE just heard. And Victor! I knew he'd hung around some shady characters, but this Cruiser is a bona fide thug.

Some guy, laughing and talking with a woman as they enter the diner, bumps into Cruiser. He stares the two of them down into quivering mounds of flesh, glances around to make sure people are watching, then leaves.

"He's a real street warrior," observes Victor, almost glowing.

"More like street trash, if you ask me."

Victor scowls. "Ain't nobody axin' you."

Nathan slides into the booth and folds his arms tight across his chest as his eyes drill into me and Victor, mostly Victor. "Why were you guys talking to Cruiser Allen just now?"

Victor's jaw tightens. "Who wants to know?"

"*I* want to know!"

"And who're you, the friend patrol? Besides, how does a goody-goody like you know Cruiser?"

"I grew up in this neighborhood too, remember? And I'm out there in the trenches every day. Word gets around."

"Well then, all'a that word shoulda told you that Cruise ain't doin' nothin' to get slammed by the po-leases. Crooked as he is, he knows bein' free is better than bein' caged."

"Victor, I'm serious!"

"So am I!"

Some people at the counter look over at us, shrug, then keep eating. Victor leans toward Nathan and speaks in a low growl.

"Look, Nate. I ain't in the mood. So don't start no mess and there won't *be* no mess."

Nate looks at me, his expression easing. "Clifford, what's going on?"

"It was nothing," I say, cutting my eyes away. "He was, uh, just giving some advice on custody."

"Custody! What could he possibly know about that?"

"Whutch'you know about it?" asks Victor.

"I know that Braddie and Bear need their mother and father." Then he looks at me, inhales, and says, "And Clifford, you know that kids that young are more dependent on their mother."

*That* pisses me off. "What're you saying, Nate? That you're on Demetria's side?"

"It's not about taking sides, Clifford. It's about what's best for Braddie and Bear."

I pull out the piece of napkin that Cruiser jammed into my shirt pocket. "I just might use this after all."

"What's that?" Nate asks.

"Another solution if I can't get advice any better than yours."

Victor chuckles. "And speakin' of gettin' advice, Cliff, I've connected you up to see a friend of mine down at PPR."

"At what?"

"PPR. Protectin' Parents' Rights."

"I've never heard of those people. What is it they do? And why didn't you check with me first?"

"Man, are you serious? It's called Protectin' Parents' Rights. Whutch'you think they do?"

"Victor, if you won't tell me, forget it! I'm not going to some jilted-lovers club to be fed a bunch'a crap about my marriage not surviving."

Victor grimaces like he's fighting to keep from boxing my ears. "Cliff, why can't you just take my word for it?"

"No info, no go!"

Victor throws up his hands in a quick gesture of surrender. "All right, man. You got it. I hooked up with PPR when I was goin' through my thang with Lynnette. They gave me the bottom-line, brass-knuckle details of what to do in court, what to expect from a custody fight, what to do if Lynnette stiffed my visitation, schooled me up on child support and mostly warned me that life was about to get real ugly."

"A lawyer'll give that same information."

"Al will give it for free."

"Free!"

"That's right, man. Free."

I look at Nate. He shrugs. Then I say, "So this person, Arnold . . ."

"Al! The director!"

"Okay! Okay! Al's a lawyer?"

"Yeah. But not one'a them pay-me-till-ya-make-me kind. Al's on our side, someone just like us who the system snatched, pissed on, then pissed off!"

"But, how can this Al be unbiased when . . ."

"Who says the rest of 'em ain't got some biasin'? Besides, it ain't meant to turn you into Perry Mason. Just school you up so you don't lose too badly."

"Lose?"

"Yeah, man. *Lose!* It ain't gonna turn out no other way."

"Why?"

"Cliff, c'mon! Soon, and *very* soon, you's gonna get hauled into domestic court where Demetria and her helpers is gonna give you a group lesson in testicle surgery. I'm tellin' ya, man! It's the only place I know where a sucka can get de-balled, mugged, and gang-banged all in the same five minutes."

"Victor, don't start that again. I've told you before, this is America . . ."

"The land of black church burnin's and brothas gettin dragged to death down country roads."

"There are laws . . ."

"That'll trickbag you every time Demetria hauls you back to court, blamin' you cuz her life ain't goin' right and wantin' more money so it can."

"And a justice system . . ."

"Where everybody in it'll tell ya, it's for *Just Us*!"

"How can you be so negative?"

"How can you be so stupid? Man, you're about to get fingered by a system that can't lock away suckas they *know* are criminals while at the same time is givin' life sentences to chumps owin' parkin' fines. But you think when you go to court, they gonna be in a good mood, and wanna hear your side, and you think they'll at least consider lettin' you have your boys, specially since Demetria's the one bustin' up ya'lls fambly. Talkin' with Al might help you keep at least one'a your nuts."

"It sounds like you have a lot of respect for Al," says Nate.

"I do!"

Victor looks hard back at me. "But that's not why I need for you to get with Al."

"Need?"

"Yeah, Cliff. Need."

Victor folds his hands, places his elbows on the table, and looks at me with withering intensity. "Cliff, you won't listen to me cuz you think I ain't smart. But Al's got some degrees like you. And even though you gonna hear the same stuff, I know you'll act'chally listen if it comes from someone whose brains you respect."

I look down and say, "What time is the appointment?"

# VICTOR

BIG BLACK *FINALLY* BRINGS OUR FOOD HISSELF, HANGIN' AROUND LONG ENOUGH FOR him'n me to sling some more insults before he trudges back to work.

While we're eatin', I tell Nate and Cliff about some'a them crazies ridin' my bus, makin' 'em laugh so hard, they sometimes can't even swallow. The only time thangs get kinda serious is when I mention Edie. But I move on to somethin' else before they start axin' questions about how we met, if it's serious, and where it's goin'.

And I'm all of a sudden wonderin' when I got jammed between this rock and a hard place. Cuz I'm missin' Edie and Karenna more than I thought, and hadn't appreciated how much I'd gotten used to seein' 'em on the bus every mornin'. And since me and Edie's finally started hangin' out, doin' a movie here'n there, some cheap restaurant action, and that free jazz festival, she knows I got a thang for her. And it feels good, *real good.* But I'm sometimes wonderin' if I oughta check myself before I start runnin' off at the mouth, talkin' about "I love you." Cuz hangin' out is one thang. Gettin' my heart carjacked is somethin' totally different.

When we go to pay for our meal, Nate and Cliff pay off the tab I owe Big. Then we head out to the parkin' lot, hug, and say 'bye.

"Victor, please be careful," says Nate.

"Nate, don'tcha think I got better thangs to do then gettin' hassled by the po-leases?"

"I only mention it out of brotherly love and concern for you."

I steal a quick look at Cliff, who's smirkin' and rollin' his eyes. Then I look at Nate and say, "Ya know, for a preacher, you's full of it."

Me'n Cliff laugh while Nate just kinda smiles. I get in my econo-cart and unlock the passenger door for Cliff. Nate walks around over to Cliff's side and leans on the car while Cliff rolls down the window.

"Clifford, will you be all right?"

"Yeah, Nate. I'll be fine. Victor's gonna drop me off at Momma's for the night."

"What about tomorrow?"

Cliff sits silent for a long time, starin' blank into space. He shakes his head, slouches into the seat, and groans. It don't take no genius to figure out that he ain't too excited about meetin' up with his tomorrows.

"I guess I'll worry about that when it gets here," he says.

"Well, you're welcome to stay at my house. Just let me check with Brenda and make sure she doesn't have other plans."

Nate sounds kinda funny when he mentions axin' Brenda about Cliff stayin' over, like he ain't too sure *he* can stay hisself. I've had enough babes throw me out to know when a sucka's gettin' curbed. But what am I thinkin'? This is Goody Two-shoes Nate. Even if him and Brenda had some words, they'll just meet each other at the foot of the Cross like he's always braggin', and everythang'll be back to huggy-kissy.

"I appreciate it, Nate," says Cliff. He looks at me for a few seconds, then at Nate. "And thanks you guys, for . . ."

"Aw, man. Just shut up," I say, startin' the car. "You's blood. Where else was we gonna be?"

"Amen to that," Nate agrees.

We holler 'bye to Nate one last time and get gone. I get on the highway, headin' for Momma's, when Cliff says, "We need to make a detour."

"A detour? Where?"

"Get off at the next exit."

"Where are we goin'?"

"Victor, *will you just do it!*"

I take the exit, pull off to the shoulder, and park. "Cliff, we ain't goin' nowhere till you tell me whuts'up."

Cliff looks straight into my eyes. "I want to check on Demetria."

I look around and get pissed. "Man, if you wanted to do that, why's you makin' me take the long way?"

Cliff grits his teeth and answers with a low, slow rumble. "We're not going to Penn Hills Commons, Victor. I want to see if Demetria's at Nolan's house."

I check out Cliff's face, feelin' proud that the sucka's finally gettin' some sense. Cuz from the way he's described the "friendship" between Demetria and that Nolan clown, that sucka's *gots'ta* be bangin' that booty.

I jet into traffic and follow Cliff's directions, makin' sure I remember every turn, street sign, light, and buildin'. After the way punk Nolan did all that wolfin' down at Demetria's job today, I *need* to know where he lives.

"Turn here," says Cliff.

I turn down Meadow Wood Lane and cruise smooth'n slow till Cliff signals me to go slower. I check out the house where he's lookin', makin' double sure I get the number, and anythang else that'll help on a future visit.

Cliff sits back and sighs. "Okay. You can drop me off at Momma's now."

"Demetria ain't there?"

Cliff shakes his head. "No. I didn't see her car."

"That don't mean nothin'. They coulda used *his* car."

"Please, Victor. I've seen all I need to see. Just drop me off at Momma's."

"C'mon, man. Whut if she's inside? We oughta go back there and . . ."

"NO!" shouts Cliff. "Will-you-please-just-take-me-to-Momma's!"

Even in the dim light, I can see that Cliff's eyes is glistenin'. "Okay, Cliff. You got it. We'll get on to Momma's and call it a day."

ON THE WAY OVER TO MOMMA'S, I DECIDE IT'S TOO EARLY FOR ME TO TURN IN. SO I DROP Cliff off and head on down to one'a my old hangout spots, The Party House. It's a hole-in-the-wall and ain't got the best music or liquor, but I ain't *never* walked out'a there without some booty for the evenin'. I check my wallet to make sure I got some rubbers, see I do, and know I'm set.

Yeah. I know Nate and Cliff is always wonderin' about my fly-by-night relationships. But they don't understand. It don't bother me if a babe skies after two or three months. If they're hangin' around longer than that, they're prob'ly pissin' me off anyway. And the fun part is knowin' I can't be dragged in front'a some judge who'll grab my nuts and squeeze for five or ten years. It's like I was tellin' Brantley. He ain't the only one who's found out that bein' in domestic court is like pickin' up soap in the prison shower. And that's why I'm worried about Cliff.

That egghead sucka's so deep into Demetria, he ain't got sense enough to get rescued. I almost feel guilty about takin' him down to PPR, where Al's gonna tell him all the funky ways he's gonna get screwed. But Cliff's gotta get his eyes opened so he can be ready for when that judge's gavel caves in his skull.

And speakin' of skulls gettin' caved in, I'd better get myself together for when I go see Jewel. Just once I wish I could visit her without havin' to deal with Lynnette. But there ain't no way of gettin' around her, so I might as well grease my throat for all the crap I'ma have'ta swallow.

I pull up in front'a The Party House, park, and sit. The Dipper's hollerin' at me, complainin' about bein' hungry, and axin' whut I'm waitin' for. And it ain't like I couldn't use some booty, specially after gettin' shafted by Justine and Simone. I'd *really* like to get with Edie, but she ain't even let me squeezed a boob and I'm still hangin' with her. Bump this! Just cuz Edie's actin' like a nun don't mean I gotta convert. So I open my door, step out, then stop.

Just before I left, Edie said, "Karenna and I are going to miss you."

Then she hugged and kissed me in a way lettin' me know that, even though we ain't done the nasty, she's as good as mine. And she's prob'ly feelin' the same about me.

I see a flash of Edie cryin', Karenna axin' her whut's wrong, and me tryin' to babble my way back into their world. I pull my foot back inside, close the door, and start the car. The Dipper's cussin' me out, axin' if I ain't losin my grip. I don't know if I am or ain't. But whut's *really* got me confused is why I don't mind.

# NATHAN

WHEN I GET HOME, I SIT IN THE CAR AND TAKE A MOMENT TO COMPOSE MYSELF AND pray, asking the Lord to strengthen Clifford for his PPR meeting tomorrow. I also offer up a prayer for Victor's safety through the evening. He'll need it, especially if he follows his usual pattern and disappears into Pittsburgh for a night of carousing. And I pray for myself, asking God to help me obey the Holy Spirit who lives in me so that my lust might be chained and slain.

I get out of the car and go inside, tiptoeing the few mile-long steps down the hallway to my bedroom door.

"Brenda?" I say softly.

"What is it, Nathan?"

"Can I come in?"

"The door's unlocked."

I go in and sit on the edge of the bed beside her. The room's dark, except for the green glow of the digital clock radio. Brenda changes her position so that her back is to me.

I reach for her shoulder, but she says, "*Don't* touch me!"

I withdraw my hand. "Brenda, it's not true, sweetheart."

Brenda turns on the nightstand lamp, sits up, and looks me straight in the eye. "What's 'not true,' Nathan?"

"Whatever you're thinking about me and Beverly Dawkins."

"Everyone seems to be thinking something, including our teenage daughter."

"Brenda, what do you want from me? Tell me what you want me to do and I'll do it."

Brenda takes my face into her hands, pulls me toward her till we're nose to nose, and whispers emphatically. "Nathan, your home is falling apart. You're getting too close to a woman who's using her personal crisis to lure you in. And if you're not careful, your ministry's going to suffer. You know what to do. The only question is, will you, before it's too late?"

"Brenda, sweetheart, why can't you trust my judgment on this? The only way something can occur is if I allow it, and that's *not* gonna happen."

Brenda sits back against the headboard, crosses her arms, and raises a skeptical eyebrow. "Do you mean that you want me to trust your judgment the same way you trust Corrine's? You want me to ignore the potential danger in your relationship with Beverly the same way Corrine ignores the potential danger with Tyrone Ballard?"

"You're comparing apples to oranges. The two situations are completely different."

"How, Nathan? You're both playing with fire. You're both going against the will of your father. You're both letting it cause turmoil in your home. And you're both letting these infatuations ruin relationships with people who truly love you." A tear rolls down along the smooth curve of her cheek.

"Brenda, why is it so hard for you to believe that I love only you?"

"I know that! What I want to know is . . . can I trust you?"

My throat tightens and I feel naked and transparent. For a miserably long second I want to tell Brenda everything and rid myself of this horrible guilt.

But rather than confess, I say, "What kind of question is that?"

"One I need you to answer."

"Honestly, sweetheart. After all the years we've been to . . ."

She turns off the light and scoots to the other side of the bed.

"Brenda, please believe me. I do love you."

"Good night, Nathan."

# JUST US!

# CLIFFORD

MOMMA'S GONE BY THE TIME I GET UP. I GO TO FIX MYSELF SOME BREAKFAST AND SEE A note from her stuck to the refrigerator.

*Clifford, stay again tonight, or for as long as you need. I love you, Momma.*

Momma's the greatest. Her note saves me the embarrassment of having to ask about today's arrangements. But who am I kidding? I'm going to be here for a while. At least until I find someplace to live, or until Demetria and I resolve this mess.

I've got to find some way, *any* way, of pulling us back from the brink. There can be no more confrontations like yesterday's. Like Nate and Momma have said, I've got to try and love Demetria through this process, no matter how unlovable she is at the moment. I want to believe that their positive perspectives will triumph, but I'm not blind to the possibility that Victor's viewpoint will prevail.

I turn on National Public Radio while fixing some coffee, and feel strangely guilty about being glad that I don't have to endure the gibberish spouted from Demetria's preferred station. The phone rings and I answer.

"Cliff, don't forget about PPR," Victor says.

"And good morning to you."

"Man, don't start sweatin' me this early."

Victor's right. There's no point trying to reverse a habit stream that's been flowing this long, so I get with his program.

"What time?" I ask.

"Around three. And be ready! Al's got lots to do and don't like to be kept waitin'."

"Okay, okay. I'll be there."

"Cool. See ya then."

"Victor, wait! Are you okay? Where'd you stay last night?"

"I camped out over at Big's. We had us a serious throw-down, specially when some of the fellas stopped by and we got to talkin' about old times, our best scams, and whatnot."

"I'm glad you had a good time."

I'm also surprised that Victor didn't pull his usual one-night-stand routine, something he'd most certainly be crowing about. I wonder if it has anything to do with this Edie he mentioned briefly yesterday. Not likely. Some things may change, but Victor will never restrict himself to one woman, missing out on "all'a that strange booty."

We talk a little longer and I hang up, start to get back to breakfast, then remember: I'm supposed to take Braddie and the Bear kite flying this morning. I look at the phone for a long time, deciding whether or not to call.

If Demetria answers, chances are good that we'll have words, and I simply don't need the headache. She might also refuse to let the boys go with me, just out of spite. That'd set me off. Then again, I'm not exactly in the mood to go running through Wyandotte Regional Park, dragging a string and fluttering paper behind me. But I promised.

I pick up the phone and dial, almost in slow motion. I sigh with relief when Bear answers.

"Hi, Dada!"

"Hey, Bear! How's my favorite cub?"

"Okay. Are we like Ryan Roberts now, Dada?"

"Huh? What happened to Ryan?"

"His mom and dad don't live together anymore. And they hate each other. Are we like them?"

My throat couldn't be more choked if a basketball had been stuffed into it.

I swallow and say, "Er, no, Bear. We're not like Ryan. Mommy and I are gonna work things out. *I promise!*"

In the background Demetria says, "Bear! Who's on the phone?"

"It's Dada!"

Demetria snatches another phone from its cradle. "Hang up, Bear," she commands.

"Okay. 'Bye, Dada. Don't forget about the kites."

Bear hangs up and Demetria says, "What do you want, Clifford?"

"Look, Demetria. I don't want to argue. I was just calling the boys to let them know what time I'd come by and get them to fly those kites."

"If I take out a restraining order on you, there'll be no point in your coming by."

The basketball jamming my throat shape-shifts into a craggy boulder. "Restraining order!" I gasp. "But . . . what for?"

"What do you mean, 'what for?' After yesterday, what do you expect?"

I'm filling with so much rage that it feels as though my scalp will blow off. But when I speak, I make sure that my voice is calm, low, and slow.

"Demetria, you know that yesterday was about as abnormal a day as I've ever had. I'm asking you respectfully to not keep my sons from me."

"Is there an 'or else' with that?"

I close my eyes tight and inhale deep. "Demetria, what're you talking about now?"

"Don't play ignorant, Clifford. Yesterday you told me to leave your family alone 'or else.' "

"Demetria, all I meant was that this shouldn't involve anyone else but you and me. This is our—"

"You need to explain that to Victor!"

This is going far afield and I need to refocus. "Demetria, you don't need a restraining order. All I'm asking is for you to not keep my sons from me." There's a long, anxious pause and I say, "Please!"

Demetria's hard breathing softens. "All right, Clifford. But here's my 'or else.' You told me to stay out of your way until this was done. Fine! But I want the same from you."

I sit down and massage my forehead. "Fair enough, Demetria."

After another long pause she says, "Well . . . all right, then. But I'm serious."

"I know, Demetria. I know."

We work out a time for me to come get the boys, then we hang up. And it hits me. Instead of simply calling out to my sons and telling them "Let's go," I'm going to have to go pick them up, like some neighbor taking them on an outing. Another thought hits. If Demetria and I don't "fix us," I'll spend the rest of Braddie and Bear's childhood picking them up rather than getting them ready. And I'll miss all those precious moments I'd once casually presumed would be there for the taking at my leisure.

I sit back and stare at the ceiling. Nate's voice whispers, *If you look to I Am during this time of trouble, He'll guide, comfort, and heal you.*

I try to fix my lips to pray, but all I can mutter is a pathetic "God, please."

BRADDIE AND BEAR MEET ME AT THE FRONT DOOR WITH THEIR KITES IN HAND. I KNEEL down and hug them tight.

"I missed you guys so much," I say, kissing their cheeks and necks.

"Why'd you stay with Grandy?" asks Braddie. "Is it because you made Mommy cry?"

I swallow the lump in my throat. "Mommy and Dada made each other cry."

I scan the living room and part of the kitchen. "Where's your mother?"

"In her room," answers Bear. "She told us to wait here for you so you wouldn't have to come in."

My knees weaken and I almost stagger into the wall.

"Dada, did you break that mirror yesterday?" Braddie asks.

I want to tell Braddie and a closely listening Bear that, no, I didn't do it. But they're too well informed to buy that fabrication, so I say, "Yes, Braddie. I broke it. But it was an accident."

"That mirror's like us," says Bear. "Broken."

I glance at their kites. "Well, let's go see if we can *fix us*."

The boys race to the car and get in. On the way to the park I steer the conversation to *anything* other than the continued decline of our family. I finally relax when we turn in to the park, and the boys get excited about flying their kites.

I scan the horizon, puzzled at the sudden appearance of clouds. I should turn back. But I don't know when I'll get another chance, or have the desire again to do this. Besides, what's there to lose? If there's any truth to what Nathan said about I Am "fixing" things, I might as well give it a shot. It certainly can't be any worse (or more ridiculous) than anything else I've tried.

I park and the boys get out and hustle to where they remember flying the kites the last day of Vacation Bible School.

"C'mon, Dada," urges Bear. "We've gotta fly one before it rains."

Braddie's bursting with excitement. He runs in circles off into the field, holding his arms outstretched like an airplane. Bear casts a wary eye at the sky, but still looks determined. I follow his gaze and hurry as bowling pins of thunder softly clatter above. I grab the kite labeled "Cloudskipper" and move into position. There probably won't be time enough to fly it and the "Windrider," so we'll do them both next time.

I lay Cloudskipper on the ground, play out some string, and start running. Wind gusts snatch it up and whip it from side to side with rough, uneven jerks. I run faster and a raindrop splashes onto my face.

"Not yet," I growl. "Not yet!"

The kite lifts higher, still jinking roughly. I circle around toward Braddie and Bear and yell above the thunder. "Get in the car!"

The boys clamber into the car as another raindrop hits my face. I start to loop back around in the opposite direction when Braddie and Bear jump out of the car and chase after me.

"Run faster!" screams Braddie. "Dada! You've gotta run faster to I Am!"

I look over my shoulder. "What! Why?"

I check to make sure I'm not about to run into anything, then look back again. Braddie and Bear are still chasing after me.

"Run faster!" they yell. "You've gotta run faster to I Am!"

This is crazy! And I know I'm a bad parent for indulging this child's fantasy when I should stop, tear this kite to shreds, and put an end to all this "I Am" foolishness. But a voice in my heart says, *I need you to believe in Me!*

My mind argues back with, "Will you please be rational?"

*Place your trust in Me and I shall give you rest.*

"If I need rest, I'll take a nap."

*Trust in Me with all your heart and lean not unto your own understanding.*

"You ask so much from one who's never seen You."

*Blessed are those who have not seen Me and yet believed.*

"But how can I see you? How can I find you?"

*You shall seek Me, and you shall find Me, when you search for Me with all your heart.*

I run faster. The kite snaps and dips, climbs and dives, then circles in tight and wide loops. Thunder drowns out the boys' voices as they chase behind. The boiling clouds get darker as the kite swoops low and levels out.

"Higher!" I scream. "I need you to go higher!"

A gusting fist of wind fills the kite's pockets and tugs it high into the air. And I run faster. Because if it takes all morning, afternoon, and night; if it takes miles of running; if it means being yanked into the clouds, I *will* move I Am to work a miracle and *FIX US*!

Nate's voice rides the wind rushing past my ears: *So Jacob wrestled with a man until the breaking of day. . . . then the man said, "let me go, for the day breaketh." But Jacob replied, "I will not let thee go except thou bless me."*

The kite swings up, swoops to the left in an arcing loop, and flattens out. Then an avenging fist of wind smashes it to the ground, crushing its fragile wooden frame, right as I slip and fall to my hands and knees. Braddie and Bear watch me in grim silence. Then the sky opens and pounds us into the earth beneath driving sheets of rain.

# VICTOR

CRUISIN' AROUND THIS SIDE OF PITTSBURGH IS THE *LAST* THANG I WANNA BE DOIN', specially when it's rainin' cats'n dogs. But baby girl Jewel's here, so I'm stuck. Lynnette's moved and I gotta drive slow to make sure I don't miss the address. When I pull up in front I recognize the place.

I use'ta drive past these town houses and wonder if I'd ever have enough cash to get one. That's part of why I was workin' a second job as mall security, and tryin' to get my janitorial thang goin' on the side. If thangs had started cookin', we'da had it made. But since the only thang that got cooked was *me*, Lynnette's got it made.

I park and take a few minutes to get myself together. I'm here to celebrate my baby girl's birthday, so, *no matter whut,* I gotta stay cool.

I go up to the door and knock a couple'a times, tellin' myself over'n over, "Stay cool, Ice. Just go with the flow and stay cool."

Ain't nobody answerin', so I pound lightly a few times, until I hear some dude hollerin' from inside. "Hold on! I'm comin'."

I'll bet he is. I knock again, harder and faster, just to piss off whoever it might be.

"Who is it?"

"Ice."

"Who?"

"Ice!"

"I don't know no Ice."

"You ain't s'posed to know me. I'm Jewel's daddy."

The inner door whips open and Lynnette's standin' there behind the storm door with the dude off to the side. He ain't the greasyhead she rolled me for. He looks like an overgrown poodle.

"Where's my baby?"

Lynnette sticks out her jaw and double-checks the storm door's lock. "She's in Atlanta with my brother and his wife."

"*WHUT?* Is you out'a your mind? You knew I was comin' early for her birthday."

"I called and left you a message."

"You ain't done no such thang!"

"Hey!" hollers the dude. "Don't be hollerin' at my woman!"

Lynnette shushes him. "Let me handle this, Arvin."

Arvin? His momma musta named him after some kinda athlete's foot.

"Lynnette, this ain't right," I say.

She crosses her arms and gives me one'a them whutch'you-gonna-do-about-it? smiles.

"Look! It ain't my fault you don't listen to your messages. Renée and Derek asked if they could take Jewel on vacation to visit our relatives in Atlanta. They were in a hurry to leave, so I called and told you. Don't blame me if you're too sorry to listen to your machine."

I punch the brick wall beside the door. "You a lie, Lynnette! I listened to all my messages before leavin' Cleveland. There wasn't nothin' from you."

"Ice, don't be callin' me a liar. I left the message. If you didn't get it, too bad!"

It feels like fire's blastin' from my ears. "You disgustin' tramp! If my baby didn't need a momma, even one like you, I'd . . ."

"All right!" Arvin shouts. "That's enough! I want you out'a here!"

I must give him one'a my worsest looks, cuz he jumps behind Lynnette.

"Lynnette! I swear, I'ma make sure I live long enough to piss on your grave!"

"This conversation is over!" says Lynnette. "Now leave before I call the po-lease."

She slams the door and I know I must look stupid, standin' here grittin' at the wall.

"He's still there!" shouts Arvin, peekin' out from behind the curtains.

I can't afford no more hassles with the Pittsburgh PD, so I hustle back to my car. It ain't no thang, cuz I'll see Jewel later. Then I see my punked-out wet eyes starin' at me from the rearview mirror and know it's a big thang, cuz I *really* wanted to see my baby.

I STOP AT THE LIGHT, RIGHT ACROSS FROM HALLIBURTON'S GUNS & AMMO. I BETCHA Lynnette wouldn'ta been givin' me no grief if I'da had her starin' down the business end of a nine millimeter. But wait! Why smoke her with hardware that can be traced? I might as well paint a LOOK PO-LEASES! I DID IT! sign on my chest. I'll swing down to The Market eight or nine blocks away at Twelfth and Brookside. The brothas down there sell everythang from zip guns to grenade launchers. And they don't ax no questions. The light turns green and I stomp on the gas.

A few minutes later, I'm still a few blocks from The Market when I park at one'a them gas station pay phones that's low enough to reach from the car. I'd love to see Lynnette's face, lookin' into mine and not seein' no mercy. I'd love for her to read my eyes, knowin' that whutever happens to her next, it'll be long, painful, and ugly. I'd love for her to smell my mad, messin' her panties once she realizes there ain't no way out. And just before blowin' her head off, I'd make her beg, just like I begged that judge.

But as mad and bad as I wanna be, I ain't got the balls. And Lynnette ain't worth it. If I spend the rest'a my life rottin' away in solitary it's gotta be for somethin' better'n her.

I reach out my car window, grab the phone, and dial Edie's number, wonderin' if I oughta be callin' her and knowin' there ain't nobody but *her* to call.

"Hello?"

This was a mistake. Whut am I s'posed to say to Edie? Whut'll she think of me whinin' about not seein' my baby girl? Even if she don't mind, whut can she do? And why should I school her up, givin' her somethin' to screw me with the day she ups and decides to leave? I know she will, cuz they all do and then I'll have'ta . . .

"Victor?"

"Yeah, Edie. How'd you know it was me?"

"I don't know. I just . . . did."

We're quiet for a few seconds till Edie says, "Victor, what's wrong?"

"It ain't no thang, Edie. Everythang's cool. I'll check you later."

Edie talks firm but real slow, sayin', "Victor, tell me what's wrong."

I flip the rearview mirror up so I can't see myself. "Talk to me, Edie. Say anythang. But just talk."

Edie don't gimme no flack but just starts talkin' about Karenna. And she keeps talkin', till I can't feel no more pain.

# NATHAN

A SHARP CLAP OF THUNDER EXPLODES ACROSS THE SKY RIGHT AS MY OFFICE PHONE rings, both of them snatching me out of my brooding. I let the call roll over to Helen's line and I sink back into my bad mood.

What am I gonna do? Brenda and Corrine are hardly speaking to me. And Nate Junior's taken to hibernating in his room. The intercom buzzes, pulling me again from my dark preoccupation.

I punch the intercom button and try not to snap when I say, "What is it, Helen?"

"Pastor, sorry to interrupt but Detective Tallametti's on line two."

"Thanks."

I punch line two. "Hi, Gino. How're things going?"

"Not so good, Rev. Can you come down to the station?"

"When?"

"The sooner, the better. I can hold him here for a while but not forever."

"Hold who?"

"That Muldoon kid you wanted me to keep an eye out for."

"Don't you mean McCoombs?"

"Huh? Oh, yeah. McCoombs. Anyway, you'd better hurry. That kid's big mouth just won him a trip to juvenile max security lockup."

"What!"

"He got picked up for illegal drug possession and trafficking, and was carrying a stolen pistol that'd been used in a convenience store robbery."

I groan.

"And if that wasn't bad enough," Gino continues, "when they brought him before Judge Hawthorne he caused a ruckus in her court and threatened her."

This is bad. And Raymond's in deep trouble, far deeper than he knows. Besides possessing a well-nurtured hatred for drug dealers and users, Judge Hawthorne's one of the most hard-nosed jurists sitting on the bench. If Raymond threatened her, the next time he sees daylight he'll be using a walker.

"Okay, Gino," I say quickly. "I'm on the way."

I hang up and dash into Helen's office. "I'll be back shortly. This is urgent."

"But Pastor, what about your meeting with that Monitor Construction guy, Syd?"

"Reschedule him. This can't wait."

Helen exhales a frustrated huff and nods.

I run out to my car and glance across the parking lot when I hear someone yelling.

"Nathan! *Nathan!*"

It's Beverly Dawkins. Hearing her yelling my name like that reminds me that I've got to find a way of getting her to call me Pastor or at least not be so familiar in public.

I wave at her and yell back. "Hi! Sorry, no time! Gotta go!"

She races up to my window, winded and gasping. "Nathan, please . . . I . . . just came from my lawyer and . . . would really like to . . . run some things past you."

Beverly's eyes hold a pleading so intense it's impossible to refuse her. But I also can't ignore the rumors that have been circulating. So I compromise.

"Tell you what," I say, glancing at my watch. "Meet me back here this afternoon. We'll talk then."

Beverly smiles and we set a time. Then it strikes me that, given where I'm going, I really can't be sure *what* time I'll be getting back.

As I start my car I say, "Take down this number."

She pulls a pen and paper from her purse and writes down my cell phone number.

"Call me just before you come," I say. "I'm hoping I won't get tied up. But if I do, we'll just meet later. Okay?"

"Thanks so much, Nathan. I really appreciate it."

"No problem."

I throw the car in gear and zip out of the parking lot. I wave at Helen, who is staring out her office window as I drive by. She waves back, but when she looks over at Beverly her frustrated expression hardens into a glare.

THIS INTERROGATION ROOM LOOKS LIKE SOMETHING OUT OF A B MOVIE: THE ONE BATtered table in the center of the room; two chairs, on opposite sides of the table, one for the person being questioned, the other for the questioner; the dull gray walls; the obligatory single light hanging from the ceiling at the end of a gnarled wire. The door opens and a medium-built, wiry young man lurches into the room. From the many pictures Mother McCoombs showed me and the fact that he's wearing her face, I know it's Raymond.

He's dressed in an eye-offending bright orange prison jumpsuit with numbers across the left breast. His hands are cuffed, his ankles shackled, and his feet covered by a pair of flimsy slippers. And my heart is suddenly so very heavy, witnessing this latest proof of how the streets are savaging the talent, excellence, and strength of this generation's young people.

Raymond's awkward shuffling is all the more pathetic since he's still trying to swagger like the king of whatever trash-cluttered street corner he used to "rule." A gargantuan guard follows, nudging him along with sharp jabs from a baton.

"Keep movin'!" the guard growls.

Raymond glances over his shoulder, giving the guard a look that's as close to a visual slap as I've ever seen. I stand as he approaches the table. He glares at me and looks me up and down with contempt-filled eyes. I fight to keep mine locked with his, not wanting to give him any reason to dismiss me as someone too weak to listen to.

"Sit down!" orders the guard.

Raymond's lips curl as he mutters a curse beneath his breath and plops down into the chair. I sit once he's situated, but only after he's looked *up* at me. The guard hovers nearby like a predator looking for a reason, *any* reason, to pounce.

"I'll take it from here," I say.

"Sir, we're not supposed to leave the prisoners un . . ."

"Do you really think he's going anywhere?"

The guard glances at Raymond's hands and feet and the cleric's collar hugging my neck. Raymond's eyes snap back and forth from me to the guard, a sneering grin creasing his lips as he enjoys the guard's moment of indecision.

"It's against the rules," says the guard, "but I'll be right outside the door." He glares at Raymond. "No funny business."

He backs out of the room, closes the door, and stands outside, peering in every few seconds through the cracked, smoky glass.

I clear my throat and say, "Raymond, I don't know if you remember me. I'm . . ."

"My name's Philly Ray, man! *Philly Ray!*"

"All right then. Philly Ray, I'm Reverend Nathan Matthews. Your gran . . ."

"Whutch'you wantin' from me?"

"I'm here to help."

"Do I look like I need your help, preacher?"

I glance at the handcuffs, the neon prison jumpsuit, the iron-muscled guard standing just outside the door, then back at Philly Ray.

"Frankly, yes."

"Look, preacher. The only thing you kin do for me is get me out'a this zoo."

"I can try and arrange that but it'll take some time."

"How much time?"

"I don't know. I'll have to get a lawyer and see what has to be done."

"Look, man!" snaps Philly Ray, slapping his palms onto the table. "Can you or can't you do somethin'?"

The guard rushes into the room, his hands gripping his baton with anxious expectation.

"It's all right!" I say quickly.

The guard and Philly Ray trade silent snarls for a few moments until the guard backs slowly out the door.

Philly Ray says, "Look, preacher. These suckas ain't givin' me my one phone call. So since you claimin' to know my grams and talkin' 'bout wantin' to help, tell her I'ma need someplace to stay when I get out'a here. After this, there ain't no way my moms is gonna let me . . ."

I stare at Philly Ray in disbelief. "You don't know?"

"Don't know what? That you sittin' there lookin' at me like I'm crazy?"

I shake my head and suppress my anger as I search for my voice. It's tragic enough sitting across from another black youth who's being sucked into the penal system's black hole. But what's even more tragic is that Mother McCoombs spent her last years praying and worrying over *this* youth, a brat so mean, self-centered, and indifferent to her suffering as to not even notice her death.

"What'sa matter with you, preacher? Why you lookin' like that?"

"Raymond, I'm sorry to tell you this but . . . your grandmother, Eleanor McCoombs, has passed away."

In an instant the loudmouthed, street-savvy urban warrior shrivels into a speechless, blinking child who's comprehending that he's not only in over his head but has lost the one person in the world who'd always loved him no matter how repulsive his behavior.

The guard steps through the door. "All right, prisoner," he growls. "Time to go back to your cell."

Philly Ray stands and starts shuffling toward the door.

"Don't you even want to know how she died?" I ask.

Philly Ray, his glistening eyes betraying his losing struggle to recapture his tough-guy persona, looks at me and shrugs. "What difference do it make, preacher? Knowin' ain't gonna make her undead."

Then he shuffle-swaggers out of the room, sniffling and wiping his eyes as he hurries out the door.

# CLIFFORD

VICTOR PICKS ME UP AND WE GET STARTED. WE DRIVE A LOT LONGER THAN I THOUGHT we'd have to, and turn in to the Wheaton Point apartment complex instead of a law office.

"Isn't this an odd location for that Protecting Parents' Rights organization?" I ask.

"This ain't it," says Victor. "We'll hit that next."

I turn and look directly at him. "If this isn't it, why are we here?"

"So you can look at some apartments."

"What!"

Victor parks and shuts off the car. "Al hooked me up here when me and Lynnette split. I woulda stayed cuz it's a nice joint. But bein' in the same city with Lynnette was still too close, so I skied to Cleveland."

I look around the complex. Victor's right about it being nice, but it's not *that* nice. Not compared to what I'm accustomed to over at Penn Hills Commons. Over there, there's not a single housing unit older than three years. We've got a park with a pond and ducks, a quaint little strip mall nearby with stores that're pricey, but so cute nobody really cares, beautiful landscaping, and an overall atmosphere that oozes affluence and upward mobility. Wheaton Point has a pockmarked parking lot and buildings styled like a housing project, and it oozes paycheck-to-paycheck struggling.

I say, "Victor, I appreciate the gesture but . . ."

"Cliff, what harm will it do? Or is you so confident that Demetria's gonna start doin' right that you ain't gotta be thinkin' about life after campin' out with Momma?"

Once again, Victor's reasoning is annoyingly correct.

He gets out and says, "C'mon, man. We can't stay long anyway. Like I told ya, Al don't like to be kept waitin'."

We stroll into the rental office and I suddenly understand the fear experienced by people who are claustrophobic. If the model apartment-office is this small, the residential apartments must be the same.

"Anybody here?" Victor calls.

"Just a sec," a gruff voice answers from the back room.

And in just about a second, a knotty-muscled older gentleman, dressed in bib overalls and sporting a nicely trimmed thick white beard, steps into the cramped so-called living room where Victor and I are waiting.

"What can I do you for?" asks the older guy.

"Buck, why you actin' like you done forgot me?" Victor responds.

The older gentleman cocks his head sideways and down, looking at Victor over his half-lens spectacles. "Victor? Zat you?"

"In the flesh."

The older guy beams. "Why you lousy can't-stay-in-touch-with-nobody rascal, how's ya doin'?"

"Still on the ropes, but fightin' back."

They shake hands and give each other a hug and pat on the back.

"Al told me I'd be gettin' a visit," says Buck. "But didn't say who. If I'da knowed it was you, I'da had my Doberman waitin'."

"Ain't nothin' that a nine-millimeter cain't handle," Victor says, and laughs. "Buck, this is my baby bro, Cliff. He's got an appointment with Al."

Buck's smile fades. "Pleased to meetcha, youngblood. Sorry you is gettin' canned."

I grit my teeth and glare at Victor, wondering if there's anyone in Pittsburgh who he *hasn't* told about my predicament.

I force a smile and say, "It's good to meet you too. I think."

Buck's smile brightens at my dry humor. "I'm wit'cha, youngblood. Been there myself. After my first marriage, I was ready to pack it in. But then I found Louise and ain't never been happier."

"Don't be rubbin' your happiness in our noses," grouses Victor. "Whutch'-you got available?"

Buck takes off his glasses, rubs the bridge of his nose, and shakes his head. "Got just a few right now. Al's been sendin' me more business than I can handle." He looks directly at me. "How soon you gonna be needin' somethin'?"

"Well, I really don't think that . . ."

"Yeah, yeah," interrupts Buck, grabbing a ring of keys off his desk. "C'mon and lemme show ya what I got. It's bein' cleaned and whatnot so you's gonna have'ta 'scuse the mess."

Victor and I hurry behind Buck, who's moving like an Olympic speed-walker. We head outside, cross the parking lot to an adjacent building, and go inside and up one flight of stairs. Buck stops in front of apartment 2C and starts searching and rattling through the keys on his ring to find the one that'll open the door.

"That Al's somethin' else," he says, his voice full of admiration. "Gettin' that tightfisted landlord to buy into lettin' PPR clients stay here for a year at a lower rent rate took some talkin'."

"Is that legal?" I ask.

Buck stops searching for the key and looks at me like I just admitted to still believing in Santa Claus. "Youngblood, ain't you heard? The law works for the folks who can afford it."

I don't need to look at Victor to know that he's enjoying the validation.

Buck says, "The landlord could afford it, so it's legal."

"And it ain't like he's losing out," Victor adds. "With as much business as Al sends over here, these apartments don't stay empty for long."

"Almost never," Buck confirms.

"And how much of a cut do Al and PPR get?" I ask, not even attempting to hide my cynicism.

Buck and Victor glare at me. Then Buck's expression softens and he says, "Youngblood, I know you's goin' through a hard time and got your jaws tight. But believe me when I tell ya, PPR ain't gettin' *nothin'* from this operation. Al's one'a the onliest peoples I know who ain't tryin' to get rich by helpin' folks."

Victor nods, his eyes telling me to be quiet before I lose the goodwill I'm being afforded by virtue of Buck's knowing him.

Buck finds the key and opens the door. "C'mon and lemme show yuz round real quick. I've gotta get back over to the office before my furnace man gets here."

Buck's right about it being a short tour. This place is so small, it can't be anything *but.*

The one bedroom is only slightly larger than Braddie and Bear's room. The bathroom is a closet with a toilet. The kitchen looks like a narrow converted hallway. The living room is standing-room-only. There's enough cabinet space to store a midsize stack of magazines. The refrigerator and stove are functional but old. The numbers on the stove's knobs have worn off and been replaced with sloppily painted ones. The caulking around the tub looks like it was applied by someone suffering from nervous twitches. The thinly carpeted floor is well maintained but nothing spectacular. A sliding glass door leads out to a balcony big enough for a small grill, or the cook, but not both. The cable and telephone connections look like they were installed by someone operating under the anywhere-will-do principle. And the walls are painted in institutional off-white.

"This don't look too bad," says Victor.

Buck nods. "And it's a steal. Only eight hundred a month."

*Eight hundred a month!* For this modified shoebox? That's only a few hundred less than where I'm living—used to live—in Penn Hills Commons. Which means that, dollar for dollar, if I were renting here, I'd be spending a lot more money and getting a heckuva lot less.

As if he were listening in on my thoughts, and trying to prove that it's really cost effective, Buck says, "Trash pickup's included."

"But not water or utilities?" I ask.

"Nope."

I lean harder against the wall. Buck glances at his watch. "Sorry 'bout this, youngbloods. I can show yuz one more, but my furnace guy's comin' and we got lots ta do."

"No problem," says Victor. "We gotta get on down to Al's anyway."

The second apartment is much like the first, some things better, some things worse, not back-flipping impressive in either case.

Buck heads for the door and glances at me. "C'mon and lemme give ya some information on the place."

"But I won't be . . ."

Buck steps off quickly into the hallway. "Victor, be sure and pull that door shut behind you," he says, looking over his shoulder.

Victor and I hurry to catch up with Buck and follow him back across the parking lot and into the rental office. He pulls some application forms and brochures from his desk and hands them to me.

"Just about everything ya need ta know is in there."

"Look, I appreciate all this but . . ."

"Yeah, yeah," interrupts Buck, rolling his eyes. "Just make sure ya don't wait too long. Like I said, these places go quick."

I just sigh and nod.

Buck extends his hand to Victor. "Good seein' ya, Victor. Try and stay in touch, you no-count roughneck."

"I'll do better," Victor says.

"Liar."

They laugh, Buck shakes my hand, and we leave. Once we're back in the car, I toss the brochures and other papers into Victor's backseat.

"You better hold on to that stuff," he says.

"No, Victor. I won't. I told you before, no matter how bad it seems, I still intend to work things out with Demetria."

Victor grumbles under his breath and takes off for PPR.

VICTOR ENTERS THE PPR FRONT OFFICE WITH THE CONFIDENT, COMMANDING STEP OF AN old visitor, grabs an outdated, palm-sweated magazine off a scratched coffee table, and sits down and starts flipping pages. The office is tidy but cramped, with a receptionist's desk, three vinyl-covered visitor's chairs, and an ancient ladderlike floral stand, sitting on a dingy, cream-color rug. I look around and wonder who, or what, in this dump could've impressed Victor enough to make him want to come back.

"Is this it?" I ask.

Victor looks up and raises an eyebrow. "Yeah. This is it. What was you expectin', a meetin' down at the mayor's office?"

I pick a flake of peeling paint from the wall. "No, nothing like that. But I also wasn't expecting . . . *this.*"

Victor tosses the magazine onto the table, grabs another, and starts flipping. "Al is gonna just love you," he says, chuckling.

Our eyes snap over to the door when from behind it a female voice yells, "But why? She's been living with him for six months! And with *my kids*! For Godsake, Al! The court's not even enforcing its own decree!"

The door flies open and slams against the wall. I jump out of the way. A crimson-faced woman stomps over to the receptionist's desk, grabs a tissue, and blows her nose. She looks at me with desperate eyes.

"It's not right!" she says, grinding out the words through clenched teeth. "It's just not right!" She grabs another tissue and stomps out the door.

"Did you see that?" I ask.

Victor tosses the magazine onto the table, yawns, and stretches. "Plenty'a times."

From behind us a voice says, "Well, well, well. Look at what the cat drug in."

Victor looks in the direction of the voice and speaking barely above a reverent whisper says, "Al."

I look—and do a double-take. Al is a woman.

AL OPENS HER ARMS. AND LIKE AN AWED PRIMITIVE APPROACHING HIS THUNDER DIETY, Victor pads across the room and folds himself into her embrace.

"It's been a long time," she says.

"I'm sorry, Al. I didn't mean to stay gone so long."

Al steps back and waggles an admonishing finger. "No apologies, Victor. I told you to go rebuild your life. If I haven't heard from you, then you've followed my instructions."

I look Al up and down, trying to discern the powers that have given her such sway over this person with his lifetime of coldheartedness. She's dressed in second-tier, no-name walking shoes, appreciably snug but not skin-tight jeans, and a plain but attractive pink sweater. She's a nice height at about five feet, five inches and doesn't look to weigh over one hundred fifteen pounds. And that's being five pounds generous. Her head's covered by an intricate network of braids, swept back into an orderly waterfall of hair that falls to just below her neckline. Her face isn't magazine-cover glamorous but it's attractive. And troubling. It's her eyes. They're not angry but they hold the memories of painful struggles. I recognize them. They stare back at me daily from my morning mirror.

Al glances at me. "Is this him?" she asks.

Victor nods and steps back, giving me and Al room to see each other. "Al, this is my younger brother, Clifford. Cliff, this is my . . . sister, Alojuwa Bell."

"Pleased to meet you," I say.

Al nods curtly, then looks at Victor. "Why don't you go and visit Mr. Chen? He's at the restaurant today and I'll bet he'd love to see you."

Victor rubs his stomach like it's agreeing with the suggestion. Al tells him what time she thinks she'll be through and they hug again.

"He's hardheaded, Al," says Victor, stepping to the door. "Make sure you do him right."

Al smiles, waits till the door clicks shut, and walking past me without so much as a glance in my direction says, "Follow me, please."

Once we're inside her office, Al points to a chair in front of her desk. "Please have a seat, Mr. Matthews."

"You can call me Clifford."

Al turns her back to me and says, "Okay. Please have a seat, Clifford," and starts rummaging through a file cabinet.

"Nice office," I say.

Al scans the office, then gives me a withering glare. "Clifford, for us to get the most out of this meeting it's best if we avoid patronizing. Agreed?"

I try not to squeak when I answer. "Agreed."

Al continues rummaging and I'm relieved that she's focused her halogens onto something else. And she's right. I was patronizing. The office is cramped, with file cabinets, a computer jammed in a corner, and stacks of folders rising from the floor like paper skyscrapers. The wall behind Al's desk is crammed, in an orderly sort of way, with photos of a boy and girl, in various stages of maturity, ending with a series of high school prom and graduation pictures. Dominating one corner of the wall is a front-page photo of Al beneath a headline:

WOMAN REGAINS CHILD CUSTODY FROM ABUSIVE, ADDICT EX

"Are those pictures of your kids?" I ask.

"Yes," answers Al, a soft smile touching her lips as she glances at them.

She spends a few more seconds rummaging, then pulls out a folder. She tosses it onto her desk and pours herself some coffee from the brewer next to the computer.

"Mind if I have some?"

Al sits down and gestures toward the brewer.

I fix my coffee and sit down, averting my eyes from her unblinking stare. I take a sip, then set my cup on the table beside me and fix my eyes on hers.

"Al, is something wrong?"

"No, Clifford. Nothing's wrong. I'm just wondering."

"Wondering what?"

"If you know why you're here."

"Yeah. I mean, well, Victor said you gave advice on helping to save . . ."

"That's what I was afraid of."

"Huh?"

"Clifford, listen closely. I *do* give advice. But not on saving marriages. When people step through my door they already know their marriage is over and are seeking shelter from the fallout."

Al sighs and slumps back into her chair, her eyes glazing over with weariness. "In a perfect world, I'd love to be run out of business. But this *isn't* a perfect world. Everywhere married couples turn they're told that divorce is a quick fix to their problems. Some people are seduced by that lie and go in search of greener pastures. When they do, their spouses are left to grapple with a life left in ruin."

She fixes me in her gaze, her eyes suddenly filling with light and energy. "I try and help the ones left behind turn the experience into a strength and get on with living."

The intensity beaming from Al's eyes is overpowering. And I sense strongly that she'd fight for me with a fierce singlemindedness that could deflect every trick and act of malice Demetria attempts. She also probably wouldn't think twice about using the law to flame Demetria into a smoking pile of ash. Part of me would *love* to see that. Another part of me still wants to protect Demetria, provide for her, and shield her from harm.

Al studies my face, then gets up and goes to the door. "Clifford, take a few minutes to figure out why you're here. If it's to save your marriage, I can arrange for you to see a marriage counselor. But if your marriage is over, we need to get busy. If you're like most people who sit in that chair, your ex has known for a while what you're just finding out and has put her plan in motion. We'll be playing catch-up but you can still cut your losses. First, you have to decide."

FIFTEEN MINUTES LATER, AL SITS DOWN AT HER DESK AND ZEROS ME DOWN WITH her eyes.

"Well, Clifford. Do you know why you're here?"

I stare at my wringing hands and say, "Let's get started. I want to pursue getting custody of my sons."

Al drums her fingers on the desktop for a moment before responding. "Okay. On what grounds?"

"What do you mean on what grounds? I'm their father."

"And she's their mother."

"As decreed by biology. That doesn't make her the best person to raise them."

"And what makes *you* the best person?"

I stare at her for a long moment. "Al, pardon me for saying so, but . . . you're not helping very much."

"And you're right to feel that way. Because the questions I'm asking you are the same ones the law will pose. And if you can't answer them with something better than 'I'm their father,' you're facing one gigantic uphill battle."

"What are you talking about? She's the one splitting up my family. Doesn't the fact that I'm not the instigator count for anything?"

"Irrelevant," says Al. "The court doesn't care about who drew first blood. Its primary concern is which parent is most fit to raise the children."

"But doesn't the fact that I'm fighting to . . ."

"You'll have to demonstrate that she's an unfit mother."

"That's preposterous!" I snap, getting loud. "If she automatically gets the kids, then the court's already concluded that she's fit and I'm not. Based on her behavior up to now, that flies in the face of common sense."

Al speaks slowly. "Clifford, listen. Unfitness is usually declared *only* when the children aren't receiving proper medical care, if they're living in an abusive, dangerous home environment, if their performance in school is radically suffering, if they're being neglected and emotionally traumatized . . ."

"Wait!" I blurt. "Are you saying that in order for me to have even a slight chance of success, my sons have to be in poor health, in physical danger, flunking out of school, and on the verge of an emotional breakdown?"

Al doesn't answer, but I don't need her to. Because from the outside, Braddie and Bear appear to be healthy, happy, and whole. If all the court's concerned about is whether or not they're wearing smiles, then I'm a dead duck.

*Is he serious?* laughs Cruiser's voice. *He's gonna depend on that blindfolded babe carryin' the sword and scales down at the courthouse?*

Al says, "You'll also have to consider the risks you'll incur."

"Risks? Like what?"

"Risks like turning your ex from being a mere rival into a vengeful antagonist. Not to mention the damage to your kids if you subject them to a custody battle. It'll hurt them more than you can know."

"Look, Al. I don't expect it'll be a walk in the park for any of us. But aren't you being a little melodramatic? My sons are strong boys and . . ."

"They'll have to be," she interrupts.

Al looks away for a moment, and when she looks back at me she has to blink her eyes hard for a few seconds.

"Clifford, listen to me," she says, speaking softly. "I wasn't always in this line of work. I was married, had a nine-to-five, and thoroughly enjoyed my family. Then I was blindsided. I don't know how my ex concealed his drug habit for so long, but the day he started using his fists instead of words to communicate I discovered the source of his problem. I tried to get him help. He wouldn't take it. The beatings continued. I left. I assumed that since *he* had the drug problem and was being abusive, the issue of who'd get the kids would be open and shut. It wasn't."

I glance up at the front-page photo on the wall.

"My lawyer said he was doing his best," Al continues. "But how could I know? I was naive, ignorant, and terrified. It was the first time I'd ever had any real dealings with the law, and I discovered quickly that it and all its absurdities were designed for turning people like me into human daiquiris rather than helping them solve their problems. My ex convinced the judge that he was in rehab and making significant progress in recovery, and that he was more capable of providing a better home life since he had the larger income. He had his case argued by some of the best legal talent in town."

"How'd it get to be a headline event?"

"At the time, it was rare for a woman to lose a custody fight. That made my case newsworthy. But that's all part of what I'm telling you. Just because more men are getting custody doesn't mean it'll be easier for you. I thought mine would be automatic. It obviously wasn't. When I lost my kids, I applied to law school."

I sit back and consider everything Al has said. She makes perfectly good sense and I don't doubt she knows what she's talking about. *But I still want my sons!* Al looks hard into my eyes, seeing more than just their color.

"Clifford, it's a lot to think about," Al says. "And we can go that route if you want. But I urge you to consider your sons. This is a terrible process to drag them through."

"Meaning?"

Al grimaces, looks down at her desk, then back at me. "Everyone's going to be traumatized by this process, especially the boys. They may be forced to choose sides, and that's a brutal position to put kids in when they love both parents. But, to borrow the court's logic, we have to be concerned with 'the welfare of the children.' The system tries to do that, but its main interest is in the administration of law, not the dispensation of justice. That's where PPR comes in. We'll approach this from the perspective that these are your sons whom you love, cherish, and would sacrifice for."

"Keep talking, Al. I like what I'm hearing."

"Don't celebrate yet. Remember, your ex will be fighting like a cornered tigress. That introduces some unpleasant possibilities."

"Like what?"

"You could lose. And if you do you'll have to deal with an ex who's evolved into a vicious enemy. She may try to restrict your access, squeeze you for more child support, claim spousal abuse, or . . ."

"Spousal abuse! I've never so much as thought of mistreating Demetria."

"That doesn't matter. In the current environment, to be accused is to be guilty."

I groan.

"That's the reality, Clifford," says Al. "I don't know of a custody battle that hasn't been nasty, or parents who've been able to resist using the kids as bargaining chips and weapons for hurting each other. That's why you need to be absolutely certain that you'll be doing it for the kids and not to get revenge."

I nod, slouch into my chair, and listen closely as Cruiser says, *Call when you want some real justus!*

AL SITS BACK IN HER CHAIR AND TAKES A DEEP BREATH. "CLIFFORD, DO YOU HAVE A SEPArate bank account?"

"Well, no. Not ex . . ."

She picks up her phone and dials. "Hi, Mallory. This is Alojuwa Bell. Yeah. I'm doing fine. Listen. I need you to set up an account. That's right. His name is Clifford Matthews. As a matter of fact, yes. He's Victor's brother. That's right. The usual procedure. 'Bye."

Al hangs up and speaks matter-of-factly. "Clifford, I know this is a rough period and that you're being hit with a lot of different issues at once. But please try and understand that the marriage part of your relationship with your ex is *over*! From now on you've got to be thinking survival."

The undeniable accuracy of Al's statement makes me look away in shame as I wonder why I didn't do for *myself* what she just did for me. Al leans forward, her expression becoming even more intense.

"Speaking of survival," she says, "I need to ask you something."

I swallow and say, "Okay."

"Do you believe in God?"

"Huh?"

"Do you believe in God?"

"Well, yeah. But what's that got to do with . . ."

"Everything!" Al closes her eyes and continues talking, soft and slow. "Clifford, if I'm going to be of any assistance, I need to make certain that you're aware of every support system available to you. And God is the one support you can ill afford to be without. Not when you're about to be boiled in legal oil."

"What do you mean?"

She steeples her fingers. "Listen, Clifford. The moment after your marriage ties are cut, you're going to need a shoulder to cry on, but it won't be there. No one, not one single, solitary person, will want to hear your complaints."

"Al, no disrespect intended, but how do you know things'll get that bad?"

"Actually, I don't. But there's truth in that old saying, 'Your friends are with you through thick and thin, but when it gets too thick, they thin out.' And it's gonna get thin, Clifford. Very, very thin."

My temples pound as if little men on either side of my head are whacking away with sledgehammers.

"That's a pretty daring assumption to make about people you don't know."

Al smiles like a wizened elder enduring a novice's stupidity. "Perhaps. But I know people, and it won't do any good to get frustrated or angry with them. They're going to be weak before being strong, cowards before being courageous, and consumed with their own problems before being concerned with yours. Twenty-four hours after that legal blender grinds you into a cocktail, you'll be desperate to share your pain with someone who understands how you feel and will let you vent for as long as you've got breath to do it."

"So what're you telling me?"

"What I'm telling you is to pray to God. He's got the time, the listening skills, and the love you'll need to carry you from one moment to the next." Al's eyes smolder with hypnotic intensity. "Clifford, do you understand what I'm saying?"

I nod.

"Good. Start praying now. Because before this is over, you'll know that a person doesn't have to die in order to go to hell."

She pulls some papers from the folder she got from the file cabinet earlier. "Has anyone talked with you about child support? How it's computed? How much you'll be paying? How it's collected? The psychological impact? How it relates to taxes? Whether or not it's tracked? Legal liabilities, etcetera?"

"Well, no. Not exactly. No one except Victor."

Al smirks. "And what did he say?"

"He says it's legalized mugging."

"Yeah. Knowing him, he would."

"Well, *is* it legalized mugging?"

Al's lips narrow into a thin, humorless line. "It's the law."

"You're evading the issue."

"It's not an issue to be evaded or resolved."

"Well, then, just exactly *what* are you saying?"

Al sits back in her chair and exhales. She seems smaller somehow. "Clifford, whether or not it's legalized mugging or something demanding resolution are moot points. It is the way it is."

I laugh nervously as a bone-chilling sword twists into my stomach. "Now *you're* sounding like Victor."

"And how's that?"

"According to him, I'm hamburger and I don't know it."

"Clifford, this isn't the most productive way for us to spend this time. You need to understand what the law is, what it means, and what it can do."

I want to press her for an answer but she's adamant about keeping to her schedule.

"In your case," she continues, "when the law does what it can, as only it can, here's what it'll mean." She picks up some of the papers she's pulled from the folder, glances over a couple, then looks at me. "What's your gross annual salary, approximately?"

I hesitate for a second, then tell her.

"And how much does your ex make?"

When I don't answer, Al gives me a piercing look. "Are you telling me you don't know?"

I shrug pathetically. Al purses her lips. "Can you at least guess-timate?"

I tell her and she punches some keys on a calculator, scans over the pages, punches in some more numbers, and hands me the calculator.

"This is approximately how much you'll be paying each month."

I look and wheeze. "That's ridiculous!"

"How old are your boys?"

"Seven and five."

"The normal pattern is for the court to have child support payments continue until a child reaches age eighteen. It's referred to as the age of emancipation."

I fall back against my chair. "For the love of God! Are you telling me that I'll spend more than a decade paying thousands of dollars a year to someone who's purposely tearing my family apart?"

"Yes."

"But I'm not the one who wants the divorce!"

Al sits back and folds her hands across her midsection. "It doesn't matter."

"What do you mean, it doesn't matter? Doesn't she bear any responsibility in this? Why am I the only one getting penalized?"

Al scowls. "Clifford, the *only* people getting penalized are your children."

That convicting truth overwhelms me into silence. I stare at the calculator, as if the power of my gaze will somehow lower the numbers.

"Isn't there anything I can do?" I finally ask.

*You got my pager number!* answers Cruiser's chuckling echo.

"As I said before, what you absolutely *must* do," says Al, "is take firm hold of the reality that the marriage part of your relationship with your ex is *over*. From here on, survival's the name of the game. So until the dust settles and the smoke clears, stay out of your ex's way. Don't get on her nerves. Keep a low profile and cooperate."

Al glances at her watch. "We'll have to continue this later. My next appointment will be here any minute."

Someone knocks on the door and Al answers. It's Victor. Before he can enter, I shamble over to him and give him a hug.

"Victor, I'm sorry," I say, holding him tight. "You were right and I was wrong."

"About what?"

"Everything."

# VICTOR

AL TELLS HER NEXT APPOINTMENT TO WAIT A SEC, THEN STANDS BESIDE ME AT THE WINdow. Cliff's weavin' like some drunk over to my car. That boy's messed up! I knew Al was gonna put the mojo on him but she's outdid herself.

"I really hated to do that," she says.

"It had to be done."

"I guess."

"Ya think he'll be all right?"

Al shrugs. "He should be. But you know how it is. It's bad enough when a stranger's destroying your life. When it's someone you love, it's double devastation."

I see from my window reflection that I'm lookin' at Al like she's lost her mind.

"You think he's still stuck on Demetria?"

"Victor, trust me. That man still loves his wife."

I look at Cliff crawlin' into my econo-cart and shake my head. "Well, he'd better get used to this, cuz he's got some whoopin's comin' like the one I got this mornin'."

Al faces me and crosses her arms, wearin' her battle face and lookin' like she's all business. "What happened this morning?" she axes.

I give Al a quick schoolin' on the details, her expression gettin' more'n more serious so that by the time I'm finished she's lookin' like she could chew nails.

"Victor, are you certain that Lynnette knew you were coming to see Jewel?"

"Al, this is my baby we's talkin' about. I made triple sure that Lynnette knew."

Al glances outside, like she's thinkin' of somethin', then looks back at me. "Has she done anything like this before?"

I do a quick scope of my memories, then say, "Not *this*. But if I had a dollar for every time I had to hassle with Lynnette about seein' Jewel, I could buy an island and retire."

Al tightens her jaw and shakes her head *reeeaaal* slow. "Those are the same kinds of games my ex used to play."

"Well, I'm *through* with games. Lynnette don't know how close she come to pushin' up daisies."

Al's eyes snap onto mine. "Stop talking crazy, Victor. Resorting to violence won't solve a thing."

"Al, I know that. But I gotta do *somethin'*. I mean, ain't there nothin' that can be done to make her stop sendin' me through these changes?"

Al starts to answer, then glances at the wall clock. "Let me look into it. Right now I've got to get to my next appointment."

We hug.

"Call me in a day or two," she says. "One way or the other, we *will* solve this problem."

I'm smilin' so big, my face is hurtin'. I get ahold of Al's shoulders, pull her into me, and hug her again. "Thanks, Al. Just lemme know whut I gotta do and I'll be back here in a heartbeat."

We let go of each other and check out Cliff in my econo-cart. We see him reach into the backseat, grab that apartment paperwork, start lookin' through it, then tear it to shreds.

Al shakes her head and says, "Victor, go take care of your brother."

NOW THAT AL'S SCHOOLED CLIFF UP ABOUT THE LEGAL CARJACKIN' HE'S GOT COMIN', he's buggin' out big time. He could use some relaxin', so I head on down to another one'a my old hangout spots, Club One.

We pull into the parkin' lot and Cliff says, "But Victor, I don't drink."

"Oh yes you do! Specially after that whoopin' Al just threw down."

He don't argue and we head on in. Steppin' into this joint is almost like bein' back at Big's Grits'n Gravy, specially with the way suckas is all over me with greetin's and friendly insults. Me and Cliff ease on over to the bar and order a couple'a beers.

"He's payin'," I say to this fine, bulgin'-cleavage, tight-bodied bartender.

Cliff pulls out a credit card. Seein' that, I order us another two beers for when we get through with the first ones.

"Ice! C'mon back here ya bullet-head chump!"

I look through the smoke and folks and see Trace, Henderson, and Billy-B. I give Cliff an elbow nudge.

"Cliff, I'll be right back. I'ma go holler at these dudes for a minute. Okay?"

"Go ahead," he mumbles. "Like you said yesterday, I've got nowhere to go."

Now I'm feelin' kinda guilty for sayin' somethin' so cold. But it was true, so I squash the guilt.

"Just stay cool, man. I'll be right back."

I'm gone longer than intended, but I look every now'n then to scope Cliff. By the time I get back, he's slumped over on the bar, mumblin' and talkin' junk.

"What happened?" I ax the bartender.

She shrugs. "He chugged two more beers and almost finished a pint of bourbon."

"And you just let him!"

She glances at the credit card hangin' loose in Cliff's hand. "His money was good. And he said you was the designated driver."

"I'm sick," groans Cliff.

I grit on the bartender, jerk Cliff up off the bar stool, and help him outside to the car.

"I need someplace to lie down," he says, grabbin' his head.

He's right, but where? I *sho 'nuff* can't take him to Momma's, cuz she'll be runnin' her mouth for days. I *won't* take him to Nate's, cuz I don't need him lookin' at me like I wiped boogers on a Bible. I *can't* take him to his crib, cuz it ain't his no more. And I *ain't* got no place, so we's just a couple'a nomads.

I get Cliff in the car, fish out his credit card, and drive him over to this four-hour motel that married suckas use for cheatin'. We'll hole up there till he sleeps it off. On the way over, I glance at Cliff and feel worser for the sucka than ever before. Cuz him and me have finally got a lot in common, and that sucks.

I AIN'T THOUGHT THEY MADE PLACES SMALLER THAN MY APARTMENT BUT WE'S IN ONE. At least it's got cable. I shoulda punched that fool at the check-in when he looked out in the car, saw Cliff, and gave me that funky smirk. But forget that clown. At least Cliff's got a real toilet to puke in, and someplace to lay his head.

I sit in the chair beside snoozin' Cliff and check out the music videos on Black Entertainment Television. Some dude callin' hisself 2-2-Cool is singin' about wantin' his babe to hurry home so he can get some good lovin'. From the way he's moanin', he oughta get a checkup. 2-2-Cool goes off and some wavy-haired, double-breasted-suit-wearin' dude named HART starts croonin' as he pours his lady a glass of wine. He gives her a rose, kisses her hand, her eyelids, the tip of her nose, her mouth, then starts cryin' about how he'll die if they ever break up.

"That's what Demetria wants," says Cliff, grittin' on the TV.

"Man, I thought you was sleep."

"What's he got that I don't?" axes Cliff, pushin' hisself up with a grunt.

"Money. A music video. And a babe fakin' love better'n Demetria ever gave you for real."

Cliff looks around and frowns, right as some babe next door starts moanin', and a bed starts slammin' up against the wall.

"Where are we?" axes Cliff, lookin' around.

I turn down the TV volume, listen, and grin. "We's at Booty Central."

Cliff shakes his head, closes his eyes tight, and rubs his forehead. "Nine years. And it comes down to this. Poof!" he says, tryin' to snap his fingers. "Everything I've worked for. Everything I've been planning for. Retirement. Braddie and Bear's college. Poof! Gone! All because Demetria wants to be a music video."

He stands like an old man hasslin' with arthritis. And it ain't till he wipes his eyes and nose that I realize he's cryin'.

" 'True love, excitement, and fun.' My life turned upside down. My sons being stolen from me. And spending more than a decade paying thousands of dollars to that slut! By the time I'm through paying child support I'll be in my mid-forties. I'll be starting over when I should be shifting into cruise."

Cliff growls out that last statement, grabs my jacket, and starts rootin' through the pockets.

"Whutch'you doin'?" I ax.

"I'm gonna make Demetria tell me why. Where are your keys?"

"Cliff, don't be stupid! All you gonna get is another lame excuse."

"So what! Before I start paying for some clown to stick it to *my wife* in *my home*, Demetria's gonna give me something better than 'true love, excitement, and fun' as an explanation."

I snatch my jacket from Cliff and block the door.

"Get out'a my way!" he hollers.

"Cliff, whutch'you think you gonna fix by doin' this?"

"I'm gonna make things right!"

"You ain't gonna do jack!"

"Don't tell me what I will or won't do!"

This is pissin' me off. Cliff's emotions is goin' haywire and I gotta get him to see the real deal.

"Tell ya whut, Cliff. I'll move if you answer me a question."

"What is it?" he rumbles, his chest heavin'.

"How many times can a man die?"

"Victor. Now's not the time for stupid word games so . . ."

"You think I'm playin'!" I holler, shovin' him back. "Well here's a news flash, Mr. Academic. The only person gettin' played is *you*! Now answer me! How many times can a man die?"

Cliff's lookin' at me like a crippled zebra suddenly spottin' a lion in the neighborhood. "Once."

I grip Cliff's shoulders and look hard into his battle-fatigued eyes.

"Cliff, you ain't got no idea whutch'you up against. By the time this is over, when you finally get past the confusion, if possible, and get over Demetria, if ever, you gonna die a million times."

Cliff's face wrinkles up like he's seriously puzzled.

"Yeah, I know it's tough to figure," I say, "but check it out. You gonna die when the judge hits that gavel, tellin' you it's over. For real. No playbacks. Nine years of life pissed into the wind. You'll die every night you lay in bed, tellin' the walls you did what you could, squirmin' when they laugh and tell you they don't wanna hear it."

Cliff fidgets and I talk faster cuz I know he ain't likin' this.

"Every time you see the boys and they're a little taller, a little smarter and wiser, lookin' more'n more like men, you'll die. On Father's Day, when you're waitin' for 'em to call, *if* they remember, *if* Demetria reminds 'em, *if* she lets 'em, you'll die. When you see 'em playin' football, knowin' that one'a Demetria's loverboys taught 'em the fundamentals, death'll be grinnin' in your face."

"Okay, Victor. That's enough."

"On them holidays when it used to be you, your wife, and the kids, but now it's your ex, the new dude, and the kids, death'll be sendin' you a Mailgram. Once you discover that Demetria likes that sex thang—*and lots of it*—death'll be whisperin' sweet nothin's in your ear."

Cliff grabs my collar. "Shut up! I don't wanna hear this!"

I break his grip and jab my finger into his chest. "You'd better hear it! Cuz the day reality hammers through all your bright-boy-self-scammin' and shows you Demetria bouncin' up and down on Nolan's dong you'll go into mental meltdown."

Cliff *really* gets crazy, punchin' me in the stomach and throwin' me onto the bed.

"Shut up, Victor! I don't care if Demetria sleeps around!"

I catch my breath and charge Cliff, tacklin' him with enough force to send us crashin' over the cheap furniture. We wrestle, kick, and punch each other until I force him onto his stomach and pull his arms behind him into a chicken-wing lock.

"Liar! If it didn't matter you wouldn't risk gettin' put in a body cast!"

"I'm gonna get you! So help me, if it's the last thing I do, I'm . . ."

I take my free hand and whack the back of Cliff's head.

"*Shut up!* You'd better learn to deal with it, Cliff! Cuz it's gonna happen! Get used to seein' it in your head. Play it over and over. Till it either don't faze you or at least don't make you wanna jump off'a bridge. Practice seein' her layin' there, legs spread wide and tremblin' with the hurry-ups."

Cliff growls and grunts, jerkin', rollin', and twistin' to get free. I whack his head again and tighten my chicken-wing lock.

"She's gonna want him inside her, more than she ever wanted you. And then they'll be movin' in ways you can't remember cuz she *never* did it like that with you."

Cliff lifts his face to the ceilin' and starts cussin'. I take my free hand and shove his face into the rug.

"And she's tellin' him stuff you used to pray she'd say to you. And doin' stuff you thought she was too stuck-up to do. And then her eyes'll roll back in her head cuz she's cummin' like tomorrow, not even thinkin' about you in yesterday."

Cliff bucks, thrashes, and kicks. Then his balloon busts, and he starts boo-hooin' in a foul, ugly kinda way. "Oh my God, Victor! What's happening? *Help me!*"

I let off some pressure, wonderin' if Cliff'll understand why I had to torture him. It don't matter. His mind needed strengthenin'. At least now I can head back to Cleveland tomorrow without bein' so worried that Demetria'll walk all over him. And I'm hopin' Cliff don't hate me too bad for shovin' the truth down his throat like this. But he'll be grateful once he realizes he's only gotta die nine hundred ninety-nine thousand, nine hundred ninety-nine more times.

# NATHAN

AFTER HOURS OF BATTLING THE BUREAUCRACY TO SEE ABOUT GETTING RAYMOND SOME help, I finally get back to the church. I pull into the parking lot and sit, trying to navigate my emotions through the double-cutting reality that not only is Mother McCoombs gone but I've as good as lost her grandson. I know it's not my fault, and his own decisions landed him where he is, and it's high time he learned that life's a full-contact sport. But I promised to look after him—a task that will be more difficult now that he's learning skills that'll better equip him for living with jackals than with people.

Beverly turns in to the parking lot and parks beside me in the spot reserved for "Pastor's Wife." It's a good thing she had my cell phone number. It saved her a trip and reminded me that I'd agreed to meet with her. I should ask her to move her car, but by this time of day everyone's gone. And it's not like Monitor Construction's equipment has left her much room to park elsewhere. Nor is it the first time someone's parked in Brenda's space.

Beverly's smiling as she gets out of her car and comes over to me in mine. One look at my face and her expression shapes into worry.

"Is something wrong?" she asks.

I sigh. "Naw, I've just got a lot on my mind."

"Wanna talk about it?"

I get out of the car and say, "Not really. At least, not right now."

Beverly walks alongside me, not saying a word as we head toward the church. Once inside she touches my arm and I stop. We both notice how close we are and ease a few steps away from each other, putting a safer margin of distance between us. Beverly looks hard at me.

"Nathan, I care about you. So if something's bothering you, then it's bothering me."

I ease back a little farther. "Beverly, I appreciate your concern but . . ."

"Please don't stop me. I don't want to be a problem, but you mean the world to me and . . ."

"C'mon, Beverly. You shouldn't be talking like this."

Beverly's eyes moisten and she closes them tightly. I hesitate for a moment, then reach out and hug her.

"It's okay, Beverly," I say, stroking her fresh-smelling shoulder-length hair.

"I'm sorry if I offended you," says Beverly, her voice muffled as she speaks into my shoulder. Then she looks up at me and says, "But Nathan, I just want you to know that I'm here for you . . . *in any way you want me.*"

Then the telephone rings. I hurry into my office, motioning Beverly onto the couch where she normally sits during our counseling sessions.

I pick up the phone and say, "Divine Temple. Pastor Matthews speaking."

"Hello, Nathan."

It's Brenda. And before I can stifle it, a gasp escapes from my mouth. It takes all my will and energy to subdue the nervous shock waves rippling up and down my throat.

"Hi, sweetheart," I say, lowering my voice and turning my back to Beverly. "How're you doing?"

"Fine."

Brenda speaks with glacial calm, her voice seeping through the phone like a freezing mist. "What are you doing?"

Like a man standing tiptoe on the edge of a cliff, I take a deep breath, spread my arms wide, close my eyes, and leap into oblivion. "I was just about to start another counseling session with Beverly."

Brenda's quiet for a long time. And the mist in her voice is now snow, swirling with gale-force winds. "I'd like for you to listen to something," she says.

A voice some distance away from Brenda echoes through the phone clear and strong, sounding like it's being projected from a microphone. "And this year's Einstein Trophy award goes to Nathan Matthews Jr."

There's cheering and applause, followed by a chilling *click!* as Brenda hangs up.

BRENDA STORMS INTO MY DEN. I HURRY IN BEHIND HER AND SHUT THE DOOR, GLAD she remembered to come here, since the den's located farther from the kids' bedrooms. They'll still hear us, but not as much, I hope.

"C'mon, Brenda," I say. "You're not being fair."

She wheels around and steps toward me, backing me up against the door. "You're right, Nathan. What I *am* being is *stupid*! For waiting on you to see that light you're always preaching about! For thinking that you'd break your neck to celebrate your son's achievement with as much effort as you exerted in going down to that jail!"

"For the hundredth time, I'm sorry. It's not like I planned on missing Nate Junior's ceremony."

"You were everywhere else for everyone else except *your family*!" Brenda rails.

"Brenda! Will you be reasonable! It's not like I was out barhopping, joyriding, or chasing skirts . . ."

"Do you mean someone else's besides Beverly's?"

"That's a cheap shot and you know it."

"What I *know* is that I'm sick and tired of you putting your lust before me and the kids and then explaining it away as doing the work of Christ."

"Lust!" I holler. "What's that supposed to mean?"

*"Beverly Dawkins!"* yells Brenda.

"There's nothing going on there!"

"Tell that to your daughter! Tell it to her and everyone else who must see me as the village idiot for ignoring what to them is so plainly obvious."

"Brenda, if I were trying to hide something would I have admitted to being with Beverly when you called? Especially since we were alone?"

"Good questions, Nathan. But an even better question is why you put Beverly before me and Nate Junior, especially after I'd reminded you over and over about his ceremony. Do you know how many times he asked whether or not you were coming? 'Mom, isn't Dad coming?' 'Mom, I thought Dad said he'd be here.' And what was I supposed to tell him? 'No, honey. Your father won't be here. He's too busy deceiving himself into adultery with Sister Dawkins.' "

"For Pete's sake, Brenda! I didn't do it on purpose. She'd just come from a lawyer and wanted to . . ."

"Nathan! Can't you understand? I don't care what she wanted! Instead of being with her, you should've been where you were needed most—*with me and your children!*"

The phone rings, the answering machine picks up, and Beverly's voice vapors out like a sensual genie.

*"Nathan, I know I probably shouldn't be calling but I was worried. If there's anything I can do, please let me know. I care for you too much to not be concerned."*

Brenda walks calmly across the room, backs me up against the wall, and slaps me so hard, I see stars.

I'M AWAKENED BY THE SOUND OF A SLAMMING TRUNK. IT'S ONLY 6:20 A.M. AND MY NECK, Lord have mercy, is stiff from my having fallen asleep at the desk in my den.

"Corrine, make sure you've got all you'll need," says Brenda from outside.

I'm emerging from the den, rubbing my neck, right as Corrine and Brenda are coming into the house, passing Nate Junior on his way out, carrying a suitcase. A knot of fear tightens in the pit of my stomach when I look into Brenda's eyes, confirming that what I think I'm seeing is exactly what's happening.

I try to keep my voice calm, but a tremor betrays my anxiety. "Bren, what's going on?"

Corrine stops beside her, both of them looking at me through angry eyes. The fact that their faces are cast from the same mold makes the effect of their disgust with me twice as bad.

"Corrine, go finish," Brenda orders.

For a split second, I think I see Corrine's anger soften and I smile, trying to tell her it'll be all right. But she only scowls.

Brenda's having no conflicting emotions. She marches past me and into the den. "Nathan, I need to talk."

I follow her inside and shut the door. "I was hoping we would."

"I didn't say anything about *we*."

I stand quietly as Brenda goes over to the window, parts the blinds, and peers out. After a moment, she turns around, crosses her arms, and sears me with an expression I've rarely seen coming from her. Or, more to the point, have rarely seen directed at *me*.

"First: Pastor Benjamin Randolph of the Everson Avenue Church of the Redemption called yesterday and requested you to come and deliver a sermon during their revival. Your schedule was clear so I told him you'd be there."

"Bren, listen, sweet . . ."

*"Second!"* she says, cutting me off. "Second: I'm spending the next couple of weeks in Ocean City with my baby sister Bianca. She's going on vacation and I asked if I could tag along. The kids will be staying with my mother. After what happened with you and Corrine, I'm not comfortable leaving them here."

"What!" I say. "How dare you insinuate . . ."

"I'm not finished!" hollers Brenda.

"Brenda! Those are my children too. You can't just arbitrarily decide to separate them from me."

"Nathan, you'd better be concerned about me separating *myself* from you."

The sheer improbability of what Brenda's saying collides in my mind with the instant reality that what Brenda's saying is not only possible but probable.

I start scrambling to implement some damage control. "Brenda, please. I'm sorry for raising my voice. Let's sit down and see if we can . . ."

Brenda raises her hand and I shut up. "I'll be back in two weeks, Nathan. That's two weeks for you to solve your problem . . ."

It doesn't escape me that Brenda says "problem" and not "problems."

". . . two weeks to gather whatever courage you need to speak to me truthfully." Her lips tremble but she firms them up, although the tremor in her voice remains. "I barely survived Syreeta, Nathan. I *won't* go through that again. You've preached about how couples have to trust the love between them. I'd suggest you pull out that cassette and listen to it. Because when I get back I want to know *all* of what's been going on. And I want it resolved!"

She stomps to the door and grabs the knob.

"Brenda?"

She stops, keeping her back to me. "What is it, Nathan?"

"What if I can't tell you whatever it is you need to know?"

Brenda turns to face me and her jaw is a smooth arc of firmness. "The next time you see Clifford, tell him I said hello."

# ADRIFT IN DADALAND

# CLIFFORD

I SURVEY MY APARTMENT, HALF LISTENING AS MOMMA SPEAKS TO ME ON THE PHONE.

"Clifford, those apartments at Wheaton Point are okay," she says, "but I still think you were too hasty. You could've stayed with me for as long as you wanted."

I sigh and slouch deeper into my chair. I don't need this hassle, not right now and certainly not in addition to this morning's dose of grief from Demetria.

"It just sounds odd," Momma continues. "I've never heard of laws requiring someone to have *X* amount of living space, and *X* number of rooms in order to have overnight visitations from their own kids."

"Well, Momma, join the club. I'd never heard of such laws either. I'm still trying to figure out how the law can justify Demetria's irresponsibly destroying my family at the same time it assumes that she's better suited to raise the kids."

I'm equally frosted about the involuntary servitude under which I'm required to pay years of child support without having the means or authority to ensure that it's *really* supporting my sons. And it's no use complaining. If I dare breathe a gripe, people act like I'm some heartless fiend who'd rather reduce Braddie and Bear to poverty than keep them in comfort.

Momma continues, "Even if that is the law, my house would've been sufficient. It's not a mansion, but it's certainly spacious enough. . . ."

This is nerve-wrecking. Momma acts like I didn't mind being told by some faceless hireling that I had to get my own place before the boys could stay with me overnight. She thinks I don't mind seeing everything I've hoped, worked, and struggled for be dissolved, dismantled, and dispersed.

". . . but it's your decision, so you have my full support," finishes Momma.

This cools my heating anger. "Thanks, Momma. I appreciate it."

"Will you be all right?"

"I'll have to be. There's not much choice."

Long seconds pass, and I hear her sniffle. "Momma, are you all right?"

"No, Clifford, I'm not. Just like *you* wouldn't be if this were happening to Braddie or Bear."

That's the rub. It just might happen. Because if there's any truth to what Nate has said about generational curses, Demetria and I could be setting a pattern that might plague our children, grandchildren, great-grandchildren . . .

"Please forgive me," I mumble.

"For what?"

"Huh? Nothing. I was just thinking out loud."

Mercifully, she doesn't press the issue. "Okay, Clifford. I have to go. Are you sure you'll be all right?"

"Yes, ma'am."

"I love you."

"And I love you, Momma. I really and truly do."

"I know, baby. Just remember, we're all in this together."

We hang up and I sit staring at the walls. We may be in this together, but right now it's just me, my thoughts, and the dread that for weeks has kept me awake with worries of what Demetria might do next.

The latest episode started with Demetria jostling me out of my sleep with an early morning phone call to complain about the division of assets. Then the faceless hireling called me on the job and announced that I was no longer allowed in my home. Then he articulated the new guidelines of my fatherhood, setting the boundaries and conditions under which I'd be allowed to carry out that role.

"I'm sorry, Mr. Matthews," he began, "but staying with your mother does not meet our independent domicile space requirements. You'll need to establish your own residence. It must have at least two bedrooms, providing adequate space for your sons to have a recreational and living area. Once you've fulfilled those criteria, you'll be permitted to keep your sons overnight. On the matter of support, your company will have to send us a letter verifying your gainful employment in a full-time capacity, and . . ."

Trevor's promise to allow me time off from work came in handy as I immediately began searching for an apartment. There were the gorgeous dwellings that appealed to my taste but were far beyond my new budget. There were the ones that I could afford but that looked in danger of being condemned. And then there was Wheaton Point.

When I entered the rental office door, Buck looked up from his desk and said, "I knew you'd be back."

We did the paperwork, sped up by Al's can-do influence. The next day, I moved in.

When I told Demetria she said, "Don't come by for your stuff until after I've dropped the boys off at day care. I'll swing back on my way to work and let you in."

She asked how long I thought it would take and I said, "I'm only getting what's mine, Demetria. It shouldn't be that long."

"Well, all right. But you might as well know, I've asked one of our off-duty security people to stop by, just to make sure everything goes smoothly."

"Demetria, there's no need for that."

"Maybe not. But I'd rather be safe than sorry."

And so Nate and some guys from Divine Temple helped me move under the watchful eye of Demetria's rent-a-cop.

Nate was puzzled. "Why is she doing this?"

"Doing what, Nate? Leaving me? Wrecking my family? Taking my sons? Making me one of the working poor? Running after her slut friends? Treating me like an enemy?"

Nate was stunned, the two volunteers from the church were embarrassed, and I wondered again about my mental stability.

"Nate, I'm sorry," I said. "It's not your fault and I shouldn't be taking my frustrations out on you. It's just that . . ."

Nate shoved me into my state-imposed second bedroom and talked me down from my anger. "Clifford, I know it's rough," he whispered, patting my back. "Believe when I tell you that I really and truly *do* understand."

And something told me that Nate wasn't just empathizing but was comprehending my situation as though he were himself a veteran of such emotional combat. And I loved him more than ever for his sensitivity, especially since I knew that he and Brenda shared a relationship that never had, and never would, expose them to the pains pummeling me.

Victor called that evening. "Cliff, I'd be there, man. But my punk boss, Corey, has got me workin' mandatory overtime all week. All I got time to do is work, wash my nuts, then go back to work."

"I understand, Victor. But don't worry. Nate and a couple of guys from his church helped, so we got it handled."

After a moment's pause, Victor said, "So howzit feel?"

And I thought: Here we go again. Victor's being Victor.

But then I remembered how he'd been loving me through this ordeal. It was a crude, clumsy, in-your-face kind of love, but it had also been strong, protective, and ever present.

So in a choked voice I answered, "Al was right. A person doesn't have to die in order to go to hell."

For a long minute, there was silence. Until Victor said, "Man, I feel bad."

"About what?"

"For years I've been wantin' you to see whut I see, and feel whut I feel. Now you do, and I'm wishin' it was somebody else."

"No, don't say that! Because now I know. All this time you've wanted understanding, and I didn't give it to you."

My throat was tight, but I kept talking. "When you split up with

Lynnette, I was around, but not there for you like you've been for me. Forgive me, Victor. Please."

"It's cool, man. I gotta go."

"No, Victor! I need you to know that I finally understand."

"Okay, Cliff," said Victor, his voice rasping. You's forgiven. *I gotta go!*"

We hung up and I sat for hours on the couch, listening to the walls laughing. I listened to their laughter through the next day as I hurried to get things in order so Braddie and Bear could spend their first night over.

Demetria called and said, "If you have boxes all over the place, that'll still cut down on the space they need."

There were so many things I wanted to say to her. So many suggestions about where to go, what to eat, and what to do with herself. But Demetria had my sons, which meant she could keep them from me. And if I sought to get them by force, the cops, the faceless hireling, and scores of other faceless, could-care-less hirelings were prepared to help her.

So I swallowed my suggestions and said, "Okay, Demetria."

She wanted to stop by a day later to look everything over. I couldn't stomach being there and asked Buck to let her in.

When I talked to him that night he said, "And how long were you married to her?"

"Nine years."

Buck grunted. "Youngblood, I'm surprised your hair ain't turned white."

"What did she say?"

"She stuck up her nose and said, 'This'll do.' "

So the way is clear for me to get Braddie and the Bear.

I notice last year's framed family picture, lying faceup on a stack of books beside me. I grab it and stare into our smiling faces.

In the picture I'm standing behind them all, smiling and oblivious, my hands holding Demetria's shoulders with a loose grip. Even then it was the three of them and . . . me.

"Why, Demetria?" I whisper. "Why does it have to be this way?"

I toss the picture off to the side, and close my eyes tight. "Please, God. Help me stop loving her. *Help me stop loving her!*"

# VICTOR

JUST BEFORE I LEFT TO GO PICK UP EDIE AND KARENNA FOR OUR TRIP TO THE CIRCUS, AL dropped me some *for-real* good news.

She said, "Victor, I think I found a way to straitjacket Lynnette concerning her interfering with your visitations."

"You're singin' my tune, Al. I'm lissenin'."

"I'll give you the short version."

Much as I wanted to hear Al's words, I was glad she was keepin' 'em short. Cuz I didn't wanna be late gettin' Edie and Karenna.

"We'll hit Lynnette from every angle," said Al, soundin' like some general layin' out attack plans.

"Whut angles?"

"*All* of them. Her inhibiting your already limited access to Jewel is in violation of the divorce decree and the stipulations attached by Childrens Services for your visitation, and it may invite criminal citation for contempt of a judicial order."

"Did you say 'criminal'?" I axed, grinnin'.

"I figured you'd like that."

I coulda done cartwheels. Cuz knowin' that Lynnette stood a chance of gettin' mulched by the same system that'd been whackin' my nuts for so long was somethin' too good to not love.

"How soon can we slam her?" I axed.

"I'll let you know," Al answered. "I've got to check out a few more details. Once I'm finished, it's possible you'll have to come back to Pittsburgh if the magistrate insists upon conducting a hearing."

"Just let me know. I'll be more than happy to help give Lynnette some'a the hell she's been handin' me."

Al gave me a few more details and told me she'd let me know if and when I'd have'ta get back to Pittsburgh. Then we hung up and I went and got Edie and Karenna.

So far, the circus has been the real deal. That, along with Al's good news and havin' Edie and Karenna with me, has me feelin' better than I have in a long, long time. Karenna and everybody else in the Cleveland Coliseum screams out a laugh when an elephant grabs a clown and twirls him in the air. The clown starts squirtin' seltzer at the people sittin' down front and I give Edie a soft jab with my elbow.

"That's why I didn't wanna sit down there."

"How'd you know?" axes Edie, her eyes glued to the elephant.

"When I was livin' in Pittsburgh, I sometimes took my nephews and niece to the circus. They do that trick with the elephants every time."

"Do you like the circus?"

"I love it. Mostly for the animals. Between the circus and the zoo, you can see some'a everythang."

"I didn't know you were into wildlife."

"Animals are cool. A lotta whut I know about people I learned from them."

Edie stares at me kinda funny, lookin' deep into me the way Momma does. "And what have they taught you?" she axes.

Karenna screams out another laugh and hugs me around the neck.

I look hard at Edie's face. I swear, with her sittin' there in that Universoul Circus T-shirt, jeans, sneakers, and a floppy hat, she's *the* most finest woman I've ever seen.

"Victor?"

"Huh?"

"Answer my question. What could we learn from animals?"

I gently stroke Edie's cheek. "How to look after each other."

She smiles and takes my hand.

ONCE THE CIRCUS IS OVER, WE JOIN THE REST OF THE HUMAN HERD HEADIN' FOR THE parkin' lot, stoppin' when I kneel down to wipe some Sno-Kone juice off'a Karenna's chin.

"Starburry's good," she says.

I smile. "That's strawberry, Karenna. Can you say that? Straw-berry."

"Starburry!"

"She's so hardheaded," says Edie, smiling.

I make a loose fist and tap Edie's forehead. "She got it honest."

Karenna sees a dancin' bear toy and says, "Mommy, can I have it?"

"Karenna, I spent all my money on the circus. Next time. Okay?"

"But the bear dances and sings."

I lean over and whisper into Edie's ear. "You mind if I get it for her?" I say, wonderin' if I should spend the rest of the money I borrowed from Clyde.

Edie looks at me for a long second and says firmly, "Victor, I don't want you spoiling her."

"And Edie, I ain't wantin' nothin' you don't."

Edie loosens up, smiles, and hugs me. I buy the bear and we laugh as Karenna gets all into it.

# NATHAN

I GRAB MY CALENDAR AND MARK OFF ANOTHER DAY, THE FOURTH, THAT BRENDA'S BEEN gone. Without her here, nothing matters. I've barely been able to pray. But I've forced myself, knowing that it's times like these, when Satan's thriving upon our misfortune, that we're tempted to avoid calling upon the One who can surely deliver us.

I've been by daily to see the kids. Nate Junior's happy enough and, except for being slightly embarrassed by the whole mess, is taking everything in stride. And Corrine, well, she's not in Ocean City but is so cold and distant she may as well be. I've apologized to her but she's really mad, showing some stubbornness that she got honestly.

Helen buzzes me on the intercom. "Whats'up, Helen?"

"Pastor, you've got a call on line one. It's Sister Matthews. She wants to know . . ."

I punch line one, hitting it so hard I jam my finger. "Brenda!"

"Hello, Nathan."

I fall back in my chair and sigh. "Brenda, I miss you so much."

She doesn't say anything for a few seconds and anxiety fills my chest.

"Nathan, be sure and give Sister Henshaw's Mahalia Jackson CDs back to her during this week's choir rehearsal. She needs them to practice for her concert and I'm sure she's just been too nice to ask for them back. And don't forget to stop by Bishop Runwalt's church. He's got a packet of information on dealing with building contractors, and with all the additions being made to Divine Temple it can't hurt to have more information. And don't forget to visit Elder Dewberry. I'm sure that after losing his mother he'd appreciate the visit."

"Okay, sweetheart. I'll make sure . . ."

"Fine. I'll talk to you later."

"Brenda! Wait!"

Glacial silence fills the space between us and I'm wondering if she's hung up.

"Brenda?"

"I'm still here."

"Brenda, no matter what you think, I love you."

"I know that, Nathan. I need more."

"Tell me what it'll take, Brenda. Tell me what you need and I'll provide it."

"Truth!"

Then she hangs up.

I KNOW CHRISTIANS SHOULDN'T GIVE COUNSEL TO THEIR FEARS, BUT I'M REALLY WORried. I've been praying and praying, but in all honesty, the human side of me doesn't want to wait on God's answer. It needs to hear something *now*.

I grab the telephone and dial the number of my pastor and mentor, the Reverend Dr. Roderick Davidson Childress. After he retired and I took over as pastor, he told me to never hesitate to call him if I felt the need. I'm *definitely* feeling the need.

While the phone's ringing I keep asking myself what made me think I could fill Pastor Childress's shoes. He was a crisis magnet, pulling problems and the people who owned them into his heart. Anyone allergic to truth knew to stay away because Pastor Childress had simply loved people too much not to share it. And that's why I need to talk with him.

"Hello?"

"Pastor Childress? Hi. It's me, Nathan."

"Nathan! How're ya doin', son?"

"Fine. And you?"

"Enjoyin' retirement." He chuckles. "Me and Sister Childress are havin' a ball, courtin' each other and actin' all giddy like the young folks."

"That's great, Pastor. You deserve all the goodness that life has to offer."

"Well, God bless you for sayin' that, Nathan. But never mind me. What can I do for you?"

I tell Pastor Childress that I've got some issues that I'd like to run past him and see what he thinks.

"Well, of course, son. I'd be glad to give you my old rusty viewpoint. You wanna do it over the phone or get together?"

"I think it'll be better face to face."

Pastor Childress is quiet for a moment. "Okay. I can meetcha at . . ."

"That's okay, Pastor! Don't go out of your way. I'll come over there, if it's all right with you."

"That's fine with me, son. You know there's nothin' I love better than keepin' my rump planted in this rockin' chair."

We talk a little longer and then I zip across town to Pastor Childress's. He meets me at the front door, hugs me, and motions me into his den.

"Thanks for agreeing to see me, Pastor."

He dismisses my formality with a quick wrist flick. "Nonsense. You're always welcome."

I smile and nod my thanks. Pastor Childress sits back in his rocking chair and gets comfortable while I take a seat on the small couch.

"So tell me," he says. "How's everythin' goin'."

I rattle off the latest news about the church renovations, the Young & Gifted program (especially the deal with Rasmussen's company), and the breakthroughs of Brenda's Intercessory Prayer Team. Pastor Childress listens intently, nodding, smiling, and grunting his approval.

"So ya see, Pastor, everything's looking up."

Pastor Childress nods, compressing his lips. "Nathan, what's the matter, son?"

I laugh nervously. "What? Why, nothing. I just . . ."

I stare at my hands, then look up into my pastor's eyes. "Pastor, I'm in trouble."

He nods again. "Okay. Let's talk about it."

I start to tell him what's *really* been going on when he holds up a rigid index finger and says, "Wait a minute, son. Let's pray first."

# CLIFFORD

BRADDIE AND BEAR GRAB THEIR OVERNIGHT BAGS AND VIDEO GAMES AND GET IN THE car, Bear in the front seat and Braddie in the back. On the way to my apartment we "talk."

"How're you guys doing?"

"Fine."

"How was school?"

"Okay."

"What's going on?"

"Nothin'."

"You miss me?"

"Yes, sir."

I'm not sure about how to best approach what I'm fixing to do. But it's crunch time and I've got to get these boys at least thinking about the idea of living with me.

"I miss you guys too. And . . . I hate being without you."

Braddie and Bear don't respond. So I say, "I wonder how it would be if we lived together."

"You mean like before?" asks Braddie. "With you and Mommy together?"

I swallow the knot in my throat and say, "Um, not exactly. I was, well, kind of wondering if you guys wouldn't mind living with just . . . me."

"Who's gonna live with Mommy?" asks Bear.

"And who's gonna feed Scratch?" adds Braddie.

"Scratch can live with us!" I say, trying to put a cheerful spin on it.

"But won't Mommy be alone?" asks Bear.

"And won't she miss us like you do, Dada?" says Braddie.

The fear and confusion in the boys' voices fills the car like an expanding balloon. Then Braddie blurts his solution.

"I know, Dada! Why don't we *all* live together again?"

This is a grand opportunity to tell them that Demetria doesn't want that and make sure they know *she's* responsible for this mess. But turning them against her in the hope that one day they'll give her the hell I haven't would make life harder on us all. Not to mention that it might backfire. So I let the matter drop. For now. We ride for a few minutes in silence.

"Dada, where are we going?" asks Bear.

"Yeah, Dada," seconds Braddie. "Where?"

I wink at Braddie in the rearview mirror and give the Bear a soft punch to the thigh.

"Someplace fun," I say.

"I know where!" announces Braddie.

I smile and glance at him over my shoulder. They're gonna love this surprise trip to the video arcade. Besides being fun it'll give us more time to get reacquainted before descending into the bog of our strange new world.

"Okay, Mr. Smartypants," I say. "Where are we going?"

"We're going to Dadaland."

Bear chuckles.

"What's that?" I ask.

"That's where all the dads go who get dumped," answers Braddie.

He and Bear laugh. I fume. Now what do I do? This isn't hardly funny and I should put an immediate lid on it. But I don't want to spend even a second of our precious little time together repairing hurt feelings. So, Dadaland it is.

# VICTOR

I LEAN AGAINST THE WALL, WATCHIN' WHILE EDIE PUTS KARENNA TO BED. THEN WE TIP-toe out, takin' a last look at the baby before closin' the door. I take gentle hold of Edie's shoulders and turn her toward me. She looks down and away instead of into my eyes.

"I don't wanna fall in love," she says.

I hug her and stroke the back of her head and neck. She kisses my cheek and hurries over to her livin' room window, crossin' her arms and leanin' against the wall. She stares outside, lookin' all dreamy-eyed.

"It's drizzling," she says.

I move behind her and put my arms around her, kissin' her neck. She moves her head sideways to give me more room.

"I'm not giving myself to you, Victor."

"Edie, I ain't axin' you to."

"But you will. So I'm telling you now, *no.*"

I step in front of Edie and look hard into her eyes. "Edie, whutch'you think I am?"

"Someone I feel good about but don't know well."

"Look, Edie, I don't know you so good neither. But I'm feelin' somethin' and . . ."

Edie covers my mouth. "No, Victor. Don't say anything you won't mean."

I put my hands on my hips like my drill instructor used to do. "Edie. I don't never say nothin' I ain't meanin'." Edie looks back out the window and I look down at my feet. "I need to finish tellin' you whut I gotta say."

"You don't have to, Victor. I've heard it all before." Tears well up in her eyes. "I haven't let anyone get this close to me since Lyle, and I can't afford another experience like him. So before you start saying things you don't mean, or making promises you won't keep, I'd rather you just leave."

"Look, Edie, don't be comparin' me with Lyle! Since you admittin' you *don't* know me well and I don't know you no better, we's both takin' a chance."

"No, Victor," she says softly. "I can't take any more chances. I don't want to play any more games."

"Edie, if you think I'm gamin', tell me to leave. I'll walk out and never look back."

Edie eases over onto the couch, grabs a tissue off the coffee table, blows her nose, and looks at me.

I step to the front door and grab the knob. "Gimme the word and I'm gone."

Edie looks into her lap, then at me, and says, "Leave!"

I fall against the door like a cannonball's been shot into my chest. Minutes later I'm on the sidewalk outside her buildin', starin' up at her window, watchin' her watch me.

# NATHAN

PASTOR CHILDRESS PATIENTLY ENDURES MY BEATING AROUND THE BUSH UNTIL I FINALLY get to the point. Once I do, the words rush out from me like water bursting from a dam. I tell him about Clifford and how my feeble prayers have yet to move the Lord on his behalf. I share the news of pregnant Keishawn. And then I mention Brenda and the widening chasm between us, and all that's happened with Beverly Dawkins. When I finish, my voice is a trembling whisper. And no matter what Pastor Childress says, I'm certain that I have to resign. I'm still too much man, and not enough spirit, to serve my Lord and Master well.

Pastor Childress scoots to the edge of his rocking chair, leans forward, and grips my arms. "Nathan, where are thy accusers?"

"Pastor, I, I don't know what you mean."

He squeezes tighter. *"Where are thy accusers?"*

I look around, trying to see what he sees. "Pastor, there's no one."

"That's right, son. There's no one here accusin' you. And neither am I."

I look away in shame.

"Nathan, many have been tempted. We survive by prayin' our temptations under."

"But I feel so vulnerable, so incapable of fighting this desire."

"That's because *you* can't! Not alone. Not by your own power. Don't you remember what the Master said about the enemy we fight?"

I nod. "He said, 'Be sober, be vigilant; because your adversary the devil, as a roaring lion, walketh about, seeking whom he may devour.' "

"And how did He tell us to protect ourselves?"

"The Lord said, 'Put on the whole armor of God, that ye may be able to stand against the wiles of the devil.' "

Pastor Childress stares deep into my eyes. "Nathan, I'm not gonna mislead you, son. You're a preacher of the Word of God. Every time you open your mouth, Satan's kingdom is shook to its roots. And that makes you a target. You *and* your family. So he's gonna come after you and keep a'comin'. He's relentless, focused, and determined to achieve your complete and total destruction."

I shudder as a serpentine chill crawls along my back.

Pastor Childress pats my shoulder and speaks softly but urgently. "Nathan, no matter what, never forget that you serve an almighty God. You'll grow in wisdom and power, but you've got to stay faithful! And while you're fighting, I'll do for you what Jesus said he'd do for Peter at the Last Supper. You remember what that was?"

"Yes, Pastor. Jesus told Peter: 'Satan has asked to have you, to sift you like wheat, but I have pleaded in prayer for you that your faith should not completely fail.' "

I TELL THE TRAVEL AGENT THAT I DON'T CARE *HOW MUCH* IT COSTS. I WANT A FLIGHT TO Ocean City today. This afternoon! This insanity's gone on long enough. I refuse to stand idly by while the love of my life and mother of my children drifts away.

I hang up the phone and start putting away my bank proposal notes when Beverly strolls into my office, unannounced. Helen must be gone from her desk because she normally guards my door like a tigress. I smile when Beverly enters and hope my face is doing a better job of communicating a welcome than I'm feeling.

"Got a minute?" she asks.

I nod and gesture for her to sit down in the chair in front of my desk. "What can I help you with, Sister Dawkins?"

A shadow of hurt passes over Beverly's face. "Why so formal?"

I laugh nervously and say, "Now, come on, Sister Dawkins. You know I refer to everyone as either my brother or sister in the Lord."

"Are you telling me that I'm lumped in the same category with 'everyone'?"

My office door's open a crack. And I see that Helen's back at her desk, sitting with her neck craned so far in this direction she's about to fall out of her chair. I get up and close the door. As I'm on the way back to my desk Beverly blocks my path.

"Nathan, have you been avoiding me?"

"I haven't been avoiding you, Sis . . ."

"Stop calling me Sister Dawkins. What's going on? I thought that after the way we'd been sharing and what happened between us, that we . . ."

"Beverly, what happened between us was a mistake and we should be grateful that it didn't go any further."

She moves closer to me and looks into my eyes. "Tell me you don't want me. Tell me I'm wrong in what I've felt coming from you."

I retreat behind my desk to safety, still feeling like a legless ant in the path of a steamroller.

"Listen to me, Beverly. Even if I did, it doesn't mean that . . ."

"Never mind what it means, Nathan. All that matters is that we both feel the same. But I want you to know, there's no need to worry. I know how to be discreet."

"Beverly, listen to me! Nothing else is going to happen. I'm sorry if you . . ."

Beverly walks up to the desk, kisses two of her fingers, and touches them to my lips.

"Nathan, we need to be honest with ourselves. Sooner or later something will happen. I just want you to understand that I'll know how to handle it."

# CLIFFORD

I'VE JUST RETURNED FROM DUMPING THE GARBAGE WHEN I OVERHEAR BRADDIE AND Bear talking in my state-approved second bedroom.

"Bear, why did we take pictures with Mommy's Nolan friend?"

"Because the pictures needed a dad."

"But he's not Dada."

"Braddie, I don't *know.* Mommy said she needed money to get new house stuff."

I step into the room and place my hands on my hips, like the brooding drill instructor in our Marine bedtime game. The boys glance nervously at each other.

"Dada, are we in trouble?" asks Braddie.

"No!"

"But Mommy is, isn't she?" says Bear.

I clench my teeth, trying to will the dizziness from my head. Cruiser's face looms in front of me, his leering grin challenging me to resist his offer. *Call when you want some real justus!*

"Dada, are you sick?" asks Bear.

"Get your shoes and coats on!"

We get in the car and minutes later I'm dropping the boys off at Momma's, zooming over to Demetria's, and charging up to the front door. She's laughing and talking with someone inside, having a jolly good time. It sounds like Tammy, and that means *no one.* I knock, pounding hard enough to make sure their jovial atmosphere is shattered.

"Who is it?" snaps Demetria.

"It's me."

"What do you want, Clifford?"

"It's about the boys."

The door whooshes open. "What's wrong? Did something happen? Are they hurt?"

"Everything. Our family blew up. And yes, they are."

"Huh?"

"Are you gonna let me in? Or should we invite the neighbors to listen?"

She steps off to the side. "Just remember that you don't live here anymore."

I step into the living room and see Tammy, smiling.

"Hello, Clifford," she says.

"Blow me!"

"Clifford!" shouts Demetria.

I head for the kitchen.

Demetria slams the door. "How dare you talk to my friend that way!"

"That's all right, Demetria," says Tammy. "I was just leaving." She gathers up her belongings and slithers out, reminding Demetria about some double date for tomorrow night.

Demetria closes the door and wheels around, her face aflame. "Don't you ever again—"

"Did you take Braddie and Bear and have family pictures taken with Nolan?"

Demetria's mouth falls open.

"Demetria, tell me you didn't do this."

She remains quiet for a few more seconds, then sticks out her chin. "So what if I did? A banker friend of Tammy's was recruiting black families for an ad campaign aimed at attracting more minority customers. They were paying top dollar. And I needed the money."

"So you forced my sons to sit in front of a camera with that degenerate Nolan. You did that knowing those photos might get plastered all over this city. You did that knowing it went against everything those boys have been taught about their *blood*!"

*You ain't gonna have much say-so,* laughs Victor's echo. *And much'a whutch'you do say'll get flushed.*

"How, Demetria? How can you hate me that much? Isn't it bad enough that you're screwing Nolan? Why'd you have to use the boys?"

Demetria narrows her eyes. "*If* I'm screwing and *who* I'm screwing is none of your business! And hate has nothing to do with it. This was just a . . ."

"*Yes, Demetria!* Hate has everything to do with it. Hate is all it could be for you to sink this low."

My body shudders with sudden release, like an orgasmic outrushing of body fluids. And it feels wonderful. Now there's nothing. No outrage. No confusion. No contempt. Like a ship that's snapped its moorings, I'm drifting into a void, floating on the essence of emptiness. I exhale and fix unblinking eyes upon Demetria.

"Demetria, I'm divorcing you. And I'm doing it posthaste."

Demetria casts me a wary, sidelong look. "Is that so?"

"Yes, from the bottom of my heart, *it is so*! "

Demetria leans against the counter, unable to suppress the smirk of victory that slimes onto her face.

"That's good news. At least you've stopped thinking we'll get back together."

I walk up to her and speak slow, calm, and steady. "Demetria, you don't seem to understand. You're getting this divorce whether you want it or not. Because I can assure you that, as of now, it's not humanly possible for you to want it more than I do."

# VICTOR

I'M SITTIN' IN MY PUZZ-MOBILE, TRYIN' TO DECIDE WHETHER OR NOT TO MARCH BACK UP to Edie's apartment and set thangs straight. But that'll be just as stupid as me thinkin' we had somethin' cookin' in the first place.

I knew it was too good to be true. I was feelin' too good. Thangs was goin' too right. I shoulda known Edie wasn't no different than the rest of 'em. I shoulda been guardin' for the moment she decided to roll me to the curb like the rest of 'em.

I hit the ignition and throw the car in gear. Just as I'm about to pull out of the parkin' space, I hear Edie scream, "VICTOR!"

I zoom into the buildin', fly up the steps, and start bangin' on her apartment door. "Edie! Edie! Open up!"

The door whips open and a shiver zooms up my spine when I see Edie holding the phone, the terror lines cuttin' across her face. "It's Karenna!" she screams. "Something's wrong with Karenna!"

I charge into Karenna's room. Her arms and legs is flailin' in wild circles and she's breathin' with loud, garglin' gasps. I pick her up and jump from worried to scared cuz this baby's on *fire*. Edie runs in and pulls Karenna from me, huggin' the baby tight to her chest.

"Oh God!" Edie moans. "Please don't let my baby die."

I scramble into the living room and grab the phone off the floor.

"Ma'am! Please tell me what's going on!" a voice yells.

"Is this 911?" I holler.

"Yes."

"We need a amb'lance!"

"What is the problem?"

Edie plops onto the couch and rocks back'n forth, boo-hooin' and huggin' Karenna.

"Listen, lady!" I yell, grippin' the phone tight. "If we knew what the problem was we wouldn'ta called you!"

In the middle of the operator's next question Edie lets out a skin-crawlin' scream cuz Karenna's hangin' from her arms like a soggy dishrag.

The operator's still babblin' and I roar, "Send the amb'lance! Now!"

# NATHAN

I'M AT HOME, JAMMING A FEW LAST ARTICLES INTO A SMALL SUITCASE, WHEN THE phone rings. I fly across the room and snatch it from its cradle.

"Brenda!"

Momma chuckles and says, "No. But I'd like to speak with her."

My body goes limp and my heart's pounding so hard against my chest, it hurts.

"Nathan? Are you there?"

"Yes, Momma."

"Well, let me speak to Brenda. I want to talk to her about organi . . ."

"She's not here."

"Oh. Okay. What time will she be back?"

"Ah, she won't be back for a while."

"Hmmm," says Momma. "That's odd."

"What do you mean?"

"It's just so unlike her to not call. Especially after the way she seemed so enthusiastic about helping to plan for this family get-together."

"What family get-together?"

"A get-together," Momma answers impatiently. "Like a reunion, but just for the immediate family. With everything that's happening with Clifford, I thought it'd be nice to remind ourselves of the love and closeness we share."

"That's a great idea, Momma."

"I thought you knew. Didn't Brenda tell you?"

"She might have. But like you said, with everything that's been happening it's probably slipped my mind."

"That's certainly understandable," says Momma. "Well, okay. I'll just talk to her tomorrow. Let me at least say a quick hello to Corrine and Nate Junior."

The phone's slick from the sweat in my palm. I swallow and say, "Momma, Brenda won't be back for at least another week. And the kids are spending a few days with her mother."

"What? But I thought that . . ."

I sigh. "Momma, things have been happening."

Momma's quiet for a long time before she says, "I know, son."

"Brenda's spoken to you?"

"No. Brenda hasn't said a word. But I've seen it in her eyes. It's something a woman will always notice if she's ever experienced it herself."

"Huh? Momma, what're you talking about?"

After another pause Momma says, "Sweetheart, come over here. There's something you need to see."

MOMMA MEETS ME AT HER FRONT DOOR, HUGS ME, THEN TAKES MY HAND AND LEADS me into her bedroom.

"Have a seat," she says, gesturing to the rocking chair beside her bed.

I sit down and watch in silence as she goes to her jewelry box, unlocks a small drawer, and pulls out a folded, yellowing sheet of paper. She stares at it for a long moment, then hands it to me.

"What is it, Momma?"

"Just read it. You'll see."

Tears spill from Momma's eyes in big, heavy drops. And fear fills the cavity forming within me as my insides turn to dust. Because, next to Christ, Momma's the strongest person I know and I'm terrified of encountering whatever's reduced her to this state.

Momma takes gentle hold of my trembling hands and speaks softly. "Nathan, read the letter."

I unfold the letter and see it's written on stationery with a symbol for the Republic of Vietnam at the top. Farther down is the slanted penmanship that Momma always joked was the result of the author's writing with his head turned sideways. Time freezes. The trembling moves from my hands to my entire body.

I look at Momma and say, "Daddy?"

She nods and leaves the room, closing the door behind her. I force my eyes down onto the yellowed page and start reading.

*May 4, 1970*

*Ellen,*

*I hope this letter finds you and the boys well. I won't waste your time with a lot of news about what's going on here. To tell the truth, the war I've been fighting has nothing to do with Vietnam and everything to do with my heart. I won't lie to you anymore, Ellen. When I return to the States, I'll be coming home to Pittsburgh but not to stay. There's someone else. And I'm certain that you've known for a long time. I didn't mean to ever love anyone but you. And I know this must hurt because it's been tearing me up, having to tell you. But I can't deny my feelings. I want to be with her. I know what this will do to the boys and I'm not unaware that they might grow up hating me. I'm sorry, so very sorry.*

*But no matter what, please believe me when I tell you that I'll always care about you and the boys. If you ever need me, I'll always come. Please forgive me, Ellen. I never meant for things to turn out this way, but . . .*

I crumple the paper in my hands as the memories rush from the past. All the football games, wishing that my dad had been on the sidelines, watching me like the other kids' fathers watched them. The questions, simple ones about shaving, cravings for women, the value of a man's word, and the consequences of a man's actions. The neighbor men, leering at Momma, hoping to get inside her house and *her* as payment for taking time to show her boys how to change the oil, replace a shingle, or trim a hedge.

I fight the impulse, but a scream erupts. I loved my dad. I remember that part too. But now this revelation brings waterfalls of anger and bitterness, because I know that our suffering would have happened anyway had not the Vietcong taken his life in ambush.

I look up and see Momma standing in the doorway, her arms crossed. She's looking grim. "Do you want that for your children?" she asks.

"No. Not ever."

I want to run away, far from my guilt and shame. But before I can flee, Momma wraps her arms around me and carries me to that spot she always took me when the world got too mean, even when I'd made it that way.

# CLIFFORD

BRADDIE AND BEAR ARE FINALLY ASLEEP. AND IT'S TIME. I GRAB A GLASS, GRAB THE whiskey, plop onto the couch, and pour myself a drink. I pour another and slug it down. The buzz comes quickly. The wall clock's minute hand lines up with the hour hand on twelve. It's quiet. But that won't last. I pour another drink and doze until I'm startled awake.

*Your wife's giving her love to someone else,* hisses a snickering voice. *You failed your sons. They'll be from a fatherless home, just like you.*

"Leave me alone," I grumble.

*Your wife has found ecstasy in the arms of another man.*

I drop the glass and chug from the bottle.

*Your sons will reject you as your wife already has.*

"Go to hell."

*From where do you think we've come?*

I slosh down the rest of the whiskey, sit back, and pass out.

# VICTOR

EDIE SHUFFLES INTO THE WAITIN' AREA, WALKIN' ARM IN ARM WITH SOME NICE-LOOKIN', sharp-dressed older babe. I hurry over. Edie opens her arms and we hug.

"Who're you?" axes the older babe.

"A friend. Who're you?"

"Her mother."

Hearin' that, I flush all my bad attitude. Edie's momma might be like mine and don't put up with no mess when one'a her kids is hurt.

"Mother, this is Victor. The one I told you Karenna's crazy about."

Crazy! Edie ain't said nothin' 'bout Karenna bein' crazy 'bout me. Hearin' that makes my chest swell two times bigger. Edie's momma don't look too happy 'bout the news.

Edie says, "Victor, this is my mother, Liz Harris. Mother, Victor Matthews."

"Yes, I remember," says Liz, grittin' on me. "You're the one nicknamed 'Ice.' "

A doctor, wearin' one'a them heart-listenin' thangs danglin' around her neck, steps through the double doors, sees us, and comes over.

"Miz Harris?"

Edie and her momma nod.

The doc looks confused for a second, guesses which one's Edie, and talks to her. "I'm Dr. Mathers," she says, speakin' with a heavy Jamaican accent.

"Where's Karenna?" axes Edie. "Is she gonna be all right?"

Dr. Mathers motions Edie and the rest of us onto them back-twistin', waitin' room torture chairs.

"Karenna's doin' fine. Just fine."

Edie, me, and Liz exhale together. I don't know about them, but I'm all of a sudden feelin' real tired.

Liz says, "Dr. Mathers, what happened?"

The doctor pulls up a chair. "Karenna has what's known as an SC blood disorder."

"A what?" I say.

"An SC blood disorder," repeats Dr. Mathers, talkin' slow. "It's a type of sickle cell anemia."

"Oh no!" says Edie, her voice full of fear.

Dr. Mathers takes Edie's hand and squeezes. "No, you mustn't think it's the full-blown disease. This is another form, less deadly and quite manageable."

"But how could this happen?" says Edie. "Karenna's had all her physicals and shots. And she's always been a healthy baby."

"And she *is* a healthy baby," Dr. Mathers answers. "Having SC disease is a matter of genetics. In other words, the combination of your and the baby's father's genes yielded this result. But even so, this condition is far from being life-threatening."

"Are you sayin' that part of why Karenna's like this is cuz'a her pumpkin-head daddy?" I ax.

"That's what she just said," answers Liz, lookin' at me and soundin' all nasty.

"We think Karenna's temperature spiked," continues Dr. Mathers. "The complications added by her SC disorder made her temperature control, if you will, short-circuit. Her brain knows her body can't survive at those ranges and began shutting down her systems to slow her metabolism and cool her off."

"Edie!" hollers a dude from across the room. It's Lyle.

Liz breaks into a smile. "Lyle! Thank God it's you."

I look at Edie. "Whut's he doin' here?"

"Victor, he's Karenna's father. He deserves to know when there's an emergency."

Lyle cruises across the room, cheezin' and steppin' like he's pickin' up his World Mr. Wonderful prize.

"He don't deserve jack!" I say, gettin' loud. "Where was he when the emergency was happenin'?"

"The same place you are when your little girl needs you," answers Liz.

"Mother!" hollers Edie.

"Well, well, well," says Lyle. "If it isn't Kareem. Tell me, el Jihad. Are you still a loser?"

Edie jumps up and slaps the piss out of him. Then she calls after me. But I ain't hearin' nothin' cuz I'm out'a there. Gone! For good!

# NATHAN

A BRISK WIND BLOWS IN FROM THE ATLANTIC. BRENDA'S STANDING ON THE BEACH, JUST far enough back from the gentle, rolling surf to keep her feet from getting splashed. She's lovely, silhouetted against the moonlit purple night sky. And I'm a fool, for flirting with forbidden fruit when the essence of beauty and love, *my wife,* still slept by my side.

I want to walk up behind Brenda, wrap her in my arms, kiss the nape of her neck, and hold her tight. But now's not the time. And I'm not worthy.

I grab some flat stones and skip them across the water. Smoky, grayish-white clouds drift past the moon, adding to the surreal loveliness of God's dusky handiwork. Brenda walks a few steps down the beach. I grab some more stones and follow. I skip them all, then sit down. For a long time we're there, still and quiet, lulled into sullen silence by the rolling waves and shimmering wind. Until Brenda speaks.

"Why'd you come here?"

"Because I had to."

"What do you mean, you had to?"

I stand up and move in front of Brenda. She sidesteps me and continues staring out across the water.

"Brenda, we're falling apart and I *refuse* to let that happen."

"Nathan, I gave you the same warning. You didn't care, so why should I?"

I pray for strength. Brenda's anger is like a focused beam that, until this moment, I'd been too distracted to experience full force.

"Because, Brenda, I need you."

She whirls around and faces me, her eyes glistening in the moonlight. She speaks softly, but with a controlled indifference that makes me shudder. "*You* need. Well, Nathan, what about what *I* need?"

Lord, please keep me calm. Please keep me from making her angry. Give me the right words to say.

"I want you to leave," Brenda says.

"No!"

Her eyes ignite with anger. "Nathan, I want you gone! I need time to sort things out."

"And you'll have your time, Brenda," I say. "But first you'll hear what I have to say."

"I'm not interested in what you have to say. Everything you've said has . . ."

"Not dealt with truth. Remember truth, Brenda? It's what you said you wanted."

Brenda keeps her eyes locked with mine. "Well?"

I take a deep breath and pray again for the right words. "Brenda, I've been a fool. I took you for granted and I'm sorry. I let other people and situations . . ."

"What 'other people,' Nathan?"

I look down, swallow, take a deep breath and push out the answer: "Beverly."

Brenda turns and begins hurrying away.

"Where are you going?" I holler.

"Back with Bianca. I don't want to hear this."

I run after Brenda and grab her arm. Momma's voice says, *Nathan! You know better!* and I let go. Brenda steps to the side and I block her. She steps to the other side and I block her.

"Get out of my way!" Her voice cracks with a sob.

"No! Not until I'm finished. Brenda, I love you. But I know that's not enough, no matter how much I want it to be. I know that sometimes in a marriage it isn't. God knows, I've seen that truth playing itself out with Clifford and Demetria."

"You hurt me!"

"I know. And I'm sorry."

I quickly hug Brenda, hanging on tight as she pounds my back with her fists, the blows getting weaker as her sobs get stronger.

"Baby, I'm so sorry," I say, my lips close to her ear. "I know I didn't hurt you just once but over and over. By not listening to your warnings. By being indifferent to your concerns. You were guarding our marriage by yourself while I watched the enemy storm the walls."

I hold her by the shoulders and look hard into her eyes. "Bren, I know it took a lot out of you. But sweetheart, nothing ever happened between me and Beverly. You've got to believe me, Brenda. *Nothing ever happened.*"

Brenda holds my face in her palms. "Nathan, I want to believe you. But how can I be sure? If the tables were turned, would you believe me?"

I look away.

Brenda says, "See, baby? See what I mean?"

I hug her for dear life. "Brenda, please. I can't lose you. I need you like I need air. Jesus saved my soul, but you saved my life. Baby, *please come home!*"

Brenda kisses me softly and says, "No, Nathan. Not until *you* come back to me."

She hurries back to Bianca's time-share. I plop down onto the sandy beach and wonder, What more can I do?

The ocean wind blows in answering, *"Go home. And let Me rule My world."*

# PAIN

# CLIFFORD

I GATHER UP MY DIRTY CLOTHES AND START SEPARATING THE WHITES FROM THE COLORS. I've got a few hours before going in to see Al, so I might as well make the best use of the time and do some laundry I've been avoiding.

The drudgery of the task is made all the worse by having to use these apartment building washers and dryers. Ugh! Knowing my clothes will be soaked and battered by the same appliances that've been layered with the stink, filth, and germs of countless others is horrifying. I should make Demetria sell our washer and dryer, take my cut, and let her get a taste of this hassle. Since we're splitting everything, I'd be within my rights. But that might hurt Braddie and Bear.

I really appreciate Trevor's agreeing to let me make up the time I'm taking to keep this early-afternoon appointment with Al, especially since she canceled someone else to squeeze me in. I'm amazed that as busy as she's been lately, she's bothering to review my rough draft copy of that blasted dissolution document. I'm especially grateful since tonight's the night I'm supposed to meet with Demetria and go over it.

I'd do almost anything to avoid the encounter, but Al says it has to be done. "That's the way it is, Clifford. In dissolution cases the soon-to-be-ex-spouses have to confer, review, and agree upon all the stipulations."

There's something wickedly masochistic about participating in a process that guarantees my getting torpedoed. But Al tells me that we need to get an idea of what Demetria's thinking and feeling, especially since she's likely to go ballistic once we slap her with my custody suit.

I stuff my dirty clothes into a laundry bag and I'm heading for the door when the phone rings. I drop the bag by the door.

"Hello?"

"Hi, Clifford. It's me, Cheri."

Cheri? It's been ages since we indulged in literary debate over lunch, one more indicator of how disrupted my world has been these last few months. I've been so consumed with Demetria and what she might do from day to day that I haven't even bothered to read a lousy newspaper, never mind the latest novel.

"Clifford, I just got a call from human resources . . . concerning you."

"Me! What about me? Are they gonna lay me off?"

Jeez! That's all I need. Getting laid off would be the final nail in my economic coffin. Especially with eleven years of child support for Bear and thirteen for Braddie hanging over me like an anvil suspended by a fraying thread. It's getting hard not to think of them as car notes.

Cheri says, "No, it doesn't concern layoffs. At least, not this time."

I plop down onto my couch and give a windy sigh. "Cheri, don't scare me like that. If it's not about layoffs, then what?"

"You know Alice Riley, the benefits specialist?"

"Yeah. What about her?"

Cheri lowers her voice and speaks quickly. "She said some lawyer called a little while ago, asking a bunch of questions about you in connection with something called a quid, no, a quadro."

"Quadro?"

"Yeah. I'm pretty sure that's what she said. It's supposed to have something to do with your pension and retirement amounts."

I spring up from the couch and stand ramrod straight. "My pension and retirement? No one's allowed to access that information."

"Hold on, Clifford," Cheri says.

I listen with mounting anxiety as Cheri patiently explains to some cave dweller how to send a fax. The person finally comprehends and she gets back to me.

"Where were we?" Cheri asks.

"I was saying that I thought pension and 401(k) information was confidential. Isn't the company liable for giving out that kind of information?"

"I don't think so. From what Alice tells me, she gets those requests quite often. She asked me not to say anything, but I knew you'd want to know."

"You'd better believe I want to know. About this and anything else that sounds the slightest bit important."

"Consider it done."

"Thanks, Cheri. I owe you."

"No problem."

We hang up and I stick a Post-it note on the dissolution document, to remind myself to ask Al about quadros. Then I sit back down on the couch and try to massage the throbbing from my pounding temples.

# VICTOR

I'M SITTIN' AT MY LOCKER WHEN BOOTS WALKS UP AND SEES ME STARIN' AT THE BAG OF lollipops.

"Hey, man. Why the long face?"

"It ain't no thang, Boots. I'm just thinkin' about Karenna."

"Havin' problems?"

"Yeah. She was in the hospital the last time I saw her."

Boots pats me on the shoulder. "Sorry to hear that, bro. Is she gonna be all right?"

I nod and Boots sighs like he's really glad. "Hey, man. That's some good news."

"I guess."

"Whuts'up? Ain't you glad she's gonna get better?"

"Boots! Quit bein' stupid! Of course I'm glad. But I still gotta get through to her momma."

"Her momma?"

"Yeah." I shake my head. "Aw, man. Whut's the use? It never woulda worked out for the three of us."

"Huh? There was three of ya'll?"

"Yeah, man. We coulda never got it together."

"Hold up, man. Is you sayin' that you was tryin' to get with the mother *and* the daughter?"

"Yeah, Boots. Ain't you been listenin'?"

Boots grins like he's close to findin' out the world's juiciest secret. "You better b'lieve I'm listenin'. Cuz this sounds like some super wild boo-tay!"

I suddenly realize where he's headin'. I ain't got the energy to set him straight, so I let it ride. Besides, it's one'a the funnier thangs that's happened since Lyle and Edie's momma blowed me away at the hospital.

That event's had me bummin' so hard, my jaws was still tight when Al called the other day, sayin' that she'd got us a court hearin'.

"It took some doing," she said. "But I called in some favors to make sure we'd get our case heard by someone who's as interested in fairness as they are in justice."

"Does zat mean I ain't gonna be found guilty just cuz'a bein' born with balls?"

Al got quiet and I was hopin' like all get-out that she wasn't pissed. But then she said, "Victor, I've told you before. Men are getting hurt by laws that other *men* wrote. It's not a question of gender, but of a judge's commitment to doing the right thing within the confines of the law."

If it'd been anybody but Al, I'da blown 'em off. But since it was her, I just said, "Well, whoever wrote the laws, ain't no doubt that they's been confinin'."

She schooled me up on the approach we'd be takin', advised me not to start no trouble with Lynnette, then topped off ev'rythang by sayin', "And we'll meet with the magistrate next week."

"Next week! That's fast."

"I was kind of surprised myself," said Al. "But once they told me that there was a slot available in the schedule, I jumped on it. Can you be here?"

I kinda chuckled and said, "Zat a trick question?"

Al laughed. "I'll take that as a yes."

We talked a little longer, then hung up, and I was wonderin' why ev'rythang was all of a sudden goin' right for me'n baby girl Jewel, but slidin' into reverse for me'n Edie.

Boots shakes his head, still tryin' to figure out my game. "So lemme get this straight," he says. "Are you sayin' that you got yourself hooked up with some mother-daughter action, all from the same fambly, and they don't mind?"

"You got it, Boots. That's *z'actly* whut I'm sayin'."

"Didn't you feel, ya know, kinda funny? Havin' both of 'em?"

I have'ta work to keep from laughin'. "Naw, man. The only time I felt funny was when I met the grandmother."

Boots's eyes boing into softballs. "You was with the momma's momma too?"

I nod slow and grin wide, lettin' Boots know it was a downtown good time.

"Ice, ain't no doubt about it," says Boots. "You's one raw sucka."

He turns to walk away, then turns back, wearin' a coast-to-coast grin. "Hey, man. You mind if I borrow some'a them lollipops?"

I toss him the bag. "Take 'em all. I won't be needin' 'em no more."

Boots catches the bag and looks at me like I just gave up the golden goose. Then he hurries and gets gone.

# NATHAN

MR. GELLEN, RAYMOND'S JUVENILE COURT COUNSELOR, MEETS ME IN THE JAIL'S OUTER offices.

"Reverend Matthews, would you follow me, please?"

"Of course, Mr. Gellen. But is something wrong? I've already pre-arranged to see Raymond and . . ."

"I'll explain everything in a moment. Come right this way."

I smile to mask my irritation. Today's schedule barely allowed time for a visit and it *definitely* doesn't have room for impromptu conferences. That doggone Drug Free Streets meeting lasted far longer than it was supposed to. And I still have to drop these renovation estimates off to Sister Anders or risk another of her "Now Pastor, our God is a punctual God" lectures. Not to mention having dinner with Momma to discuss this little get-together she wants to have. I know she'd prefer to have Clifford and Victor there too, but Clifford's got far too much on his mind. And even though Cleveland's only a few hours away, that's still too far for Victor to drive for something like this, so she understands.

The more I've thought about this mini reunion, the more I'm convinced Momma's right in her reasons for having it. With Clifford's divorce looming, my marital problems putting on weight, and Victor away from home, we've been feeling pretty fragmented. The most exciting part is Victor's announcing that he'll be bringing his new girlfriend, Edie. Momma's really looking forward to meeting her. And who knows? Victor just might be serious, because he hasn't brought anyone home since—my gosh—Lynnette.

What irony. For years, Clifford and I smugly assumed that Victor would be an emotional nomad. But now, all this madness has suddenly put him closer to stability and happiness while Clifford and I are left to ponder the barren wastes of late-thirty and forty-something bachelorhood.

I follow Mr. Gellen into his office and take a seat as he positions himself on the corner of his desk.

"Are you and McCoombs close?"

"Not really. But I promised his grandmother that I'd try and look after him."

"Is she well? I mean, she doesn't have any, ah, heart problems or anything, does she?"

"She's deceased."

Mr. Gellen suppresses a yawn before responding. "Sorry to hear that."

I acknowledge the condolence, then glance at my watch. "Mr. Gellen, I'm on a tight schedule, so I'd really appreciate knowing what this is about."

Mr. Gellen crosses his arms and faces me directly. "Raymond McCoombs is dead."

My mind empties, so much so that I can't utter a sound.

"It happened last night. Somebody used a homemade pick to turn him into Swiss cheese."

My throat goes dry, making me have to cough out rasping blasts of air as I ask, "But, but, who? Why?"

He answers like a bored sportscaster describing a punchless boxing match. "We don't know exactly. But we're doing everything possible to find out."

I wipe my eyes and try to control my voice. "This is unbelievable. Didn't anybody see anything? Wasn't someone on duty?"

Mr. Gellen shrugs. "The usual staff. But Reverend Matthews, try and understand. Jail is a different kinda world. It's dangerous to have the wrong people as enemies and not so smart to have any if you can help it."

"Pardon my naïveté, Mr. Gellen, but Raymond just got here. How is it possible he could've made the kind of enemy who'd want him *dead*?"

Mr. Gellen closes his eyes and massages the bridge of his nose like a man who's delivered this speech one too many times. "Reverend Matthews, I repeat: Jail is a different world. If he'd gotten here a hundred years ago or in the last half hour, if somebody had a score to settle, his goose was as good as cooked."

"A score to settle?"

"I'm told that during his first couple'a days in lockup, McCoombs spent a lotta time shootin' his mouth off about the dirtbags he use'ta terrorize."

Mr. Gellen shakes his head. "Bad mistake," he says. "Very bad. They could've been somebody's cousin, friend, who knows? McCoombs probably bragged to the wrong people, somebody made a connection and decided he'd look better as a wind chime."

I sit back and collect my swirling thoughts. My God, my God. Why did this have to happen? Raymond was so young, still so new to life. And now he's dead, gone before the world could be blessed by what he might've become if he'd turned himself around. But what's worst and most frightening of all is that Raymond died without Jesus.

# CLIFFORD

I STUFF MY COLORS AND WHITES INTO SEPARATE WASHERS, PRESS QUARTERS INTO THE soap-caked change trays, and start the machines. One of the trays, too caked with dried soap, doesn't move until I lean against it and shove it in.

I grab a mangled magazine from the pile on the table and stand guard next to the dryers, waiting for someone to come empty one. Today must be my lucky day, because it's a short wait. The door opens and I'm hoping that this person's here to collect their clothes. Then I see her.

"Hi," she says.

"Huh? Oh. Hi!"

Her smile is one of both salutation and amusement, probably from the gawk I feel myself wearing. She starts pulling clothes from a dryer, glancing at me every few seconds and smirking.

"Are you all right?" she asks, speaking with the most lilting, intoxicating accent.

"What? Oh! I'm sorry. I don't mean to stare. It's just that . . ."

She finishes loading her basket and sets it on the table. "Just that what?"

"You're . . . gorgeous."

There, I said it. And if I say so myself, not too bad for a guy who's nine years out of practice. Her smile widens and my adrenaline surges. It's the Fourth of July along my neural pathways as flickering memories of passion flame back to brightness. She extends her hand.

"My name is Mykomo Onanga. My friends call me Mikki. With two *k*'s and an *i*."

"I'm Clifford. Clifford Matthews."

"Pleased to meet you," says Mikki.

"You have a very unusual name."

"It's Nigerian."

She pulls out several undergarments and starts folding. "Well, Clifford. Since you're in this building's laundry room, I guess we're neighbors."

"Yeah. I guess so."

Mikki folds some pairs of panties, each of them a soft feminine color in the pink-to-lavender range.

". . . been here?" says Mikki.

"What? I'm sorry, Mikki. I didn't hear you."

"I said, how long have you been here?"

"A few weeks. How about you?"

"Just a few days. But I won't be staying in these apartments long. They're okay, but I prefer something more modern."

She's hit that nail on the head.

"So are you making Pittsburgh your home?" I ask.

"Temporarily. I live in Seattle."

"What's brought you all this way?"

"I work for a computer systems troubleshooting company. We have a major account here and I'm assigned to monitor their software conversion."

"Sounds intense."

"It can be. So Clifford, what do you do?"

"I'm getting divorced."

Stupid! Where did that come from? My brain must be autopiloting in the ozone.

Mikki laughs and continues folding her clothes. "Is that a full- or part-time occupation?" she asks.

"Never-ending."

She stops folding and her smile softens. "Kind of rough, huh?"

"Very."

Mikki pulls out several bras and lays them off to the side. They're enticing, with their mixture of sexy colors and lace. Especially the black one. She holds it up by the straps.

"Does that look faded to you?"

"No, Mikki. It looks, ah, okay."

She shrugs and keeps folding. "How long were you married?"

"Nine years."

"That's a long time."

"Don't remind me."

Mikki finishes up the last of her clothes. "Well, congratulations on your freedom."

"No offense Mikki, but it's hardly worthy of celebration."

Mikki heads for the door, stopping to look back at me just before leaving. "Clifford, does your wife also sorrow over the loss of your happy marriage?"

She holds me in her eyes, darker now and filled with magnetic intensity. I blink and stare at her in startled silence.

"I see," says Mikki.

# VICTOR

VERNON FINISHES WIPIN' THE BAR COUNTER AND SAYS, "HOW'S THINGS GOIN' WITH Edie?"

"I don't wanna talk about it."

"Ya blew it, didn't ya?"

"C'mon, man. I really don't wanna talk about it."

"I warned you not to mess that up, didn't I?"

I look up at Vernon like he's grown a second head. "Vernon, do you got mud in your ears? For the last time, man. I *don't* wanna talk about it!"

"You ain't gonna find many like her."

I shake my head and say, "You sure are one stubborn clown."

"And you're just a clown."

That pisses me off. "Vee, how do you know Edie woulda been good for me? I told you whut went down at the hospital. So why're you up here talkin' like I'm the century goat cuz Edie decided to keep hangin' with Lyle?"

Vernon sets down that gotta-be-dry-by-now glass he's been wipin' forever and leans onto the bar to make sure I hear him rag on me.

"Ya know, Ice, you ain't the only dude to ever get scorched by love."

"Whut's your point, Vernon?"

"My point, *punk,* is that you ain't the only sucka who's been made a sucka. And for as many scams as you've run, you ain't got *no* room to be judgin' Edie for keepin' a little action on the side till she's sure you oughta be the only game in town."

"Vernon, whutch'you want from me, man? I as much as told Edie I wanted to be with her. I was gonna go the distance."

Vernon slaps me up'side my head. " 'As much as told' ain't the same as sayin' so, is it? And whutch'you expect her to do when the dude is the baby's father, ya double-standard-havin', poutin'-cuz-thangs-ain't-gone-your-way turd?"

"Whut double standard?"

"Man, don't try chumpin' me. You know good'n well that if somethin' ever happened to Jewel and Lynnette didn't tell you, you'd be headin' to the joint for homicide."

"All right, Vee! I'm hearin' ya, but it don't matter. I mean, c'mon, man. How am I gonna compete with a college-degreed sucka like that, drivin' a

BMW, wavin' hundreds like they was dollar bills, and he's wantin' to hang around and Edie's lettin' him?"

I finish the rest of my beer and grab a handful of peanuts. "So I hear whutch'you sayin', Vee. But when a babe makes her choice, I let her go. I ain't in the mind-changin' business."

Vernon says, "Man, you are *too* stupid! If Edie's still carryin' a jones for this dude, why's she been callin' you so much?"

I sit up straight and look hard at Vernon. "How'd you know she'd been callin'?"

"Because, numbnuts. She told me."

"Told you! Whut? When?"

Vernon just smiles and goes back to dryin' that glass.

# NATHAN

I'M STILL REELING FROM THE NEWS ABOUT RAYMOND, BUT GOD'S GIVING ME THE strength to push on through the day. I get out of my car and hurry to the church's front door. Just as I unlock the door, a horn toots and I see Beverly Dawkins, swerving out of traffic and into the parking lot. I don't need this, not now! I'm nearly at my office when she yells down the hallway.

"Nathan! Wait up!" she says, huffing as she hurries toward me. "Well! That was some warm hello. It's a good thing I wore sneakers so I could catch you."

I give her a weak smile. "Hi, Beverly. What brings you this way?"

"I was actually on my way to the market. But then I saw *you*." She emphasizes "you" in a way that once would've left me oozing with hormonal desire. Now it's just annoying.

"My goodness," she says. "You look like the world's coming to an end."

"Someday it will, Beverly. And on that day, I intend to be right with my Master."

She frowns. "Nathan, is something wrong?"

"Yes, Beverly. Something is *very* wrong."

"What is it? You know I'm here for you."

"Let's talk inside."

I don't know if now is the best time to do this. But God's chosen this moment and I must move in accordance with His will. Instead of going into my office, I motion Beverly into the conference room. She takes a seat and I sit down on the other side of the table opposite her, clear my throat, and search for a way to do what should've been done weeks ago.

"Beverly, our relationship has gone way past where it should have and I'm putting an end to it."

She sighs with relief and smiles. "Is that all? From the way you looked I thought it was life-threatening."

"It *is* life-threatening. For this one and the one beyond the grave."

"Nathan, I told you. There's nothing to worry about. I'll never do anything to interfere with your ministry."

"Beverly, my ministry isn't just another money-grubbing job. I'm working for God the Father, and I've compromised that work and my integrity by letting this relationship get out of control."

Beverly's jaw stiffens. "Why all the sudden worry? You're the one who's always insisting that nothing really bad has happened."

"And we should thank God that it hasn't! But even so, it doesn't make what *did* happen acceptable. Either way, I'm putting the brakes on this foolishness."

"What about me?" she challenges. "Don't my feelings count?"

I soften my tone and choose my words carefully. "Of course your feelings count. But please try and understand that *I have to do this*."

"No, Nathan, you don't. I told you I'd be discreet. I told you that I don't want to break up your marriage."

"Beverly, you don't have the power to break up my marriage. Not unless I allow it, and that's not going to happen."

Her eyes narrow. "Don't get nasty, Nathan. Just because you're nervous and scared . . ."

"The only thing I'm scared of is how my behavior has dishonored Christ. And the only worry I have is whether or not Brenda will forgive me."

Beverly gasps. "Are you saying that you've told her?"

I slump in my chair as a vision of Brenda's angry face fills my mind. "Not yet."

"What do you mean, not yet? If she doesn't know, there's no need to . . ."

"Yes! There *is* a need. Brenda deserves to know and it's the right thing to do."

Beverly looks truly puzzled. "But, but why're you doing this? What about us?"

"That's what I'm telling you, Beverly. There never was, is, or can be an 'us'! I'm in love with Brenda. She's my wife and the mother of my children. I promised God to love her for the rest of my life and I'm going to. My spirit belongs to Christ and my heart belongs to Brenda. There's no room for anyone else. Period!"

Beverly's lower lip trembles. I feel lousy seeing her so wilted and dejected. And I feel even worse knowing that her anguish could've been avoided if I'd done this sooner.

"Beverly, please forgive me," I say. "I was supposed to be your pastor, shepherding you as the Lord gave guidance, but I let the boundaries of that relationship blur and almost made a terrible mistake."

"Are you saying that making love with me would've been a mistake?"

"Even *thinking* it was a mistake."

Beverly sniffles and pulls a tissue from her purse. I crush the impulse to comfort her.

"I guess I should've known," she says.

"Known what?"

"It's written all over you."

I look down at the table to avoid the hurt in her eyes. "You're right, Beverly. Like King David wrote in Psalm Fifty-one after he killed Uriah to have Bathsheba, 'my sin is ever before me.' "

"What're you talking about?"

"I'm agreeing with you. This situation has convinced me that I'm not fit to . . ."

"Don't be silly!" Beverly interrupts impatiently. "You aren't 'fit' to do anything other than serve Christ. That's why I love you, Nathan. Because I *know* you love the Lord and have seen how you share that love. All my life I've had men like Percy who'd talk about love, wanna make love, buy, control, and manipulate love, but *none* who understood it. But then I met you, and saw how you loved Brenda, and I, I . . ."

Tears stream down Beverly's cheeks, collecting at the point of her chin before falling in huge droplets onto her balled-up hands.

"Oh, my God," she says, her voice warbling. "I just wanted so desperately what Brenda had. How can I ever make this up to her?"

From the doorway that connects my office to the conference room, Brenda's voice emerges. "You can start by *leaving my husband alone.*"

Beverly's eyes widen in shock.

I swallow several times before I finally manage to squeak out my surprise. "Ba, Brenda, I wasn't expecting . . . I mean, how'd you . . ."

"Your visit convinced me to come back early. On the way home I saw both your cars in the parking lot and decided to find out for myself just how bad things were."

Beverly stammers out, "This, this isn't what you think. He loves you, Brenda. *Only you.*"

"I know," answers Brenda, looking hard at me. "Now, I know."

She's standing like a bantam fighter who's surging with adrenaline. "Nathan, I want you to leave."

"But Brenda! You heard for yourself. I thought you'd . . ."

"Nathan! I want to talk to Beverly. Alone!"

Beverly's eyes dart around the room, looking, I guess, for something with which to defend herself.

Brenda notices and shakes her head. "Beverly, I only want to talk."

"About what?"

"First, about how you're gonna make this up to me. And second, about how I'm gonna help you find a new church home."

# CLIFFORD

AL TURNS ANOTHER PAGE OF THE DISSOLUTION DOCUMENT AND LOOKS UP AT ME WITH wide, unblinking eyes. After a moment, the disbelief on her face melts into disgust.

"Am I reading this correctly? In addition to wanting the child support, the new car, the new living room set, and eight of the solar system's nine planets, she also wants *you* to carry both kids on *your* medical and dental insurance?"

I nod. There's perverse satisfaction in knowing that Al can still be stunned.

She flips through the rest of the pages and shakes her head. "I guess it's a good thing you're going to file for custody of the kids," she says, glancing back at the document. "Your ex is a real work of art."

"Greek? Roman? Gothic? Renaissance? Baroque or modern?"

Al smiles wanly. "I was thinking Paleolithic. You know, old Stone Age. Rough, crude, and primitive."

"I can hardly disagree."

We laugh for a few moments, then Al gets serious. "The biggest question is why you're agreeing to carry both kids on *your* insurance."

"She says her employer's health package isn't as comprehensive as mine."

Al shakes her head like a wearied instructor having to correct her hard-headed student once again.

"Clifford, Clifford. Will you please get an understanding of the person you're dealing with before you're plundered into poverty?"

"You sure have a way of making a point."

"You'd better start getting the point! She's not the innocent princess you fell in love with. And in her eyes you're not only a frog but one she wouldn't kiss even if you were guaranteed to become a prince. Right now, you represent the incarnation of everything that's wrong in her life and you're deserving of punishment to the maximum extent the law allows. And believe me, the law allows much."

"Al, have you been living under my couch?"

"What do you mean?"

"Never mind." I chuckle. "I'm just constantly amazed at the accuracy of your observations."

"Well, you'd better start listening to them. I know her lawyer, Drake Burchy, and he's no slouch."

"He's a pretty tough customer, huh?"

"To say the least. He takes no prisoners. He glories in his role as the gunslinging legal hit man who can paint the courtroom in blood and still sleep well that night. It's no accident that he and your ex found each other."

A centipede of fear races from my forehead and down my back. This SOB was undoubtedly the "hit man" who called about my pension and retirement amounts.

"Al, what's a quadro?"

Al grimaces. "Clifford, you need to get this dissolution over with quickly."

"Well, whatever it is, it doesn't sound good," I say, forcing a chuckle.

Al's expression hardens into a form that could qualify her for a place among the presidential rock-faces at Mount Rushmore.

"Quadros, also known as qualified domestic relations orders, are used when an ex's lawyer calls the former spouse's employer, requesting 401(k) and pension information."

The last of my fading smile vanishes. "And once they have that information, then what?"

"It's filed with the court to get an actual dollar figure to be split between the two of you. At the time of your retirement, the decreed pension amount is to be paid, which, as you can probably guess, cuts into the pittance most companies pay a retiree."

"But isn't there a Privacy Act statement, a law, statute, *anything* that'll prevent this kind of prying?"

"Clifford, the law doesn't see it as prying but rather as another element in the division of assets. The saving grace is that we can request her records for similar purposes."

My head's aching like someone's whacked it down between my shoulders. "This is utterly fantastic!"

For a moment, I'm too numb even to feel my clothes against my skin. A moment later, my hair's on fire. Al sits back in her chair and folds her arms across her chest, quietly watching the explosion that she knows is coming. My brain's cognitive corner reminds me that Al's been through this and knows I need to vent. And if I were emotionally equipped at the moment, I'd thank her for letting me. But right now, *I'm just too mad!*

"What kind of system is this?" I bellow. "Demetria's the one instigating this disaster. And for all her trouble, the court's gonna make me reward her with monthly tribute payments and a blueprint for raiding my savings and pension. *Jesus!*"

Al speaks softly. "Clifford, I know this is upsetting but there's no point in . . ."

"Do you know what my tax guy told me?" I shout. "He says that the money she gets from me isn't considered part of her income, and the money I'm paying her isn't deducted from mine. The IRS pretends that her income isn't boosted and that mine isn't reduced. Demetria's getting *free money* in a system that'd lock me up if I sold T-shirts from the trunk of my car without reporting the income. How can they do that, Al? *How?*"

Al points to the old newspaper clipping behind her and, sounding as grim as ever, says, "Because they can."

ONCE I'VE CALMED DOWN, AL AND I MOVE ON TO THE MOST IMPORTANT MATTER: Braddie and Bear. And like the other times we've talked about my getting custody of them, Al's not saying all of what I want to hear.

"Clifford, if you want to pursue custody, that's your choice. But as I've already mentioned, you need to be absolutely certain. There are *no* guarantees. Your ex will most likely interpret your attempt as an act of spite, vengeance, selfishness, and rage all balled into one. And she'll have no inhibitions about responding in kind."

"But Al, none of that stuff is why I'm exploring this. Doesn't it matter that I want to raise my sons in an environment that has a more stable, secure, and substantive foundation than one built upon some vacuous search for 'true love, excitement, and fun'?"

"And Clifford, I'm telling you that your ex won't care. She's as convinced as you are that *she* can provide the best environment for those boys. The moment you confront her with the possibility of losing them she'll go for the throat. Believe me, I know what I'm talking about! She could slander you. Make false charges full of criminal innuendo. And petition the court to place all sorts of restrictions upon your visitation rights."

"But all those would be acts of desperation, just to keep me from having them."

"And how could you prove that your motivations wouldn't be equally biased?"

"But . . ."

"And the most important people you keep forgetting about are *the boys*. What about them? As much as you love your sons, are you willing to subject them to a custody battle that'll turn their parents into bitter enemies? Isn't it bad enough that they've lost their home? Shouldn't you be exploring strategies that'll keep relations between you and your ex civil so the boys won't have to choose sides? And believe me, Clifford, *they will*! It'll damage your relationship and leave them emotionally scarred. With those kinds of possibilities lurking, are you really willing to risk a custody fight?"

An oppressive silence coils around me as I inventory, again, the incredible series of events that have led to me sitting here across from Al, scrambling, searching, and scheming to find *any* means of saving my skin. Braddie and Bear's faces flash before me and the guilt that's been nipping at my heels starts chomping.

*Dada, you let us down,* says Braddie and Bear's echo.

"But I didn't want it this way," I mumble.

*We don't care. Your failure made us grow up like you.*

Al's voice snaps me out of my waking nightmare. "Clifford! Are you okay?"

I nod. Al studies my face for a moment, then glances at her watch and says, "Clifford, we need to wrap this up, so listen close. You've got to try and suspend hostilities long enough so the two of you can review the document together and ensure that you're in total agreement. *And be alert!* It's essential that every *i* be dotted and every *t* crossed."

"What if she wants to argue every little point?"

"If you can't reach agreement she may file for divorce, which, as I've told you, is lengthier and more expensive, and can get nasty."

"But aren't dissolutions supposed to keep the process civil?"

"Yes, Clifford. Theoretically. But the difficulty with a dissolution is that it depends upon the people separating to mutually agree to everything."

"This feels like some sick practical joke," I say. "Now, *at the end,* we're supposed to find the flexibility, cooperation, and listening skills that could've saved the marriage all along."

Al answers with several seconds of silence. Then she says, "Just try to review the document in as cooperative an environment as possible. In the end, you'll save time. So don't antagonize and don't be argumentative. But *do* pay attention! That way, if issues arise, you two can try and resolve them on the spot."

"And that's the cruelest irony of all," I say.

"What?"

"That destroying our marriage will go more smoothly if we cooperate and do it together."

# VICTOR

VERNON'S REALLY PISSIN' ME OFF! HE'S HAD ME SITTIN' HERE FOREVER, TAKIN' ME through all kinds'a changes, and still ain't answered my question.

"C'mon, Vee! Whut'd Edie tell you? *When* did she tell you?"

The bar phone rings and Vernon answers. "Benny's. Who? Yeah, he's right here."

He covers the phone and grits on me. "Ice, why're you tellin' your babes to call here? You know how Benny feels about suckas usin' the bar phone."

"Vee, pull that corn cob out your butt and gimme the phone!"

He grits and hands me the phone. I move down one bar stool to get some privacy.

"Yeah. This is Ice."

"Hey, baby." It's Simone. And her voice is drippin' love lube.

Whatever thoughts I was havin' about Edie are blocked out by memories of Simone's mega-mountains. I glance at my watch. "Where's you at? We was s'posed to hook up ten minutes ago."

"I got a 'mergency," says Simone, whisperin'. "My boyfriend's here. He's in the shower. I thought he'd be on the road for another two days but he came back early."

"So whut's this mean?"

"Don't be catchin' no attitude. You know what this means. It'll have'ta be later."

Havin' to wait, *again,* to gnaw Simone's pyramids has my head spinnin'.

"Simone! How many times you think I'ma put up with this?"

Vernon yells from down the other end of the bar. "Ice! Benny don't play yellin' in his phone!"

"You ain't got to put up with it at all!" Simone says.

"Don't even go there!" I say. "You know I want to . . ."

"What you wantin' right now don't matter. It ain't gonna happen. I'll call you later."

Simone hangs up right as I'm hollerin', *"WHEN?"*

# NATHAN

ON THE DRIVE HOME, I'M HOLDING THE STEERING WHEEL IN A DEATH GRIP BUT MY HANDS are still shaking. I tried reading Brenda's face before I left, but to no avail. What makes it worse is that, despite her calm exterior, I know she's seething.

The only thing weighing in my favor is that Brenda heard me slam the door on Beverly's dreams and my lust. At least, I think she did. But what if it's not enough? What if I'm too late? What if Brenda feels I shouldn't have let things get this far? What if I've pushed her beyond where she's willing to reconcile, no matter how enlightened I've suddenly become? What if she divorces me? What'll happen to the kids? What'll happen to my ministry? *What'll I do without Brenda?*

I pull into my garage, shut off the minivan, and try to calm myself. It's no use. My insides are knotted up with emotion. I'm angry at myself for enjoying Beverly's ego-stroking attention and arrogantly assuming that Brenda would accept it passively. I'm ashamed for giving her ample reason to distrust me, and for damaging our relationship. I'm scared of what Brenda might do, and horrified by the wrath awaiting me from my angry God.

The image of Clifford's face fills my mind's eye. He told me about the fight between him and Victor, and what Victor said about dying a million times.

And then there was what he said the other day at his apartment: "Moving in here is one of my million deaths."

Am I destined for that future? Will I become Clifford, staring vacantly through eyes that have seen too much, bearing a burden that'll only get heavier?

I knew divorce was bad, but it wasn't until Clifford's ordeal that I realized it could be so profoundly miserable. "Nate, whatever you do, hold on to Brenda. You don't wanna know what I know," he said.

Please God. I don't want that to be my future. And forgive me, Clifford, but *I don't want to be like you.*

# CLIFFORD

I DRIVE SLOWLY OVER TO DEMETRIA'S, CRAWLING ALONG AS EACH PASSING MILE BRINGS me closer to a destiny I don't know how to avoid. Demetria meets me at the door with the dissolution document in hand. She's dressed for a night out on the town, cradling a box of roses in one arm, and she has her head tilted to keep the cordless phone tucked snugly between her ear and shoulder. She points through the darkened living room toward the kitchen, where I'm to sit at the table and do my part in accomplishing this marital suicide. She stays in the living room for a few more minutes, talking low but her voice carrying like a canyon echo.

"Nolan, don't worry," she says. "I'll be there on time. Just as soon as I'm through here and my baby-sitter arrives, I'll be on my way."

I try tuning Demetria out, but end up listening closer to what she's saying. "Nolan, I do not walk throwing my hips. . . . Okay, maybe just a little, but it's for your own good." She laughs softly, then says, "Look, I've gotta go. . . . Because Clifford's here. . . . Okay. See you in a bit."

I scan the pages of the dissolution document while Demetria arranges the roses in a vase. Each word leaps off the page and slaps me again and again into numbing resignation, each blow a searing reminder of how powerless I am to stop this madness.

> The parties request that, upon hearing, the Court finds said Separation Agreement to be complete, fair, and equitable, to have been voluntarily entered into by and between the parties, and that the marriage be dissolved by law and the Agreement approved. . . .

Demetria finally joins me at the table as I flip through the last of the pages. And I start laughing. First, it's just a chuckle. Then I'm laughing so hard, my stomach muscles are hurting. After a few moments, I compose myself for rational discussion.

"Well, Demetria! It's amazing, don't you think?"

"What's amazing, Clifford?"

I hold up the document. "This! It's a work of art! A masterpiece of condensation! A miracle of miniaturization! A testament to minimalism!"

"Clifford, what're you talking about?"

I shake the papers at her, waving them inches from her nose. "This. *This!*"

Demetria speaks very soft and very slow, operating, I guess, from the belief that soft music, or voices, will soothe the savage breast. "Clifford, what *about* . . . this?"

I toss the papers onto the table. "This document, Demetria. Your lawyer's managed to reduce the nine years of our marriage down to less than twenty-five sheets of paper. Don't you think that's amazing? I know I do."

Demetria stares at me with the calm, confident gaze of one who is certain of victory. I try reading her face but there's nothing. No concern. No remorse. No hesitation. Just an iron will to get what she wants.

I shake my head and chuckle. "I never stood a chance, did I?"

"What're you talking about?"

"Come off it, Demetria. You never wanted to save this marriage."

"Clifford, I've told you from the start what I wanted. I never misled you or gave you any reason to hope."

"And let me congratulate you on a job well done. But you see, Demetria, I'm not as stupid as you might think."

I shuffle the papers into a neat, compact stack, then drill her with my eyes. "I heard you loud and clear when you said you wanted out. I also heard that fiction you pumped down my neck about 'suddenly' knowing the 'truth' after talking with Nolan. Well, here's a news flash, Demetria: Divorce isn't something that sneaks up and attacks during the night! You'd decided this long before you ever verbalized it."

"Well, Clifford! That's amazing, isn't it? How can we explain your being perfectly content to let this marriage stumble along until you knew I meant business?"

I laugh. "That's what I'm saying, Demetria. It wouldn't have made a difference. You'd already made your decision. So nothing would've mattered. Not the romantic *Phantom of the Opera* weekend we spent in Toronto. Not doubling up on courses so I could finish school early and spend more time with my family. Not when I'd show up on your job to take you to lunch or just say 'I love you.' Not when I'd decided to keep hammering at our problems till they were fixed. And for certain not when I decided that, no matter what, I was gonna stay in this marriage even though you were frequently impossible to live with."

Demetria blinks like a surprised chipmunk.

"What did you think, Demetria? That you were married to yourself? Yeah, I know you believed that. Well, let me assure you, love cup, for as miserable as you think I made you, it can't begin to compare with the crap I've put up with from you!"

Demetria snaps out of her trance and her expression darkens. "Look! I've said what I said and if you don't like it, tough!"

"You've got that right! This has made me tough. And thanks to you, I'll be a lot tougher before it's over. But I just wanted you to know, Demetria, I'm no fool. That day when you said that you wanted 'true love, excitement, and fun,' I thought you were stressed and just couldn't find words to express yourself. But you were serious! All that garbage about me being gone so often, hibernating in my office, being intellectually condescending, and pestering you about sex, and your already feeling like a single parent—all of that was the camouflage *you* needed to make sound sensible what even *you* knew sounded ridiculous. I could've come home every day, fixed dinner, sewn you a new wardrobe, and laid down as the mat for you to wipe your feet on and the result would've been the same. Any reason would've been just as good as the stupid, selfish, shallow one you gave because, in the end, *you weren't gonna be there anyway*!"

"Screw you, Clifford! I don't care what kind of analytical spin you've put on this to ease your conscience. We were in this together and we're both responsible."

"I couldn't agree more. I'm completely and totally responsible for my half of what went wrong." I lean forward and level my gaze. "But Demetria, I'm responsible for *only* my half."

She springs up from her chair. "I don't even know why I let you drag me into this. I'm ending this conversation. I'm tired and—"

"I know. I know. You're going to bed. Because you're tired and got a headache and feel your stomach tying itself in knots and don't feel like hearing my mouth and don't wanna have sex and feel smothered and have got more important things to do and don't have'ta take my crap and are too busy with the kids and need to go meet Tammy and wish I'd buzz off and don't have to waste your time and have been over this before and wish I'd get a life and don't know what we have in common and need more than I can give, blah, blah, blah."

"Clifford! *Drop dead!*"

"I did, Demetria, being married to you. But now that that's ending, I'm alive again."

Demetria crosses her arms tight over her chest and wipes a tear from her cheek. "I want those papers back tomorrow."

"You'll get 'em back after I've had the revisions reviewed."

"I don't know why. Everything's in order."

"And of course I trust you and your desire to secure my highest good. If only I could ignore you holding that dagger stuck in my back."

Demetria's cheeks are glistening and she suddenly seems so small, fragile, and vulnerable, holding on to herself tight, as if to keep from shrinking further. She sways a bit, then totters back a step. I race around the table and catch her, holding her in a full, firm embrace. The scent of her hair fills my nostrils and my legs weaken as nine years' worth of emotion-charged memory bolts through my mind. Our first kiss. The first time she said "I love you." The doctor pulling Bear from her womb. Braddie's smile the day he was born. Playing with them in my Santa suit. Our anniversary at Niagara Falls. All of us crying when Scratch got hit. The Caribbean moonlight on Demetria's face.

A tear spills onto my cheek and I stagger. Demetria steadies me, as I steady her.

"Demetria, how did we come to this?"

She whispers, "I don't know, Clifford. I honestly do not know."

I look into her eyes and we kiss, hard and with desperate passion. She hugs me, holding on with the clutch of someone being sucked into a maelstrom, fearful of the journey, and even more so of what's on the other side. Then, slowly, she pushes me away.

"It's too late, Clifford. It's too late for that and thoughts of what might've been."

Demetria hurries off into the dark living room.

I walk to the edge of the darkness and say, "No, Demetria. There'll be plenty of time to think of what might've been."

I LOOK IN ON THE BOYS BEFORE LEAVING. THEY'RE SITTING SIDE BY SIDE ON THE FLOOR, playing one of their many video games. They're gazing at the TV as they try to outmaneuver, bludgeon, or vaporize each other's screen warrior. There's an air of intense concentration about them, but there's something different about them, different from their usual competitive banter. *There isn't any.* And my insides are shriveling as I wonder how much they might've heard of that awful conversation I've just had with Demetria.

I walk softly across the room and kneel down between them. "How's it going, guys?"

"Okay," answers Bear, sounding dejected.

Braddie says, "Dada, will we have to go away now?"

"Huh? What're you talking about, Braddie? Nobody's going any . . ."

"You went away!" says Bear. "You used to live here, but now you're in Dadaland."

He tosses aside his game controller and starts crying. Braddie does the same, and jumps up and wraps his arms around my neck so tight that I have to struggle for breath.

"Hey, c'mon, you guys," I say softly. "What's going on here? What's the matter?"

Braddie speaks first, his words coming in fits and starts. "My . . . my friend, Ryan Roberts . . . his dad came and took him away and . . . now he'll never see . . . his mommy again."

"Nobody knows where he is," says Bear, tears spilling from his eyes.

I gently shush the boys into silence. "C'mon, you guys," I say. "I'm sure Ryan's dad will bring him home. Why're you crying?"

"Because you . . . you asked us about living with you," says Braddie. "And since you're so mad at Mommy . . . you might not let us see her anymore."

"Why can't we see both of you?" asks Bear.

I hug the boys tight, and have the queasy sensation that on this custody issue, Al just might be right.

# VICTOR

I LOOK AT VERNON AND POINT TO MY SHOT GLASS. "HIT ME!"

He pours some vodka and I slug it down. "Hit me again!"

Vernon snatches the glass away. "You ain't gettin' another drop!"

"Whuts'a matter with you, man? I'm a payin' customer."

"I don't care what you payin'. Benny don't like suckas gettin' scraped up off the road cuz they was too juiced to drive. Besides, I don't know why you're wastin' so much energy on a babe who's makin' a career of shaftin' you."

Whut Vee's sayin' is right. But bein' denied Simone's weather balloons again is frustratin' the daylights out'a me. I slap some money down on the counter and head for the door, stoppin' when Vernon calls.

"Ice! Ice! Hold up a second."

I wait while Vernon searches beneath the counter. His face lights up and he pulls out an envelope.

"I almost forgot. When Edie passed through she asked me to give you this."

I snatch the envelope and stare at it, rubbin' my fingers back'n forth along the edges. Seein' Edie's handwritin' is the closest I've been to her in days and, I swear, I'm all of a sudden missin' her so bad my legs almost give out. I stick out my hand to Vernon and he stares at it like I'm handin' him a bear claw.

"What's this for?" he axes.

"For bein' my friend, punk."

Vernon smiles, we shake, and I leave.

IT'S A BATTLE MAKIN' MYSELF WAIT TILL I GET HOME TO READ EDIE'S LETTER. MY HEART'S gongin' when I tear the letter open, handlin' it like it's thousand-year-old paper that might crack and crumble. I pull the letter out and start readin'.

*Victor,*

*I tried calling over and over but it's clear you don't want to be bothered. I'm sorry about what happened at the hospital. I gave Mother and Lyle a royal chewing out. I guess I can't blame you for being angry. But understand, Victor. I'm not out husband-shopping to find a father for my baby. I'd love to raise her in a two-parent home, but I refuse to cast my pearls before any more swine. I'd need to be absolutely certain that you were ready to love me. I now know you aren't. You see, I tried contacting you through your job. Mr. Corey Jackson said you'd be on sick leave until your VD cleared up. Good-bye, Victor. I don't know if it was nice knowing you. But I do know I never want to see you again.*

*Edie*

I race up to Edie's momma's door and knock. Edie prob'ly forgot she told me where her momma lived, but thanks to the Marine Corps I pay attention to details. This ain't the time to be bashful. Specially after the lady hollerin' through the door of what use'ta be Edie's apartment told me that she'd moved out. Her momma don't think I'm good enough, specially compared to Lyle. But I ain't losin' Edie—not without a fight!

The porch light comes on and my legs get the wobblies.

"Who is it?" says a female voice that ain't Edie's.

"Ice."

"Who?"

"Ice! The dude at the hospital. The one Karenna's crazy about."

Edie's momma don't answer right away and I'm wonderin' if she's callin' the po-leases. There ain't a black dude over the age of two who don't know them suckas just *love* crackin' our skulls, so I ain't too thrilled about a possible meetin'. But I ain't goin' nowhere! If the po-leases come, they'll have'ta wait till I'm through with Edie.

"What do you want, Mr. Ice?"

"I want Edie!"

"She doesn't want to see you. Now go away before I . . ."

"Look, Miz Harris. You been around long enough to know I ain't no stranger to the po-leases. So you know I don't need them kinda hassles. But I'm tellin' you right now, I ain't leavin' till I talk to Edie."

She don't say nothin' again and now I *know* she's callin' 'em. This sucks! Once they check them computers and find out whut happened in Pittsburgh, I'm dead meat. I back up a couple'a steps and almost sprint to my car, cuz ain't nobody's lovin' worth all this. But Edie ain't just nobody. She's the one I want. The one I've been lookin' for. The one who can put out the fires that's been burnin' up my brain.

"Mr. Ice, I don't want any trouble," says Liz. "But if you don't leave I *will* call the police."

"Toss me the phone and I'll call 'em for you. I ain't leavin' till I talk with Edie."

"She has nothing to say to you."

"Good! That means she'll be quiet while I talk."

"You didn't return her calls."

"I was bein' a fool."

"You left her at the hospital."

"I was hurt and jealous of Lyle."

"What about your . . . disease?" axes Liz, soundin' like she's confused about the question herself.

That fool Corey better be watchin' his back, cuz he's sho'nuff got some payback comin'. I lean close to the door and talk slow so Liz hears all'a whut I'm sayin'.

"Liz, Edie knows that was a lie."

A minute goes by. Two. Then the door opens. And behind Liz stands Edie, holdin' Karenna.

Karenna wiggles down from her arms and runs to me. "Bus driver!"

She hugs me hard around the neck, looks back at Edie, and says, "See, Mommy! Bus driver loves us!"

Edie looks grim. "What do you want, Victor?"

"You."

"I'm not a toy."

"I ain't playin'."

"I don't love halfway."

"I ain't half-steppin'."

"I won't be one of many."

"Edie, it's you and *only* you!"

Then, slowly, she smiles.

# NATHAN

I'VE BEEN AT HOME, WAITING FOR OVER AN HOUR AND PACING A TRENCH INTO OUR LIVing room carpet. I pull back the curtains, glance out the window and up the street. Still no Brenda, so I go back to pacing.

My thoughts collide and rampage like stampeding elephants. On the one hand, I'm glad that Brenda heard me tell Beverly that I was going to fix a situation that I'd let get out of control. On the other hand, I'm horrified that Brenda heard me tell Beverly that it was necessary to fix a situation that I'd let get out of control. It means that Brenda could be both glad and furious. It also means I could be either spared or skewered, depending upon which portion of this mess she chooses to focus on.

A car pulls into the driveway and I zip to the window. It's Brenda! I hurry to the front door, ready to prove that I'm so very sorry and want to make this up to her any way I can. It's not the strongest bargaining position, but that's not important right now.

What's important is that my wife is home, and I've got another—maybe last—chance to give her a reason to stay.

I open the door and Brenda walks past me, not saying a word or even glancing in my direction.

"Brenda?"

She turns the corner and starts down the hallway toward our room.

My racing heart's whacking against my chest. "Brenda? C'mon, baby. Let's talk."

"We will, Nathan. In here."

I follow her into the room. She's sitting on the edge of the bed, her expression so calm it's almost menacing.

My throat tightens and I have to shove out my words. "Brenda, listen to me, sweetheart. I'm so sorry. I . . ."

"Come over here," says Brenda, softly patting the bed beside her.

I sit down and she takes firm hold of my chin. "Nathan, I want to know everything."

My stomach flip-flops, leaving me nauseous. "Brenda, are you sure?"

She nods, tightening her grip on my chin. "And speak only truth, Nathan. The moment you lie, *I'll know.*"

She gets up and goes over to the window, crossing her arms and keeping most of her back to me. I ball my hands into fists to stop their trembling. It works, but barely. Brenda turns and looks at me, her expression still calm but resolute.

"Well," she says, "I'm waiting."

I take a deep breath and search for a beginning. "Brenda, no matter what, please believe me when I tell you that I love you."

She turns back to the window. "Stop stalling, Nathan."

And so I start, doing my best to silence the howling voices warning me that this is the stupidest thing I've ever done. Another part of me shouts that it's the right thing to do. And still another part of me prays that the Lord will see me through.

I talk on, giving Brenda only a sketchy outline to spare her the steamy details. ". . . but the moment our lips touched, I pulled away. I just couldn't . . ."

Brenda's head snaps around and she locks her angry eyes onto me. "Nathan, don't forget that I just finished talking with Beverly. I'd suggest that you tell me *everything*."

I lower my head, take a deep breath, and comply. Brenda listens quietly, looking steadily out the window, mercifully shielding me from the agony that must be etching onto her face. Then the moment comes when all that there is to tell has been told.

I look at Brenda still gazing out the window. A menacing silence fills the room, its dark presence extinguishing the light, love, and warmth that once reigned here.

"Brenda, I'm sorry," I say. "Please forgive me."

My heart shatters when Brenda chokes back a sob. "Did you . . . did you make love to her?"

"No, Brenda! As God is my witness, it never went that far."

Brenda turns slowly toward me, the expression on her face removing any hopes I'd had that things would somehow turn out all right.

"Don't bring God into this," she says, her voice resonating with rage. "He was your witness the day you were groping Beverly and that didn't stop you. So don't you dare speak to me about *God*!"

"Brenda, please. I know you're upset but . . ."

"No, Nathan! You have *no* idea of how upset I am."

She stomps over to my closet, gathers a mass of my clothes into her arms, and with a mighty grunt lifts them off the clothes rod and throws them on the floor.

"Brenda! What're you doing?"

"What does it look like I'm doing?" she says, throwing my shoes onto the pile.

I rush over and grab her, holding her tight in my arms. "Stop, Brenda! *Please.* We can't let this happen."

"Let go of me!" she shouts, struggling to get free.

"Baby, listen to me. You're moving too fast! We've got to sit down and . . ."

"No!" Brenda gathers all of her strength, breaks free from my arms, and grabs one of my shoes.

"Brenda, this is insane. Nothing's going to be solved by . . ."

She hurls the shoe and it slams into my face, dazing me and knocking me back a step. I shake my head to clear the vision of two Brendas dumping the contents of my dresser drawers onto the clothes pile. She tosses the last drawer aside, storms into the bathroom, then storms out, throwing my shaving kit onto the heap.

We stand on either side, looking at each other over this lump of clothes, shoes, and toiletries that may as well be Mount Everest. Brenda's nostrils are flared, her chest is heaving, and her lips are jammed tight together. Tears stream down her cheeks in wide paths of watery sorrow.

My voice cracks as I say, "Brenda, please don't do this."

"I'm going to pick up the kids. When we get back, *I want you gone*!"

Brenda heads for the doorway, stopping when I say, "Brenda, I can't do this. How am I supposed to live without you?"

"In pain, Nathan," she says.

And then she's gone.

WHERE DO I GO? I'VE BEEN DRIVING AROUND PITTSBURGH FOR NEARLY TWO HOURS, TRYing to answer that question. My first thought was to camp out in my office down at Divine Temple. But when I considered all the questions and gossip that'd be generated by me spending not just a lot but *most* of my time there, I tossed the idea.

I started for Clifford's house in Penn Hills Commons, but then remembered that he's now living at Wheaton Point.

When I called him on my cell phone, his voice was pulsing with anger. "Hello!"

"Clifford, hi. It's me, Nathan."

"Hey, Nate," he said, his tone barely civil. "What can I do for you?"

"Ah, well, you crossed my mind and I just thought I'd check and see how things were going."

"They stink! I spent the first part of my evening reviewing that lousy dissolution document with Demetria. I've spent the last part arguing with her about the boys."

Clifford was clearly in a bad mood and I was about to let him go when he said, "Sorry about the bad attitude, Nate. But I can't believe her! It's like she's on another planet!"

"What happened?"

"It's unbelievable," he growled. "I called over there to speak to Braddie and Bear, just to reassure them, and . . ."

"Reassure them about what?"

"That I wouldn't kidnap them."

"What!"

"That was my reaction too. And I was truly puzzled, until they explained that one of their friends had been kidnapped by his father."

I almost said something like "Those poor kids," but I bit my tongue, knowing that Clifford didn't need me to acquaint him with Braddie and Bear's pain.

Clifford continued, saying, "And when I considered that they had probably heard me and Demetria fussing over that dissolution document, their fear made a lot of sense."

"So what did Demetria have to say about this?"

"About what?"

"The dissolution document."

"Plenty! But that's not what we've been just now hassling about. I was getting on her case about having some guy baby-sit the boys."

"Some guy?"

"That's right! She went out and left my sons in the care of some stranger."

"Oh. You mean that Nolan character."

"No, Nate! I *do not* mean 'that Nolan character.' From what I could gather of their phone conversation, Nolan was Demetria's *date*! This other clown is probably some romantic hopeful, positioning himself to pounce the moment Demetria boots Nolan out."

I was flabbergasted. "Were the boys all right?"

"Yes. But that's not the point. As soon as I found out they were there with a stranger, I picked them up and brought them over here."

"C'mon Clifford. If this guy's putting the moves on Demetria, he can't be a stranger to her."

*"He's a stranger to me!"* bellowed Clifford. "Jesus, Nate! Whose side are you on?"

"Yours, Clifford! I was merely pointing out that . . ."

"I know you don't understand. But put yourself in my place. What would you do?"

The question hit with the same dizzying impact of the shoe Brenda had hurled. With it came the realization not only that Clifford and I were close to being in the same place, but that I could one day be the person shouting at his end of the phone.

"I'll tell you just like I told Demetria," railed Clifford. "Braddie and

Bear are my sons! The moment I suspect something negative happening to them, whoever's responsible is going to have to deal with *me*!"

"What did she say?"

"She blew me off, of course."

I shuddered, imagining Brenda doing the same with me. I turned in to Wheaton Point, pulled into a parking space, and left the car running.

"Let's talk about something else," sighed Clifford. "Are you on your way over?"

I looked around the Wheaton Point complex. The day I helped Clifford move in, I tried to get him to see that these apartments weren't so bad. Now that I had no place to go, I could see that they weren't all that great.

I shifted the car into reverse, started backing out of the parking space, and said, "Naw. I was just calling to check and see how you were doing."

"I think I've answered that question," said Clifford, sounding incredibly weary.

I headed for the exit, passing his apartment on the way. I saw his silhouette behind his thin living room curtain. He was pacing and, from the looks of it, massaging his forehead.

"Try and take it easy, Clifford. Things'll get better."

"If you say so. Thanks for calling, Nate. Sorry about losing my temper. I guess Braddie's not the only one who needs an anger-management class."

"What?"

"Never mind. I'll talk to you later."

And then we hung up.

I keep driving, picking up the phone to dial my mentor, Pastor Childress. I know he'd let me stay with him, engulf me in his love, and never let me feel even the breath of condemnation. And that's exactly why I can't stay there. I couldn't bear to see the reflection of myself staring back from his spirit-filled eyes, his very presence a constant reminder of what I could've been and how I've failed. I put the phone down and keep driving.

I pass a number of motels, eventually turning in to one and sitting for a few moments. I could check in and gut it out for a few days until this mess straightens out. But given the gravity of my situation and the depth of Brenda's anger, that could run into a lot of time and money. Not to mention that staying at a motel might also send a very wrong message to Brenda, causing her to think that motels might have been a part of this chaos with Beverly. I can't afford to have Brenda make that association. I pull back out into traffic and leave.

Another hour passes and for a moment—a very brief moment—I consider taking a few days off and driving to Cleveland to stay with Victor. But that's a bad idea. Not because Victor wouldn't let me, but because he would savor the chance to remind me of every criticism, admonishment, or disapproving statement I've ever made about him and his lifestyle.

He'd tell me, "See there, Nate. When it's all said'n done, you ain't no better'n me."

I pull into a burger joint drive-through, ordering food that Brenda, if she were here, would lovingly remind me is a cholesterol injection. That's so much like her, taking notice of every little thing, loving me and the kids in a way that always left us feeling secure in the knowledge that she'd be there and that no one came before us.

"Brenda, how am I supposed to live without you?" I ask softly.

*In pain, Nathan.*

The memory of Brenda's tortured voice fills my ears. My eyes water. I toss the burger back in the bag and keep driving, willing myself into composure. I have to endure this like a man, a man who's learning that a love like Brenda's is never to be taken for granted.

I pull into Momma's driveway and park. As with Pastor Childress, I'm not looking forward to seeing my reflection in her eyes, especially since I know she's experienced the hurt I've caused Brenda. But there's nowhere else to go. And no matter how disappointed Momma might be, no matter how angry that I've driven away my wife and her daughter, I know she'll love me. And right now, I need that love, even if it's clothed in her anger.

I get out of the car, gather up some of my belongings, and head for the door. Momma opens it on the first knock.

"Where have you been?" she asks, irritated.

"Driving around. I'm sorry, Momma. I didn't know you were looking for me."

"Not me. Brenda."

"Brenda!"

"She's been calling here looking for you."

My heart, so incredibly heavy a moment ago, is flying. Momma says, "Wipe that smile off your face! She only wanted to make sure you were safe."

I nod and lower my eyes. Momma shakes her head. "The guest room's available. You can use the downstairs office to sort through all that material."

"What material?"

"I'm not sure. Brenda stopped by with an armload of papers and said something about the next phase of church renovation."

Momma sees my effort to keep myself in emotional check and pulls me into her arms. "I know you're hurting, Nathan. But your pain is *nothing* compared to what you've put Brenda through."

"I know, Momma. And I'm so desperately sorry, but Brenda doesn't believe me."

"Don't be so sure about that. If my guess is right, she might eventually let you come home. But it'll be different this time."

"What do you mean?"

Momma takes my face into her palms. "When Brenda loved you before, she gave her love freely. You'll have to provide her with some solid and substantial reasons before she'll risk investing her heart in you again."

She pulls me close and kisses my forehead. "And Nathan, don't underestimate her anger. You're on dangerously thin ice. If you want her, I'd suggest you get to work *now.*"

I hug Momma, grab the phone, and call Brenda. She answers on the first ring.

"Hello."

"Hi, Bren. It's me."

"I recognize your voice, Nathan. What do you want?"

I swallow and keep talking. "I just wanted you to know that I'm over at Momma's. I'll be staying here until . . ."

"Until what?"

"Until you tell me I can come home."

"Don't hold your breath."

"I'll do that and anything else it takes to win you back, Brenda. I know that sounds hollow right now, but you'll just have to take my word for it."

"Take *your* word! That's a laugh."

I grimace. "I deserved that, Brenda. And I understand that you're angry and God knows you have a right to be. But hear me well. I'm not going quietly into the night. I love you. I need you. And I refuse to live without you, unless you insist that it be that way. But before that happens, you're going to know that I have, shall, and always will love you. Good night."

I hang up and glance at Momma. She smiles and goes into her room.

# THEIR BROTHER'S KEEPER

# CLIFFORD

I MISS BRADDIE AND BEAR. SO BEFORE I LEAVE WORK, I CALL TO SEE IF DEMETRIA WOULD mind my stopping by to see them. I *hate* having to do that. After watching them enter the world, protecting and guiding them without help from the state, and providing for them out of the abundance of my love, I've got to get permission like I'm suddenly of questionable character.

I drum my fingers on my desk, waiting for Demetria to pick up. When someone does, it's not her.

"Hello?"

"Hello," I say. "Who am I speaking with?"

"Tammy. Who are you?"

Tammy. The moment I hear her voice, I think about Victor's thug friend, Cruiser. If there were ever someone who needed "doin'," it's Tammy. But there's no point in considering the merits of unleashing Cruiser against her. After all, Demetria's the chief perpetrator of this drama. Tammy's just an irksome sidekick.

"Where's Demetria?" I say, speaking with minimum civility.

"Gone."

I roll my eyes. "When will she be home?"

"As soon as she gets back."

It's apparent that Tammy has no more love for me than I do for her, and I imagine her wearing the same smirk that's constantly plastered onto Demetria's face.

"Ask her to have the boys call me when they get home," I say.

"They're home right now."

"What! Braddie and Bear are there with *you*?"

Silence answers from the phone, and it should. Because if I were Tammy, and knew that Demetria's soon-to-be-ex-husband wouldn't even pee on me if I were on fire, I'd be kicking myself for letting him know that I was babysitting his sons who are precious to him beyond measure.

"Let me talk to Braddie and Bear," I demand.

"Er, ah, now listen, Clifford," stammers Tammy. "I don't want any trouble."

"Don't you mean that you don't want to *be* any trouble?"

"Clifford, I know you blame a lot of this on me, but . . ."

"Let me talk to my sons!" I bellow.

Several people on the way out of the office hear me and try to look without looking. I glare at them and they quicken their pace and get out.

Braddie's first on the phone. "Hi, Dada. Aunt Tammy said you . . ."

"Braddie, listen to me. Tammy's not your aunt *anything*. Okay?"

"But Mommy said . . ."

"I don't care what she said!"

I'm immediately sorry about being rough with him, but this is no time for subtlety. "Braddie, Tammy's not part of our blood. Do you remember what I told you about our blood?"

"That we're proud, strong, and should always do the right thing."

"That's right! And Tammy's *none* of those things. Understand?"

"Yes, sir."

Bear picks up the other phone. "Hi, Dada."

I say hello and immediately set Bear straight on this "Aunt Tammy" business.

"Is that the same for Uncle Nolan too?" asks Bear.

Hearing that, my scalp almost blows off. It's bad enough that I've had to fight Tammy's and Nolan's shadows, lurking in the background of my marriage. But now Demetria's invited them onto center stage, giving them direct access to and power over my sons. And I'm not having it!

"Braddie! Bear!"

"Yes, sir."

"Get your school stuff together. I'll be there in a minute."

"But mommy told us . . ."

I hang up and am on the way.

# VICTOR

AS USUAL, I HAD TO HASSLE WITH MY PUNK BOSS COREY ABOUT GETTIN' SOME TIME OFF so I could come back to Pittsburgh for this hearin' Al's set up. But I played it different this time.

As soon as Corey started goin' into his "Mr. Jackson" routine, I got quiet and stepped off for the front office. That rattled him somethin' serious cuz he ain't had no idea of whut I was about to do. Specially since I'd told him that I knew he'd fed Edie that lie about me havin' VD.

He came huffin' up behind me and said, "Now hold on, Ice. What're you fixing to do?"

"Nothin', Corey," I said, grinnin' and steppin' fast. "I'ma just talk to our bosses about some funny thangs I've been noticin'. Like people screwin' on company property."

Corey couldn't talk fast enough. He jumped in front'a me, wipin' his forehead and lickin' his lips.

"Wait, Ice! No need to do that. Tell you what. Why don't you take some time off? Go to Pittsburgh. See your family. Take care of that business you were telling me about."

I stepped around him and kept stridin'. "Never mind, Corey. This stuff's really important. I betcha even Claudia's ugly, muscle-head husband will wanna know."

"No!" he hollered, grabbin' my arm.

I looked down at his hand, then up into his wide eyes, and said, "If you wanna keep ev'rythang from your hand up to your elbow, you'd best let go of me."

He shifted into fourth-gear-friendly, shufflin' and apologizin', and urgin' me to take some vacation days with pay.

"Are you sure, Corey? I don't wanna be causin' you no budget troubles or nothin'."

I messed with his mind a little longer and he was too glad to see me gone. But Corey knows he better be sleepin' with one eye open. Cuz somehow, some way, I'ma get some payback for him tellin' Edie that lie. But later for that. Right now I'm havin' too much fun listenin' to Lynnette get whooped.

I lean forward a little bit so's I don't miss a word of whut the magistrate, Judge Bentley, is sayin'.

She looks over her half-lens spectacles at Lynnette and says, "All right, Ms. Porter. Suppose you tell me again why you permitted your relatives to take your daughter to Atlanta, interfering with her father's visitation."

Lynnette's lawyer, some scarecrow dude, wearin' a nice-lookin' blue suit and soundin' like someone's puttin' a steady squeeze on his nuts, stands up. "Your honor, I'd like to . . ."

"Sit down, Mr. Dixon!" snaps Judge Bentley. "You'll get your chance. I want to hear what Ms. Porter has to say while I consider citing her with a contempt violation."

I lean over to Al. "Gettin' cited with that contempt thang, that's pretty bad. Ain't it?"

Al nods slightly, keepin' her eyes locked on Judge Bentley. I bite my lower lip to keep from smilin' too big.

"Well!" says Judge Bentley, gettin' kinda loud. "Don't you have anything to say, Ms. Porter?"

"I, I told him about Jewel's goin' out'a town. You just gotta know Ice. He do what he wants to do, not thinkin' about nobody but himselves."

Judge Bentley rolls her eyes. "Well, according to his travel records, he brings 'himselves' back to Pittsburgh quite often to see his daughter. But *you* let relatives take her to Atlanta, depriving her of an opportunity to further bond with her father, who, unlike so many others, wanted to be there."

That travel stuff like mileage, toll receipts, and whatnot is one'a the thangs Al got me to doin' a long time ago, just in case of days like today. And I'm so glad that, for once, I wasn't bein' hardheaded about followin' advice. Cuz with the way Lynnette's squirmin', it was worth every toll charge paid, every gallon of gas pumped, and every mile traveled.

Judge Bentley takes off her specs and points 'em at Lynnette. "Listen to me closely, Ms. Porter. It's obvious that you and Mr. Matthews have had some disagreements regarding your relationship. That's unfortunate, but quite frankly it's not the concern of this court."

She puts her specs back on and starts shufflin' through papers. "What *is* of major concern is that your daughter be provided with as much of a loving, balanced childhood as possible. *Understood?*"

"Yes, your Judge-ness."

Judge Bentley shakes her head and keeps flippin' pages. "A balanced childhood means ensuring that your daughter has access to her mother *and* her father. It also means that you two should treat each other with some degree of respect so that the child's being from a broken home isn't further compounded by having to endure arguments, accusations, and slander like Mr. Matthews being called 'a good-for-nothing Negro.' "

Judge Bentley's kinda smirkin' when she says that, but it's cool. For the way she's kickin' Lynnette's butt, she can call me anythang she wants! And like always, I'm double-impressed with Al. Cuz I ain't thought she remembered me complainin' about Lynnette's bein' the cause of Jewel callin' me "Nero." But since Judge Bentley mentioned it, that's proof that Al not only remembered but somehow convinced the judge to bust Lynnette's chops about it.

"I deal with too many fathers who aren't even thinking about their children," says Judge Bentley. "So I'm not going to ignore the plea of one who's trying to do right." She stops flippin' pages and zeros Lynnette down with her eyes. "And Ms. Porter, as long as Mr. Matthews is fulfilling his obligations *you* will comply with the judgment of this court. Am I making myself clear?"

"Yes, your Judge-ness."

Judge Bentley looks at Lynnette's scarecrow lawyer. "Mr. Dixon, make certain that your client understands the ramifications of refusing to obey this decision."

"Yes, Your Honor."

Judge Bentley looks at me. "And Mr. Matthews, don't take my statements to Ms. Porter as a sign that you're somehow free of fault. Both of you are responsible for bringing a precious child into this world, a child who's now suffering because the two of you had a change of heart. I strongly recommend that you keep living up to your end of the bargain or you'll also find yourself on my bad side. Is that clear?"

I start to answer but Al cuts me off, sayin', "We understand completely, Your Honor."

Judge Bentley bangs the gavel, looks at the court clerk, and says, "Next!"

Outside in the hallway, I pick Al up and twirl her around. "You's one bad lawyer!" I say. "From the bottom of my heart, thank you!"

Al laughs and says, "You're welcome. Now put me down."

I set her down and give her a hug. "Al, that was great. Ev'rythang! Even the part where the Judge was slammin' Lynnette about that 'good-for-nothin' Negro' stuff."

"Consider it a bonus," says Al. "I found out that Judge Bentley's mother once suffered a nervous breakdown from all the name-calling and other verbal abuse of her father. Knowing that, I worked that part of your issue into the language of our complaint. I wasn't sure if the judge would allow it, but the gamble paid off."

"You'd better b'lieve it paid off. I just wish there was somethin' I could do for you."

"There is," says Al, lookin' all of a sudden real serious. "Go see your daughter."

I smile and say, "Consider it done," then step off to go see my Jewel.

# NATHAN

BEFORE GOING HOME TO MOMMA'S, I STOP AT THE GROCERY STORE NEAR DIVINE TEMPLE to pick up some items she wants me to get for this mini reunion she's still planning. Given the current state of affairs in our family, I think she's being overly ambitious. But who knows? Maybe an overly ambitious display of love is what we need to regroup and fight the disintegrations that've been causing so much havoc.

After three days of fasting, being around all this food is tough. But I intend to persevere, denying my hunger as a means of disciplining myself to deny other fleshly appetites. The first day and a half was rough. After that, my body adjusted and it felt good being in control. That denial of flesh combined with getting deep into God's Word has left me more fulfilled than if I'd consumed a world-class meal. My only regret is that I didn't do this sooner, and that it might be too late.

Brenda's still not speaking to me, always handing the phone to one of the kids whenever I call. Corrine's still angry, limiting her responses to monosyllabic grunts. And even though he's more talkative than Brenda or Corrine, Nate Junior's in a tough spot and spends most of our conversations trying to get off the phone.

I've stopped by a few times, hoping that an in-person visit might somehow make it more difficult for them to ignore me. I was wrong. And poor Nate Junior, caught between being glad to see me and sympathizing with his mother, tries his best to put me at ease, but always retreats to the politically safe territory of his room.

Not being around them has left me miserable. It's also left me understanding better the rage that's been so apparent in Clifford's voice recently, and the anger that's always simmered inside of Victor. Even the best attitude would be soured by the gauntlet they're running.

They've had their lives and their relationships with their children colonized by strangers who seem to be constantly issuing rules, quoting regulations, and telling them what they can or can't do. And according to Victor, the only choice they have is to "obey and pay." As much as I'm praying that that isn't my fate, if it happens I'll have only myself to blame.

I try focusing on more positive thoughts, park my grocery cart alongside the meat counter, and start looking for some reasonably priced steaks and spare ribs. Even though Momma's reduced her meat intake, the rest of us are still very much carnivores, especially Victor. Which means that if we're going to have a family gathering, we may as well do it right and have a barbecue.

Even while I'm comparing prices and quality, I'm missing Brenda so much that I can almost hear her voice. Someone laughs and I stop in my tracks. She laughs again and I have no doubt that that voice is real and it belongs to Brenda. I hurry over to the aisle her laughter's coming from and turn the corner.

Brenda's standing with her back to me, but I can see that it's definitely her. And talking with her is some stud of a guy who can only be described as tall, dark, and handsome. From his body language and the sly grin on his face, it's obvious that he's not discussing matters of health and nutrition.

I hustle behind a large cardboard display for children's cereal, shielding myself from view and listening as my heart jackhammers against my chest. My anger's igniting as the shock of what I've seen wears off and its meaning sets in.

This pretty boy's putting the moves on *my wife*. And from the sound of the conversation, Brenda's not struggling to get away. An anger more pure and potent than any I've ever felt explodes in my stomach and fans out, until even my fingertips are pulsing with heat.

"It's too bad you feel that way," says the guy, his voice smooth and oily. "All I can say is that he's a fool for letting someone as gorgeous as you come out in public alone."

Brenda laughs softly, sounding like she's actually *enjoying* this. And each of the pretty boy's words hits me like a brick to the jaw, sounding painfully familiar to words I spoke to Beverly on the way to our transgression.

After what I've done, I have no right to be angry. I have no right to blow my stack over Brenda's merely having a grocery-aisle conversation. But this *isn't* just a conversation. It's a beginning, an invitation to skulk and slink, pretend and posture, lie and evade. I know this because it's how I brought myself to ruin, and I can't let that happen to Brenda. I've got to stop this—and now!

But who am I kidding? I'm not doing this for Brenda. I'm doing it for *me*, to protect my pride and spare myself the horrible vision of Brenda making love to another man. And even though all that's true, and my indignation's hypocritical, I still have to "save" her.

I move to step from behind the cardboard display, stopping when Brenda says, "Well, it was nice meeting you, Darnell, but I'm married. So thanks, but no thanks."

"I understand, beautiful. But why don't you take my number anyway. After all, you never know. Things could change."

"I'm flattered, but *no*," says Brenda sternly. "I appreciate the attention, but I'm not interested."

"Aw, c'mon," croons Darnell. "Don't be like that. If you're worried about him finding out, I know how to be discreet."

I wince at the memory of Beverly's speaking those words to me. Hearing this creep speak them to my wife is more than I can stand. I speed toward them.

"Are you hard of hearing?" I say, my voice low and rumbling. "She wants to be left alone."

Brenda's head snaps around, her eyes locking onto mine. I hold her gaze, staring back at her with a love matching her anger.

"And who're you?" asks Darnell.

"Someone who's going to be charged with assault and battery if you don't stop hassling *my wife*!"

Darnell backs off. "Hey, man. I, I didn't know."

"Neither did I," I say, still staring hard at Brenda. "But now I do. And I understand how horrible it must've been and I'm sorry."

"Huh?" says Darnell. He looks from me to Brenda, then back to me. Then he eases away, grousing and grumbling about "crazy babes" and "jealous husbands."

"I didn't need your help," says Brenda.

"Yes, Brenda, you did. Just like I needed yours, only I was too blinded by my arrogance to accept it."

Her lower lip trembles, but she quickly firms it up. "From now on, I'd prefer that you let *me* handle my business. After all the practice I've had recently, I've discovered that I like it that way."

"Whatever you say, Brenda. But if I get the slightest feeling that you're ever in trouble, hurting, or in need, I'm going to be at your side. That's where I belong."

Brenda forces a chuckle. "That's funny. I thought you were more comfortable at Beverly's side. Or did you like it better on top of her?"

I lower my eyes, take a deep breath, and sigh. It takes everything I've got to stay rooted to my spot as she wrestles with her pain and anger. Comforting her now would be the wrong thing to do, when she needs to unleash more of her frustration at me for poisoning the precious, fragile relationship that was our heaven on earth.

Brenda jerks her cart around and shoves it toward the checkout line. I keep watching her, calling out to her with my heart, mind, and soul, asking her from the depths of all that I am to please, please forgive me.

She gets to the checkout line, empties the contents of her basket onto the conveyor, pays the clerk, and heads for the door.

"I love you, Brenda," I whisper.

She stops at the door, glances back at me, and leaves.

# CLIFFORD

"YOU KNOW DEMETRIA'S NOT GONNA TAKE THIS LYING DOWN," SNARLS TAMMY AS I leave with the boys.

"I don't care if she takes it standing up! She knows how I feel about my sons being around disgusting, negative influences. Present company included!"

Tammy slams the door. The boys are quiet on the way over to my apartment, their confusion and fear clearly advertised on their faces. I'd explain what's going on, but how am I supposed to make them understand that I'm trying to protect them from the same forces, and people, who've already caused us so much trouble? And even if I knew what to say, I'm too angry right now to tell them. Fortunately, their batteries are low and they succumb to sleep.

As upsetting as this episode has been, there's something weird going on inside me. There's something different about the level, intensity, and duration of my anger. With each passing mile on the way to Wheaton Point, layers of understanding envelop me as I realize the power, peace, and goodness of returning to a place where there's *no Demetria.*

Awaiting me in my drab, cramped, overpriced apartment is a sense of harmony and exquisite self-reinforcing intellectual solitude that could never have been achieved with Demetria. The walls that once whispered taunts of my failure now shout in celebration of my liberation from Demetria's malignant mentality. In that stuffy shoebox I call home, mornings and evenings are now ruled by Vivaldi, Bach, Beethoven, and Handel, not Demetria's gibbering radio.

A warm satisfaction spreads through me as I turn in to the Wheaton Point complex. These apartments aren't the most aesthetically pleasing, don't offer all the creature comforts, and are held together by an old grouch named Buck. But for all that they aren't and all they could be, Wheaton Point is my turning point, a chance for me to reclaim myself, my dignity, and my life.

I wrestle my drowsy sons upstairs, pull out the sofa bed, and wait for Demetria's phone call. She doesn't disappoint and I take the phone into my back room to avoid disturbing Braddie and a snoring Bear.

"Are you out of your mind?" shouts Demetria. "You had *no* right to walk into *my* home and take those boys."

"Demetria, I've got every right under the sun. I'm their father!"

"Their father who no longer lives with them."

"Only because you decided to recapture your glory days at the skating rink and high school prom."

She laughs. "Is that what you think? Well, just so you'll know, I left in hopes of finding a *man* to replace a pathetic mouse."

"A mouse I may have been, Demetria. But a lion I've become. Which is more than I can say for your de-evolution into pond scum!"

Even at our worst, Demetria and I were rarely this vicious with each other. But this exchange makes it plain that not only is the disaster we once called a marriage truly dead, but Demetria's once-stated crap about post-marital "friendship" was a fantasy.

An oppressive silence hangs in the air until Demetria says, "Clifford, I'm coming to get the boys." Her voice is flat and subdued, maybe even tired.

"No, Demetria. I'll take them to school tomorrow. And since we're *not* living together, and they *are* here with me, there's no need to get into a prolonged discussion about it."

"There's a parent-student outing tomorrow," she says. "If the boys don't have a parent show up, they can't go. Do you have tomorrow off?"

Demetria's question catches me off guard, and for good reason. I can't afford to ask Trevor for any more time off. He's been great thus far, but sooner or later he'll have to put on his "boss" hat and my concerns will bow to the needs of the company.

My silence answers Demetria's question and she says, "I didn't think so. I'll be over in a little while."

I start to tell Demetria that since the boys are already sleeping, she can save herself the trip, and that I'll bring them back in the morning. But then I remember that I'm scheduled to conduct early-morning training for first-shift employees. They start at 7:00 A.M., which means I'll have to be set up and ready by 6:30. That'll require me to rise at 4:30 or 5:00 so I can have enough time to get dressed, eat, and get to work before rush hour gets heavy.

And so, in another one of my million deaths, I'm again compelled to relinquish my sons to Demetria. But I don't want Demetria to come over here. I don't want her presence poisoning my space.

So I say, "Never mind, Demetria. I'll bring them back."

"When?"

"Now."

She hangs up and I roust the boys. They're not happy, nor should they be. And I feel like a large pile of something vile and smelly for failing to protect them from all they've endured on just this one night.

It's a quiet trip over to Penn Hills Commons and Demetria answers the door, looking grim and weary.

"How long have they been asleep?" she asks, taking Braddie from my arms.

"Almost from the moment I picked them up."

She heads upstairs as I go get a still snoring Bear from the car. I lug him up the steps and tuck him in, just as Demetria's finishing with Braddie. We stand there in the glow of their night-light, side by side and miles apart, staring at the children we created—both of us, I think, pondering the pain we're putting them through. Demetria turns to leave and I linger, snapping a few more mental shots for my Dadaland photo album.

Downstairs, Demetria's standing by the open door, anxious for me to get out. I oblige her, then stop when she calls my name.

"Clifford."

"Yeah, Demetria. What now?"

"After tonight, the gloves come off."

I chuckle and shake my head. "What're you gonna do, Demetria? Leave me? Take my sons? Set me back financially fifteen years? Hire a pimp for your new lifestyle?"

"You'll find out."

"I guess I will. And since you're taking off the gloves, I'd recommend that you use brass knuckles."

"Oh, really. Why?"

"Because after tonight, that's what I intend to use."

IT JUST SO HAPPENS THAT I'M CLOSE ENOUGH TO NATHAN'S FOR A QUICK VISIT. THE LAST few times we've talked, I've left him headless. I need to apologize and tell him that I appreciate his concern, and that he's still my favorite theologian.

Brenda answers the door, looking thin and like she's just been spat from a dryer. Her eyes are puffy and her face isn't emitting what I've always joked was her angelic glow. She looks downright hard, reminding me of Demetria and sending a chill down my spine.

"Hi, Bren," I say. "Is Nathan . . ."

"Nathan's not home."

"Oh. Okay. Well, just tell him I stopped by and that I'll call later."

Brenda presses her lips tight together as her eyes fill with tears. She wipes them away quickly, composes herself, and speaks with a strong, determined voice. "Nathan's over at Momma's. He's not going to be home for a while . . . if ever."

"If ever? What do you mean?"

"Clifford, your brother's been playing with fire. And *she's* burning him up."

"Do you mean . . . another woman?"

Brenda nods gravely, the tears spilling from her eyes like huge, shimmering diamonds. The absolute impossibility of what she's saying leaves me staring at her wide-eyed and slack-jawed.

I hug her and say, "Brenda, I'm sorry. I'm so very sorry."

She's stiff at first, then loosens up, burying her face in my shoulder and sobbing. But even so, she doesn't cry long. She straightens up and gently pushes me away.

"Talk to your brother," she says. "Make him understand what you're going through."

I take firm hold of Brenda's shoulders. "I will, Brenda. I swear to you that *I will make him understand.*"

I hug her again, hustle to my car, and rocket off to Momma's.

# VICTOR

THIS WAS ONE'A THE BEST VISITATIONS EVER. I MEAN FROM START TO FINISH IT WAS THE real deal.

I strolled up to Lynnette's front door, rang the bell, and waited. Jewel saw me out the livin' room window, started jumpin' up'n down, and screamed, "Nero!"

Lynnette was already throwin' me a serious grit when she opened the front door, but I stayed cool.

"Hello, Lynnette," I said.

I was fightin' hard to not look like I was gloatin'. Cuz with Judge Bentley talkin' all that yang about bein' nice and livin' up to my end of the bargain, I wasn't even tryin' to give Lynnette no reason to come gunnin' after me.

She unlocked the screen door and said, "Come in."

"Why, thank you, Lynnette," I told her, speakin' all nice'n friendly.

She clenched her teeth so hard, I could hear 'em grindin'. And I was thinkin' that if bein' nice to her was pissin' her off that bad, I was gonna make it a habit.

I stepped inside and Jewel ran up to me shoutin', "Nero! Nero! Nero!"

I scooped her up and said, "Hi, baby." She laughed and squirmed as I kissed her all over her face. Then I set her down, got on one knee, and looked into her eyes. "Baby, I'd really like it if from now on you called me Daddy instead'a Nero. Could you do that for me?"

She thought about it for a hot second then said, "Okay . . . Daddy."

I almost broke down but stayed cool.

She hugged me again. "I missed you, Daddy."

"I missed you too, baby. And guess what I brought?"

"Magic Maiden?"

I nodded and Jewel was squealin' tons'a happy. Then she got serious and said, "Did you bring her castle and flying horsey?"

"I sure did."

Jewel hugged me around my neck so tight, I had to work at breathin'. But I didn't care. Cuz if she'da squeezed the life out'a me right then'n there, I'da died one happy sucka.

---

BEFORE I GET ON THE TURNPIKE AND HEAD BACK TO CLEVELAND, I *GOTS'TA* STOP BY Momma's and tell her about today. She's gonna be cheek-bustin' happy with the results.

For a sucka who ain't never had no whole lots'a luck, these last few days have been smooth'n slick. Me'n Edie are hooked back up and crankin' strong. I've seen my precious Jewel. Corey's so freaked about me blowin' his action, he's dyin' to be my friend. And that stankin' slut Demetria's evictin' herself from my fambly. Cliff's bummin', but that won't last. Like I told him, when he sees how good his world is without Demetria, he'll be kickin' hisself for not flushin' the skank sooner.

I cut across the expressway, grab the cell phone Edie bought me, and dial her number. I'da called her sooner, but was too excited to think about anythang else but seein' Jewel.

The phone rings once and Edie says, "Hello?"

I like her answerin' quick like that. Cuz even if Edie wasn't sittin' by the phone waitin' on my call, it feels good thinkin' she mighta been.

"Hey, baby," I say. "It's me."

"Hi, Victor! How'd it go?"

"Let's just say that Lynnette won't be hasslin' me for a while."

"That's wonderful!" says Edie. But then all the happy drops out her voice and she axes, "Wait a minute. Why only for a while?"

"Cuz I know Lynnette. And sooner or later her attitude'll be stankin' up the joint."

"That's too bad. I'm sorry that you might have to deal with her again."

"Ain't no point in you bein' sorry, Edie. I'm the one that laid down with Lynnette. Now I'm scratchin' her fleas."

Edie laughs. "Well, don't worry about it. The next time, we'll handle her together."

Hearin' that, I could almost feel bad for Lynnette, goin' up against both Edie *and* Al.

"When're you coming back to Cleveland?" Edie axes.

"As soon as I tell Momma the good news."

"Well, hurry home. I miss you."

The Dipper warns me to be careful cuz Edie might just be another schemin' babe. But later for that! How I feel is how I feel, and I'ma break it down to Edie.

"I miss you too, baby. And . . ."

"And what, Victor?"

"And, I love you."

Edie don't say nothin', and I'm sweatin' bullets. Then, in a shakin' voice, she says, "I love you too, Victor. Please hurry home."

We say 'bye and I step on the gas. I'ma hurry'n do what I gotta do so I can jet back to Cleveland and Edie.

# NATHAN

I'M SITTING IN THE LIVING ROOM WATCHING THE NEWS WHEN MOMMA CALLS ME FROM the front door. "Nathan, I'm going to get in a quick workout at the spa before it closes. If anyone calls, tell them I'll be back shortly."

I look up at her and smile. "Momma, this is the fourth time this week you're going down there. Are you preparing for a body-beautiful contest or something?"

Her eyes fill with mischief. "Of course! How else do you expect me to qualify for next year's Sexiest Grandmas calendar?"

I laugh. "That should be as popular as the one featuring Playboy Pastors."

The moment the words leave my mouth, Momma and I are both sorry. I slump back against the couch.

Momma walks over, sits down beside me, and takes hold of my hand. "Nathan, you've got to stop this."

"I'm trying, Momma. I really am. But I've let so many people down, maybe even caused some to lose their faith. And worst of all, I've hurt Brenda and the kids."

"I know it's hard, sweetheart. But you have to believe in the words you've preached. The Lord promised to forgive us if we confessed our sins. Don't you think He was including you?"

"I don't doubt the Lord, Momma. It's myself that I'm having questions about."

"Meaning?"

"Meaning, I don't think I'm the best person to do His work."

Momma starts to speak, stops herself, then pats my hand and stands. "Nathan, the Lord doesn't make mistakes. If He called you to work in His vineyard, then that's where you're supposed to be. But no one can tell you that. It's something you have to know for yourself."

She walks back to the door and looks back at me. "Think about Saint Peter. He betrayed Jesus three times, even swearing and cursing that He'd never known Him. But after all that, Peter was *still* the rock upon which Christ chose to build His church."

I consider what Momma's saying, get up and go give her a hug. "Thanks, Momma. I guess I'm just going to have to pray about it."

She strokes my cheek. "You're a Christian, Nathan. That doesn't mean you're perfect, just saved. So feel bad if you must, but don't blame Christ. He loves you, has forgiven you, and, if you let Him, will grow you into the warrior He needs you to be."

She glances at her watch and gasps. "I need to go! See you in a bit."

"Have a good workout, Momma."

"I will. There's stiff competition for that calendar."

I smile as Momma gets in her car and starts up. Once she's out of the driveway, I return to the couch and stare at the phone. I want to call Brenda so badly, I ache. But I'm afraid of pushing her too hard. I'm also afraid of not pushing her hard enough. And how many times can I apologize before "I'm sorry" loses its meaning? Maybe it has already. Maybe it was irrelevant the moment I first said it.

"I'm sorry" from Brenda would've meant little or nothing to me if she had accepted the offer of that jerk in the supermarket. After what happened between me and Beverly, it's ludicrous to think she'd be satisfied with limp apologies. But nothing else communicates my profound sorrow for hurting Brenda in this way. Nothing better sums up my anguish for bringing her such misery.

I'm reaching for Momma's cordless when I hear a car turn into the driveway. This can't be Momma. Not this soon, unless she's forgotten something or has run into trouble. I hurry to open the door and see . . . Clifford.

He charges inside, shoves me back into the living room, and roars, *"Have you lost your mind?"*

## CLIFFORD

NATE STUMBLES BACKWARDS, FALLING ONTO MOMMA'S COUCH. HE SCRAMBLES TO HIS feet but I shove him back down.

"Clifford, what's the matter with you?" he yells.

"Never mind me! What's the matter with *you*? What have you done to Brenda?"

"You've seen her?"

"Answer me!"

"It's none of your business!"

"The hell it isn't! Brenda's as much my sister as she is your wife. Tell me what's going on!"

Nate exhales and collapses into the cushions. "It's a long story." He drops his head, resting his chin on his chest. "Clifford, I messed up. I messed up and . . ."

"No!" I shout. "Don't tell me there's someone else. *Please don't tell me that!*"

He looks up at me, his eyes imploring. "There *isn't* anyone else."

"Then why . . ."

"It was a mistake."

"*What* was a mistake?"

"Beverly Dawkins."

"Who's that?"

"One of my parishioners. I, I was counseling her and things . . . they just got out of control."

"No, Nate! Let me tell you what 'out of control' is. Out of control is when someone's tossing you to the trash heap for 'true love, excitement, and fun.' It's when you've debased and humiliated yourself in a fight to maintain your family, and someone spits in your face. It's when invisible hands are reaching into your life, dictating where and how you'll live, *if* and when you see your kids, and robbing you blind and calling it legal. *That's* out of control!"

Nate groans and slumps into the couch, looking truly miserable.

"Nate, you're obviously in deep trouble," I say. "But you've still got a chance."

"How can you say that? If you've talked with Brenda, you know she's . . ."

"She's trying to get you to open your eyes, Nate. That's what *I'm* trying to do. She asked me to make you understand. She wouldn't have said that if there weren't still a chance. Maybe it's slim. Maybe it's near hopeless. But it's there and you need to take it."

"But how can I? She's refuses to even talk to me on . . ."

"Maybe talk isn't what she wants. Maybe she needs to *see* in order to believe. Maybe she needs you to step out from behind the Bible and talk to her as a man. A man who fooled around and is dying inside for the pain it's causing his wife and family."

Nate says, "What am I going to do?"

From Momma's front door, Victor says, "You's gonna suffer, Nate. For a long, long time."

# VICTOR

NATE SPINS AROUND, LOCKS HIS EYES ONTO ME, AND IS SHO'NUFF WORRIED. CLIFF GIVES me a glance, then looks back on Nate.

"Look, Victor," says Nate, firmin' up his voice. "I'm already stressed out, so I don't want you . . ."

"Aw, man, just shut up! Cuz if I'm hearin' whut I think I'm hearin', you ain't got no room to be tellin' nobody *nothin'*!"

Nate's lower jaw is quiverin', but he ain't blubberin' his way out'a this whoopin'.

"You gots'ta be the dumbest sucka alive!" I say. "And I hope you's been keepin' *yo'self* prayed up. Cuz you's about to find out whut it's like to get hacked into wood chips. Ain't that right, Cliff?"

Cliff nods. I go over to Nate and give him a light slap up'side his head. "Whuts'a matter with you, man? How can you have somebody like Brenda and think there's somethin' better?"

Cliff sits down beside Nate and rubs his shoulders. "Brenda loves you, Nate. And it's real love. The kind that'll endure and weather the storms. Laugh with you through the good times. Cry with you through the bad. Comfort you when you're hurting. Watch your back when trouble comes nosing around."

"That's right," I say. "Unlike Demetria and Lynnette, who only watched our backs to find a good spot for the knife."

"Brenda's a thousand times more woman than they are," soothes Cliff. "So I don't care who this Beverly is or what she's offering, it's not worth it, Nate. It's simply not worth it."

I join my brothers on the couch, sittin' so that Nate's between me'n Cliff. "Nate, you and Brenda *hasta* work thangs out," I say. "Ya'll're the only reason that I ain't gave up on love."

Cliff looks at me like I just confessed to wearin' panties. "Whutch'you lookin' at?" I ax. "I ain't never told you I wasn't in'trested in love."

But later for Cliff. I gotta get through to Nate. "Look, man. I don't know how much you's been prayin', but it ain't enough. I don't know whutch'you been sayin', but it ain't enough. I don't know how much you's been hopin', beggin', and pleadin', but it ain't enough!"

"You've got to do whatever it takes," Cliff puts in. "No matter how long, no matter how painful. You've got to do it because Brenda's worth it."

Nate jumps up and stomps off from me'n Cliff. "Don't you think I know all of this?" he shouts. "Don't you think I want to go home to my wife? Don't you think I've been trying?"

"No!" I holler back. "I don't know nothin' like that! Except that for all'a your high'n mighty talk, you's just a reg'lar booty hound like the next sucka."

Nate's face twists and turns into somethin' pissed-off and nasty. "Victor, you can take a flying leap!"

I follow Nate's advice, fly off the couch, grab him by his collar, and jerk him close till we're nose to nose. "I'ma fly right down your tonsils if you don't shut up and listen to whut we's sayin'!"

Cliff pushes us apart. "Knock it off!" he orders. "This isn't helping anything."

Nate's sad as all get-out. But so whut! If he don't get his action straight, he's gonna be sadder than he ever thought.

"Nathan, you have no idea what you're up against," warns Cliff. "There's an entire industry out there, ready and willing to separate you from your kids, your home, and your money and generally make your life miserable."

"And besides havin' the laws to back 'em up, they love their jobs," I say.

"I'm sorry, you guys," Nate says sadly. "I know you're only trying to help."

"Tryin' my foot!" I say. "We's gonna get this thang together. Get your stuff and come on."

"Huh?" blurts Nate.

Even slow-gettin'-it Cliff figures out whut I'm plannin'. He grabs Nate's arm and says, "Let's go!"

"What're you guys doing? Where are you . . ."

"To Brenda, stupid!" I answer. "I know you been buggin' God to cut you some slack. Now we's gonna see if He's really pissed, or has just been makin' you sweat."

We get into Cliff's car, blow out'a Momma's driveway, and rush my jughead big brother to his home and his wife.

# NATHAN

CLIFFORD AND VICTOR SIT IN THE CAR, WATCHING GRIMLY AS I KNOCK ON THE DOOR. Brenda answers, sees me, and scowls. She glances past me and looks at Victor and Clifford. Her expression softens for an instant, then re-hardens when she focuses back on me.

"Why are you here?" she asks.

"Brenda, I want to come home."

"Shouldn't you be over at the Dawkins residence?"

"No, Brenda. My place is here. With you and the kids."

"It's too late for that, Nathan. I . . ."

"You didn't do anything, Brenda. It was me. *All me.* I forgot about who we were and the many other things that made us special. I got comfortable with your love, and careless with it as well. I let my eyes and desires wander when everything I wanted and needed was at home."

"That sounds good, Nathan. You're good with words. You always have been. But I'm not interested in words. Not now. Before, when I was warning you, trying to get you to see where we were headed, words might have worked. But this is now."

"What is it you need me to do, Brenda? Do you need for me to be punished? If so, you're too late. I don't know if I'll ever be through punishing myself for hurting you the way I have. For wounding you and the kids. For rejecting the Lord's strength and choosing to be weak."

Brenda's face softens, but only slightly. "Nathan, I'm just not sure."

I reach carefully for her hand. She jerks slightly but doesn't pull it back. "Brenda, more than anything else, I want you to be happy. Even if it means being without you. I don't want to lose you, but I deserve to."

I wipe a tear from her cheek and say, "I'm sorry." Then I turn to walk away.

Someone yells, "No!"

I look past Brenda and see Corrine. "Mom, please!" she says. "I know Daddy's been a *jerk*, but you know you love him."

Nate Junior walks up from behind Brenda, takes her hand, and says, "Please, Mom. I don't want Dad to leave."

Brenda's eyes are awash in tears. She looks at me and says, "Neither do I. But your father has to want to come home. All of him. Body. Mind. And spirit."

I slowly, tentatively reach out for Brenda and wrap her in my arms. "I'm here, Brenda. And here I will always be."

We all look at Clifford when he starts his car and drives off, him and Victor smiling and giving a thumbs-up.

# SHADOW PEOPLE

## CLIFFORD

SOMETHING TOLD ME NOT TO DO THIS. ESPECIALLY NOT TODAY, SINCE, ACCORDING TO Victor, Momma's having this mini family reunion because of me and my turbulent situation.

"Cliff, try and not be bummed out," he said, a couple of nights ago on the phone. "Cuz you know how Momma is. If *you* ain't happy, she'll be runnin' off at the mouth and everybody'll be miserable."

I glance at the wall clock. I've still got a few more hours to rehabilitate my attitude, but how? How can I do that with all that's confronting me?

I scoot closer to my pygmy kitchen table and stare at my anemic checking account statement, my bills, a repair estimate for my car, pricing paperwork for Braddie and Bear's school trip, two threatening letters from creditors, and a copy Al gave me of the projected child support payments that I'm *already making*.

I keep staring and despairing, trying to balance the reality laid out before me with what Braddie and Bear said the last time I picked them up.

I was backing out of the driveway when Braddie, bouncing with excitement, said, "Dada! Dada! Guess what!"

"Tell me!" I answered, overjoyed that he was too happy to notice he was coming over to "visit" and not stay.

"We're going back to Disney World!"

"Yeah!" added Bear. "And Mommy said this time we're gonna stay in the *really* good part."

I slammed on the brakes and hollered, *"WHAT!"*

The outburst left them wide-eyed and trembling. I quickly shoved my enraged emotional genie back into his bottle. It took everything I had, but I plastered a smile onto my face and said, "Wow! That should be lots of fun!"

My ear-to-ear smile melted their fear and rejuvenated their excitement.

"And next year we go to some islands," said Bear.

"The hommas!" added Braddie.

I kept smiling, backed out, and started over to my apartment. "You mean the Bahamas, don't you?"

"Yeah!" Braddie agreed. "That's what Mommy said."

The telephone rings. I'm in too foul a mood to talk and let it roll over to the answering machine. After a few seconds, the caller's flat voice drones out.

*"Hello. This is Mr. Lipscomb calling from Fast Pay Credit Collections. This is my SECOND attempt. Please return my call at 312-666-0666."*

I get up and stomp into the bathroom to urinate and I see termites in the tub. *Again!* A prickling shiver moves from my forehead down my back as I watch the squirming mass. This is ridiculous! I've set off two "bug bombs," called Buck at least three times, had to take off from work twice to let the exterminator in, and I'm no farther ahead than when I first complained.

I'm still itching at the memory of that first time when I woke up, went to take a shower, pulled back the shower curtain, and saw the bottom of my tub covered with bugs. Bile shot into my throat as I stared at the creeping, crawling mass, making me retch and heave into the toilet. I staggered out of the bathroom and called Buck, who grumped about being disturbed so early in the morning.

He showed up in a plaid robe and battered slippers, took a look, and said, "Termites. We've had this problem before." He yawned. "They come up through the drains. Only happens at certain times of the year, though. The rest of the time they're hibernatin' or somethin'."

He looked at me as if expecting me to say "Oh! Is that all? Well, since it's only certain times of the year, this'll be all right."

What I actually said was, "That's very interesting, Buck. What do you intend to *do* about this problem?"

Surprised, he frowned and started scratching his whisker-covered face, his eyes darting from me to the tub and back. "I guess I'ma have'ta call my exterminator."

"Now there's an original idea," I said.

He snorted and huffed out of the apartment, mumbling something about smart-alecks.

I clean up and march down to the rental office. Buck's on the phone, so I lean against the wall and wait.

"Hey, youngblood," he says, hanging up. "What can I do you for?"

"Buck, I hate to be a pain, but those termites have returned."

Buck grimaces. "I keep tellin' the landlord to get rid'a that bargain basement bozo and hire me a professional exterminator."

I sympathize with Buck's frustration, but I can guarantee that mine is greater than his. "Buck, something's *got* to be done," I say. "At eight-hundred-dollars-a-month rent, the only thing that should be in my tub is the dirt washed from my body."

"I'm doin' the best I kin. Whaddya want from me?"

"To fix it so I can walk into my bathroom without getting creeped out by an insect carpet in my tub."

Buck grabs the phone and dials. "Hello! Lemme talk to Hank!"

He waits for Hank, then launches into him. "Hank! This is Buck Stiles over at Wheaton Point. . . . Never mind how I'm feelin'. My tenant in 2C's still got termites comin' up his bathtub drain. . . . So! It wouldn't be a headache if you'd do the job *right*!"

While Buck and Hank joust on the phone, I figure out roughly how much it would cost to move out of here. It's a short calculation.

With the penalty I'd incur from breaking the lease, having to pay rent till someone else moved in, scrounging enough cash for first month's deposit and rent on a new place, I'd be strung out to the max. Those realities lumped together with the stack of bills sitting on my kitchen table make it clear that I'm not going anywhere. At least, not anytime soon.

". . . I don't care what kinda species critters they are!" howls Buck. "I just want 'em dead! Well, if you ain't gonna do it right, I'll find somebody who can!"

Like the last time, Buck harasses and cajoles Hank into making another trip to add more chemicals to the ones he's already sprayed, and the ones I've unleashed. And I ask myself again what's worse: living with the bugs or exposing me and my sons to an ever-increasing buildup of insecticide?

Buck hangs up, his knotted brow smoothing out with satisfaction after he's tongue-lashed Hank. "Okay, youngblood. He'll be out tomorrow. And this time he's comin' with stuff that'll kill bears."

I sigh. "Buck, if he just comes with stuff that'll kill the termites, that'll be good enough."

I spin around and stomp out, promising myself that *somehow* I'll get out of here as quickly as I can make it happen.

I DRIVE DOWN TO THE BOOKSTORE, HOPING DESPERATELY THAT A LITTLE LITERARY browsing will help me forget, even for a moment, the depths at which I lurk. If only I could quiet the noise in my head.

*We're going to the hommas!* echoes Braddie.

*After we stay at Disney's World's REALLY good part,* adds Bear.

"Be quiet," I grumble, stopping at an intersection.

The boys keep talking, their voices echoing louder. *Dada, your house is too small. Dada, I don't like this couch bed. . . .*

"I said to *be quiet*!"

*. . . Dada, there's nowhere to play outside. Dada, guess what! Mommy's Nolan friend bought us "Troll Warrior III." Yuk, Dada! There's bugs in your tub!*

*"BE QUIET!"*

A horn blows from behind. I glance up into the rearview mirror. The driver behind me is furious, his face contorted. I hurry through the intersection, swerving slightly as the irate driver zooms past, jams down his horn, and gives me the finger. Forget that jerk! I travel a little farther and turn in to the bookstore parking lot.

I feel better the moment I step inside the store. I've always been a reader, but books are now truly an escape luxury, especially since the life I was living has been pounded into the life I must survive.

I grab the latest technothriller from the display, get some coffee, find a chair, and lose myself in the story.

"If it's that good, you should just buy it," says a female voice from above and behind.

I turn around and look straight into Mikki's smiling face. I'm glad to see her. *Really glad.*

"Hi," I say, standing up and extending my hand. "What a nice surprise."

Mikki takes my hand, squeezes it tenderly, and doesn't let go. The soft warmth of her touch sends waves of desire vibrating through me.

"So what are you reading?" asks Mikki.

I hand Mikki the book and she reads the back-cover description. "Oh, Clifford," she says, smiling. "This is so macho. Are you going to be a hero?"

"Who says I'm not already?" I answer, chuckling.

"Touché." Her voice lowers ever so slightly into the smoky nether regions of possibility. "And I'll bet you know just what to do." She glances at my empty cup. "Did you get coffee?"

"Yeah. It was some Afro-Brazilian blend. It was pretty good."

"Oh, yes. I've had that one. I like it."

I screw up my courage and say, "Would you like to get some coffee and talk?"

Mikki's eyes sparkle. "I'd like that very much."

I step aside, let her walk past, and follow her. My eyes caress the seductive motions of her rear end and I smile as forces stir within me that had been driven into dormancy by Demetria.

# VICTOR

I CLOSE THE TRUNK ON MY PUZZ-MOBILE AFTER PUTTIN' IN THE LAST SUITCASE, GET IN, and wink at Edie. She's grinnin' from ear to ear, excited about this trip to Pittsburgh. And since these next couple'a days is my scheduled time off, even punk Corey couldn't stop me from goin'. I hope he ain't foolin' hisself into thinkin' I ain't gonna get me some payback for him tellin' Edie I had VD. Yeah. When I get even with that sucka, I'ma make sure he gets the full treatment.

"Did you remember Karenna's dancing bear?" axes Edie.

"Got it."

"Don't forget we have to stop by the drugstore and pick up her prescription."

"Already in the plan."

"Did we give Mother the number to your mom's house?"

"Gave it to her myself."

"What about . . ."

I pull Edie close and give her a quick kiss. "Stop worryin', baby. Momma's lookin' forward to meetin' you. And she knows you ain't no flake, cuz I don't let just any-old-body get close to my fambly."

Edie looks in the visor mirror and starts messin' with her already perfect hair. "Victor, who was the last person you let get close to your family?"

I hit the highway and watch in the rearview mirror as Cleveland shrinks in the distance.

"Victor?"

"Yeah, baby."

"Who was the last person you let get close to your family?"

Edie's starin' at me like she ain't gonna quit till I answer. So I lay it on the line and say, "The last person I let get that close, I married."

# NATHAN

I FINISH THE ROUGH DRAFT OF MY RESIGNATION LETTER TO THE CHURCH BOARD, THEN SIT back and stare at it. I've had some good times with these saints. We've worshiped together, sung together, buried friends and relatives, christened the newest, most precious members of our community, supported each other through crises, kept each other lifted up in prayer, and generally sought to do as the Lord commanded, loving each other as we loved ourselves.

I hate to leave them, but this is the price I must pay. After nearly losing my wife, breaching the confidence of someone who trusted me as her counselor, and shaming myself before my children, I have no other choice. And there's still so much to do, in my personal life and in this ministry.

I'm back at home, thank God. But Brenda's still very cool toward me. I'm prepared to wait till the thaw, whenever it comes. She's agreed to let Pastor Childress conduct marriage counseling for us, and will let me know when I can stop sleeping in my den.

The kids seem to be doing okay, but Corrine's still irritated with me. Nate Junior's happy about no longer being a diplomatic bridge, and would just as soon forget any of this ever happened. I'd like to, but can't afford to forget. I need to remember that, although I've worn the holy cloth of a pastor's robe, I'm nothing but a weak creature of flesh. That doesn't excuse my failure, but instead informs me that I'm only safe when shielded by Christ. So things are better than they were, but my family needs to heal.

As for the ministry, the urban garden planted by the Y&G kids needs to be expanded, especially since it produced enough food to allow a donation to a homeless shelter. Our Christian theater ministry is getting calls from as far away as Cincinnati, Ohio, to come and share the message of Christ through drama. Twelve new members were added last month. The property adjacent to the church has finally gone up for sale, numbering the days of the crack house sitting on that land. And through the power of prayer, the real estate agent for the seller who'd rejected our first offer called and let us know we could have it for even less than we'd proposed.

Yes, God has truly been blessing. And I threw it all away by listening to my lust and pride rather than the voice of Him who loved me before my mother knew me. But through prayer and by His power, I know that the Lord will restore me. And I have to remember the blessings I still have.

Brenda and the kids. My faith back on track. And the sobering knowledge that as spirit-filled as I thought myself to be, my humanity is too powerful a force to arrogantly ignore.

I reread and start editing the letter. Once I'm finished, I'll get with Sister Anders, chairperson of the finance committee, finalize some details to secure the funds from the bank, and the next phase of church expansion will be set. After that, I'll meet Brenda and the kids over at Momma's and start barbecuing. If all goes well, everything will be nice and ready by the time Clifford and Victor arrive for our mini reunion.

# CLIFFORD

MIKKI'S DOING HER BEST NOT TO LAUGH TOO LOUD AS WE JOKE AND TALK OUR WAY through another cup of coffee.

"What happened next?" she asks.

I lean close and talk low. "Victor looked at Big and, in a voice the world could hear, asked if the cops had ever caught the people who'd been stealing restaurant equipment. After that our food was as good as sitting in front of us."

Mikki laughs. "Your brother sounds like so much fun."

"He can be," I answer, chuckling. And then I think about how Victor's been there for me throughout this crappy ordeal, how despite his crudity he's shown me nothing but love, and say, "He's also one of the biggest-hearted people I know."

"I can tell that you love him dearly."

I smile. "Please don't ever say that to Victor. It would ruin his day to know someone thought well of him."

We laugh and keep talking, the conversation slowly getting around to us sharing some of the bizarre features of our lackluster love lives.

"Are you kidding me?" I say, stunned by Mikki's revelation concerning her last boyfriend.

"I'm serious, Clifford. This guy would pee in the shower."

"That's disgusting!"

"Not to mention unsanitary."

"Is that why you broke up?"

Mikki shakes her head no, then says, "He woke up one morning overcome by feelings of love for his ex-girlfriend. That and the fact that we'd already been having problems made it easy to say good-bye."

"Jeez. What an airhead," I say, remembering Demetria's classic non-excuse excuse.

"Who could've known?" asks Mikki, shrugging. "When I met Sherrod, he'd just finished an environmental impact study on agricultural expansion in the Amazonian basin."

"I know what you mean. When I met Demetria . . ."

"Is that her name? It sounds pretty."

"You'll understand if I don't share your appreciation."

Mikki nods with regal grace.

"Anyway, when I met Demetria she was wrapped up in student politics, protesting environmental racism and petitioning universities to pursue gifted black scholars with the same energy they used to pimp gifted black athletes."

"Wow! She must've been dynamic."

"She was, Mikki. She really and truly was. To be honest, I didn't see myself as having a chance with her. Considering how things turned out, I guess I was right after all."

"Do you really believe that?"

I shrug. "I guess so. It's just that I admired Demetria so much. She was sure of herself and her identity, unlike me, who read biographies, looking for an identity to emulate."

Mikki takes firm hold of my hand. "Stop that."

"Huh? Stop what?"

"Stop beating yourself up," she answers, squeezing my hand.

I squeeze back and look hard into her eyes, marveling at the way their light brown color perfectly complements her rich, dark skin.

"Look, Clifford," says Mikki. "Being studious is who you are. Don't apologize for following the desires of your heart. Scholarship requires its own brand of discipline."

I smile inwardly as I recall my favorite passage from Isaac Asimov's *Prelude to Foundation*, when the hero, Dr. Hari Seldon, promises himself: "If he ever found another companion, it would have to be one who understood scholarship and what it demanded of a person."

Mikki loosens her grip. "Besides, just like my friend who golden-showered *in* the shower, your ex turned out to be someone totally different than you thought. Just like *we* must've seemed to *them* after a while."

"Good point, Mikki. But *I* married Demetria. So no matter how much I might want to bash, berate, and blaspheme her, it's *my* judgment that ultimately doomed me to Dadaland."

"Dadaland?"

I chuckle. "Braddie and Bear say it's where all the dads go who get dumped."

Mikki looks stunned.

"Their words," I add, smirking.

"Cute, but sad."

I sip some coffee and say, "There is one good thing about Dadaland. I can finally be with my sons without interference. No more debates about when, if, and how they should be disciplined. No more arguments about teaching them the kind of manhood lessons black boys can't learn soon enough. And no more being suckered into the divide-and-conquer scenarios that leave parents at each other's throats instead of backing each other up."

"Is she aware that your boys call your home Dadaland?" Mikki asks.

"Your guess is as good as mine. Demetria's convinced that no matter what the psycho-emotional damage, one day we'll all get over it, let bygones be bygones, and laugh and frolic into the future like inebriated characters in some Mother Goose rhyme."

Mikki's expression clouds with disgust and she shakes her head. "My God. I hope she finds what she's looking for."

"I hope so too, Mikki. For what it's costing all of us, I hope so too."

# VICTOR

KARENNA SAYS, "MICE, HOW MUCH LONGER?"

I chuckle and shake my head. Between Jewel callin' me Nero and Karenna callin' me Mice, I'ma end up like one'a them split-personality dudes.

I glance back at Karenna, sittin' in her car seat, and smile. "We're almost there, Karenna. Just hold on, baby."

She goes back to lookin' out the window and I step on the gas, speedin' up so's I can get to Momma's before Karenna axes me a million times instead'a just a thousand. I look over at Edie, who's finally sleepin'.

She was all knotted up and fidgetin' when we took off from Cleveland, prob'ly worried about meetin' Momma, Nate, and Cliff. I prob'ly shouldn'ta told her nothin'. But as crazy as my fambly can be, there wasn't no way I was gonna let her walk in there blind. So I told her about Momma bein' one seriously sweet-but-tough sister, and that I was really proud of her for doin' her school thang, even though I ain't got no idea whut it's about. Then I warned her that even though Goody Two-shoes Nate was prob'ly gonna try and baptize her, the way to get him off her case was to go find Brenda. One look from her and Nate won't even *think* about steppin' out'a line. And Cliff. There wasn't nothin' much to say about him except that he's gettin' dumped, ain't likin' it, but someday'll figure out that Demetria's doin' us all a favor.

I get into the Pittsburgh city limits and wonder again if I'm doin' the right thang, if this ain't too much, too soon. Cuz everybody's gonna know that me bringin' Edie home means she ain't one'a my reg'lar fly-by-night babes.

Part of me ain't certain. The other part of me remembers all'a that hassle from Fran, Jizelle, Dorinda, Renée, Anika, Pearl, Clarita-Jean, and Justine. Ev'ry last one of 'em gave up the booty by the second date, which was just fine. But not crazy Edie. She *still* ain't let me even squeeze a boob, and I'm achin' for her so bad my *teeth* hurt. And I must be crazy too, cuz this waitin' feels kinda good. Not that the Dipper's happy, but this ain't about him. At least not yet.

"Mice, are we there yet?" axes Karenna.

I shake my head and smile back at the cutie-pie. "Almost there, Karenna. We's almost there."

# NATHAN

SISTER ANDERS AND I FINISH OUR PHONE CONFERENCE WITH THE BANK AND IT'S A DONE deal. Our plan to repay the loan in two years is approved and the money's ours. Now I can rest easy in the knowledge that whoever takes over as senior pastor will have a good foundation from which to keep expanding the Lord's temple.

I escort Sister Anders out of my office, close and lock the door, then start packing up a box with some small, not-easily-missed items. I glance at the clock and stop. It's time for me to get to Momma's.

I stuff the box way back in the corner of my private closet. Everyone will know soon enough about my decision to resign. There's no reason to start a lot of rumors by leaving evidence lying around.

I zip across town to Momma's and see Brenda's car, so she's already here with the kids.

"Knock, knock!" I say, stepping through the front door. "I'm here."

"C'mon in, Nathan," says Momma.

I hear Corrine in the kitchen, on the phone. And Nate Junior's downstairs, adding his throaty noises to the sound effects being generated by whatever video game he's playing.

I hear the muffled sound of Momma's voice and Brenda's coming from Momma's room, and stick my head inside.

"Hello."

Momma and Brenda stop talking and look at me with intense, almost irritated expressions.

"Nathan, we're kind of busy right now," says Momma.

Brenda's no-nonsense expression tells me that they want to finish talking *about* me, not *to* me.

And so, with nothing else to do, I stroll outside to the grill where Momma's already got everything set up, light the fire, and start barbecuing.

# CLIFFORD

I CASUALLY GLANCE AT MY WATCH AND STIFLE A GASP. I'VE BEEN SO ENGROSSED IN CONversation with Mikki that I hadn't even noticed how close I am to being late in getting to Momma's.

"Mikki, this has been great, but I've gotta go pick up my sons. We're meeting my mother and brothers for a mini family reunion."

Mikki's eyes light up. "Really! That sounds like fun."

"Yes! I think it will be," I answer, smiling and feeling mildly surprised at my sudden enthusiasm.

After my latest termite encounter, spending a few hours gazing into Mikki's soft eyes has done wonders for my attitude.

"Do you have time to give me a ride back to the apartments?" asks Mikki. "I took the bus down here for a little adventure. It was interesting, but I prefer not being asked twenty times for my number on the way back."

Taking Mikki home will probably, no, it *will* make me late. But not that late.

"It'll be my pleasure," I say, standing. "And were there only twenty?"

"Only twenty what?"

"Only twenty people who asked you for your phone number? If I'd known the competition was that strong, I'd have put in my own request."

Mikki arches an eyebrow. "Is that what you're doing now?"

The question catches me off guard. I've just asked for a woman's phone number for nonprofessional reasons. And it feels good.

I answer with firmness. "Yes, Mikki. I am. I'd like very much to have your phone number."

"And I'd like very much to give it to you."

There's a stirring in my crotch that I should ignore, but it's been so long. And the erotic double meaning of Mikki's statement is just too enticing to resist, so I permit myself a fantasy moment.

She writes her number on the back of a card and hands it to me. "Don't wait too long, Clifford. After all, there were twenty in front of you."

"That may be true," I say. "But *I've* got the number."

We get in my car and continue laughing and talking on the way back to Wheaton Point, mostly comparing notes about our all-time favorite books.

"Have you ever read David Bradley's *The Chaneysville Incident*?" I ask.

Mikki frowns and shakes her head no. "I've checked a number of places, but no one seems to have it."

"I've got it at the apartment. Would you like to borrow it?"

"Is that a trick question?"

I smile and pat Mikki's hand. "Case closed. Consider the book yours. To borrow, that is."

Mikki laughs and gives my hand a quick squeeze. "Thanks so much, Clifford. If it's as good as I've heard, I'll have it back to you in a day or so."

I park and we hurry to my apartment. On the way in, I keep my fingers crossed in hopes that those termites have followed their normal pattern and crawled back down the tub drain. I start to ask Mikki if she wouldn't mind waiting outside, but that might make her think I've got something to hide, which I do with regard to those doggone termites. But maybe it'll work out.

We go inside and I head straight for the bathroom. "Excuse me, Mikki. I need to check and see how much progress Buck's made on some tub repairs."

"No problem," she answers, strolling over to peruse the contents of my bookshelves.

I close the bathroom door, check the tub, lean against the sink, and sigh. The termites have descended back into their subterranean pit, saving me from certain embarrassment.

I go back into the living room, and over to my bookshelves.

"Did he get much done?" asks Mikki.

"Not much. You know Buck."

"Yes, I do," she says with a trace of annoyance. "Especially how it takes him forever to finish anything."

"Truer words were never spoken."

I search the shelves, but *The Chaneysville Incident* isn't where I'd normally keep it. But then, it wouldn't be. Especially since I haven't had the time to organize my books the way I had them over at Penn Hills Commons.

I continue my search, fuming as I'm reminded of how Demetria's defection has sent shock waves even into the literary corner of my life.

The doorbell rings. What now? I ask myself, glancing at my watch.

The moment I open the door, the cutest little girl launches into a spiel about needing to sell candy so she can go on her school trip to the Smithsonian. Her mother, standing behind her, beams proudly. The little girl is too darling to turn down, so I reach for my wallet.

"Sure," I say, smiling. "I'll buy a box."

I pull some money from my wallet and Cruiser's number falls out. I snatch it up, pay the little girl, and hurry toward the bathroom, stopping by Mikki on the way.

"Want some chocolates?" I ask.

"Of course I do." She takes the box, sniffs along the edges, and purrs. "The only weakness in my otherwise healthy diet."

I smile and step inside the bathroom. "Excuse me for a second, Mikki. Nature calls."

She nods and starts opening the box as I close the bathroom door. I stare long and hard at Cruiser's number.

*Call when you want some real justus!* growls his echo.

I love Braddie and Bear so much. More than my life! But I can't do this. It's not worth me spending years rotting in jail. Besides, no matter how repulsive Demetria is to me, to Braddie and Bear she'll always be Mommy. And Al's right. I can't honestly say that trying to get custody of those boys isn't partly motivated by the desire to crush Demetria. And in the long run, that would hurt *them.* So in another of my million deaths, I'll have to hold my peace and support Demetria's pirated authority.

I tear up the number, drop the scraps into the toilet, use the bathroom, and flush. The phone rings while I'm washing my hands.

"Mikki! Would you get that please?"

"Are you sure? I don't want to be the cause of confusion."

I laugh. "Trust me, Mikki. My little black book is blank. There'll be no confusion."

I listen through the door while she answers.

"Hello? Yes, he lives here. *What?* Oh my God! Hold on. I'll get him."

Mikki shoves the phone at me when I open the door.

"Hello?"

"Dada! He hit us!" cries Bear.

*"WHAT!"*

"Mommy's Nolan friend. He hit me and Braddie."

I glance at the gurgling toilet, hear Cruiser's watery chuckle, then toss the phone to Mikki and fly out the door.

# VICTOR

CORRINE'S ON THE FLOOR PLAYIN' WITH KARENNA AND IT LOOKS LIKE BOTH OF 'EM ARE havin' some serious fun. And with the way Momma, Brenda, and Edie have been carryin' on, yakkin', laughin', and whatnot, somebody could mistake 'em for long-lost buddies. Which is fine with me.

When we first got here and I introduced Edie to Momma, they hugged and Momma looked at me over Edie's shoulder and winked. A few minutes later, she pulled me off to the side, held my face in her hands, and kissed both'a my cheeks.

"Victor, I'm so proud of you," she said.

Momma's sayin' she was proud of me felt so good, I just kept quiet and listened to her tell me why.

"Edie's a sweet woman, Victor. And you've done well in finding her. Please, *behave!*"

I almost axed Momma how she knew Edie was so sweet, but didn't want her goin' off into her mumbo-jumbo about bein' able to "feel" Edie's goodness. Cuz if she'd said that, I'da axed her how come she didn't warn me about "feelin' " all'a that stanky bad attitude sloshin' around inside'a Lynnette. But then I remembered—she did!

So I just said, "Momma, it ain't no thang. Edie's the real deal and I'ma handle my business right."

Nate takes a break from barbecuin', steps inside, and says, "Any word from Clifford? I thought he'd be here by now."

Cliff's gonna just love Nate for remindin' Momma that he ain't here yet. I start toward the kitchen so I can call Cliff and tell him to hurry up. The sucka knows how evil Momma gets when the food's ready and we ain't.

I glance at my watch. I'd best go and pick up Jewel. She can't wait to play with Braddie and Bear—that's *if* Demetria lets 'em come over. Seein' as to how she and Lynnette crawled up out the same swamp slime, Cliff's prob'ly gonna have'ta get Al to jack her up like I had to do Lynnette.

Then Momma says, "I'm going to call Clifford and see if he's still comin'."

Momma know she ain't gotta ax that question. Cuz Cliff knows it'd be easier swimmin' in quicksand then dealin' with Momma for missin' dinner.

She gets up from where she, Brenda, and Edie have been sittin' and yappin'.

"He's probably at home sulking and feeling alone. That's one of the reasons we're having this reunion."

I step aside, hopin' that Cliff's on the way. Nate Junior walks past and grins. I stick out my palm and we slap each other five. He's headed to some corner downstairs to listen to the latest Bone thugs-n-harmony rap CD I bought him. Those brothas are tough and Big Nate would throw a fit if he knew I'd slipped it to the kid. But just cuz he pretends like he never use'ta listen to crazy George Clinton, Funkadelic, and wild Rick James don't mean Nate Junior's gotta suffer. For all Big Nate knows, God might have his own rap label and love throwin' down with Puff Daddy and Dr. Dre.

Momma dials and I'm waitin' to hear whuts'up. She says, "Hello? Is this the Clifford Matthews residence? . . . I'm his mother. *Who are you?*"

Everybody stops in their tracks and starts gatherin' around Momma cuz her voice is bulgin' with worry.

"Whut's happenin?" I ax.

Momma waves me off and keeps talkin'. "What! When? How long ago?"

She starts cryin' and slams the phone down. "We've gotta get over to Demetria's! *Now!*"

"Momma, what's wrong?" axes Nate, steppin' inside with a platter of ribs.

Momma's cryin' so hard, she ain't hardly understandable. I grab her shoulders and feel her tremblin'.

"Momma! Tell me whut'sup! Whut'sa matter?"

She shoves me away. "That person on the phone was a friend of Clifford's. Bear just called. *Some man hit him and Braddie!*"

# NATHAN

VICTOR AND I EXPLODE OUT THE DOOR. MOMMA AND BRENDA ARE HOT ON OUR HEELS.

I stop Momma and say, "What're you doing? Stay here until Victor and I . . ."

Momma snatches my keys and shoves me aside. Victor glances at Edie, who's standing in the door holding Karenna in one arm and hugging Corrine with the other.

"Go ahead," she says. "I'll watch everything here."

Momma starts the minivan and hollers, *"COME ON!"*

She backs out of the driveway, slowing down just enough for me and Victor to dive into the back before she takes off.

Victor and I scramble into our seat belts as Momma zooms through traffic.

"I'll bet it was that Nolan sucka," Victor growls. "If he's hurt Braddie and Bear, he's gonna have more'n Cliff to worry about."

"His name sounds familiar," says Brenda.

"It should," Victor confirms. "He's the dude who Demetria's been givin' all her . . ."

"Time!" I blurt, jabbing Victor with my elbow and cutting my eyes at Momma. "He and Demetria have been spending a lot of time together."

"That doesn't give him the right to hit Braddie and Bear," says Momma. "Please God, let us get there in time."

I give her shoulder a reassuring squeeze. "Don't worry, Momma. We'll make it."

"We'd better," says Victor. "Cuz after that fight me'n Cliff had, I know whut he can do."

"Fight!" says Momma. "When did you all fight?"

Victor explains the altercation he and Clifford had a few weeks ago and Momma steps on the gas.

Brenda grips the sides of her seat as Momma weaves in and out around cars, pounding the horn when she gets behind slow-cruising vehicles. I look around, checking for cops, grateful that none are around but wanting them close, just in case.

"Momma, did that person you talked to say whether or not Demetria was there?" I ask.

"They didn't say and I didn't ask."

"She'd better not be," answers Victor. "Cliff's likely to go after her first."

Momma shakes her head. "This feels like a bad, bad dream."

Brenda cuts her eyes at me and says, "I know what you mean."

Penn Hills Commons is coming up fast, but not fast enough, so Momma stomps on the gas.

I say, "Momma, when we get there let me go in first so . . ."

"No!" she snaps. "You're free to wait outside, but I'm going in."

"I'm wit'cha," adds Victor.

Brenda looks at me, her expression softer. She holds out her hand to me and says, "We'll do this together."

I take her hand and look into her eyes. "Together."

# CLIFFORD

BEAR CHARGES OUT THE FRONT DOOR AS I SCREECH TO A STOP.

"Where's Braddie?" I ask.

"He's in the living room, wiping up Scratch's poop."

"What?"

"We didn't let Scratch out when Mommy's Nolan friend told us. Then Scratch pooped on his slippers."

"Slippers!"

*NOOO!* Please don't tell me she's had him sleeping here! *Not under the same roof with my sons!*

"Where's your mother?" I bellow.

"At the store."

The pounding in my head blurs my vision as everything comes together. *"She left you guys here? Alone? With him?"*

Bear nods, sniffling and wiping his eyes. I point to the car. "Get in!"

I dash into the house and see Braddie on his hands and knees, crying and scrubbing a slipper. He sees me, runs, and leaps into my arms.

"Dada! Dada! He hit me!"

"Where is he now?"

"Downstairs, hitting Scratch with a newspaper."

And then I hear it—Scratch yelping. I put Braddie down and grip his shoulders. "Get in the car with Bear. I don't want you to see this."

# VICTOR

MOMMA SLAMS ON THE BRAKES AND THROWS NATE'S MINIVAN INTO PARK, GIVIN' US all group whiplash. Cliff's car is jacked up on the curb, part of it in the grass, part of it in the street. Braddie and Bear are in the front seat, cryin' and lookin' scared. We pile out, bumpin' into each other as we hustle to the house.

"Where's your daddy?" hollers Momma, runnin' past Cliff's car.

"In there!" answers Bear, pointin'.

"That man hit us!" cries Braddie.

Hearin' that, my brain catches fire. Cuz this could be Jewel. And for all I know, it has been. I streak past everybody through the front door, lettin' out Cliff's mutt, Scratch, as I charge into the war zone that use'ta be his livin' room.

The TV's smashed, sparkin' and fizzin'. The wall mirrors are busted. Furniture's sittin' every which way but right. Books are tossed everywhere. The rug's stained with blood. The phone's danglin' off the hook with that "Please hang up'n try again" message repeatin'. And crouchin' and whimperin' in a corner is that Nolan sucka who was sellin' them wolf tickets down at Demetria's job.

A thick line of bloody drool is hangin' from the corner of his lip. His nose is bleedin', his left arm's hangin' limp, his jaw is puffy. One eye's startin' to swell and his good eye is locked on Cliff, who's standin' over him with chest heavin' and eyes lookin' wild. Cliff's shirt's ripped from neck to waist. And the sheen of sweat on his skin makes it look like he's glowin'.

And I'm scared. Cuz there ain't much that can punk me, but *I ain't never seen Cliff like this*. He's got that combat-fatigued-thousand-yard stare of a sucka who ain't got nothin' to lose, and no reason to pretend.

Momma charges in with Nate and Brenda and hollers, "Clifford!"

Nolan calls out to Momma, "Help me! *Please!*"

*"SHUT UP!"* screams Cliff, kickin' him in his side.

Loverboy doubles up and starts crying. Cliff grabs a lamp so he can send Nolan on a permanent Twilight Zone vacation. But that'd get *him* sent away, and I can't have that. So I tackle him, makin' sure he don't clonk me instead. Cliff roars, throws me into a wall, and the world is spinnin'.

# NATHAN

INCREDIBLE! VICTOR SLAMS INTO THE WALL AND BRENDA RUNS TO HELP HIM. MOMMA starts toward Clifford, but I pull her back.

"Let me go!" she yells, jerking her arm away.

I shove her behind me. "Let me handle this!"

I move quickly up alongside Clifford and he shoves me backwards. I topple over a chair, but scramble to my feet as Clifford starts moving toward the cowering man, balling and unballing his fists.

"Clifford!" shouts Momma.

Clifford stops, then starts moving again. The cowering man hunkers deeper into the corner, collapsing inward on himself.

Momma moves cautiously toward Clifford and speaks softly. "Clifford, what're you doing?"

"He hit Braddie and Bear. In *my* home."

"Clifford, listen to me," says Momma, her voice soothing. "This is no longer your home."

Clifford's fists tighten. He glares at Momma for long moments. She reaches out, tentatively at first, and strokes his cheek. She keeps stroking, slowly and with much love, over and over until the rage in Clifford's face begins to subside.

"Clifford, I love you," she says.

"I know, Momma."

"Then try and understand, baby. *This is no longer your home.*"

Clifford looks around the room. His eyes widen in amazement, like a museum patron suddenly discovering that these artifacts once belonged to him. Then he looks at Momma as if for the first time.

"Momma?"

She opens her arms. And then Demetria runs in and shouts: "Clifford! What're you doing?"

Clifford's face explodes into a volcano of emotion. He leaps toward Demetria and almost reaches her before Victor blurs into the scene, tackling him again.

"She ain't worth it!" yells Victor. "You got too much to lose, man. Think about Braddie and Bear! *Braddie and Bear!*"

Hearing their names boosts Clifford to new levels of resistance. Victor tries pinning him down and I jump on to help, but the adrenaline surging through Clifford is too much and he throws us off.

The cowering man scrambles upstairs and slams the bedroom door. Clifford stomps toward Demetria, stopping when Braddie and the Bear jump in front of him.

"Dada! Don't hurt Mommy!" shouts Bear.

"Get in the car!"

"We don't want you to hurt Mommy!" screams Braddie.

Clifford shoves them aside, knocking them down and reaching for Demetria. The boys hit the floor and start crying. Momma rushes in front of Clifford and slaps him. His head snaps sideways and back. His eyes narrow, his nostrils flare, and he exhales in powerful snorts.

"Move!" he shouts.

Momma slaps him again, harder. "Clifford! Listen to me! You don't belong here anymore!"

"But she's *my* wife! They're *my* sons! It's *my* family!"

Momma's face contorts as she fights her tears. She grabs Clifford by the shoulders and looks hard and deep into his eyes.

"Clifford, let her go. *LET HER GO!*"

"But, Momma. It's . . . it's not fair."

"I know, son. But it's over. *It's all over.*"

Momma pulls Clifford into her, hugging him tight. He struggles for a few seconds, then stops and jams his face into her shoulder, burying his pain in the only person other than Christ who loves him unconditionally.

# MANHOOD

# CLIFFORD

OUR MINI REUNION'S OVER. VICTOR'S BACK IN CLEVELAND. NATE'S PROBABLY PRAYING for me at this moment. And it's almost time to enter the courtroom. Al hovers over me, patting my shoulder and whispering reassurances.

"Clifford, you've got to trust me. It's going to be okay. It'll be all right."

I look up at her and smile. "Al, just this once, I don't believe you."

A pudgy, dull-eyed clerk steps into the outer area and bellows his announcement. "Now hearing case number 99-DR2912! Matthews versus Matthews!"

A shock wave hits. Nine years ago, the Reverend Dr. Roderick Davidson Childress announced: "Ladies and gentlemen, I now present to you for the first time in public, Mr. and Mrs. Clifford and Demetria Matthews."

Now we're case number 99-DR2912. Demetria walks past, staring straight ahead and not even acknowledging my presence. Al and I follow, taking our places behind a small table on the far side of the court, adjacent to that of Demetria and her counsel. The judge glances at his watch, stifles a yawn, and bangs his gavel. In a shadowed corner, lurking like some perverse god of the underworld, an imposing statue of "Just Us" smirks and points its sword at my throat. The bailiff orders everyone to stand, mumbles some sacrilege about the nobility of the proceedings, then defers to the judge.

The judge flips quickly through the dissolution document, asking, every few pages, whether the parties are in full agreement with this or that. Demetria tells the truth and I perjure myself as we answer that, yes, we agree. Another shock wave hits. Demetria and I aren't husband and wife anymore. We're the "parties."

And I can't help laughing at something Victor once said: *Cliff, there's plenty'a people like you, not believin' in the system! But it's out there, man, just waitin' for you to bend over and tie your shoes.*

The judge glares at me and bangs his gavel. "Order!"

I glance at the wall clock and laugh at another Victorism: *Cliff, domestic court's the only place I know where a sucka can get de-balled, mugged, and gang-banged all in the same five minutes.*

"Order in the court!" says the judge, raising his voice.

Al leans close and whispers. "C'mon Clifford. You've got to hang in there for me."

"No, Al. I've got to hang in there for my boys."

The judge gives me a final glare and bangs his gavel. "This marriage is hereby dissolved!"

And so, nine years of life and love are blasted into oblivion. I tug on Al's sleeve.

"What's the matter?" she asks.

I point at the clock. "Victor was off by fifteen minutes."

Al shakes her head, grabs my hand, and leads me out to the court clerk's office so I can pay for my "Just Us." Demetria approaches slowly, finally deigning to let her eyes fall across my path. She opens her mouth to speak but clamps it shut when Al slips between us and steps forward, making Demetria take a step back.

Then speaking with a ferocity I simply can't muster right now, Al tells Demetria, "Go away. *Just go very far away.*"

# VICTOR

ME, CLYDE, AND BRANTLEY DUCK INSIDE THE TRANSIT AUTHORITY MAINTENANCE SHACK just a few yards from Corey's office. Brantley eases up beside the window and peeks out.

"This is right on time," he says. "We'll see everything from here."

I move to the other side and me and Brantley slap five. Clyde grabs a smudged newspaper off somebody's tool box and starts flippin' pages. Brantley peeks again, grins, and rubs his palms together like a bank robber lookin' at an open vault.

"Ice, this payback's gonna be the cold-blooded real deal," he says.

"You'd better b'lieve it," I agree, grinnin'. "But it's Corey's own fault. He never shoulda lied to Edie about me."

Clyde looks up from readin' the paper. "Don't you youngsters know that revenge ain't all it's cracked up to be?"

"Naw, man," says Brantley. "I don't know *nothin'* like that."

Clyde looks at me like he's waitin' for a better answer. He's waitin' for nothin', cuz I say, "The only thang I know is that it feels good."

Brantley says, "Well it must'a felt *real* good when you thumped that Nolan clown back in Pittsburgh."

"You got that right."

Brantley sticks out his hand and we slap five again. "I oughta put that Cruiser dude on Tawnee's case," Brantley says. "I'll betcha she won't be jackin' me around no more about Tyrell. Gimme his number so I can hook it up."

"No can do, Brant. Last I saw Cruise, he said he was cuttin' out'a Pittsburgh. Said thangs was gettin' too hot."

And they were. That night after Clifford got through whoopin' up on Demetria's loverboy, Nolan, I got ahold of Big, who helped me find Cruiser. It didn't take no whole lotta explainin' and Cruise was down with the plan.

"I been kinda bored anyway," he said.

So I left Edie and Karenna at Momma's, tellin' Edie I had to take care'a some stuff for Cliff. After all that'd happened she didn't ax no questions. So I kissed her 'bye and told Momma I was gonna go help Cliff out. She didn't ax no questions either, prob'ly thinkin' I was headin' over to Cliff's apartment to pat his head.

Cruiser met me down at the Grits'n Gravy and we breezed across town to Loverboy Nolan's crib.

"How's you knowin' where this sissy lives?" axed Cruiser.

"The Corps taught me about payin' attention to details, man. I was all eyes the night me'n my baby bro drove past to see if his ex-ho's car was here."

"Was it?"

"Naw, man. Which was too bad, cuz I'da loved bustin' that slut doin' the big nasty."

We parked way down the street, diddy-bopped real smooth up to Nolan's house, then ducked into some bushes. It wasn't no long wait, and Nolan soon pulled into his driveway, checked his mail, and limped to his front door. He was just about to stick his key in the door when me'n Cruiser grabbed him and slammed him facedown on the ground.

"Don't hurt me," he begged, soundin' like some whinin' puppy.

"Shut up!" said Cruiser, growlin' and talkin' low.

I kneeled down behind the chump where he couldn't see me, grabbed his hair, and snatched up his head. "Are you scared?"

"Yes! Yes, I'm scared."

"Good! Now answer this! You wanna be a missin' person?"

Nolan started beggin' and Cruiser punched him in his kidneys, makin' him cough and cry.

"Answer me!" I said, whisperin' hard. "You wanna be a missin' person or not?"

"No! Please I—"

"Shut up!" I said, slappin' him up'side his head. "Remember this, fool. A bad day above ground is better'n a good day below. You's better forget whut happened today. And stay the hell away from those boys. *Got it?*"

"Yes! I won't say a thing! And I'll stay away. I promise. Just please don't—"

I whacked him up'side his head. "Stop beggin', *worm*!"

Cruiser yanked Nolan to his feet and spread his legs apart, and I slammed his balls from behind. Then we zoomed out'a there, leavin' Demetria's hero doubled over, hackin', spittin', and moanin' on the ground.

"I BETCHA THAT FOOL COREY WON'T GO AROUND TELLIN' VD LIES ON NOBODY ELSE!" I say, easin' up to the window to see if anythang's happenin'.

Brantley switches his position to get a better view. "Man, this has been a long time comin'."

"That's what I've been sayin' all along," Clyde mutters.

"Since when?" I ax.

"Since when what?"

"Since when has you been sayin' it?"

Clyde rolls his eyes and nods at the paper. "I'm talkin' about this article in today's 'We the People Speak' section, fathead."

"What about it?" says Brantley, checkin' out the window every few seconds.

"And why you gotta be callin' me 'fathead'?" I ax.

Clyde don't pay me no mind but instead reads the article. "This brotha says we need to finish up the revolution that was started back in the sixties. He says . . ."

"Bump what he's sayin'," Brantley interrupts. "The revolution ain't done *squat* to get them child support buzzards off my back."

I laugh. "And it was one'a the so-called brothas from the revolution that I caught in bed with Lynnette."

Brantley holds out his palm and we slap five. "And if I remember correctly, it was one'a the brothas from the revolution who drilled me in domestic court."

Clyde's lookin' at us like we just took off our disguises to show our real Martian selfs. "Ya'll're some bitter, bad-attitude suckas," he says.

Brantley checks out the window, stiffens up, and eases back a little. I take a quick peek, give Brantley a thumbs-up, and look at Clyde, who's already grinnin'.

"What about the revolution?" I ax.

Clyde tosses the paper off to the side and says, "Later for that. Let's have some fun."

We move into position to get the best view, coverin' our mouths to keep from bustin' out laughin' when Francine steps into Corey's office. A minute later, Claudia screams and flies out the door, lookin' over her shoulder like a platoon of Big Foots is on her case. She opens her car, dives in, then rockets into Cleveland. A chair smashes through Corey's window and he's yellin' and babblin' for his life.

"Ba, ba, baby. Pleeeeze!"

"You no-good, two-timin' weasel!"

Corey zooms out the front door, barely ahead of the coffeemaker and phone flyin' after him. Francine fires off a string of cuss words, insultin' Corey's relatives all the way back to Africa. And me, Clyde, and Brantley howl when Corey hurry-hobbles past, blinkin' his puffy eye and pullin' up his drawers.

# NATHAN

I'M SHRINKING BY THE SECOND AS BEVERLY TALKS. SHE'S IN THE LIVING ROOM CHAIR opposite the kids, who are sitting on the couch. Brenda's standing off to the side, arms crossed and eyes on Beverly like a hawk plummeting to its mouse dinner.

Beverly is saying, "And I want to apologize to you kids for whatever problems were caused. Will you please forgive me?"

Corrine and Nate Junior glance at each other, then Brenda, then me. I signal with my eyes for them to check with Brenda. They do. She nods. They look at Beverly and jab each other, both trying to urge the other one to speak first.

"Yeah," says Nate Junior. "I guess so."

"No!" snaps Brenda. "No guessing. Do you or don't you?"

Nate Junior huffs in frustration at having to do again what was hard enough the first time. "Yes, Sister Dawkins. I forgive you."

Corrine glares at me, then looks at Brenda again. Brenda gives an emphatic nod. Corrine pouts. "Yes, Sister Dawkins. I forgive you."

Smiling nervously, Beverly stammers out her good-byes and hurries to the door. Brenda escorts her out. Once the door's closed she looks at me.

"Well?"

I grab the chair Beverly sat in, pull it close so I can look straight into my children's eyes, and take the next step on the long road back to earning their trust. But before I can do that, I have to make all things right.

I kneel in front of Corrine and take her hands into both of mine. With the way she's scowling right now, she looks like Brenda almost twenty years ago, when she forgave me for Syreeta. Just as she has for Beverly. I must never give her reason to have to do so again.

I take a deep breath and say, "Corrine, I want to apologize again for hitting you, baby. Please forgive me."

Corrine's scowl cracks, then crumbles into a smile. Her eyes mist over and she hugs me. "Yes, Daddy. I forgive you."

"I love you, baby."

"I love you too."

I sneak a peek at Nate Junior and Brenda, just in time to see them glance at each other, look at me and Corrine, and smile.

# CLIFFORD

I DESPERATELY WANT TO BELIEVE THAT THIS ORDEAL IS FINALLY OVER. BUT VICTOR assures me that Demetria's hand will keep reaching from the nightmare of my recent past, palm up, fingers snapping. She'll keep demanding that I respond like a husband and getting offended when I remind her that she's an ex.

*Cliff, she's gonna be a bigger pain now than when ya'll was married,* I hear him say with a laugh.

I swing past Wal-Mart to buy Al a card and a small gift. I take my time shopping, picking over the items carefully because now it matters that those who are precious to me know it.

"Hi, Clifford," says a female voice.

I turn around and see Tammy, Demetria's counselor and running buddy.

I nod, turn away, and go on shopping.

"I'm sorry to hear about you and Demetria."

"Excuse me," I say, moving around Tammy and heading toward the exit.

In my married life, I was forced to share my space with Demetria's repugnant friends. As of today, I'm no longer married. And I've paid the price, and will be paying monthly, to decide who'll inhabit my space. Tammy's not in danger of being invited.

I'm halfway to my car when I hear Tammy calling again. I pick up the pace, and she does the same.

"Clifford, listen," she huffs. "I know you may not care for me . . ."

"Now what would make you think that?"

She ignores the sarcasm and continues, ". . . but I told Demetria not to divorce you. Honest. I told her how hard it is out here and that you were a good man and she should work with you. But she just wouldn't listen."

I study Tammy's face and recall the words from one of Nate's sermons: "Now the serpent was more cunning than any beast of the field which the Lord God had made."

Tammy pulls a pen and notepad from her purse, scribbles out her number, and offers it to me.

"Clifford, if you ever wanna talk or, you know, get together, I'm more than willing."

I look at Tammy, the paper, back at Tammy, then look skyward and laugh. I get in my car, start up, and leave Tammy fuming in my exhaust, her look of surprise and indignation genuine and complete. And I'm tickled and overjoyed because, today, after many days of wondering whether it would ever matter again, I finally remembered how to laugh.

# VICTOR

I'M JUST GETTIN' BACK TO MY APARTMENT AFTER RENTIN' SOME VIDEOS FOR ME AND Edie to watch this evenin' when my phone starts clatterin'. I hurry inside and answer it.

"Yeah. This is Ice."

"Whutch'you doin'?"

It's Simone. She's got some balls callin' like ev'rythang's smooth'n buttered.

"Whutch'you want, Simone?"

"Why you got an attitude?"

"After all'a your games I can have any kinda attitude I want."

"What! I *know* you ain't *even* tryin' to flick me off."

I make a sound like a toilet, suckin' a big, Simone-sized turd down its pipe.

"Okay," says Simone, suddenly soundin' calm and up-to-no-good. "I guess it ain't no point tryin' to change your mind."

"None!"

"That's too bad. Cuz my sorry boyfriend's out'a town for the next few days. And I told my girlfriends I was goin' to D.C. on business."

Simone pauses and I'm feelin' every corner of the brick she just rammed down my throat.

"Ya know why I did all that?" she axes.

I lower my voice and make sure it's got plenty'a don't-care in it. "No, Simone. Why?"

"Cuz I know you still want 'em."

"Want whut?"

"You know 'whut'! You still want these big thirty-eight-double-Ds. Don'tcha?"

Man, later for this! After all Simone's junk, listenin' to her lies, gettin' built up and let down, over and over, I ain't about to get chumped again. Besides, me and Edie are cookin' real good and I ain't gonna let skeezin' freak Simone mess up my good thang. So thirty-eight-double-Ds or no thirty-eight-double-Ds, *no*! Not even if it means missin' out on slurpin', slobberin', and squeezin' them blimps. Not if it means trashin' my chance to work my tongue all over them bowlin' balls. And bury my face between them mountains after lickin', snugglin', and playin' with 'em. None'a that matters cuz the answer's *"NO!"*

Simone says, "Well?"

"I'll see ya in twenty minutes."

FINALLY I'MA GET MY CHANCE TO LOCK MY LIPS ONTO SIMONE'S SACKS. I ALMOST fainted when she showed me that lingerie she was puttin' on. I'ma blow a gasket when I see her in it.

"Is you excited, baby?" Simone axes, talkin' from the bedroom.

"Yeah! C'mon out here and . . ."

"C'mon and what?"

Gunnery Sergeant Daniels's voice rings through my head, blarin' so loud it blocks out everythang else. *Recruit Matthews! How does a Marine get his balls blown off in combat?*

*Sir! I don't know, sir!*

*By puttin' 'em in harm's way, douchebag!*

I grip the sides of my chair, look around Simone's apartment and . . . understand! *This* is harm's way, where suckas get trickbagged into losin' ev'rythang that means anythang to 'em. And it ain't somebody else who trickbags 'em. *They do it to theyselfs!*

I get up and start backin' to the door. I need to get to Edie. She's where safety is. She's where ev'rythang makes sense. She's where I'm finally gettin' a break. She and Karenna is where I can get back the fambly I lost. Simone opens the door and steps out. Them juicy-jugs is bouncin', jigglin', and ringin' the dinner bell.

"You wanna play with 'em?" axes Simone, leanin' over so I can see that mile of cleavage.

"Play with 'em yourself!" I holler.

Then I bust out that apartment and blitz to my car.

I ZOOM INTO BENNY'S AND STRAIGHT UP TO THE BAR.

"Whut'sup with you?" Vernon axes. "You look like you just seen *Blackula.*"

"It was worser than that. I looked in his face and saw *me*!"

Vernon looks at me funny and moves back a couple'a steps. "Man, are you okay? You ain't workin' at the post office or nothin', are you?"

"Naw, Vee. Just gimme a brew."

The bar phone rings and Vernon answers. "Benny's. Who? Yeah, he's sittin' right here. Hold on."

He grits on me while handin' me the phone and says, "Ice, you know Benny don't play suckas gettin' personal calls on his phone."

I take the phone, cover it, and ax, "Who is it?"

"Sounds like that Simone babe you been slobberin' after," says Vernon, grinnin'.

I hand the phone back. "Tell her I just left. Tell her I got drafted. Tell her I got a boyfriend. Tell her anythang! Just get rid of her."

Vernon takes the phone and mumbles some lies, pullin' the phone from his ear every few seconds as Simone gives him the royal cussin' out she meant for me. Then he hangs up and shakes his head.

"Lemme get this straight. You had Hortense Hooters down to the silk and split?"

I nod, hardly believin' it myself. "That's right, man. And don't be thinkin' I didn't want them pontoons, cuz I did. But dog, Vee. It ain't worth losin' Edie. *Nothin' is!*"

Vernon gets out one'a his best German brews, pours me a glass, and extends his hand.

"Whut's this for?" I ax, lookin' at his hand.

"For you finally bein' a man. Punk!"

We shake and I take the beer and enjoy.

THE MARINE CORPS CALLS IT BEIN' IN A HURT LOCKER. AND I GOTTA SOMETIMES FIGHT TO keep from feelin' I'm in one, cuz now Edie knows more about me than any woman on the planet, includin' Momma. But whut's worsest is that she's seen my skid marks, which means she's close, *reeeaaal* close.

The Dipper keeps axin', Whut's goin' on? Don't I realize I'ma wake up one mornin' and find myself standin' in front'a some preacher? But the Dipper don't know that me and Edie have talked about that. A lot! Cuz I'm tired of goin' through whut I've been puttin' up with the last few years. All'a that strange booty was nice but it was a lotta times *too* strange. Besides, I ain't lookin' for no more greener grass, specially since most of it's green cuz'a bein' fertilized by bulls.

Edie holds her arm out straight, lookin' at the engagement ring on her finger.

"It's beautiful," she says.

"Are you sure you like it?"

She smiles brighter'n a truckload of stage lamps. "Victor, it's wonderful."

I look at the cheesin' clerk. "Okay. Wrap it up."

Edie gives the ring back and hugs me. But in her eyes, somethin' ain't right.

"Whuts'up Edie?"

"Victor, are you sure you wanna do this?"

"Yeah, I'm sure. Ain't you?"

"Baby, yes!" she answers quickly. "But it's just that, I don't want to make a mistake."

I hold Edie by her shoulders. "Edie, do you love me?"

"Victor, you know I do."

"And I love you. Ain't no guarantees, Edie. It's just a risk we gonna have'ta take."

# NATHAN

I LOOK INTO THE GRIM FACES AROUND THE CONFERENCE TABLE. SOME STARE AT ME IN anger, others in disbelief. Some of the people stare at the table, others wipe away tears. And demonic laughter rains down from the rafters. But more than demon spirits it was my lust and pride that seduced me into flirting with a power *no* man can defeat without God. And now I must stand firm. I straighten up, take a deep breath, and finish what I've begun.

"I apologize to all of you from the bottom of my heart and pray you'll find it within yours to forgive me. Effective immediately, I'm resigning as pastor of Divine Temple. I've enjoyed my time here and want all of you to know how privileged I've been to work in God's vineyard with some of the finest saints in the kingdom."

My voice quavers for an instant and I stop to compose myself.

"You dear people need a leader you can trust to do the right thing. You need someone whose all-consuming desire is to serve God by serving, caring, and shepherding you as God gives guidance. As my final act I'm recommending that Sister Josette Lyman take over as interim pastor until . . ."

"Now hold on just one minute," interrupts Carlene Newman. She looks around the table at the rest of the council members. "I'm not gonna just sit here and let Brother Matthews walk off and rob me of his love and care." She looks at me and says, "And how dare you not know how much love there is for you in this church? My daughter Keishawn says that if her baby's a boy, she's gonna name him after you."

Brother Loudon clears his throat. "Pastor, what makes you think we's gonna let you just run off like this? If it wasn't for you helpin' me write a résumé and practice interviewin', and teachin' me to get past bein' afraid of them computers, I'd still be bustin' suds down at that diner."

Marla Edgar stands and leans forward, placing her palms flat on the table. She glances into the face of each council member before speaking. "Now Pastor, I ain't sayin' that I like what you told us. But you was man enough to step forward. And far as I'm concerned, that's doin' the right thing. You was tempted and beat it back. You took a little longer than I wished you had, but praise God, you took responsibility like a man."

My secretary Helen speaks next. "Pastor, you don't know how much I've worried about you."

"We've *all* been worrying about you, Nathan," says Brenda, sitting at the far end of the table, her face a mixture of pride, impatience, and love.

"You're a good man," adds Helen. "Anyone can see that the Lord's hand is upon you."

"That don't mean we're blind to wrongdoin'," Marla Edgar says.

"But it also doesn't mean we're gonna condemn anyone for being tempted," Carlene Newman puts in. "If that's the case, everyone at this table had better resign."

Brother Loudon says, "Pastor, you's the one who taught us that the devil's gonna always be comin' after us. Ain't you said that's his job? That's what he does? That he ain't got nothin' else to do? That nothin' makes him happier? Ain't you said that he enjoys his work to the point where he don't even take time to sleep?"

Marla Edgar speaks again. "The devil came after you, Pastor. And you told him to get lost. Next to acceptin' Jesus, that's a good first step."

The room grows quiet until Carlene Newman says, "There's so much love for you here, Brother Matthews. And we know you love us. Please stay."

I look into the earnest face of each council member seated around the table, smile at the love beaming from Brenda's eyes, then glance outside at Tyrone Ballard and Corrine, talking and laughing in the parking lot.

I look at this church council which the Lord has given back to me and say, "Let's join hands and pray."

I NOW KNOW THE SORROWS OF ONE WHO HAS LIVED IN THE VALLEY OF THE SHADOW. IT was a deep valley, the shadow was long, and I wasn't always certain that I'd see the light of day. But just as God guided Moses in the desert, spared Daniel in the lion's den, and ordered Lazarus to rise and defy death, so He spared me destruction by my own hand.

I don't understand the love that was so large it moved Christ to sacrifice himself so that I might live. I don't understand why I had to drink from the cup of despair to mature my thirst for hope. I don't understand the compassion that, with all the realm of creation to concern itself with, spent time caring for me.

When I stand in the pulpit, looking upon God's people, I see where His heart lies. They're precious to Him, each and every one, with all their troubles, weaknesses, oddities, defects, and secrets.

*Dost thou love me?*

"Lord, you know I do."

*Then feed my sheep.*

And in so doing, I respect the fragility of this flesh housing my spirit. I'm strong, because I've been weak. But because I've been weak, I don't rely upon *my* strength. For that, I need Him. And Brenda. Learning to love her right taught me to love others well, and teaching me to love others right and well is the essence of how God loves me.

After service, Sister Noreen Hammond hugs me and says, "Pastor, would you mind stopping by and blessing my new home?"

"Why of course, Sister Hammond. When did you have in mind?"

She leans close, too close, and whispers, "Anytime this week. I'll even fix dinner."

I give Sister Hammond's hands a tender squeeze.

Brenda shows up, right on time. "Nathan, did you call?"

"Yes, honey, I did. Sister Hammond wants *us* to bless her new home."

Brenda hugs Sister Hammond and congratulates her. "What time did you want us to come by?"

"Er, anytime'll be fine. I don't want to be any trouble."

Brenda smiles. "You won't be, Sister Hammond. You'll be no trouble at all."

# GENESIS

# CLIFFORD

I DRIVE THROUGH PENN HILLS COMMONS, PARK IN FRONT OF MY FORMER HOME, AND steel myself before going in to get Braddie and Bear. In some ways this is the hardest part, having to return to this fog of toxic memories I'd love to forget.

For the next few years, I'm going to have to find the strength, somehow, some way, and from somewhere, to keep a smile on my face so Braddie and Bear will never know that when I pick them up, a little more of me is dying. I'll have to find the discipline to not growl and snap when they mention, as they have several times already, the existence of yet another man.

*That's how it is,* chuckles Victor's echo. *Some other sucka gets to slam your ex-booty, and you get to pay the bill.*

And that's not the only bill I'm paying. Demetria's constantly badgering me about this or that unpaid medical or dental bill, the boys needing clothes, shoes, allowance, school pictures, spending money for a field trip, or *something*. The worst was when she called asking for copies of the canceled child support checks, saying that without proof of regular support, the bank wouldn't consider loaning her money to buy a house.

*And while loverboy's tappin' that yummy in the new house,* chortles Victor, *you'll be in your tuna can mumblin', "How'd I get here?"*

All I could do was stare at the phone and ask myself again, *how* under the light of God's bright blazing sun did I fail to see these traits in Demetria? Then it struck me that if the boys had a house, life would be better for them. So like so many other times throughout this mess, I reinterpreted reality, telling myself that Demetria's getting a windfall was an unfortunate, but unavoidable, part of ensuring Braddie and Bear's happiness.

I'd complain about having to constantly play such mind games, but Al was right. No one wants to hear my gripes.

*And I'll tell you why,* says Victor. *It's cuz half the suckas don't care about your problems, and the other half is glad you got 'em.*

I get out of the car and knock on the door. Scratch barks and Demetria says, "Just a minute!"

When she opens the door, my legs turn to rubber. Demetria's stylish hairdo, makeup, and the sexy dress on her svelte body offer me a vision of the loveliness she's always possessed. The loveliness that someone else now enjoys.

Demetria gives me a stiffly civil smile. "Hello, Clifford. The boys are almost ready."

"Okay. I'll just wait here at the door."

I step inside, hoping with all my heart that Braddie and Bear will hurry up *just this once.* But it's not to be, not with the sound of roaring creatures and video game explosions coming from their room. Competing with that noise is the radio, tuned to Demetria's favorite intelli-crap-excreting station. Some soap opera's on TV, but the volume's turned down, strangely emphasizing the intensity of the actors' expressions. And it smells like some bacon was just recently burned.

Demetria moves briskly to the stairs. "Braddie! Bear! I told you guys to get ready ten minutes ago. Now your father's here."

"Okay, Mommy," they answer. "We're coming."

"Don't make me tell you again. I have to leave too!"

Demetria sits down on the couch we bought before our trip to Disney World, grabs the cordless, and keeps talking.

"Where were we?" she says, to whomever. "Oh, yeah. So then he starts telling me about how he's planning to have a heart-shaped jacuzzi installed in his bedroom. Well, he'd better think again. It's gonna take more than some bubbling water to . . ."

I tune Demetria out and hurry over to the steps. "Braddie! Bear! Would you guys *please* hurry and come on!"

Nate must be praying for me right now because they burst from their room and race downstairs with Scratch bringing up the rear.

I kneel and hug them. "Hi, fellas. I've missed you."

They hug me back, but Bear's hug is different. I look into his eyes. They're still the eyes of a child, but they're harder and more informed, like he's comprehended more of the price he's paying for me and Demetria collapsing his world.

"Bear, are you okay?" I whisper.

He nods. I'm unconvinced, but now's not the time to seek this truth, so I just hug him and Braddie again.

"C'mon, you guys," I say. "Let's go fly this last kite."

"Okay, Dada!" says Braddie. "This time we'll do it right!"

"This time we'll fly it high!" adds Bear.

This time they know it's not so that I Am can "fix us" but just to spend some time together and have fun.

"Okay, boys," I say, forcing a smile. "Let's go."

The boys rush to Demetria, who's still droning away on the phone. They kiss her cheeks and she smiles and waves a perfunctory good-bye.

I kneel down and pat Scratch. "You're a good dog," I whisper. "And I've missed you."

Scratch whines and licks my palm. I march quickly to the door, getting there just as Braddie and Bear race outside. I look back at Demetria, still on the phone and somehow concentrating through the TV's turned-up volume and the radio's gibberish.

"Well, he might be disappointed," says Demetria into the phone. "But like I told him, I'm looking for true love, excite . . ."

I exit quickly and glance at some geese flying overhead. My steps get lighter and faster as I realize that I'll never again have to endure the mean-spirited havoc lurking behind Demetria's door. And this isn't some self-deluding positive perspective, for I'm well aware of all that I've lost.

But even though I've lost much and miss my sons terribly, and my apartment's small, and I'm occasionally hassled by termites in my tub, and the court and the IRS will for the next few years pirate, pillage, and plunder, with all that's gone wrong, the *one* thing I did right was *divorcing Demetria.* Now there's no cancer killing my dignity. There's no malice mangling my heart. There's no puppeteer plaguing my mind.

What lies before me is the grand opportunity to create a new world of any size, shape, and character I want. I can stride confidently into the future, trusting in the words Nate spoke when he said: "Clifford, have faith. For this too shall pass."

I TURN INTO WYANDOTTE REGIONAL PARK, GET OUT, AND FOLLOW BRADDIE AND BEAR UP a slight rise onto a brilliant emerald field of grass. My chest swells as I notice how tall and masculine they've gotten. They move with the confidence of travelers who know where they're going. We get to the top and they sit down.

There's a pleasant eeriness to this place, as if in the midst of all Wyandotte's hugeness a small piece of acreage has been set aside as, well, holy ground. I lay the kite down, play out some string, take firm hold of the line, and, just like Braddie and Bear are doing, stare into the clouds and wait.

One minute turns into two, five, then fifteen. Leaves rustle in the trees behind us as the breeze picks up. I shamble into a slow lope, trying to get some wind beneath the kite. A powerful gust pulls it into the dazzling blue, snapping and pulling at the paper, urging the kite to come play where the air is thinner.

The kite sails higher, swaying from side to side, then settles onto an air cushion and floats. I glance at the boys and smile. They're watching the kite. The wind slackens suddenly and the kite dips. Then a new gust fills its pockets, jerking it upwards until the string pulls nice and taut. And finally the kite is flying, high and graceful, sailing along on the wind currents.

And then . . . the string snaps.

I watch in silence as the kite floats away. The thin, fragile string dangling from my hand sways in the breeze. It's a miracle that these thinly twined threads had ever connected us, me to her, her to me, seducing me with an illusion of control. But now that the string has snapped, the kite is fleeing toward a distant horizon, as is my desperately departed Demetria. And now, having eyes with which to see, I turn toward the sun, open my arms, and give myself over to the One who controls the wind.

EVERY NOW AND THEN, NO MATTER WHERE I AM, NO MATTER WHAT I'M DOING, I'LL STOP and stare, my eyes wide, unblinking, and utterly amazed at how easily it all unraveled, so effortless and hypnotic in its inevitability. Then the catatonia descends, one onion-thin layer at a time, wrapping me tight in a numbing cocoon, shielding me from a blurry vision that can't see agony's end. And I'll miss Demetria so much, the sorrow fills my bones, making each step forward an excruciating journey.

I'll miss her laugh and the haunting certainty that she celebrated with all her being. The glint in her eyes before we'd make love. The scent of her sex, lingering in our bedsheets. The way she'd walk, stepping with symphonic grace. The way she'd love Braddie and Bear, so total, hard, and complete. Her feel, moist, welcoming, and warm inside; soft, tender, and sweet outside. I'll miss watching her sleep, the way she'd exhale the breath of morning.

Then the walls drop the curtain on my memories, cutting off their light to match the darkness in Dadaland. The tears no longer come, and I tremble for fear of having dried up inside. But then I hear of a child who dies, an innocent set free, or someone rescued from a fire, and I care, glad that I can still feel.

I sip from my glass of wine and watch as darkness descends upon Pittsburgh. And then, slowly and one at a time, the stars flicker on across the night sky, restoring the hope in my heart.

# ABOUT THE AUTHOR

FREDDIE LEE JOHNSON III grew up in the Washington, D.C., metropolitan area. He attended Bowie State College, earning a bachelor of science degree in history and teacher education before going on to serve in the United States Marine Corps as a communications-electronics officer and infantry officer with the reserves.

A former auto industry production scheduler and telecommunications company systems analyst, he worked full-time as a training coordinator for Aircraft Braking Systems Corporation in Akron, Ohio, while completing his master's and doctor's degrees in history at Kent State University. He currently resides in Holland, Michigan, where he teaches history at Hope College.